D1300067

Icebreaker

Content Warning:

Icebreaker is intended for adult readers only

*It contains mature themes and sexually explicit content and
is not intended for readers younger than 18 years old.
This book also contains a focus on eating habits.*

Icebreaker

HANNAH GRACE

SIMON &
SCHUSTER

London · New York · Sydney · Toronto · New Delhi

First published in Great Britain by Hannah Grace, 2022
This edition published in Great Britain by Simon and Schuster Ltd, 2023

3 5 7 9 10 8 6 4 2

Simon & Schuster UK Ltd
1st Floor
222 Gray's Inn Road
London WC1X 8HB

Simon & Schuster Australia, Sydney
Simon & Schuster India, New Delhi

www.simonandschuster.co.uk
www.simonandschuster.com.au
www.simonandschuster.co.in

A CIP catalogue record for this book is available from the British Library

Paperback ISBN: 978-1-3985-2568-9
eBook ISBN: 978-1-3985-2569-6
Audio ISBN: 978-1-3985-2570-2

Printed and Bound in the UK using 100% Renewable
Electricity at CPI Group (UK) Ltd

For Erin, Kiley, and Rebecca

Thank you for believing in me.
This book is for you guys.

Playlist

CRUEL SUMMER | TAYLOR SWIFT	02:58
KISS ME MORE (FEAT. SZA) | DOJA CAT	03:29
TALKING BODY | TOVE LO	03:58
SHUT UP | ARIANA GRANDE	02:38
IDGAF | DUA LIPA	03:38
ENERGY | TYLA JANE	03:20
MOTIVATION | NORMANI	03:14
ONE KISS (WITH DUA LIPA) | CALVIN HARRIS	03:35
DANCE FOR YOU | BEYONCÉ	06:17
NEEDY | ARIANA GRANDE	02:52
WHO'S | JACQUEES	03:06
LOSE YOU TO LOVE ME | SELENA GOMEZ	03:26
KISS ME | SIXPENCE NONE THE RICHER	03:29
BOYFRIEND (WITH SOCIAL HOUSE) | ARIANA GRANDE	03:06
RUMORS (FEAT. ZAYN) | SABRINA CLAUDIO	03:46
MORE THAN ENOUGH | ALINA BARAZ	02:31
YOU SHOULD SEE ME IN A CROWN | BILLIE EILISH	03:01
I'M FAKIN | SABRINA CARPENTER	02:55
MAKE ME FEEL | JANELLE MONÁE	03:14
CAN I | KEHLANI	02:48

"Skating was the vessel into which I could pour my heart and soul."

—*Peggy Fleming*

Icebreaker

Chapter One

ANASTASIA

"AGAIN, ANASTASIA!"

If I hear the words *again* and *Anastasia* together in a sentence one more time, it might be the thing that finally tips me over the edge.

I've been on the edge since I woke up this morning with a hangover sent directly from the pits of hell, so the last thing I need right now is more grief from Coach Aubrey Brady.

I focus on suppressing my annoyance, like I do every training session when she makes it her mission to push me to my limits. Rationalizing it's her dedication that makes her such a successful coach, I decide throwing my ice skates at her is something that should stay in my imagination.

"You're being sloppy, Stas!" she yells as we fly straight past her. "Sloppy girls don't get medals!"

What did I say about not throwing skates at her?

"Come on, Anastasia. Put in some effort for once." Aaron snickers, poking his tongue out at me when I shoot him a cold glare.

Aaron Carlisle is the best male figure skater the University of California, Maple Hills, has to offer. When I was offered a spot at UCMH and my skating partner wasn't, Aaron was luckily in the same position, and we became pairs. This is our third year of skating together and our third year of getting our asses kicked.

I have a theory that Aubrey is a Soviet spy. I don't have any evidence, and my theory isn't well developed. Developed at all, actually. But sometimes, when she's screaming at me to straighten my spine or lift my chin, I swear a slight Russian accent slips out.

Which is peculiar for a woman from Philipsburg, Montana.

Comrade Brady was a figure skating superstar in her heyday. Even now, her movements are delicate and controlled, and she moves with such grace it's hard to believe she can shout as loud as she does.

Her graying hair is always pulled back into a tight bun, which accentuates her high cheekbones, and she's always wrapped tight in her signature faux-fur black coat, which Aaron jokes is where she hides all her secrets.

The rumor is she was supposed to go to the Olympics with her partner, Wyatt. However, Wyatt and Aubrey were practicing those lifts a little too often, and she ended up holding a baby instead of a gold medal.

That's why she's been in a bad mood since she started coaching twenty-five years ago.

"Clair de lune" fades as Aaron and I finish our routine nose to nose, our chests heaving against each other as we try to catch our breath. When we finally hear a single clap, we move apart and skate toward what will undoubtedly be the source of my next headache.

I haven't even stopped moving when her green eyes lock on me and narrow. "When are you going to land your Lutz? If you're not going to deliver, it needs to come out of your long program."

Aside from Brady, successfully doing a quadruple Lutz and not landing on my ass is the current bane of my existence. I've been practicing for God knows how long, but I can't quite manage to nail it. Aaron can execute it flawlessly, which is why I convinced the choreographer to put it into our routine in the first place.

Pride is a foolish thing. It's incredibly foolish when it comes to figure skating, since when you get it wrong, you bounce your face off solid ice. I'd take face-planting over the annoying, fake-disappointed face Aaron pulls anytime it's suggested we take it out.

"It's coming, Coach," I say with as much fake enthusiasm as possible. "I'm getting there; it's not perfect yet, but I'll keep practicing."

It's a minor lie, a harmless one. I *am* getting there. What I've failed to mention is I'm only getting there off the ice, specifically when I'm attached to equipment that helps me get there.

"She's getting there," Aaron lies, throwing an arm around my shoulders. "Just a bit longer, A.B."

It's nice for Aaron to be on my side and show a united front to KGB Aubrey. What he says in private is that the only way I'm going to pull it off is if I start doping and build a time machine to get my prepuberty body back.

She mutters something inaudible and waves us off flippantly. "I'll see you two back here tomorrow, and if you could both not be hungover, that would be great. I'm fairly certain eating Kenny's before training isn't going to get either of you onto the Olympic team. Understood?"

Shit. "Yes, Coach," we say in harmony.

Aaron is staring at his phone, waiting for me in the lobby when I finally exit the women's locker room.

"I fucking told you she'd know." I groan, swinging my bag toward him as soon as I'm close enough to hit him in the stomach with it. "I didn't even have anything!"

He grunts at the impact, tugging the bag from my hands and flinging it over his shoulder. "The woman has the nose of a bloodhound."

Like most things in life, skating is far easier when you're a man because nobody is picking you up and launching you across the room twice a day.

Freshman year, I gained the freshman fifteen. Well, it was more like the freshman five, but Aaron said I was getting too heavy to lift, so I haven't put on an ounce since.

I try to stick to my meal plan religiously, with the odd party here and there to keep me lucid. My best friend's twenty-first birthday yesterday was the perfect opportunity to let loose a little, even if it did mean braving Brady with a hangover.

We climb into Aaron's new G-Wagen, the latest guilt gift from his adulterous but wealthy father, and head home. Aaron and I decided it would be cool to live together, with my best friend, Lola, at the end of freshman year. Our schedules are similar, and our lives revolve around skating, so it made sense.

Aaron takes the turn onto Maple Avenue and looks over at me while I rummage through my purse for my most prized possession. "What does the planner say you're doing tonight?"

I roll my eyes, ignoring his teasing tone. "Getting laid."

"Ew," he says, the tip of his nose wrinkling as he grimaces. "It's bad enough you plan what time you sleep and eat, but do you need to plan having sex?"

He's not lying about the sleeping and eating thing—every minute of my life is meticulously scheduled in my trusty planner, which my friends find equal parts hilarious and ridiculous. I wouldn't necessarily say I'm a control freak, but I'm a woman who needs to be in control.

There's *definitely* a difference.

I shrug, suppressing the urge to point out that at least I'm getting some, unlike him. "Ryan is a busy guy and I'm a busy girl. I want to see him as much as I can before basketball season."

Ryan Rothwell is six feet six inches of pure athletic perfection. UCMH point guard and team captain, he's as serious about his sport as I am, which makes for a perfect no-strings-attached situation. The added benefit is Ry is the sweetest guy, so we've become great friends through our mutually beneficial arrangement.

"I can't believe you're still fucking around with him. He's, like, double your size, how does he not crush you? No, wait. I don't want to know."

"I know he is." I giggle, pinching his cheeks until he bats me away. "Sorta the whole point."

Most people assume Aaron and I are more than partners, but we're more like siblings. It's not that he isn't good-looking, we've just never had any romantic interest in each other.

Aaron is much taller than me and lean like a dancer with his sculpted, muscular body. His black hair is kept short, and I swear he wears mascara because his sky-blue eyes are framed with the darkest, jealousy-inducing lashes, contrasting prominently against his pale skin.

"I officially know too much about your sex life, Anastasia."

Aaron can't decide if he likes Ryan or not. Sometimes he's cool with him and Ryan gets to see the Aaron I see—the one who's fun to be around. You'd assume Ryan had personally ruined Aaron's life or something the rest of the time. Aaron can be so abrupt and harsh that it's embarrassing. It's unpredictable, but Ryan brushes it off and tells me not to worry about it.

"I promise to not talk about it for the rest of the drive home if you promise to give me a ride to Ryan's later."

He contemplates for a minute or so. "Okay, deal."

LOLA LOOKS UP FROM THE salad she's stabbing aggressively with her fork and huffs. "I'm just saying, who's dick is Olivia Abbott sucking to get the lead role for the third year in a row?"

I can't help but cringe at her harsh words, but I know she doesn't mean it. She was already feeling delicate this morning after the copious amounts of alcohol we consumed last night for her birthday, so today wasn't the best day to find out she didn't get the part she wanted.

I've watched every show for the past two years, and Lo knows as well as I do, Olivia is an exceptionally talented actor.

"Can she not just be very talented? And not be sucking someone's dick?"

"Anastasia, will you please let me be petty for five minutes and pretend I don't know she's better than me?"

Aaron throws himself into the chair beside me and reaches over to pick a carrot stick from my plate. "What're we being petty about?"

"Olivia Abbott," Lola and I respond in unison, the distaste in her tone evident as hell.

"She's hot. Might be the hottest girl on campus," he says nonchalantly, clearly not paying attention to how Lola's jaw drops. "Is she single?"

"How am I supposed to freaking know? She doesn't talk to anyone. She swans in, gets the role I want, and carries on being an anomaly."

Lola studies performing arts, and it must be an unwritten rule that you have to have a larger-than-life personality, because everyone I've met in her major is like her. It's usually an exhausting battle for attention, even as a spectator, but Olivia keeps to herself, and for some reason, it seems to bother people.

"I'm sorry, Lols. There's always next time," I offer. We both know it doesn't mean anything, but she blows me a kiss anyway. "If it makes you feel any better—I still can't land my Lutz. Aubrey is going to work it out soon and banish me to Siberia."

"Oh no. You're officially a failure, how can you ever step foot on the ice again?" She grins, her eyes shining as I scowl at her. "You'll get there, babe. You're working hard." Her eyes move to Aaron, tapping away on his phone, totally uninterested in our conversation. "Hey, Ice Princess! You gonna help me out here?"

"Huh? Sorry, yeah, you're hot, too, Lo."

I'm surprised I don't see the steam leave Lola's ears as she yells at him about not listening to her.

I slowly retreat to my bedroom, eager to not draw attention to myself and get caught in the crossfire of my roommates' argument. Living with Aaron and Lola is like living with siblings who always wanted to be only children.

Aaron, like me, is an actual only child. The miracle baby to his two aging, midwestern parents desperate to keep their marriage together. Living with other people after being his parents' pride and joy for eighteen years was a big transition for him, and for us, who are the ones who have to live with him and his mood swings.

Now he's not in Chicago, things between his parents aren't great, and we always know when they're extra bad because Aaron gets an obnoxiously expensive and unnecessary gift.

Like a G-Wagen.

In contrast to the two of us, Lola is from a huge family. Being the youngest and the only girl guaranteed her the number one spot in her house, and she has no problem putting Aaron in his place.

I'm still hiding out in my room when my phone buzzes, and Ryan's name flashes on my screen.

RYAN

The boys wanna throw a party tonight. Your place instead?

They were supposed to be going to a pep rally or some shit, but now they're staying home.

Just wanna be alone w you.

Sure, roommates are in though.

Will have to be quiet.

Ha

Should probably give yourself that instruction in a mirror.

You free now?

Yeah, come over.

Omw. Bringing snacks.

"Everyone friends again?" I call out cautiously as I make my way from my bedroom to the living room. They're both fixated on the *Criminal Minds* rerun on the TV, but I get a faint "Yeah" in response, letting me know it's safe to approach.

I lean over the couch for a handful of popcorn from the bowl resting between them, making a mental note to add it to my food tracker when I get back to my room. "So, the basketball team is having a party. I was wondering—"

"If we will go with you?" Aaron interrupts, sounding uncharacteristically hopeful.

"No?"

Lola spins to face me, her red curls bouncing around her shoulders and delight written all over her face. "If we mind that Ryan wants to come here?"

"Yeah. How did yo—?"

"Cough up, Carlisle," she laughs, holding out her hand. He presses a few twenties into her palm, muttering something under his breath as she counts them out. "We heard about the party, and I didn't think you'd wanna get railed with drunk freshmen making out on the other side of the door. We're going to walk there."

Our home is one of Aaron's dad's better *forgive me* presents. It was either after his affair with his secretary or before he decided to have sex with the interior designer. Maple Tower is a beautiful condo block on the edge of campus, and our place has a great view and tons of natural light.

The building isn't exclusive to students, so it's a peaceful place to live, but it's close enough to everyone else that stumbling home from parties is easy.

Aaron and I aren't supposed to be at parties, but what Aubrey doesn't know won't hurt her.

I'VE ALREADY WATCHED LOLA TRY on ten different outfits when Ryan texts to let me know he's finally on his way up, giving me an excuse to leave her and her ten almost identical black dresses.

The butterflies I get when there is a knock at the door and I know Ryan is on the other side of it were strange to me at first, but now it's cute.

He's practically filling the doorway when I open the door to let him in. His messy blond hair is still damp, and he smells strongly of orange and something I can't quite put my finger on, which is now weirdly comforting to me. His head dips to mine, and his lips press against my cheek lightly. "Hello, beautiful."

He hands me the bag of snacks he always insists on bringing because apparently, I don't eat enough, and I don't have anything good to eat when he's here. Ryan eats more than any person I know, and his version of good is loaded with sugar.

For some reason, Aaron and Lo are watching us from the living room like they've never seen other human beings before. Ryan laughs when he spots them; fortunately, he's used to their antics by now, and he offers them a quiet "Hello" as I lead him in the direction of my bedroom.

"Hey, Rothwell?" Lola shouts as we reach my door.

He lets go of my hand, turning around to face her. "Yeah?"

She's leaning over the back of the couch, and I know from the mischievous look on her face I don't want to hear whatever she has to say.

"Since my bedroom is next to Stassie's and I'm going to be listening to your grunting and balls slapping all night"—my eyes widen as far as they can go from behind him—"can I have the code for your room, so I don't have to fight for the shared bathroom at the party at your place?"

Campus housing has electronically coded locks on bedroom doors for security. Ryan's room has a private bathroom, so Lo's request is a good idea since the bathroom line gets ridiculous the drunker people get.

It's her delivery that's going to require some serious work.

"Sure, I'll text it to you. No snooping, Mitchell. I'll know if you have."

She holds up a peace sign. "Scout's honor. Enjoy all the sex."

"*Jesus*, Lols." I groan loud enough for her to hear as I drag Ryan into my room away from her. "I'm so sorry."

"I like her. She's funny." He chuckles, taking my face between his hands and tilting my head up so he can kiss me.

It's soft at first, then more urgent as his tongue moves against mine. His hands travel down my body gently until they reach my thighs, scooping me up in one quick motion. My legs automatically wrap around his waist, my body familiar with his after doing this so many times.

There's banging outside of my room, which I *think* is my room-mates leaving, but every hot kiss Ryan places on my neck steals my attention away. I should check if it is them going, but it suddenly plummets to the bottom of things on my mind when Ryan lowers me to the bed and climbs on top of me.

"How was your day?" he mumbles beneath my ear.

He always does this. He kisses me perfectly, positions his body between my legs, applies enough pressure to have me squirm, scrambles the thoughts in my head, and *then* asks me something mundane like how my day was.

The second I try to formulate a response, his fingers journey beneath my T-shirt, and he traces the curve of my jaw with his nose. Every inch of my skin feels like it's buzzing, and he hasn't even done anything yet. "It was, uh, uhm, fine, I, mhmm, skated . . ."

His body rocks as he laughs. "You mhmm skated? Sounds interesting. Why don't you tell me more, Allen?"

I hate him. I really, really hate him.

I incoherently mumble something about ice and Russians as he strips us of our clothes until we're both in our underwear. Ryan's body would make a Greek god weep; tanned skin from his summer home in Miami, and a torso with more abs than I can count.

Forget a Greek god, it makes *me* want to weep.

Gripping my panties on each hip, he waits until I nod before slowly pulling them down my legs, throwing them behind him, and spreading my legs wide.

"Stas."

"Yeah?"

His forehead creases. "Can Lola really hear my balls?"

Chapter Two

NATHAN

THERE'S A HAND NEAR MY dick that isn't mine.

She's fast asleep, snoring loudly with her hand wrapped around my waist and tucked into the band of my boxers. I gently untuck and examine it—long fake nails, Cartier rings, and a Rolex strapped to her slender wrist.

Who the fuck is it?

Even after a night of God knows what, she still smells expensive, and there are strands of long golden-blond hair draped over my shoulder from where she's lying behind me.

I shouldn't have gone to the party last night, but Benji Harding, and the rest of the basketball guys, are persuasive little shits. As much as I love throwing a party, nothing beats going somewhere else and coming home to a quiet house not full of other people's mess.

Unless you're talking about this kind of mess. The kind where there's a woman in your bed, and you can't remember who the hell it is.

The commonsense part of my brain tells me to roll over and look at her, but another part that remembers all the silly situations we've gotten ourselves into keeps reminding me that drunk Nate is a dick.

That part of my brain has real concerns this is going to be someone's sister, or worse, someone's mom.

"Can you stop moving about?" the mystery guest snaps. "What is it with fucking sports guys and early mornings?"

That voice. It's one I wish I didn't recognize.

Oh fuck.

I slowly roll over so I can confirm my own worst fear: that I did have sex with Kitty Vincent last night.

And I do.

She looks peaceful when she's trying to sleep; her facial features are soft and delicate, lips blushed and pursed. From how calm she looks right now, you wouldn't know she's an absolute raging bit—

"Why are you staring at me, Nate?" Her eyes fly open, and she disintegrates me with one look, like the fucking dragon she is.

Kitty Vincent is everything wrong with rich girls with Daddy's credit card, a subspecies of women at UCMH I happen to be an expert on. Expertise I've gained from having sex with practically all of them.

Except for this one.

I was never supposed to do it with this one.

There's nothing wrong with her visually. To be frank, she's an absolute knockout. She's just an absolutely terrible human being.

"Are you okay?" I ask carefully. "Do you need anything?"

"I need you to stop staring at me like you've never seen a naked woman in your bed before," she snipes back, pushing her body to lean against the headboard. "We both know you have, and you're creeping me out."

"I'm shocked, Kit. I, uh, don't remember how this happened . . ."

I remember being at the party and trying to get Summer Castillo-West to give me her number, but tragically being rejected for the fourth September in a row. I also remember playing beer pong with Danny Adeleke and losing, which I'd rather not remember, but I still don't remember how *this* happened.

"Oh shit. Wait, aren't you dating Danny?"

She rolls her blue eyes and reaches for her purse sitting on the table beside my bed, cursing when she finds her phone battery is dead. Brushing her hair from her face, she finally looks over at me, and I have never known a woman to look so irritated by my existence. "We broke up."

"Right, right. That sucks, I'm sorry. What happened?"

I'm trying to be polite, a gracious host, some would say, but she raises one of her perfectly sculpted eyebrows at me and frowns. "Why do you give a fuck?"

I rub my jaw nervously with my palm as I attempt to think of a reason to give her. She's right; I don't care. I just hate cheaters and I panicked, but since they broke up I don't have anything to worry about. "Only trying to be nice."

She gives me the fakest smile I've ever seen, swings her legs off the bed, and struts butt-ass naked toward my bathroom. It's hard to concentrate on how good she looks because, with one last disinterested look over her shoulder, she scowls at me. "If you want to be nice, get me an Uber."

Thank God. "Sure."

"Exec only, Nate. It's bad enough I'm going to be seen leaving here. Don't make me suffer further by being cheap."

When the bathroom door slams shut and I hear the shower turn on, I know it's safe to scream every curse word I know into my pillow.

I'm standing at the front door watching Kitty climb into her Uber, Exec obviously, because of all the potential shame.

Raking a hand through my hair, I can't decipher how I ended up here after swearing this year would be different.

I distinctly remember saying to Robbie, my best friend, on our drive back to California from Colorado, that senior year was going to be different. I must have said it at least twenty times on our two-day coffee-fueled journey.

I lasted three weeks.

I'm quickly dragged from the pity party I'm throwing for myself by the sound of muttering behind me. Robbie and my other roommates, JJ and Henry, are all sitting in our living room sipping their mugs of coffee like the cast of *The View*.

"Well, well, well," Robbie says smugly. "What happened here, you little ho?"

Robbie has been personally terrorizing me since we were five years old. Robbie's dad, whom I still call Mr. H sixteen years later, was the coach of our local ice hockey team back in Eagle County, where we grew up. That's where we met and became friends, and he's been a pain in my ass ever since.

I ignore him and head straight past their prying eyes to the kitchen, pouring a mug of coffee and giving him the finger instead of the satisfaction of a response.

Gulping down my coffee in what feels like two seconds, I can still sense their eyes on me. This is the worst part of living with your teammates—nothing is a secret.

JJ, Robbie, and I are all seniors who have lived together since we shared a dorm freshman year, but Henry is a sophomore from the team.

The guy is incredible at hockey but has a bit to go with the whole social pressure side that comes with being on a sports team. He hated living in dorms and struggled to make friends outside the team, so we offered to let him move in here.

We've always had a spare bedroom because our garage was converted into a wheelchair-accessible bedroom for Robbie, and Henry was more than grateful for the offer.

Even in the three short weeks he's been here, we can already see him more confident—which is probably why he no longer has a problem helping JJ and Robbie give me abuse.

"Why did you have sex with Kitty Vincent?" Henry asks over the rim of his coffee mug. "She isn't very nice."

Oh yeah, and the kid has *zero* filter.

"I'm going to pretend I didn't, buddy. She wasn't very excited about it, either, and I don't remember one second of it, so it doesn't count." I shrug, walking over to the living room and throwing myself into a recliner. "How the fuck did you three let this happen?"

Am I old enough to not pass off the blame for my mistake? Sure. Will it stop me from trying? No.

"I tried to stop you from leaving with her, bro," JJ blatantly lies, holding up his hands defensively. "You said she smelled nice and her ass felt good. Who am I to stand between you and true love?"

I groan loudly, making my own head thump from the noise. If Jaiden claims he tried to stop me from leaving, he probably requested the Uber and put me in it with Kitty.

JJ is an only child from middle-of-nowhere Nebraska, so messing with the people around him was his only source of entertainment when he was growing up.

His parents always visit in June so they can join the rest of us at LA Pride with JJ, proudly wearing their pansexual flag ally pins. The time they spend at our house has allowed me to get to know them well, which is how I know JJ's dad is exactly the same, to the point I don't know how his mom coped with having two of them in the house.

Mrs. Johal is an amazing woman with the patience of a saint. She always makes sure she fills our refrigerator full of different curries and sides before they leave, and she has amazing taste in horror films, which might be why I love her so much.

She might be the only reason I haven't murdered Jaiden yet.

Robbie maneuvers beside me and wraps what I think is supposed to be a comforting arm around my shoulders. "Your focus on school and hockey lasted longer than I was expecting. Now come on, sort your shit out. You have to drive us to class."

I HAD NO IDEA WHAT I wanted to study when I got accepted by Maple Hills. I'm graduating in less than a year and I'm still not sure studying sports medicine was the right choice.

I was drafted to the Vancouver Vipers when I finished high school and it was a hard choice to put my education first, especially when joining the NHL has been my dream since I was a kid. All I want to do is play, but I know shit goes wrong in hockey all the time; one bad injury or one unavoidable accident and your career is over.

Even with a spot on my dream team waiting for me as soon as I graduate, I still wish *something* I've learned in the past three years had stayed in my brain so my backup plan felt worth it.

My dad wasn't a fan of me heading out of state for college, and he was even less of a fan about me signing with a hockey team, never mind one in Canada. He wanted me to *learn the family business* and run the ski resorts until I'm old and gray like him. The idea of turning into my father has always been enough to kick my ass into gear and get my goals.

I'd have better luck understanding cell structures if I wasn't con- stantly exhausted from practice, not to mention keeping my clown teammates out of trouble. When Greg Lewinski graduated and handed the captain torch to me last year, he didn't prepare me for how much babysitting it takes to keep butts on benches ready to play.

Robbie helps me out since he's assistant to Coach Faulkner. After a skiing accident in our junior year of high school, Robbie didn't regain movement in his legs and now uses a wheelchair. He trans- ferred his skill of shouting shit at me on the ice to shouting shit at me from the edge of the ice.

He loves nothing more than waving his oversized clipboard in my direction and telling me to do better. The guys on the team love that I take the brunt of Robbie's abuse because it gives the rest of them an easier time.

A perfect example is days like today. On Fridays, JJ and I have classes in the science building, so we have a tradition of dragging ourselves over to the rink for practice via a Dunkin' for a pre-workout doughnut.

It's our little secret, but JJ knows if we get caught, I'll get the blame anyway, so he doesn't mind the risk. The last class of the day on a Friday is my least favorite thing in the world, so I don't mind the risk, either.

I'm lazily scrolling through my feed, waiting for JJ outside his lab, when I hear his cheery tone getting louder as he approaches me. "You ready to get your hungover ass kicked?"

"Nothing a rainbow sprinkle ring can't solve. Sweating out alcohol is good anyway. Will get me fresh for tonight."

His brows furrow together. "What are you talking about? Have you not seen the group chat?"

The last thing I saw was Robbie deciding we were throwing a party tonight. Our first game isn't for another two weeks and it's tradition for us to bring in the season with a party or five.

The second I pull out my phone I can see the messages I haven't read yet.

PUCKBUNNIES

BOBBY HUGHES
Might be dying.

KRIS HUDSON
God speed, buddy.

ROBBIE HAMLET
Drinks at ours tonight?

BOBBY HUGHES
In the words of Michael Scott, I am ready to get hurt again.

JOE CARTER
I'll bring the tequila roulette board.

HENRY TURNER
Email from Faulkner says go to the awards room, not the rink.

JAIDEN JOHAL
Wtf?

HENRY TURNER
Sent an hour ago.

The awards room is a function room in the central area of the sports building. Most of us don't spend much time over there unless we're in trouble; it's where the coaches work outside of practice and games. It's where ceremonies are held at the end of the year. If we're being called there it means someone has massively fucked up, and I hope it wasn't me.

"I don't know what's going on," JJ says as we climb into my car. "Y'know Josh Mooney, the baseball guy in my class? He said their practice has been canceled, too. They have to go to the awards room, but they've been told to go thirty minutes after us. Fucking weird, man."

It's the third week of term, how much trouble could we be in?

We're in so much fucking trouble.

When we walk through the door, Coach doesn't even look in our direction. Half the team is already sitting in front of him, each wearing an identical look I recognize: fear. JJ takes a seat next to Henry and gives me a look that says *Find out, Captain*.

Neil Faulkner is not a man you want to get on the wrong side of. Three-time Stanley Cup winner before a drunk driver knocked him off the road, shattering his arms and right leg, instantly ending his NHL career. I've watched his old game tapes countless times, and he was—no, still is—one scary motherfucker.

So, the fact he's sitting on a chair in front of the team, red-faced like he's going to implode but saying nothing, is triggering my fight-or-flight. But my team needs me, so I reluctantly poke the bear.

"Coach, we we—"

"Get your ass on a seat, Hawkins."

"W—"

"I'm not going to tell you again."

Stumbling back to my teammates with my tail between my legs, they look even worse now than they did a minute ago. I'm racking my brain, trying to think what we could have done because there is no way he's angry over the house party we went to last night.

Apart from Henry, most of the underclassmen weren't there. They're not old enough to drink, so we don't invite them to parties with us. Not to say they're not all out getting wasted on frat row instead, but at least I'm not the one putting the beer in their hands when I'm supposed to be their responsible leader.

When Joe and Bobby arrive and sit, Coach finally makes a move—well, a huff, but at least it's something.

"In my fifteen years at this school, I have never been as ashamed as I was this morning."

Fuck.

"Before I go on, does anyone have anything to say?"

He's looking at each of us like he's waiting for someone to stand and confess, but I genuinely don't know what we're supposed to confess to. I've had the *I've never been so ashamed* speech *so* many times since I joined the team—it's a Faulkner special—but I've never seen him look this angry.

Folding his arms across his chest, he leans back in his chair and shakes his head. "This morning, when I arrived at the rink, I found it destroyed. So, who has been causing trouble?"

College sports are full of traditions. Some good, some bad, but traditions all the same. Maple Hills is no different, and each sport has its own quirks and superstitions that get passed down from year to year.

Ours are pranks. Reckless, childish pranks. Against each other, against other teams, against other sports. I've been in enough of these Faulkner verbal beatings over the years to know I wasn't letting it happen during my time as captain. Egotistical guys were fighting to outdo each other, and even themselves, until it got to the point the school was being forced to get involved.

So, if our arena has been trashed, it means someone hasn't been listening to me.

I creep forward slightly to get a better view of my teammates, and it takes approximately 0.2 seconds to spot Russ, a sophomore who's been playing with us for the last year, and right now looks like he's seen a ghost.

Faulkner's voice gets louder to the point it's echoing around the room. "The director is furious! The dean is furious! I'm fucking furious! I thought we'd drawn a line under this prank bullshit! You're supposed to be men! Not kids."

I want to say something, but my mouth is dry as hell. I clear my throat, which does nothing to help, but manages to capture his attention. Taking a sip of water, I finally manage to speak. "We have drawn a line, Coach. We haven't done anything."

"So, someone spontaneously decided to smash the generator and cooling system? My rink is on its way to being a swimming pool, and you expect me to believe you clowns have nothing to do with it?"

This is really, really bad.

"The director is holding a meeting with every student athlete in five minutes. Buckle up, gentlemen. I hope none of you want to make hockey your career."

Have I said *fuck*?

Chapter Three

ANASTASIA

MY PLANNER IS IN TOTAL, irreparable chaos and I'm irritated as hell.

This is the opposite of the Friday feeling people so famously love. Today was going to be a problem-free day; I woke up under a beautiful man, and the rest of my day was planned to perfection. Gym, college, training with Aaron, dinner, and finally, dancing until my feet hurt at whichever party sounded the most fun.

I even had the option to see Ryan again and concentrate on scratching those mutual itches while he's still got time.

But according to the very passive-aggressive email I received, David Skinner, Maple Hills Director of Sport, doesn't give a flying fuck about my planner or my training schedule, and he certainly doesn't give a fuck about my sex life.

Why else would he universally cancel training and drag every student athlete to the worst corner of campus?

This building is where all the coaches lurk and plot how to make us all miserable. When I posted a picture this morning that said *Just enjoy where you are now*, I didn't realize where I was going to be was a huge line of students trying to get into the awards room.

I'm lost in angry, borderline murderous thoughts when two muscular arms wrap around my waist from behind, and I feel lips press gently against the crown of my head. Instantly knowing it's Ryan, I settle into his embrace and tilt my head back to look at him. He moves to peck a kiss to my forehead, and sure, I might feel a little better. "Hey, beautiful girl."

"I'm stressed," I grumble, looking ahead to watch the line shuffle along. "And you're cutting in line. You're going to get into trouble."

Gripping my shoulders, he spins me around to face him. His long finger nudging under my chin, tilting my head up to meet his gigantic height. When I think he can't be any freaking cuter, he brushes my hair from my face and smiles at me. "You control the planner, Stas. The planner doesn't control you."

"You're still cutting in line."

He chuckles, shrugging. "You were holding my spot for me. That's what I told everyone I pushed past. Come on, what sickeningly motivational quote did you post today? Do we need to revisit it?"

Ryan and I started hooking up last year when we met at a party and were beer pong partners. Naturally, we won because we're the most stubborn and competitive people within a hundred-mile radius of Maple Hills. The next day he slid into my DMs, joking he wasn't expecting to find someone who plays drinking games so aggressively preaching about *positive vibes only* on their social media pages.

Since then, whenever I'm grumpy or fed up, he reminds me I'm supposed to be a ray of sunshine.

Dick.

"Well?" he asks, guiding me along as we get closer to the entrance.

"It was about stopping to enjoy the moment you're in."

His smile widens when he realizes he's got me. "Okay, yeah, I can work with that. It sucks practice was canceled, *but*, if you enjoy the moment, you're hanging out with me and I'm great."

Folding my arms across my chest, I try my hardest to stop the smile threatening to break through, continuing to pretend he's not having any impact on my mood. "Hmm."

"Tough crowd, *jeez*. As soon as we get out of here, I'll take you for food, and later, there's a hockey party we can hit to let you blow off all your stressy energy."

"What else?" I let him spin me back around now that we're only a few people away from finally getting into the room, and his hands stay on my shoulders.

"I'll take you home and let you take out any remaining stress on my body?"

"With a bat?"

His fingers sink into my tense muscles, rhythmically working out every knot as I roll my head side to side. "Kinky. Will you dress up as Harley Quinn, too?"

He grunts loudly as my elbow sinks into his ribs, which is ridiculously dramatic, because my elbow is definitely hurting more.

After what feels like a lifetime of waiting, we finally make it through the entrance to the awards room. Instead of normal round tables, the room has row upon row of chairs all facing the stage.

What the hell is going on?

Ignoring my immediate concern, Ryan insists I enjoy the moment, which roughly translates to me being forced to sit with the basketball team. So now I'm wedged between Ryan and Mason Wright, his teammate, who make my respectable five-foot-four-inch body look like one of an overgrown toddler.

"Chip?"

I struggle to look at the bag of Lays being shoved under my nose, but they smell like barbecue flavor, which Ryan knows is my favorite. "I'm good, thanks."

He leans forward to dig in the bag at his feet, rustling loudly, not caring people are staring at us. Throwing himself back into his seat with a huff, he holds out a packet. "Cookie?"

"No, thank you. I'm not hungry." I'm trying not to draw attention to us again, but it's hard to ignore the look of disappointment on his face. "Don't look at me like that. Regionals are right around the corner; I can't gain weight."

Ryan slouches in his seat so our heads are level, and he leans in to give us more privacy. His breath dances across my skin as his lips hover beneath my ear, sending a wave of goose bumps across my entire body.

"As someone who throws you around quite a lot, I feel like I'm qualified to say this: if that jackass isn't able to cope if your weight fluctuates a few pounds, which is perfectly normal, by the way, he shouldn't be your partner."

"We're not having this conversation again, Ryan."

"Sta—" he starts, cutting himself off when Director Skinner finally strolls onto the stage, squinting under the spotlights. Ryan sits back up straight and rests his hand on my thigh, squeezing softly. "Maybe we will need a bat later."

The high-pitched squeal of the microphone turning on echoes around the room, causing everyone to wince. Skinner has taken his place behind the podium but hasn't managed to force a smile yet.

He's aged a lot in the time I've studied at UCMH. He previously looked approachable and eager, but now, with the disdain he's sporting deepening the lines on his forehead, he looks anything but.

"Good afternoon, everyone. Thank you for taking the time to come here on such short notice. I'm sure you're all wondering why you're here."

I don't know why he's pretending like the email didn't have the word *compulsory* in bold, capital letters.

Skinner shrugs off his suit jacket, hanging it over the chair behind him, sighing as he turns to face us all again. He drags a hand over his thinning gray hair, which I swear was thick and black when I was a freshman.

"There's a certain expectation when dealing with college students. It's a given there will be some level of chaos as you begin your lives as adults away from home." He sighs again, his exhaustion clear. "When you add competitive sport into the mix, the balance changes as you try to manage your skill against the authentic college experience."

Well, this is patronizing. It feels like he made his secretary write this little speech, and he practiced it in the mirror a few times. If Lo were here, she'd be highly critical of his performance.

"Some of you have been enjoying the college experience a little too much."

Here. We. Go.

"In the five years I've been Director of Sport, I have dealt with countless avoidable situations. Out-of-control parties, medical expenses due to students behaving recklessly on campus, more pranks than I can count, unplanned pregnancy, an—"

The noise of Michael Fletcher's chair scraping across the floor rings out as he springs to his feet.

"Mr. Fletcher, please take a seat."

Fletch ignores him, bending to grab his bag from the floor instead. He stomps toward the exit, pushing both doors open forcefully and leaving the room.

I don't know a lot about football, but everyone says Fletch is the best linebacker this college has ever seen and is practically guaranteed a spot in the NFL when he graduates.

More importantly, he's an incredibly proud father to his little girl, Diya, who he had with his girlfriend, Prishi, last year.

Prishi was on the skate team with me before she accidentally became pregnant at the start of her junior year. When I asked her if she'd be returning, she said her bladder isn't what it used to be after pushing out a nine-pound baby, and she didn't fancy peeing on the ice in front of an audience.

They live together with their friends, and everyone takes turns looking after the baby to allow Fletch and Prishi to go to class. The fact Skinner is using them as an example in his delinquent student–bashing exercise is shitty of him.

Twenty minutes pass and he's still going. I rest my head against Ryan's shoulder and close my eyes, accepting the cookie he sneaks into the palm of my hand.

". . . To summarize."

Finally.

"Going forward, there will be a zero-tolerance approach to misappropriation of your status on this campus."

I feel like I'm missing a huge part of the puzzle here because—despite his long-ass, still-not-over speech—I have zero idea what prompted this rude interruption to my schedule.

"For the seniors hoping to join professional teams at the end of this school year, it would be prudent for you to take note of this message."

Beside me Ryan snorts, shoving another cookie in his mouth. When I open my mouth to ask what's so funny, he shoves one into mine, grinning like a fool because I have no choice but to eat it.

Skinner finally runs out of energy. He leans against the podium and his shoulders sag. "I don't care what your potential is. If you don't fall in line, you will be benched. I'd like the skating and hockey team to stay behind, but the rest of you are dismissed."

Ryan grabs his bag from the floor and stands, stretching and letting out an overexaggerated yawn. "I'll wait for you outside. Food?"

I give him a nod, creeping onto my tiptoes to wipe the cookie crumbs from the corner of his mouth with my thumb. "Hopefully I won't be long."

Everyone, bar the fifty-ish of us, filter out of the room. Ironically, about five times quicker than they filtered in.

Brady and Faulkner, the ice hockey team coach, join Director Skinner on the stage. "Come closer, everyone, I'm tired of this microphone."

As we all head to the front of the room as requested, I spot an annoyed-looking Aaron in the crowd and move to his side.

"You okay?" I ask quietly as we take a seat in the front row.

"Yep."

It doesn't take a genius to know he isn't in a great mood, but this feels directed at me, not at Skinner. "You sure?"

His lips are pulled in a tight line, and he hasn't looked at me yet. "Yep."

Skinner steps out from behind his podium and pushes his hands into his suit pants pockets, his tired, sunken eyes scanning those of us left. "I'll make this quick. Following what can only be labeled as a colossal shit show, Arena Two is out of action for the foreseeable future."

Oh God.

"An investigation is underway into how the extensive damage was caused, but I'm told there will be significant delays when it comes to repairs, due to a shortage of parts for our particular equipment."

The realization doesn't wash over me, it fucking drowns me. The hockey team is known for causing trouble with rival teams, and each other usually. The spoiled, rich-boy-to-hockey-team pipeline thrives at this school, and I'd put money on one of them being the culprit.

"What this means for you," Skinner continues, "is you will need to share a rink until repairs are complete, and I expect you all to work together to make this situation work."

Clearly knowing the number of questions about to come his way, Skinner proves he doesn't actually care about us, and immediately dips. He's not even off the stage before I'm storming over to Coach Brady.

"We have regionals in *five* weeks!"

"I'm well aware of your competition schedule, Anastasia," Coach Brady drawls, waving off some of the underclassmen when they attempt to crowd around when I'm very close to having a meltdown. "We have no other option, so it isn't worth getting upset over."

Is she for real? "How are we going to qualify if we can't practice?"

Ten feet away, Coach Faulkner is flanked by his own team, I would imagine fending off the same concerns. Not like I care—they obviously caused this mess, and now we're the ones who are going to suffer.

I'm trying to not catastrophize, to not blow this out of proportion in my head. I'm concentrating on breathing in and out, and not bawling uncontrollably in front of strangers, while I listen to my teammates voice the same concerns. When I let my eyes drift back over to the hockey team, most of them have gone. There's one guy talking to Faulkner, and he must feel me watching him, because his eyes meet mine. He's looking at me with a weird expression on his face, a forced pity grimace, I think.

Frankly, he can take his fake sympathy and shove it up his ass.

"We'll talk about this at practice, Stassie," Brady says, offering a rare—almost borderline friendly—smile. "Enjoy a Friday evening off for once. I'll see you both on Monday."

After another small protest, I finally listen to Brady's pleas for me to leave her alone, and head toward the exit. I'm trailing behind Aaron, dragging my feet, and feeling sorry for myself, when I hear a "Hey" and feel a hand land on my bicep.

It's Mr. Sympathy, still sporting—you guessed it—a pity pout. "Listen, I'm sorry. I know this sucks for all of us. I'm going to do what I can to make this as easy as possible."

He lets go of my arm and takes a step back, giving me the chance to look at him up close for the first time. He towers over me by at least a foot, broad shoulders, thick muscles straining against the sleeves of his Henley. Even beneath a dusting of stubble, you can see the sharpness of his jawline. I'm trying to work out if I've ever met him before when he starts talking again.

"I know you're probably feeling stressed, but we're having a party tonight if you want to come."

"And you are?" I ask, forcing my voice to sound calm. I can't ignore the twinge of satisfaction I get when his eyebrows shoot up for a split second.

He gains his composure just as quickly, amusement lighting up his deep brown eyes. "Nate Hawkins. I'm captain of the hockey team." He holds out a hand for me to shake, but I look at it, then back up at his face, folding my arms across my chest.

"Were you not listening? Party time is over according to Skinner."

He shrugs and reaches around to rub the back of his neck awkwardly. "People will show up regardless, even if I tried to stop it. Look, come over, bring friends or whatever. It'd be good if we could all get along, and I swear, we have good tequila. Do you have a name?"

I refuse to be charmed by a pretty face. Not even one with little dimples and nice cheekbones. This is still a disaster. "Do you meet a lot of people who don't have names?"

To my surprise, he starts laughing. A heavy, rich noise that makes my cheeks flush. "Okay, you've got me there."

His eyes flick behind me as an arm lands across my shoulders. I look up, expecting to find Ryan, but instead find Aaron. I shrug off his embrace, since stuff like this is what makes people assume we're dating, when I'd honestly rather eat my skates. "Are you coming?" he snaps.

Nodding, I take one last look at my new rink *friend*. He doesn't bother introducing himself to Aaron, instead he mouths, *Remember the party* to me.

God, Lola is going to love all this drama.

Chapter Four

NATHAN

THE ENTIRE HOCKEY TEAM POURS through the front door and immediately heads toward the liquor cabinet.

I wait until Russ is about to walk past then grip his arm, stopping him in his tracks. "My room. Three-nine-nine-three."

His face drops and he forces a nervous laugh. "You're not my type, Cap."

I tighten my grip when he attempts to walk off toward the rest of our team members, who are passing around beers in the living room. "It's been a long fucking day. Don't make me do this in front of the whole team."

His shoulders drop in defeat, and he trudges up each step like a naughty schoolkid, his head hung low. I mean, technically right now he *is* a naughty schoolkid.

Sharing a rink right before the start of the season is a logistic fucking nightmare—not to mention when we have home games. *Fuck.* I feel like I have a migraine coming on already and we haven't even attempted to work out a schedule yet.

The brown-haired figure skater was seething earlier. I'm surprised a vein didn't pop out of her forehead when her coach told her to not worry about it. I was trying to discreetly listen in, which wasn't hard since she was yelling. I feel like doing the same when I think about "not worrying about it," so at least she and I have something in common. Her boyfriend looked totally unfazed, so maybe he'll help her calm down, or maybe not, judging by the way she shrugged him off.

She's a funny little thing. Immediately sassing me, holding her head high, but I *think* she might have been warming to me. Minutes earlier, she was clearly on the brink of tears. I'm hoping she takes up my offer and we can have a drink, form a friendship of some sort. It'll make this whole situation easier.

I decide to let Russ wait for twenty minutes, hoping the guilt will be eating away at him, and it won't be hard to find out what's happened. He'll be upstairs listening to people laugh and joke without him, but he won't realize people are laughing about how fucking awful this season is going to be.

I feel sorry for them.

So much so, I'm not even kicking the rookies out as they drown their sorrows in their beer bottles. I feel like I need to make a motivational speech or something, cheer everyone up, but first I need to work out exactly why we're in this mess.

Russ is sitting on my desk chair, spinning in circles, when I finally join him. I expect him to make a snide remark, moan about waiting so long—something I would have done when I was a cocky little shit—but he doesn't say anything. He sits silently, waiting for me to make the first move.

"What did you do?" He rubs his hands together, leaning forward to rest his elbows against his knees. He's uncomfortable. His face is pale, and he looks ill more than anything. "Buddy, I can't help you if you don't tell me what I've gotta help with."

"I didn't do anything."

I run my hand across my face, trying not to lose my patience. "I know you've done something, and I can't fix it if you lie to me."

When I first started playing hockey at Maple Hills, our captain was a dick, and everyone hated him for it. I never expected to become captain, but I knew if I did, I wouldn't be like him. Russ has a shitty home life, and I know he didn't work his ass off to get himself out of that situation to come here and be treated the same way by me.

Maybe I wouldn't be this patient with some of the other guys on the team but being a good leader means knowing how to get through to your men.

Taking a seat on my bed across from him, I slowly watch about ten different emotions hit him all at once. "It wasn't a prank, I promise."

"Right, keep talking."

"There's this girl at UCLA. I met her at a party a couple of weeks ago. We started screwing around, and then every party I was at she'd be there. I thought she was single but . . ." He looks at his hands, picking at the calluses on his palms.

"But?"

"But she has a boyfriend. He found out somehow and sent me a message saying I was gonna fucking regret even looking at her. Then this happened so it must be that, right?"

"You still talking to this girl?"

He shakes his head. "I blocked her on everything as soon as I found out she had a boyfriend."

"You don't tell anyone this, okay? You'll get kicked off the team," I say seriously. "I mean it, kid. When they ask why you've been up here, tell them you got shit going on at home or something, and you wanted to talk to me."

"Okay, Cap."

I nod toward my door. "Get yourself a beer."

I wait until he's out of the room and stomping down the stairs before I scream every curse word I know into my pillow, for the second time today.

A FEW HOURS AFTER MY best attempt at being a responsible captain, the house is overflowing with people, empty bottles, and red cups. Part of me is expecting David Skinner to walk through the door, or worse, Faulkner.

I doubt Coach would be too thrilled we decided to end the worst day ever with a party we were told not to have. Normally Friday parties are full of tired athletes, aching from Friday games or practice, looking to unwind and watch other people make some questionable choices. But tonight, there's something different in the air. It's almost like being reminded we shouldn't be misbehaving is making everyone want to go wild.

I spot Briar, Summer's roommate, pouring herself a drink at the kitchen counter, which immediately makes me feel better. Those girls are inseparable, so if B is here, Summer will be here somewhere. She can't reject me twice in one week, right?

Summer jokes the only reason I want her is because she's not interested, and she's the only woman who's ever rejected me. Hearing her say she's not interested makes me want her more, so thinking about it logically, she's probably right. As much as I want a chance with her, we are good friends, which makes her rejection sting a bit less.

I push past the masses of people and put on my friendliest *I wanna marry your best friend* face. Briar's so engrossed in the random liquor she's mixing, she doesn't even notice me as I lean against the counter beside her. "That looks like you're gonna be throwing up on my lawn later, Beckett."

Her head snaps up, long blond hair swishing as she finds me next to her. "It's a good job I'm not drinking alone then, isn't it," she slurs, her accent an unusual mix of British and American.

Her green eyes are glassy, and her smile is more of a lazy, drunken smirk as she winks at me and pushes the cup in my direction, immediately reaching for a new one. "I heard you had a shitty day. I did, too, we can be sick together."

I wait until she's mixed another disgusting concoction before tipping my cup to hers. "To dipshit sophomores."

She snorts. "To dipshit ex-girlfriends."

I throw back the drink and *fuck* does it sting. *"Jesus Christ."* I choke as the fluid burns its way down my throat. "Who the fuck taught you to mix drinks?"

"My uncle James. He calls it a magic cocktail. You looking for Summer?" She rolls her eyes at me when I nod. "She's playing beer pong with Cami in the den."

"I'll remember this beautiful moment when I'm making the speech at mine and Summer's wedding." I knock back the rest of my poison, trying not to gag, but failing.

"No you won't!" she shouts after me. "She knows you fucked Kitty last night!"

Fuck.

Summer is bent over the table, lining up a shot, when I push my way through the crowd to stand next to her. She's playing Ryan and CJ from the basketball team with her other best friend, Cami.

"You winning?"

"Go away, Nathan," she laughs, not bothering to look up at me. "You're going to distract me."

"Rude. What if I'm your good-luck cha—" I don't even get to finish my sentence because I'm eating my words as she sends the ball bouncing across the room by accident.

She finally looks up at me, her eyes murderous in a way I find weirdly sexy. I clear my throat. "I'll cheer you on from over here."

She rolls her eyes, muttering under her breath knowing I won't understand her, *"Tienes suerte de ser guapo."*

Scanning the den to see who turned up, I immediately spot Miss I-don't-have-a-name. She looks significantly more relaxed than she did earlier; her long light brown hair is curly, bouncing around her face as she throws back her head and laughs at something her friend said. Her cheeks are flushed, ocean-blue eyes bright; she looks happy.

I like it.

She spots me before I reach her, and I might be imagining it, but I swear she checks me out. "You made it!" I say cheerfully, although she doesn't react. I try her friend instead, who's staring at me with an intrigued look on her face. "I'm Nate."

"Lola." She flicks her finger between the two of us, eyes narrowing. "Do you two know each other?"

"We met earlier," I confirm, watching her ignore my attempt to get her to look at me. She takes a sip from what I can see—from my height advantage—is an empty cup. "Didn't get your name, though, sadly."

She stops pretending to drink and finally looks at my face. She only looks like she wants to hit me with a hockey stick a little bit now, which is a huge improvement from earlier.

"Anastasia. Or Stassie. Whichever, it doesn't matter."

"Can I get you guys a drink?" I ask.

"I can get my own, it's fine."

Lola huffs and rolls her eyes at her friend, smiling up at me. "Ignore her, she doesn't know how to play nicely with others. Only child thing."

"*Jesus*. Okay, I'll help *you*, though," Anastasia says, walking off toward the kitchen, dragging her friend behind her with her free hand. I jog after them, scooping the empty cups from her grip. "A drink isn't going to charm me into not being mad about the rink, y'know."

I can believe that. Nothing about this girl tells me she's going to be easy to crack, and it's made this whole rink situation a bit more interesting. "You haven't even seen how charming I can be yet," I tease, grinning ear to ear when I catch the corner of her mouth creeping up. "You're going to be impressed."

She takes the cups back from my hands and moves in front of me to place them on the counter, getting to work making two drinks. "I'm immune to hockey player charm."

Robbie wheels his chair to my side and digs me in the leg, mouthing *What the fuck* behind the girls' backs with wide eyes. He clears his throat and they both turn to face him. "What about charming assistant hockey coaches?"

"Oh, she's *definitely* immune to those, but I'm not. Hi, I'm Lola."

"Robbie."

Lola elbows Stassie who mumbles a "Hi."

"This is Stassie. She acts like she's grumpy but she's actually very nice."

"Thanks for coming to my party," he says, not taking his eyes off Lola. I don't know whether to cringe or stand in awe as she flutters her eyelashes at him and giggles.

Unbelievable.

Anastasia has the same blend of confusion and amusement on her face as she looks between our friends. "Lols, I'm going to get into line for the bathroom. Are you coming?" Lola's eyes flick to hers then back to Robbie's, before shaking her head. "Okay, I'll meet you back here."

I hold out a hand to lead her toward the stairs. "Come on, you can use my bathroom." She looks at my hand once then back up to my face, eyes narrowing suspiciously. "I have a password-protected door and a private bathroom. You can join the line if you want," I say, pointing toward the people drunkenly draping over the staircase.

She sighs in defeat and drops her hand into my palm, weaving her fingers between mine. "This isn't me forgiving you."

"Obviously."

I navigate us through the crowd, keeping her body close to mine, her free hand resting gently on my waist, until we reach the stairs. She walks around me to go first, and I immediately realize letting her go in front of me is a mistake, because as soon as she gets a few steps ahead, I've got her ass in my direct vision, swaying side to side as she takes each step.

I usher her in and point toward the bathroom, getting a weird sense of déjà vu watching her after this morning's antics. At least she's clothed. *Wait, why am I saying it like it's a good thing?*

She exits the bathroom after a couple of minutes, stopping in her tracks when she spots me waiting for her on my bed. I hold up my hands defensively. "I didn't want you to get lost."

"It's fine." She folds her arms across her chest and tilts her head to the side in a way that almost looks playful. "I'm disappointed you're here; I was going to snoop."

It's nice to see a different side to her after the one I met this afternoon. Not that there's anything wrong with showing emotion, I just prefer to see her more relaxed.

For the first time, I get a real look at what she's wearing. Tight leather pants that look like they were freaking painted on, and a black lace corset, showing her body in a way I'm not sure I even know how to describe. What I'm saying but not saying is she's hot, and maybe getting to know her a little better won't be a bad thing.

"Don't let my presence deter you from snooping," I joke. "I'll wait right here."

The sound of her heels clicking echoes around the room as she walks slowly toward my desk, not taking her eyes off me. Her fingers travel across the pile of biology books littering my desk. "What're you studying?"

"Sports medicine, you?"

"Business." She picks up a picture from my desk, analyzing it thoroughly before looking back at me. "West Coast kid?"

"Mountains."

"Wyoming?" she asks, putting the photograph down and picking up the one next to it.

"Close." I stand and walk over to the desk, taking the picture from her hand and replacing it with one of me and Robbie at our first hockey game when we were five. "Colorado. Eagle County. You?"

"I'm from Seattle. That's Vail, right? Rich-kid hockey star from Eagle County is a bit predictable, isn't it?" I sit on the desk so we're at eye level, folding my own arms to match her guarded stance. "A little bit cliché?"

I can't keep the smirk from my lips as her ocean-blue eyes lock with mine. "You think I'm a star?"

Turning quickly, she scoffs and heads across the room, sitting on my bed. I want to follow her like a little puppy, but I force myself to stay put, watching as she places her hands behind her and leans back, letting her silky brown hair drape over her shoulder.

"I've never watched you play," she says with a bit more cheer than I'd like. "I *strongly* dislike hockey."

"I'm offended, Anastasia. I'll have to get you tickets for rinkside seats at our next home game."

"I don't need tickets for an event in my own arena. That's if you guys don't fuck up before then and your team gets axed."

There is almost a bit too much optimism in her tone when she says the word *axed*. It's like being verbally abused by Tinkerbell.

"Who did you guys terrorize enough to deserve getting your rink trashed?"

This isn't going to be the last time I get asked this question, so I need to get used to it, even though I hate lying to people. It's a white lie, but I'm not a fan of starting a friendship with a negative. "We haven't done anything, so I'm not sure." Her eyes narrow because she clearly doesn't believe me, so I panic. "I promise, Anastasia."

Her eyes soften and I immediately feel like shit. *Why the fuck did I promise?*

"Should we head back downstairs?"

"Sure. Robbie has probably charmed the pants off your friend by now."

She chuckles and it's borderline embarrassing how happy I feel finally getting her to laugh. "Trust me, Lola is more than happy to be charmed by a hot guy."

This time I'm smart enough to walk in front of her down the stairs, resting our interlocked hands on my shoulder for her to use me to balance. It's not until I'm on the bottom step that I see her boyfriend—who I'd forgotten existed—standing there, staring at me like all hell is about to break loose.

Chapter Five

ANASTASIA

NATE STOPS ABRUPTLY IN FRONT of me, almost sending me tumbling down the stairs.

"What're you doing?" I ask, confused when he practically rips his hand from mine. He steps to the side, and as soon as his massive body is out of the way, I see what he can see.

"Your boyfriend looks like he wants to murder me."

"Well, that's odd," I muse, moving so we're on the same step. "I don't have a boyfriend."

He's right, though; Aaron does look ready to murder someone. It doesn't change as he approaches me and Nate when we step off the last stair. "Hey," I chirp. "I thought you were staying home tonight."

Aaron is still staring at Nate, even when I place my hand on his arm and give it a squeeze. Aaron's eyes finally meet mine, eyebrows raised. "What were you doing upstairs with him?"

I feel Nate beside me, the ghost of his touch hovering around the bottom of my back. I decide to play nice instead of tearing Aaron a new one for being so weird and rude in front of an audience like I want to. "Aaron, this is Nate. Nate, this is Aaron, my skating partner."

The testosterone oozing out of them is practically palpable as they shake hands, each of their hands turning white when they try to crush each other's bones. *Pathetic.* When they eventually let go and the blood returns to their fingers, I turn to Aaron and force a fake smile, even though he doesn't deserve it. "You good? Where have you been?"

"I asked you first."

"I was peeing, is that a sufficient answer?" I snap, finally losing my composure.

It's been a long-ass day and I've already had to tolerate Aaron's bullshit once, when he decided Ryan was public enemy number one after the meeting.

Ryan wanted to take me for food, you know, a normal activity between friends. Aaron kissed his teeth as he reminded me I have an outfit to fit into for regionals. Like I could ever possibly forget, especially being around him. Ryan was pissed, so told Aaron if he couldn't lift me, he needs to work harder in the gym.

Of course, Aaron didn't like that so fired back, and in the end, I was so tired of the drama Ryan ended up giving me a ride home. Unfortunately, my chicken salad didn't taste as good with the knowledge that Ryan would have convinced me to eat a burger or something.

So now I'm irritated and hungry, a bit drunk, and once again watching Aaron be an ass and embarrass me.

Aaron quirks a brow, clearly not believing I was using the bathroom. "Thought you were collecting team captains like Pokémon. Where's Rothwell? He's normally the one draped all over you."

His words hit me right in the chest like he wanted them to, and I can't stop the lump forming in my throat. Nate's hand settles on my back as he takes a step closer. "If you're going to be a dick you need to leave, dude. People are trying to have a good night."

"You're intruding on a private conversation, *dude,*" Aaron responds bluntly.

"You're in my house and you're being rude to my guest. Lighten the fuck up or leave."

Nate is a big guy, much bigger than Aaron. He's a good half a foot taller, broader, more muscular. Not to mention he's a freaking hockey player. Aaron is built like a ballet dancer, strong, too, but lean. Plus, he has never been in a fight in his cushy, privileged life, which is why it's so surprising to me that he starts shit with people who have.

"I'm sorry, Stas," he says, my name slurring slightly. "I suppose I'm upset now I know why the rink was trashed."

"Nobody knows what happened," Nate answers quickly.

Too quickly.

Aaron laughs, but there's no humor to it. "I do. Rookie couldn't keep it in his pants. Knocked up someone's little sister. Ghosted her." He turns to me, the shock on his face clearly fake. "How bad is that, Stas? Ghosting the freshman you knocked up? And now *we're* suffering."

"That isn't what happened," Nate says coldly.

God, I feel foolish right now. I shouldn't have believed his promise; of course he knows. My body stiffens under Nate's hand, and he removes it quickly, moving away to give me space. "Well, this was fun," I say flatly, trying not to show any emotion, since it's clearly what Aaron was hoping for. "I'm heading home."

"Cool, we can ride together. I'll go find Lo."

He's a different guy in a matter of minutes. It's like being friends with Jekyll and Hyde sometimes, especially after a drink when his nasty side comes out. It's disappointing because most of the time he's great, but he's so fucking good at hiding the nice side of himself.

Nate pinches the bridge of his nose between his fingers, blowing out a frustrated sigh as we both watch Aaron disappear into the crowd. "I didn't want to lie to you."

Putting some distance between us, I turn to face him. He looks like he's got the weight of the world on his shoulders right now, and he might for all I know. But I have goals, too. I love my sport and my time on the ice is as valuable as his.

He drags his hand down his face and forces a smile. "I don't want this to affect our friendship—well, like, the friendship we could have."

"You think a good friendship starts with a lie?"

"No, well," he says, stumbling over his words. "I didn't want to lie to you. But my team doesn't even know, and I swear, it isn't what happened. Your partner is lying, too."

I wish I hadn't come to this party. "Great, so everyone is lying to me. *Fantastic*," I say sarcastically. "Forget it, it's fine. The hockey team can look after themselves, and the rest of us will, I dunno, go fuck ourselves or something."

I doubt Dr. Andrews, my long-suffering therapist, would be impressed with me right now. *Communication is king* is what he's said every session for over a decade. Technically, I am communicating, not very well, but it still counts. I don't know how to tell Nate how stressful this whole situation is for me without seeming dramatic. Maybe I'm not trying hard enough to not react the way Aaron was hoping, but I blame the alcohol and lack of decent food.

Nate catches my arm as I turn to walk away. Looking at him over my shoulder, I see his face soften. "I promise, he only hooked up with her. She's got a boyfriend and he didn't know. Nothing about a pregnancy."

He looks like he's being genuine, but he did earlier as well. Turning to face him, I take a step back to keep enough distance between us but his hand stays on my arm. "No offense, but your promises don't mean shit. You have zero idea the pressure I'm under, the sacrifices I've had to make. You don't understand how it feels, knowing it all hangs in the balance because some kid doesn't know how to wrap up his dick."

His brows furrow together, confusion, maybe. "'Hangs in the balance'? You're blowing this out of proportion. If we don't overreact and we work toge—"

It's like I can physically feel my blood boiling. Clearly he has no idea of the impact of his team's mistakes. He has a full team to help him win, but it's just me and Aaron. If we don't practice enough, we don't win. If we don't win, we don't go to the Olympics. If we don't go to the Olympics, what was the fucking point?

There is a reason Maple Hills has two rinks. There is a reason it produces some of the best athletes in the country. It's because the school makes sure we have enough space to get the time we need to be the best.

"You think I'm being dramatic? You know what, Nate," I say sharply, shaking off his hand. "Forget it. Stay out of my way and I'll stay out of yours."

"Stassie!" he shouts after me as I head into the crowd.

But I ignore him, the start of what is going to be a lot of me ignoring him.

At the end of what is possibly the worst day ever, my level of irritation continues to rise because trying to find Lola in this house is like trying to find Waldo.

Aaron is also nowhere to be seen, although I can't quite decide if it's a good thing or a bad thing after his little performance.

I track down Ryan easily; it isn't hard since he's still in the den with his basketball friends. However, I wasn't expecting to find him sitting on a couch, whispering into the ear of Olivia Abbott.

Weirdly, my first thought is *I wonder if Lola knows her archnemesis is here*, but after I shake that off, I'm in shock.

I don't think I've seen Olivia at a party before, ever. She's even more beautiful up close than she is on the stage; long golden-blond hair styled like an old Hollywood icon, eyeliner that would take me three weeks to perfect, and a perfect red lip. She looks like she should be going on the red carpet, not sitting at a college party.

"Hey, I'm sorry to interrupt," I say as I approach them. Ryan stops whispering and looks up at me. "Have you guys seen Lola?"

Ryan immediately looks concerned, even though he doesn't need to be. Well, unless I murder Aaron tonight and he has to help me hide the body. "Everything okay?" Ryan asks cautiously.

"Aaron being Aaron. We're heading home."

"I saw her go into Robbie's room with him quite a while ago," Olivia says quietly. "I can make sure she gets home okay if you need to go. I'm not drinking and my car is right outside."

"Do you need my help with Aaron?" Ryan asks cautiously.

"Olivia, if you could I will love you forever," I promise, breathing a sigh of relief now I know Lo is covered. "Aaron will be fine now he's got all his bitchiness out. I'm sorry I didn't get a chance to talk to you tonight, Olivia. You look beautiful. Next time we can get to know each other properly. My Uber is outside, though, so I need to go."

She gives me a shy smile. "That would be nice. See you soon."

"Text me when you get home, 'kay?" Ryan shouts as I walk away. "I mean it, Stas. Don't forget."

I know it might be weird to think about the guy you have casual sex with and your best friend's fake archnemesis together, but an Abbott + Rothwell relationship would be the type teenage girls cry over because of how perfect it is.

Ryan and I work so well because I don't want a relationship, and he doesn't care. If he found someone he wanted to date, I would never stand in his way. He deserves to be loved like that and he deserves to be happy, because he's such an amazing guy.

He would be Olivia's greatest supporter, and maybe he'd bring her out of her shell a little. I don't know Olivia yet, but even when she gets the role Lola wants, Lola can't deny Olivia seems like a nice girl.

I can't wait to see where this goes.

I STARTED WORKING AT SIMONE'S Rink freshman year when Rosie, a friend of a friend, mentioned her mom was looking to hire help.

The cost of textbooks was mounting up and I couldn't ask my parents for money, since they were already paying for all my skating stuff. Simone, the owner, paid for me to do a coaching qualification, which meant I could teach Saturday classes to kids under ten.

"All good?" Simone asks, walking into the break room where I'm sitting, contemplating what to eat.

"Yeah, great. I'm gonna go grab some lunch before my next class, I think."

"There is a very handsome man in reception asking for you," she says with a wink. "Looks like he has food with him."

Venturing out to the reception desk, I see Simone was right, there is a very handsome man.

Ryan looks super out of place with the energetic six-year-olds circling him, screeching. The second he spots me, his tired eyes soften, and the corner of his mouth tugs up. He holds up paper bags in each hand. "Wanna be my lunch date?"

"I've got another class at one p.m.; can you eat all that in thirty minutes?"

"I can achieve a lot in thirty minutes, Anastasia, you should know that by now."

We settle down at a table in a quiet corner next to the concession stand, and he begins to unbox the food. "Before you shout at me, I got you a Cobb salad . . . but I also got you a side of bacon cheese fries and nuggets, because I saw your post this morning about how important balance is."

I roll my eyes because I'm not sure which of us is becoming more predictable. "Balance is important, stop teasing me! Anyway, thank you. You didn't have to bring me lunch—well, two lunches—but I appreciate you. Where did you end up last night?"

Ryan takes a bite of his cheeseburger and stuffs in some fries, groaning happily. "West Hollywood at The Honeypot. I overdid it."

"With Olivia?"

I swear his cheeks blush a little. "No, Liv headed home, unfortunately. Stop looking at me like that."

"Oh, she's 'Liv' now is she? I'm excited for you. I'm allowed to be excited, so you can't stop me. You haven't dated anyone in so long, and she seems like a nice person from the little I know."

"I'm not dating her, drama queen. We exchanged numbers."

"The first step of any marriage."

He huffs, shrugging and wiping his hands on a napkin. "We'll see. Why can't you marry me, Allen?"

"Why did you skip over being your girlfriend and go straight to marriage?"

"Why date when we're already best friends? Dating is scary. Mind-blowing sex and someone who doesn't get pissy with my schedule? Sign me up, I'll put a ring on it right now. Will you accept an onion ring instead of a diamond?"

"I don't get pissy with your schedule because I'm too busy to notice you're busy," I say, leaning over to nudge him in the arm. "Olivia is nice, Ry. Take her out and see how it goes. Worst-case scenario, you can tell your future kids you went on a date with a famous movie star or Broadway star, whatever she ends up becoming."

"Do you think it's a good idea for me to take advice from you? A huge commitmentphobe?"

He might have a point there.

"I'll ask her out, but if it goes horribly wrong, Anastasia, I'm blaming you."

"That's fair."

"Want to tell me what went on with Aaron?" I can tell by the tone of his voice he's trying his best to seem calm and uninterested. In actual fact, based on the twelve texts he sent me at various stages of the night, I know he's very interested.

"He asked me if I was collecting team captains like Pokémon," I drawl, unboxing my nuggets and throwing one into my mouth. "Saw me coming downstairs with Nate Hawkins and assumed I'd fucked him."

"What the fuck is that guy's problem?" Ryan mutters, stabbing his fries into ketchup aggressively. "I don't know how you spend so much time with him. Even if you had been hooking up with Hawkins, it's no one else's business. You're a single woman and you can do what you want."

"I know, I know. But then Aaron revealed he'd found out what happened with the rink trashing, and Nate had promised me he didn't know minutes earlier, so it caused a bit of an argument."

"Aaron is a dick, Stassie. It's not great Hawkins lied, but at the same time, he's gotta put his team first. It's not the same as me lying to you or something, you guys don't have trust yet. Surely you understand?"

"Yeah, of course I do, but when I was trying to explain how much this impacts me, he made out I was being dramatic. And whether I was or not doesn't matter. How are we supposed to be equals when he doesn't even try to see my point of view?"

"Being captain is a tough gig, take it from me. You've gotta think of twenty-plus people as well as yourself. They're all looking for you to have their back, no matter what senseless shit they've done. It can fucking suck sometimes. Hawkins is a good guy, though, don't hold it against him."

I'm having an intense staring contest with my nuggets because I can't look at Ryan's face while he talks sense.

He snickers, leaning forward to grab my attention. "You're going to hold it against him, aren't you?"

"Definitely, without a doubt. Forever. Even longer than forever if I can manage it. They threw a huge curveball into the mix, and I'm going to stay away from all of them."

He's laughing at himself before he even says anything. "You know curveballs are baseball not hockey, right?"

Chapter Six

NATHAN

THE LAST THREE WEEKS HAVE been some of the most stressful of my life.

Aaron Carlisle—God, even his name sounds dickish—ran his mouth off to anyone who would listen. Including his coach, who told our coach, who then threatened to start tearing off limbs if someone didn't explain to him what the hell was going on.

I've spent more time getting screamed at with the team than I have playing hockey with them recently. The guys who trashed the rink were on the UCLA hockey team, our closest rival college. Aaron wasn't fully lying; the girl is pregnant, but it has nothing to do with Russ.

The poor kid didn't know anything about it; he thought he'd been hooking up with someone's girlfriend. She blamed him when her older brother found out, and she panicked. I suppose it was easier to blame a stranger, and I doubt she expected him to drive over here and fuck up our arena.

Russ has aged about ten years since this started. The relief on his face when we told him the real story was unbelievable. Faulkner and I had a meeting with the UCLA coach and captain, and they were able to tell us the full story. I've known Cory O'Neill, the captain, for years and he was as pissed about this as I am.

I felt like Dr. Phil giving the results of a paternity test—well, Jerry

Springer is more accurate for this bunch. Safe to say, we're all on thin ice with Faulkner. He said the next person to do something irresponsible will get benched for the rest of the season. He said he didn't care about our postcollege prospects; he'd forfeit every game until we learned how to behave.

I'm on my best behavior for the rest of the year because I'm not sure Vancouver will still want me if I get expelled or delimbed, and there is no fucking way I'm going back to Colorado after I leave this place.

Is it a cliché being a guy who grew up with immense privilege and also has daddy issues? Yes. But in my defense, my dad is a massive jackass. I'm pretty sure he didn't get hugged enough as a child and now he's making it my and my sister's problem.

Luckily, I managed to move a thousand miles away, but poor Sasha is still stuck with him since she's only sixteen. Even when she turns eighteen, I doubt he'll let her leave. She'll be stuck being an underappreciated, overworked skiing prodigy.

Dad is prepared to throw money at every coach in the northern hemisphere, if it means Sash gets to be the next Lindsey Vonn. Ideally without the injuries, but I'm not sure he's concerned about her safety anyway; he just wants her to win.

Thankfully, he hates hockey. *Careless, violent sport for people who lack discipline and crave chaos*, he says. It was Mom who signed me up for Mr. H's team all those years ago. She was pregnant with Sasha at the time and needed something that would tire out her energetic five-year-old.

I didn't take to skiing like my dad had hoped, and I can proudly say I've been disappointing him every day since. He wouldn't even be surprised if I told him what has been going on recently, but it would involve answering his calls, and that isn't something I tend to do.

Plus, he'd only find a way for it to be my fault.

The intensity of Robbie's stare feels like it's burning into my skin, which jolts me from my thoughts.

Annoying him is my favorite thing to do, and it makes me realize why JJ likes being an asshole so much. Robbie keeps dropping things on the floor, banging his phone against the TV remote to make a clanging noise, and after about ten minutes of getting no response, he's started coughing loudly.

I keep my eyes on the TV and smother the urge to smirk. Mike Ross is about to nail another case when Henry elbows me in the side. "Robbie is trying to get your attention. Are you ignoring him on purpose?"

"Great question, Henry, thank you," Robbie shouts dramatically. "Are you ignoring me on purpose, Nathan?"

When I finally look at him, he's staring at me like an unimpressed mother. "Sorry, buddy. Did you want something?"

Robbie mutters something under his breath, followed by a loud huff. "Have you organized my birthday party?"

"You mean the surprise birthday party? The one you *specifically* said you didn't want to know anything about? So it was, y'know, an *actual* surprise?"

Six weeks ago, Robbie told me he wanted a surprise party for his birthday, claiming hosting parties is very stressful and time-consuming. He didn't want to deal with the problems of his own birthday, so I needed to do it. I told him if it was such a hassle, he didn't need to organize our parties anymore. He called me a dipshit and told me to grow up.

"If the surprise is you haven't arranged anything, I don't fucking want it."

Henry immediately stands, his eyes darting between me and Robbie, and rushes toward the stairs. Robbie follows his fleeting frame with narrowed eyes before flicking back to me. I shrug it off, acting like I don't know Henry has been worried about spoiling the surprise for weeks. The kid doesn't have a poker face, and he's convinced himself with only a few more days to go, he's going to fail at the last hurdle.

"You need to relax, Robert," I say, knowing using his full name will rile him up a little bit more. "Stress isn't good in your old age."

I think that's the end of it, but instead, he scratches at his jaw and makes an *uhm* sound. It's not like Mr. Confident to struggle with his words, so now he has captured my attention like he wanted to. "Did you . . . Did you invite Lola?"

Oh, this is fun. "Who?"

I narrowly avoid the cushion he launches in my direction. "Don't be a dick, *Nathaniel.* You know who she is."

Three weeks ago, when I was royally fucking up with Stassie, Robbie was getting better acquainted with her best friend. He won't tell me what happened, claiming he's a gentleman, but it's hard not to draw your own conclusions when she left on Saturday afternoon wearing one of his T-shirts.

I haven't seen her since, so I thought it was a one-night thing but judging by the nervous look on his face, maybe not. "Would you want her there? In the hypothetical situation where there is a party?"

"We've been talking, so yeah. Hypothetically."

Robbie has no problems with women, but I can't pretend he doesn't rotate them when he gets bored. The fact he's talking to her and not only hooking up with her is a good sign.

"Noted. Ready for practice?" I ask him, carefully changing the subject before I give away party secrets.

"Yeah, let me get my sweatshirt first."

Shit. Now I have to find a way to get Lola here.

JJ IS SPRINTING DOWN OUR street as I'm putting Robbie's chair into the trunk of my car. Pressing the button to lower the falcon-wing doors, I climb into the driver's seat and put the car into reverse, automatically locking all the doors.

He bangs on the window, panting and mumbling something inaudible. I lower the window a little so I can hear him. "Don't leave without me, you douchebag."

"Hurry up!" I bark back, watching him frantically run toward the front door to get his stuff. I'd feel sorry for him if I didn't know he's been tucked up with one of the football cheerleaders since last night.

This whole situation with sharing a rink means we're training at different times each day. Since it's technically their arena, Coach Brady demanded we work around the skaters' scheduled training. A lot of them have competitions coming up and she argued anything less than our total agreement wasn't going to work for her.

Aubrey Brady is a fucking terrifying woman, and she has Faulkner's balls in an iron vise. As soon as she found out why our rink was trashed, she used it to bully Skinner into bowing to her every demand, and now she owns us.

I can't blame her, she's looking out for her athletes, but awkwardly brushing past Stassie every day got old quickly. Seeing how hot she is in her skating stuff got old quickly. Watching her joke around with her dickhead skating partner, you guessed it, old.

Quickly.

She looks at me like she wants to set me on fire most of the time, or alternatively, she doesn't look at me at all. The girl knows how to hold a grudge, with everyone except Henry, apparently.

Last week, Henry saw Anastasia studying in the library alone. He bought her a coffee, explained about the Russ situation, apologized profusely, saying he totally understood why she was so upset, and now he's the only one of us in her good graces.

"Why do you always want girls who don't like you?" Henry asked me as she stomped past us one afternoon, still managing to flash him a sweet smile. "Summer, Kitty, Anastasia . . . Why?"

"Jeez, Hen," JJ spluttered out, choking on his water. "Kick the guy while he's down, why don't you."

"I don't know, kiddo," I confessed, wrapping my arm around his shoulders as his cheeks flushed at the guys laughing. "You find me a nice girl who likes me back and I'll give it a shot."

JJ snorted. "He's not a fucking miracle worker, Hawkins."

Robbie claims he could be in her good graces if he wanted to be, and Jaiden said he prefers being the mysterious bad boy anyway. As for me, I could bow down at her feet and apologize, but I think she'd use it as an excuse to kick me in the head.

Parking outside the rink, I let the guys know I'll see them in there, quickly climbing out to jog toward the door. She's throwing her skates into her bag when I push through the doors—her eyes flick up in response to the noise, but she grimaces when she realizes it's me.

Charming.

I sit on the bench beside her bag and clear my throat. "Anastasia?"

Her eyes lock with mine, plush lips immediately pouting. "What do you want?"

"I need a favor."

"No."

"You haven't even heard what it is yet."

"Don't need to. The answer is no."

"What if I told you it's super important to both of our best friends' happiness?"

She sighs, a noise I'm used to hearing now, putting her hands on her hips. "I'll bite. Go on."

"It's Robbie's twenty-first birthday on Saturday and I'm throwing him a surprise party. He'd like Lola there—could you pass on the message? You're invited, too, obviously."

"Fine."

Success, maybe. "Sweet, thanks. It's Vegas themed, so black tie. Free bar, poker tables, all the fun stuff. I hope you guys come; it'll make Robbie very happy."

"Okay." She struts off toward the opening doors, the guys coming through at the same time. She pats Henry's arm and murmurs "Hi" as she passes him, and the kid's cheeks flush again.

When she's officially out of earshot, JJ traps me in a headlock, cackling as I fight him off. "You're losing your touch, Hawkins. The kid has more game than you."

"I'm not trying to date her," Henry says quickly, scratching at his jaw nervously. "I'm trying to be nice to her, y'know, so she likes us again. She's got a boyfriend anyway."

"He's her skating partner, not her boyfriend. She doesn't have a boyfriend, she told me so herself."

Henry shakes his head. "Not him, Ryan Rothwell. I saw them hugging last week."

"Hugging someone is hardly the sign of a relationship, Hen. Kris and Mattie would be in a relationship with half the campus if that were the case," Robbie says with a snort.

"They were making out and he was grabbing her ass," Henry adds.

Great.

Aaron is still fucking about on the ice when we're all ready to start practice. He's an obnoxious prick and I truly cannot stand the guy. It's got nothing to do with Stassie, either—he gives me the worst vibes imaginable, and it's enough for me to hate him. Obviously, it doesn't help he fucked us all over with his big mouth.

I know I said it wasn't about her, but one thing I don't like about him is how he speaks to Anastasia when they're skating. I gave him the benefit of the doubt at the party because he was clearly wasted, but because of their class schedules, a lot of the time their session is pre or post ours.

When we're either early or finishing up, I hear him telling her not to be sloppy this session or telling her she'll get it one of these days in the world's most patronizing tone.

It's shitty, but it's none of my business. She's not the type of girl who needs defending, and if I were to try, it'd probably land me higher up on her hit list.

When he hears us coming, he finally skates to the edge. He's wearing the smuggest grin when he spots me. He's already massively testing my patience, and he hasn't even opened his mouth. I'm sure if I punched him, I'd feel better. But thinking back to what Faulkner said about behaving, I take a deep breath instead. See? I can be an adult.

"She's not going to fuck you. You're wasting your time."

"Excuse me?"

Don't punch him. Don't punch him. Don't punch him.

"You heard me." He sits on the bench and starts to unlace his skate, not bothering to look at my shocked face.

The guys are dragging the goals onto the ice and Robbie is talking to Faulkner, otherwise I'd be looking for confirmation I was hearing this jackass correctly.

"You might think she's playing hard to get, but she's not. The iciest thing about her is her heart. She'll drag you along like she does Rothwell, so save yourself the trouble."

This fucking guy.

"You're a dick, do you know that?" I tell him brazenly.

He throws his skate in his bag and switches to the other one, looking up at me to grin. "Truth hurts, buddy."

"I'm not your fucking buddy." I clench my fist, desperately trying to keep my temper at bay. "And if you talk about her like that again, you're going to be picking your teeth up from that rink."

He gives me a sickly-sweet smile. My fingers crunch, I'm clenching my fist so tightly, but he's unfazed enough to bump into my shoulder as he passes me. As he reaches the exit, he turns to face me. "I'm going to enjoy watching her turn you into a simpering fool, just to drop you like she does everyone else. Happy skating."

Chapter Seven

ANASTASIA

TEAM BUILDING.

Two words. Twelve letters. Two hours of hell.

"We're going to be doing some icebreaker activities," Brady announces to the room. She sounds as enthusiastic as I feel; I know she doesn't want to do this because she bitched to me about it on the way here. Coach Faulkner is standing by her side, also looking like he'd rather be anywhere else.

David Skinner—who is becoming a pain in my ass—wants to see an improvement in the *dynamic* between our two groups. Brady told me Skinner happened to drop in when Ruhi, one of the younger solo skaters, was arguing with one of the hockey guys for interrupting her skate. Skinner got to witness Ruhi's creative use of hockey-based insults.

So now, we're team building.

What a great use of time I could be spending doing *anything* else. I may as well throw out my planner since nobody seems to give a shit about my routine anymore.

Faulkner clears his throat, looking to Brady for guidance. He looks out of place anywhere that isn't an ice rink, and if I wasn't so miserable about being stuck in the awards room again, I'd probably find it funny.

"I'm sure all of you have heard of speed dating," Brady says. "My skaters, you're going to each sit at a table. Hockey team, you will move from table to table every five minutes."

"A reminder: this is not real dating," Faulkner bellows, finally saying something. "The goal is to get to know each other better. Discuss your aspirations, your hobbies, your dog's name, I don't care, but keep it respectful. Hughes, Hudson, Carter, and Johal, to be clear, I'm specifically talking to you four."

The four guys each pretend to be shocked, gaining a laugh from the rest of their teammates.

"This is a joke," Aaron groans. "We're not kids."

As much as it pains me to agree with Aaron, I sort of do. He's been on his best behavior for the past three weeks, and he's been an absolute dream to be with. He even treated me and Lola to dinner at Aiko, a fancy Japanese restaurant I wouldn't be able to afford otherwise.

He seems to have turned things around and I'm so grateful. I haven't seen Ryan a lot because he's been spending a lot of time with Olivia, but when he does come over, Aaron has been polite. I try to see the positives so Aaron doesn't get grumpy. "It might be fun. Some of them are nice."

I have the *softest* soft spot for Henry Turner, one of the sophomores on the hockey team. I was stressing over my corporate social responsibility essay in the library when he approached me last week, sporting a worried look. He introduced himself, explaining he was on the team and he'd heard what happened. He said he couldn't tell me too much, but he wanted to explain.

Then he proceeded to tell me everything about everyone.

Henry started with explaining that Nathan put an end to the prank traditions the minute he became captain. He promised there was nothing the team—including Nathan—could have done to prevent this disaster.

Russ, the impregnator—or not impregnator as it turns out—has a difficult home life, which he's managed to escape by working exceptionally hard to get a full-ride scholarship.

Nathan knew that if people found out, Russ might lose his scholarship, and with his parents being unable to cover his tuition, he'd
have no choice but to head back to the life he's worked so hard to get
away from. Nathan didn't even trust his own team with the information, that's how protective he is of Russ, despite his indiscretions.

Henry wanted me to know that Russ isn't some cocky trust fund
kid, he's quiet and tries to keep out of trouble, and Henry can relate
to that because he's the same. He didn't make any friends freshman
year; even though he's from Maple Hills, college was overwhelming
for him.

He hated dorms but without friends to live with, he was going to
have to stay on or move home. Nathan offered him a room in their
house, even though a sophomore living with seniors is unheard of on
their team. That was his basis for telling me how much of a good guy
his captain is, and while I'm mad now, I should try to give him a chance.

After telling me gossip about all the team members I don't know
yet, he finished off his speech by telling me I was the most beautiful
figure skater he'd ever seen. He quickly followed that by clarifying he
meant my performance, not my appearance, and that when I'm not
landing on my ass or looking like a baby giraffe, my performance is
exceptional.

And if I wasn't enamored with him enough, he bought me a coffee and helped me study.

Brady claps her hands to get us all moving. I take a seat on the
other side of the room from Aaron. He might be being friendly at
the moment, but it doesn't mean I want to have him listening in on
my conversations.

I can do five-minute conversations, right? That's only two and a
half minutes each. I can talk about myself for that long. It's going to
be fine.

I think.

My first "date" takes a seat in front of me, immediately making me feel relaxed with a huge smile. His buzz cut is bleached blond, the golden-brown skin of his arms is covered in intricate black tattoos, which I can see because the second he sat down, he rolled up his sleeves and winked at me. His jawline is covered in short stubble and he has a small silver nose ring. He looks like the type of guy you could get into heaps of trouble with, but in a good way.

He holds out a hand for me to shake, which feels oddly formal. "Jaiden Johal, but you can call me JJ."

This feels awkward, but I go for it anyway. "Anastasia Allen. Stassie is fine, too."

"Oh, I'm more than aware of who you are. I make it my mission to know any woman that puts Nate Hawkins in his place. I'm a big fan."

I'm blushing, *great*. "Thanks? I think. Tell me about yourself. We've gotta fill five minutes somehow."

The room is filled with the sound of people chatting, which is a positive sign. JJ stretches out his legs, getting comfortable in his seat. "I'm twenty-one. I'm a Scorpio sun, moon, and rising. I'm from Nebraska, which if you've ever been to Nebraska, you'll know there is nothing to fucking do." He rubs his palm against his face, pausing to think of what to say next. "I play defense, I'm going to the San Jose Marlins when I graduate, I hate pickles. Faulkner said we weren't allowed to talk about sexual stuff, so I don't know what else to say."

Looking at the clock on my phone, we've covered ninety seconds.

"I'm twenty-one. I'm from Seattle, I'm an only child, I work at Simone's Rink. I've been figure skating since I was a kid, always pair skating, and I've been skating with Aaron since freshman year." I shift in my seat uncomfortably, wishing JJ were still talking about himself. "Our goal is Team USA, we wanna be at the next Olympics." *Why is this so hard?* "I study business. You wanna know my big three?"

He nods enthusiastically. "Obviously."

"Virgo sun and rising, Cancer moon." He hisses and shakes his head immediately. "What?"

"Cancer moon. Red flag."

"From the triple Scorpio?"

Jaiden holds up his hands defensively, widening his hazel eyes. "I'll have you know we are incredibly misunderstood."

Looking at the clock again, we've got one minute left. "Sixty seconds. Anything else?"

He rubs his hands together in a way that makes me worried about what he's about to ask. "Would you rather . . . have a fish head but your body, or would you rather have your head but a fish body?"

At least thirty seconds pass where I stare at him, unable to formulate a response. He taps at the watch on his wrist. "Tick tock, Stassie. Time's almost up."

"I don't know."

"Ten, nine, eight, seven . . ."

"Fish head with my body. I think. God, that's disgusting to visualize."

"Great choice," he praises, looking satisfied with my answer. Brady blows her whistle, indicating for everyone to switch. He winks at me again and I'm definitely blushing. "I hope to see more of you soon."

Time flies as each guy sits at my table before moving on. Three freshmen asked for my number, a guy called Bobby spent our five minutes talking about a girl instead of himself, and when a guy called Mattie realized we share a class, he spent five minutes asking me to explain our latest assignment and writing the answers on his phone.

Robbie approaches my table when the whistle blows, and it's nice to see someone I kind of know. "Anastasia."

"Robbie. Fancy meeting you here."

Lola and Robbie might be a thing, I'm not sure. *She's* not even sure. The second she found out we'd be "team building" together, I was given strict instructions to find out. "How are you?"

"I'm good. I'm hoping you're going to spend the next four minutes and"—he looks at his watch—"twenty-eight seconds talking about your roommate."

She's gonna lose her mind when I get home. It's the easiest four minutes of my life; Lo is an open book, what you see is what you get. Talking about her to someone else is easy, because she likes everything and she's the most loving and supportive friend ever.

I'm ashamed to say, Joe and Kris are very funny and had me slapping my hand over my mouth to stop laughing, which is so annoying because I had no intention of adding other hockey players to my approved list.

It was going to be Henry only, forever.

Ten minutes of laughing was well-timed, because I'm in a good mood when Russ sits at my table.

It feels pointless describing hockey players at this point, because the only word that ever comes to mind is *big*. Russ is no different, but the one thing that sets him apart from his friends is his baby face. Unlike the rest of the team, there is no stubble in sight. His eyes are big and soft—like a puppy.

I've never noticed before, but I've also never seen him up close. He looks nervous as hell, too, and I think back to what Henry told me about him being a quiet guy. "I'm Stassie. Russ, right?"

He nods, the tips of his ears reddening. "Yeah. It's nice to meet you. Do you wanna talk about yourself or something? I don't have anything interesting to tell you."

Oh, Russ, why did you have to be like a timid animal when I want to be mad at you?

I launch into the same spiel I've given every other guy; he asks follow-up questions that keep me talking, and by the time the whistle goes and he's moving on, I still don't know anything about him. "It was nice to meet you," he says gently as he leaves.

The activity is nearly over, and I'm incredibly annoyed that it's sort of had the desired effect. It's hard to begrudge letting the guys share the rink after you've heard all about their aspirations and motivations.

I mean, I said it's hard. It's not impossible.

Through the process of elimination, I know I've only got two people left. My social battery is wavering, but I try to push through, because I know it's worth it when Henry drops himself into the seat in front of me.

"This is unnecessary, isn't it?" he mutters, placing his elbows on the table to rest his head in his hands. "Why do I need to know what someone's childhood pet is called or when their birthday is? The only person who cares about that information is a hacker. And I don't even like computers."

I'm in shock.

During the few one-on-one encounters we've had, Henry was calm and so laid back he was practically horizontal. It appears Skinner has found the thing to get under his skin—forced socialization.

"Please don't tell me about your pets, Anastasia," he begs, brushing his hand over his short, auburn curls, sighing heavily. "I don't have the energy to pretend to care."

"You wanna sit in silence? You only have one more person after me. You can have a little pre-finale break."

"That's a good idea, thanks."

Henry shuts his eyes and I have no choice but to just watch him have a micronap. I feel like a creep, but equally, what else am I supposed to do? He could go into modeling if hockey doesn't work out for him. Perfectly symmetrical face, smooth, glowy brown skin, the most defined cheekbones I've ever seen on a man. He's beautiful.

"I can feel you staring at me. Can you stop?"

I'm glad he keeps his eyes closed, that way he can't see the very aggressive shade of red my face turns. Brady's whistle blows and Henry struts off with only a glance in my direction.

There's only one person I haven't faced yet and it's the one person I've been dreading. He takes forever—or what feels like forever, at least—to take a seat. He's in a Maple Hills Titans T-shirt and gray sweats, and I hate myself for being a woman swayed by a man in gray sweatpants. *Shit*. No, there will be no swaying.

"Hi," he says cheerfully. "I'm Nathan Hawkins."

"You're playing it like that, are you?"

He ignores my question and quirks an eyebrow. "And you are?"

"Nathan, what are you doing?" I ask, folding my arms and leaning back in my seat. He mirrors me, folding his own arms. To an outsider, we probably look like the least approachable table, which to be fair, we might be.

"We're starting over. Everyone loves a fresh start, right? Let's have one. You can't stay mad forever."

"I was planning to stay mad longer than forever, so I feel like you're massively underestimating me." He starts laughing and I don't know what to do with myself, because my face is fighting to smile, too.

Damnit.

"Your commitment to the cause is admirable, Allen," he teases. "I already know you're a figure skater, you're studying business, and you're from Seattle. I've found out that you can be terrifying, but you can also be sweet." My eyebrows immediately shoot up, confused, so he clarifies. "To Henry, not to me."

"Henry has been nice to me."

His face sinks a little, the charming façade slipping. "I want to be nice to you. Look, I'm sorry I lied to you. My hands were tied and I had to put Russ first. I honestly do want to be your friend, Anastasia."

"I know, I get it. You don't know me, can't trust me or whatever, and that's fine. I understand that, but I tried to share how I was feeling so you could see my side, and you immediately brushed it off as an overreaction."

I feel naïve sharing this, but I've had enough therapy in my life to know I should try to communicate my feelings. Well, when I'm not being petty. People keep telling me Nathan is a good guy, so I'm giving him the opportunity to be one.

"I can see why that would make you want to stay away from me." His hand sinks into his hair, tugging with what looks like annoyance at himself. "I'm sorry, it's not okay that I did that. Can we start again?"

Brady's whistle blows for the final time, but he doesn't move. He waits for me to answer, his brown eyes practically staring into my freaking soul.

"You're on probation." I sigh.

Heat creeps back to my cheeks when he gives me the brightest smile. "I'm gonna nail it."

"You better."

Shit, shit, shit.

Chapter Eight

NATHAN

Robbie was right; party planning is hard.

However, dealing with him has been the hardest part today. We had an arrangement that Joe and Mattie were going to keep him busy all day, while the rest of us waited for everything to be delivered and set up.

It was a perfect plan.

Until Robbie decided he needed to stay home for the delivery of something he'd ordered. Me staying home wasn't enough, he had to stay home himself.

After Joe, Robbie is the smartest guy I know, which is how I know he 100 percent was doing it to stress us all out. Eventually, he went with the guys and thirty seconds later, the delivery driver pulled up with the tables. The delivery Robbie was supposedly expecting never arrived.

Prick.

Every time I think I know everything there is to know about my friends, we do something like try to turn the house into a casino, and I learn how annoying they all truly are.

The house looks fantastic. I haven't spared an expense and I don't regret it one bit. As much as he irritates the hell out of me, Robbie deserves it.

The smartest decision I made was to hire a fully stocked and manned bar. They set up on the decking, outside of the French doors from the kitchen, and it looks amazing. Bobby and Kris had a great time naming the cocktails, and I think when Robbie hears someone order The Jersey Chaser or The Judge Judy, he's going to be happy.

We've all collectively agreed to not explain The Judge Judy's origin. It's more fun to let people guess, but the real answer is, when Robbie was in the hospital after his accident, all he watched for weeks was *Judge Judy*.

Now, when he's hungover, he lies on the couch in the living room and watches his favorite show. Nobody is allowed to talk during it, and nobody is ever allowed to disagree with her decision.

Henry didn't realize what was happening when he first moved in with us, and I'm not sure he does now, but he knows to stay quiet like the rest of us.

"We look hot," JJ praises, looking at each of us in our tuxedos. The guys are due back right before the party starts, so they will have time for a shower and to change into their tuxes. We all wanted to be ready to give the full Vegas effect when Robbie gets back.

"Do you think Lola and Anastasia will come?" Henry asks, fiddling with his bow tie.

"I hope so, buddy. Robbie wants Lola here and I don't wanna let him down on his birthday."

"Nothing to do with you wanting to kiss and make up with Stas, then?" Bobby laughs.

My eyebrow raises. "Since when was she 'Stas'?"

"We're friends now. Icebreaker shit worked; I like her."

Oh great.

Luckily, the guys get back, and shortly after, the party is in full swing, which doesn't give me time to dwell on my friends being so-called *friends* with Anastasia.

Making this party invite-only was one of my smarter ideas. To start with, you would never mutter the words *free bar* on this campus unless you wanted to be bankrupted.

Second, it meant I could stick Tim, one of the rookies, on the door with a guest list. Now I don't need to worry about troublemakers getting in and ruining things.

Tim's success as gatekeeper is heavily reliant on him being next to the front door, so the fact I can see him striding across the den with his clipboard doesn't give me much hope about security. "What's wrong?"

"Nothing's wrong, Cap. Sorta. Those girls you told me to watch out for arrived. Lola Mitchell and Anastasia Allen."

Thank God. "Right, what's the problem?"

"Well, I told them to come find you, like you told me to, an—"

"Spit it out, Tim."

"Lola, well, she told me to tell you if you want to give her orders, you should put her on the goddamn team."

"Message received. Where are they now?"

"The bar, Cap."

Sending Tim back off to his post, I keep an eye on the doors to the backyard while I carry on with my game of poker.

The house is full of people crowding around various game tables, drinking, laughing. I tried hard to make sure nothing looked tacky, even when JJ tried to convince me to hire an Elvis impersonator who can do weddings. Me accidentally ending up married to JJ felt like too much of a risk, so I put my foot down and said no.

I haven't seen them come back inside and it's been over an hour. When I finally make my way to the bar, Henry, Robbie, and Jaiden have already beaten me to finding the girls.

"You look very nice today. Not at all like a baby giraffe," I hear Henry saying to Stassie as I approach the five of them. JJ begins to choke on his drink, but she doesn't seem to mind being compared to a giant, wobbly animal.

"Do you feel better now you can't spoil the surprise?" she asks, eyes flicking over to me as I stop beside him, then back to Henry.

I feel like everyone, except Robbie, knows how worried Henry has been and has been rooting for him.

"I feel much better, thank you."

Now that I'm up close I can see how fucking breathtaking she looks. Hair in perfect curls down her back, silk navy-blue dress cut low at the front and back, with a split all the way up to the top of her thigh. But above all else, she's grinning ear to ear. Happiness is practically radiating off her as she chats away with my friends.

I can't help but watch her with a goofy smile on my face, and I know she must notice it because every now and again her eyes float over to me, but I'm too scared to say anything and ruin this moment.

Looking at her makes me want to be the funniest guy in the room, so I can be the one to make her laugh. But I'm going to have to settle for her not scowling at me for now.

This whole thing was about getting Lola here for Robbie, and I've achieved it. She's pulled up a chair beside him and they're whispering away together, in their own little world. I'm happy for him, albeit a little jealous.

Anastasia rubs her hands up and down her arms, and I quickly realize for someone wearing not that much, it's cold out here. "Here," I say, shrugging off my tuxedo jacket. "Take this."

Her mouth opens and I recognize that look; I have a fight coming my way. But to my surprise she closes it, accepting my offer. She drapes it over her shoulders and tightens it across her front. "Thank you, Nathan."

"Let's get a drink, Hen," JJ says, patting him on the back.

"But I have a drink and so do you."

JJ sighs, dragging Henry toward the nearest server, muttering something about discretion.

I've never been nervous to talk to a woman before. I know I need to try hard with Anastasia if we're ever going to be friends. I can't stomach the next few weeks, or months, with the weird tension between us. Especially now all my teammates are making progress with her.

Plus, she said I'm on probation so I've got to try something.

"You look beautiful." *Weak start, Hawkins.* "Are you having a good time?"

"Yeah, I am. It's a shame you had to be the one to throw it. Having to give you credit is my only criticism."

Her words seem harsher than they actually are. They're defiant, but what they don't show is the way her eyes are fucking gleaming, and the way her teeth sink into her lip while she waits for me to respond.

God bless, Patrón.

"I thought we had a truce. I'm on probation, you're supposed to be being nice." I chuckle, watching her try not to laugh.

"This *is* me being nice!"

"This is your version of nice? You fucking suck at it, Allen."

"I said *you* were on probation, not me."

I tut playfully. "I'm going to teach you how to be nice."

"I'm sure there are *plenty* of things you can teach me, Nathan, but being nice isn't one of them. I'm a delight."

"Mhm. I think 'delight' might be a stretch." She smiles. A real one that lights up her whole face, and I finally feel like I'm getting somewhere. "What things would you like me to teach you?"

She nods toward the house. "How about we start with poker?"

Before I can respond, Henry reappears, now carrying a drink in each hand. "I'm up for poker."

"Great." I force a smile, trying not to outwardly grimace at the interruption. "Let's set up a table."

Everyone settles around a table in the den, and cards are dealt. In record time, it takes roughly twenty minutes for the birthday boy to ditch us in favor of alone time with Lola.

I'm grateful because it means he misses Anastasia hustling me out of two hundred bucks. *Teach her how to play poker, my ass.* I'll add acting to her list of skills because I truly believed she'd never played before. She called the club a clover, for fuck's sake; she was very convincing. Well, up until she put down her cards and wiped the floor with me.

"Where are you going?" I ask Stassie as she stands from the table.

"To use the bathroom. I'll be back."

Standing, too, I give my chips to Bobby. "The line will be huge. You can use mine, come on."

She accepts my outstretched hand without hesitation, and this all feels familiar. I'm hoping this night ends with us being friends, though, instead of how it ended a few weeks ago.

Apparently, I didn't learn my lesson last time and now I have Anastasia's ass in my face again as we walk up the stairs. The stilettos she's somehow managing to walk in are huge, so she navigated my hands to the curve of her waist to help her get up the steps safely.

The silk of her dress is soft under my fingers, her body warm. Every step she takes, her hair swishes in front of me and the strong honey and strawberry smell of her shampoo invades my nose.

There are worse problems to have.

Reaching my room finally, I punch in the code and usher her through the door. In a way, it's nice to have her alone to hopefully talk with her. The guys are like golden retriever puppies, all fighting for her attention.

It must get exhausting for her. It's exhausting to watch, plus it fucking sucks for me because I'm definitely runt of the litter as far as she's concerned.

Stopping in her tracks when she exits the bathroom and spots me sitting on the bed, her hands go to her hips. "I wasn't going to snoop."

"I thought you might want some peace and quiet from your fans."

Her shoulders drop, her body relaxing. "I like them all, but social settings sometimes drain me."

"I get it. They're a lot. You get used to it, though, and if you don't, I can always help you escape them."

"What if I'm trying to escape you?"

"You definitely don't need my help. You're on, like, expert level now or something."

She laughs and, my God, that noise. I've never enjoyed making someone laugh as much as I do with her. It's because she makes me work for every laugh and smile—the competitive side of me buzzes when I manage it. Taking a seat at my desk, she tells me about shows she did when she was younger, and how draining it was being surrounded by hundreds of other overexcited kids.

I sit and listen to her, nodding and laughing, freaking mesmerized at her confidence and her commitment, how she views things and explains them.

When she's done, even she looks like she doesn't know where that came from. She concentrates on the contents of my desk, prodding at a textbook about God knows what.

"I don't mind if you snoop, y'know. You didn't check everything last time."

"I don't need to snoop. I know everything I need to know about you."

I can't stop the sigh that escapes me when she stands from her seat and walks toward the bedroom door. Her hand reaches for the handle, and I instinctively lean forward, gripping her arm lightly.

Spinning to face me, her back presses into the door.

"Are you ever going to forgive me?" I ask hopefully.

"I told you, you're on probation."

Raking a hand through my hair, the groan that slips out is pure frustration. "That isn't a yes. Do I need to get on my knees and beg you, Anastasia? Is that what you want?"

She shakes her head and laughs. "The only time I ever want to see a grown man on his knees in front of me, Nate, is when his face is between my legs. So no, I don't want you to beg me."

Oh fuck.

Standing from the bed, I immediately watch her change. Her breathing deepens, thighs squeeze together, tongue pokes out to wet her lips. I can't help but smirk because I've just realized the attraction might not be as one-sided as I thought it was.

"You don't hate me like you pretend you do, do you? If you want me on my knees, Anastasia, we can make that happen."

My hands press against the door on either side of her head; I lean down so we're eye level, her ocean-blue eyes now dark. By the way she gulps, I suspect if I pressed my mouth to her neck, I'd feel her pulse hammering erratically against my lips.

"I'm not pretending."

"You are." Watching her fight herself is the hottest thing—even if she sticks to her guns, I'll be leaving this room a happy man. Leaning forward, I let my mouth linger near the shell of her ear, my breath tickling her neck. "Ask me nicely. Let me show you how much I like it when you're nice."

"Why would I do that when I don't like you?" Her words are strong, but her delivery is strained and wispy, giving her away.

"You don't have to like me to scream my name, Anastasia."

I lightly trace her jawline with my nose, enjoying the way her breathing hitches.

"I could give you a map to my G-spot, and you still wouldn't be able to get me off, Hawkins."

"I don't need a map."

"You do."

My mouth is millimeters from hers and I'm not going to be the one to make the first move. I don't need to be; if she wants me, she's about to show me.

The idea I'd need a map to get her off is laughable. Her thinking I wouldn't spend every moment learning her body better than my own is also laughable.

The thing I like about her is she's competitive, but I'm competitive, too; I always have been. It's how I've gotten so good at winning, and right now, we're competing to see who can hold out the longest.

Lowering my voice to a whisper, I give her one last chance. "Let's test that theory, shall we?"

Chapter Nine

ANASTASIA

THERE IS A REAL CHANCE I could spontaneously burst into flames at any moment.

Nate's voice is barely above a whisper as he suggests testing his theory, but I feel every syllable all over my skin as goose bumps spread down my neck and across my chest. I have been betrayed by my body from the second he put his hands on both sides of my head and leaned in.

He's barely touched me and yet I'm ready to melt into a puddle at his feet.

I don't know whether it's the proximity, the sheer adrenaline, or the tequila, but every rational thought disappears, and I crush my mouth against his.

He wastes no time sinking his hand into the hair at the nape of my neck, gripping tightly. His free hand slips around my body and palms my ass, making me moan into his mouth.

Nate is everywhere at once; all I can do is hold on to him and take it, and when his mouth travels down my neck, sucking and nipping, I'm practically panting.

I didn't think this would happen when I followed him up here, I swear. He just looks so good in his tux and watching him nervously check the party is going well all night has been sort of endearing. And he's hot as fuck, have I said that before? All dark hair, dark eyes, and muscles upon muscles, upon muscles.

He sinks to his knees in front of me, tugging at his bow tie and undoing the top button of his shirt. With messy hair from where I've held on to it and flushed cheeks, he looks up at me. His hands run from my ankle to my knee, then back down again, and yep, still close to melting territory. "You sure?"

"Do you have a pen and paper for me to draw you a map?"

I'm making jokes. Why am I making jokes? Why do I find how unimpressed with me he looks right now so funny? And hot?

"I don't joke about consent, Anastasia," he says softly, leaning forward to kiss the inside of my knee.

"I'm sure." I don't know why I'm sure. I'm sure I shouldn't be sure. I shouldn't like how he looks hooking my leg over his shoulder. I'm definitely sure I shouldn't be enjoying his tongue running up the inside of my thigh.

He pulls the material of the dress to the side, and when I put on this dress earlier, this is not how I saw the evening turning out. I hear a groan of approval when his mouth gets closer to the apex of my thighs, and he realizes I'm not wearing any panties.

The anticipation is killing me. I know he's doing it on purpose, getting closer and closer, but not doing anything meaningful.

I'm about to open my mouth to tell him to hurry up when his tongue runs between my folds, circling my clit slowly. A loud, desperate moan echoes around the room. I don't even realize the noise came from me until I feel his shoulders move because the jackass laughs.

Fingers tickle up the back of my thighs until they can't go any farther. His huge hands sink into my ass, squeezing at the same time he sucks my clit into his mouth in a way that makes me feel like I'm floating.

I'm a wreck. A writhing, moaning, shaking wreck. *Shit*. I don't even need to be looking at his face to realize how arrogant he is right now, not that I could—it's buried pretty deep between my thighs.

Sinking my hands into his hair for something to hold on to, a satisfied groan rumbles in his throat and the butterflies in my stomach freaking multiply.

I want to say something smart, sass him in some way. Not give him the satisfaction of knowing he's turned me into a whimpering mess in a matter of minutes.

One of his hands moves from my ass cheeks, and when I look down, a pair of brown eyes are staring back at me. They stay burning into me, watching me closely as two of his fingers slide into me, finding my G-spot in 2.5 seconds.

It's game over.

His pace increases as he pumps his fingers in and out of me, perfectly coordinated with his tongue, and if he wasn't holding up my entire body with his mouth, I'd have toppled over by now.

The feeling keeps building, hands tug harder at his hair as I cry out, stiletto heel digging into the hard muscles of his back as I desperately try to move my hips to ride his fingers. "Nathan . . ." I whimper. I'm wound so impossibly tight I can't breathe. "Nathan, I'm going to co—"

I don't even get the words out as every part of me spasms and I scream, everything tingling and throbbing as I tighten around him, bucking and thrashing, pleasure and heat flooding my entire body.

Removing his fingers and mouth, he leans back so he can look up at me properly, wearing the smuggest expression I've ever seen as he sucks his fingers into his mouth, not once breaking eye contact.

Oh fuck.

IT'S BEEN DAYS SINCE THE party and every day I learn something new about myself.

A disaster will do that to a person.

The first thing I learned was I'm good at running in heels; I found that one out when I sprinted from Nate's room. I've learned I'm not good at keeping a low profile, even when I'm actively trying to avoid someone. I've also learned I'd be a terrible criminal; I'd end up getting caught. I'm too jumpy and paranoid, which is why my instinct is to immediately panic when I wake up to the sound of heavy banging on my bedroom door.

Ryan's arm tightens around my waist, head burrowing deeper into my neck, his deep groan of annoyance vibrating against my skin. "Make it stop."

There is only one person in this house who is confident enough to slam their fist against someone else's door this early in the morning.

"What do you want, Lola?"

"Are you two fucking or can I come in?"

Ryan and I didn't even hook up last night, we watched a movie and fell asleep. We agreed the benefits aspect of our friendship was over now that he's looking to ask Olivia to be exclusive with him. I don't feel sad about it because I always knew it'd come to an end. I'm happy I managed to gain a best friend out of what's been an amazing situation.

Ryan untangles our bodies and rolls onto his back with a huff. "If we were fucking, you just killed the mood."

"Okay, I'm coming in! Put your dick away, Rothwell."

Carrying two boxes on her hip, Lola bursts through the door and throws herself onto the bed. She shields her eyes dramatically when she gets a look at Ryan's exposed chest.

He looks at me in disbelief, tugging the duvet up to cover himself. Hooking up or not, I'd have a picture of Ryan's body as my bedroom wallpaper if I could. Lola is ridiculous.

"How is my favorite not-couple this morning?" she asks cheerfully, throwing one of the boxes at me. "We have presents!"

Ryan yawns, ensuring he keeps his body covered as he stretches. "Better if you'd woken me up with breakfast instead of a headache."

Lola making breakfast is Ryan's favorite thing about staying over. Charming, isn't it?

Lo tuts. "Nobody likes a drama queen, Rothwell."

"Who are the presents from?" I ask, examining my surname on the box in big letters.

"Nate." She taps away on her phone, the signature video call sound starting. "We have to open them on a video call."

Video call? "Lo, wai—"

"Good morning," Robbie says. "You're beautiful in the morning."

"She's got an audience," I grumble before the phone sex starts.

"So have I," he responds. Lola turns around so her back is to me and Ryan. She holds her phone up and manages to get the three of us in the shot.

Robbie does the same thing, showing he has Nate and JJ on either side of him, eating what looks like cereal. JJ looks up from his bowl to the camera and chokes. Nathan looks up, too—his expression is blank. Robbie ignores him and talks louder over the noise. "Open your presents now."

"Here, Rothwell," Lo says, turning back around and leaning to hand Ryan the phone. "Make yourself useful and be the cameraman."

Finally, after what feels like hours since Lo crashed her way in, I rip the box open. I feel weird opening what is supposed to be a gift from Nathan while sitting in bed with Ryan. I have no reason to feel weird, but I do.

Oh wait, it might be because I've been avoiding Nate since he gave me the best head of my life five days ago, and the first time he sees me afterward, I'm in bed with someone else. Maybe that's it.

Dipping my hands into the box, I pull out its contents—a Titans hockey jersey.

Lo squeals excitedly, holding up her matching one. *Mitchell* is printed on the back and when I flip mine over, *Allen* is staring back at me in big white letters. "Thanks, Nate!"

"I was told this is all it takes to make you two listen to me. Welcome to the team."

The poor rookie on door duty at Robbie's party obviously reported Lola's message.

"Put them on," Ryan says from behind the camera. "I can't believe I'm in bed with two hockey stars. I feel so lucky."

"Could have made it three if you'd given me the heads-up," JJ says with a snort.

"Shut up, dipshit, that's my girl you're talking about."

Lo winks at me right before pulling the jersey over her head. We have both read enough romance novels and watched enough bad romance movies to know we love a *she's mine* type of man. "I love it."

"We gotta go to practice. I'll speak to you later, yeah?"

"Sure, bye."

"Bye, guys," Ryan and I add.

Just before Ryan disconnects the call, we hear Henry. "Is that Anastasia? I thought she was avoiding you, Nathan."

I manage to not react to Henry's words, other than one long, loud internal scream, but it doesn't stop two pairs of eyes burning into me. It was funny when Lola and Ryan both started intensely staring at me, but now, minutes later, it's a little sinister.

"What aren't you telling me?" Lo says in her most serious voice.

What happens in Vegas stays in Vegas is supposed to be a real thing. I know technically it was a Vegas party in Maple Hills, but the rules should still apply. I should be allowed to be a little irresponsible and a little slutty, and not have to share with my friends. Unfortunately for me, the secret keepers of Vegas haven't met Lola. "Tell us or I'm calling him back to ask."

I sink into the bed, pulling the duvet up over my head so I don't have to look at anyone.

"HewentdownonmeatRobbie'sbirthdaypartyandIranoff."

"Huh?" they both say in unison.

I huff and cling on as Ryan tries to tug the duvet back down. He's stronger than me, so I eventually give up. "He went down on me at Robbie's birthday party, blah blah blah." I ignore their gasps, Lola's genuine and Ryan's pretend one, to play along with her dramatics. "It was an accident, a moment of weakness, and I've been avoiding him."

"You are not going to *blah blah blah* me. It's been almost a week!" she screeches, arms flailing around dramatically. She turns her attention to Ryan. "Did you know about this?"

"No, I was on a date with Liv on Saturday, so I couldn't make the party," he says, completely missing the way her face twists when he mentions Olivia. "I'm interested to know how people accidentally have oral sex, though, Stas. Share with the group."

"You're a dick." I groan, hitting him in the chest with a pillow. "I was using his bathroom. He was trying to get me to admit I wanted to be friends, asked if he needed to get on his knees and beg."

"Classic," Lol says, rolling her eyes.

"Said I was only pretending to hate him."

"Yeah, this sounds like the start of any good hookup," she says sarcastically, scrunching her nose up with annoyance. "Get to the good part."

"Well, when he asked if he needed to get on his knees, I was honest. I said the only time I want to see a man on his knees is if his head is between my legs."

Lola can't breathe, she's laughing so hard, and Ryan is nearly as bad. I'm surprised Aaron hasn't shown up because that would be *perfect*.

"You guys are annoying," I mutter, hitting them both again with a pillow. "Anyway, he took it as an invitation. Said ask me nicely, and was all 'I don't joke about consent, Anastasia,' super sexy and brooding and yeah, practically ruined my vocal cords screaming."

"Took it as an invitation?" Ryan repeats back, jaw slack. "Stas, you practically told him you wanted to ride his face."

"I did not!" I definitely did not. I was simply making a point that I don't see anything good in a man begging at my feet. I'm not sure how it became so misconstrued in conversation.

If anything, I blame Ryan for this situation. If he had been there when Lo disappeared off with Robbie, I'd have had someone to make sure I didn't do reckless things with reckless, hot hockey players.

"Anastasia." He takes my face between his hands and turns my head so I'm only looking at him, not Lola, who is wiping away tears. "If a woman is telling me the only time she wants me on my knees is when my face is in between her legs, respectfully, I'm making a move. I'd have kissed you, too."

"Well, technically," I mumble, shaking my face free, "if you want to get into the specifics, I kissed him."

"You little slut," Lola says in delight. "I can't believe you weren't going to tell us!" Her eyes flick to Ryan, nose scrunching again. "Well, me. You two are weird. I don't know what you share, but I can't believe you weren't going to tell me!"

"It's not happening again, Lols, so calm down."

Ryan groans beside me and drags his hand down his face. "Stas, you know I love you, but you've got to stop being so fucking stubborn. Hawkins is a good guy, fuck him, don't fuck him, but since when do you avoid people you hook up with?"

"You should definitely fuck him," Lo says, far more enthusiastically than I'd like.

"I agree. You probably should at least once, Stas. For science."

The performing arts major and the English literature major, the two least STEM people I know, both look at me, synchronized nodding and talking. "For science."

Chapter Ten

NATHAN

HAVE YOU EVER SEEN A woman sprint in stilettos? I have.

Last week. I hadn't even gotten off my knees before Anastasia's hand was straightening her dress and reaching for the door handle. She gave me one last look, post-orgasm glow warming her cheeks, then she got the fuck out of there like Road Runner.

She was moving so quickly, I'm surprised there wasn't smoke behind her. All I could do was let her leave, otherwise, I'd have been stepping out with a throbbing boner into a house full to the brim with people.

Did I know that was what was going to happen when I took her upstairs? No. The best-case scenario was she'd think I was looking out for her, maybe she'd agree to finally be friends. Did I think there was a chance that she'd end up crying my name, and I'd be sucking the taste of her off my fingers? I don't think any normal man would, under the circumstances.

Is that memory on repeat in my head every time I jerk off? Obviously.

She clearly regrets it, since every time she sees me, she darts off in the opposite direction. I thought at first it might be embarrassment, but after seeing her in bed with Rothwell yesterday, I'm back to believing the interest is one-sided.

I thought maybe she was dating Rothwell, like Henry seems to think she is. Maybe I was a mistake, a moment of weakness, but I had to stop because I was making myself feel ill. I hate cheaters and my gut was telling me that wasn't the case with her. I felt immediately better when I spotted Ryan looking close with Liv Abbott.

I don't know what type of relationship Stas and Ryan have, but whatever it is, they're clearly not exclusive.

I've decided today is the day we're going to talk it out. She's good at communicating her feelings, she's proved that a few times. She's obviously not good at facing men whose faces she's come on.

The plan is to catch her straight after training, since she trains with Shithead before us on a Friday. JJ is furious we're not going to have time to stop for Dunkin', mumbling something about his constitutional rights. I promise to buy him two doughnuts next week, and it seems to placate him. He's excited to ambush—his words, not mine—Stassie with me, and watch me get shot down.

Bold of him to assume that I'll get close enough to be shot down.

Focusing on how to win over Anastasia has been enough of a distraction to not wonder why my dad has been blowing up my phone for three days and is currently showing no signs of slowing down.

Assuming he's calling about the significant dent in my available funds after paying for Robbie's party, I don't want to speak to him anyway. I'm sure a guy with a normal dad would assume it's a good luck call, since our first game of the season is tomorrow. But sadly, my dad isn't normal.

Mr. H has been more of a dad to me than mine, and having the Hamlets in town for Robbie's birthday has been great. Great for me, maybe not great for Lola, who had an impromptu meeting with them on Sunday morning, while only wearing Robbie's T-shirt.

Mrs. H looked like she was going to combust with happiness,

while Mr. H gave Robbie a double thumbs-up. Lo looked like a deer caught in headlights, and Robbie was just as bad.

JJ had a look on his face that I've never seen before. He looked like it was the best moment of his life, and that only increased when Henry asked Lola loudly if she regretted not putting on pants.

Having the Hamlets here reminds me of home, but the good memories, the ones before Mom died. Talking out strategies with them reminds me why I love hockey, and now I'm pumped for the start of this season.

I know I've said it before, but I mean it this time. This year is going to be different.

I ALWAYS KNOW SHIT IS going down when my phone incessantly buzzes. Ignoring Professor Jones's painfully boring recap on macronutrient metabolism, I pull my phone from my pocket.

PUCKBUNNIES

ROBBIE HAMLET
I'm dead.

BOBBY HUGHES
Weird way to announce it but go off.

KRIS HUDSON
Can I have your room?

JOE CARTER
Can I have Lola's number?

ROBBIE HAMLET
Shut the fuck up, Carter.

NATE HAWKINS
RIP

ROBBIE HAMLET
Here he is. Man of the hour.

NATE HAWKINS
Wtf are you on?

ROBBIE HAMLET
Did you know Stassie, Summer, and Kitty all live in the same building?

NATE HAWKINS
You're fucking joking.

ROBBIE HAMLET
Wouldn't joke about something as funny as this.

JAIDEN JOHAL
Maple Tower? Shit. I might move.

HENRY TURNER
I don't get what the problem is.

KRIS HUDSON
They're neighbors, Hen.

HENRY TURNER
Yeah . . . But none of them want to fuck him anyway, so why is it a problem?
It's not like he's going to be invited over.

MATTIE LIU
Shots fired.

KRIS HUDSON
I just know Hawkins is so tired rn.

JOE CARTER
Tired of waiting for Turner to say it was a joke lmao

JAIDEN JOHAL
Can anyone else hear crying?

NATE HAWKINS
Switching to basketball. Bunch of pricks.

HENRY TURNER
Might have a better chance with Stassie if you switch.

NATE HAWKINS
And why's that?

HENRY TURNER
She definitely has sex with Ryan Rothwell.
Maybe basketball players are her type.

NATE HAWKINS
You don't know that.

HENRY TURNER
I do. She told me.

NATE HAWKINS
And why the fuck would she tell you that?

HENRY TURNER
Because I asked?

JAIDEN JOHAL
Not to tip you over the edge, Cap . . . But Rothwell
has definitely fucked Summer too.

NATE HAWKINS has left PUCKBUNNIES
JOE CARTER has added NATE HAWKINS to PUCKBUNNIES
NATE HAWKINS has left PUCKBUNNIES
MATTIE LIU has added NATE HAWKINS to PUCKBUNNIES

NATE HAWKINS
Dicks.

I've always liked Ryan Rothwell, until now.

I make the strategic but easy decision to put my phone back in
my pocket and try to concentrate on learning something, or at least
learning something *not* about Ryan Rothwell and where he's sticking
his d—anyway.

Actually, concentrating seems to help the class go by quickly, but I
wish I'd stayed behind as soon as I spot JJ. From the minute I meet him
outside his lab, to when I pull up outside the rink, he laughs at me.

Thankfully, though, he opts to let me fail in private and promises
to wait in the car until the rest of the guys get here.

"Clair de lune" is blasting over the arena speakers when I walk
through the double doors. There are other skaters hanging about but
only one pair on the ice, which means I'm here at the right time.
Dropping my hockey bag on the benches, I make my way to the edge
of the rink, giving Brady a polite "Hello" when she spots me and
scowls.

I've never seen Anastasia skate before. Usually, one of us is arriv-
ing as the other is leaving, so I don't ever get to see her at work, but
today I'm twenty minutes early.

She's fucking mesmerizing. I've been on the ice since before I
can remember, and I've never, ever moved the way she is moving

right now. She doesn't even look like she's skating, she looks like she's floating; I can't take my eyes off her.

Her arms reach out toward Shithead. They're not even looking at each other but they still connect perfectly. Before I know what's happening, she's up in the air, resting on one of his hands, spinning, gripping the blade of her skate to hold her leg above her head.

I think he's about to drop her as he quickly lowers her, but somehow, she's spinning through the air, a combination of limbs that I can't even keep track of. I wipe the sweat from my brow when her skates are back on the ice and let go of the breath I didn't even know I was holding.

The pair pick up speed, flying across the rink flawlessly. I can tell something is about to happen by the way Brady's posture changes; her fingers grip the boards, and she holds her breath.

Stas and Aaron are moving in perfect rhythm, both turning to travel backward. They hit the toe of their boot against the ice, spinning at a speed my brain can't even register. My eyes don't even realize what's happening as Aaron lands, his leg flying out gracefully to finish the move, and Anastasia's body skids across the ice, slamming harshly into the board on the other side of the rink.

Fuck.

I've been slammed into more boards than I can remember, but that's when head to toe in hockey equipment. She's in leggings and a long-sleeved sports crop top, doing nothing to protect her, even if she hadn't hit it with force.

The music abruptly stops as Aaron pulls her to her feet, checking every inch of her in a frenzy, looking at the crown of her head as she points to it. She pushes him off as he tries to scoop her up, instead accepting his hand, letting him guide her as they skate toward where Brady and I are standing.

I feel like I should make myself scarce, but my heart is about to fall out of my ass. I need to hear her say she's all right, even if it's not to me.

The short journey across the ice feels like a fucking lifetime. They eventually reach the side, and she looks at me but it's almost like she doesn't realize it's me, because there isn't any emotion on her face. Not even disgust.

She must be properly injured if she isn't even annoyed by my existence. *Fuck.*

Brady grips her face—it's almost protective, like a mother in a way, tilting it every which direction until she's satisfied. "It's coming out, Anastasia. You'll do the triple."

"What?" she squeaks, genuinely looking confused. "It's fine! Give me a minute; we'll go again. I'll land it. You know I can land it."

"Anastasia, I've just watched you violently slam into a solid structure! This isn't up for discussion."

Stassie looks to Aaron, her jaw slack, tears beginning to line her eyes. He wraps his arm around her shoulder, tugging her body to his as she begins to sob. "Triple is still hard, Stas. There's no shame in dropping the quad—so many people can't even do the triple, and yours are perfect."

Her entire body is shaking as she brings her hands to her eyes to wipe away the tears, wincing as she raises her left arm, the side of her body that took the impact. "But I can do the quad. I've been working toward the quad for so long. I need to go again; I didn't take off right. I can fix it."

Her eyes land back on me as she wipes the falling tears on her sleeve. I try to give her a comforting smile, but it sinks into horror as a dark red stream of blood escapes from her hairline and runs down her temple.

It's like we all see it at the exact same moment. We all lunge for her at once, confusion on her face intensifying as the three of us inspect her.

"Coach, I'm trained in first aid," I say quickly. "She needs to go to the hospital but the open wound needs cleaning and wrapping before she goes anywhere."

Brady's lips are pinched into a hard, concerned line but she gives me a tight nod.

"Stas," I say softly. "I'm going to pick you up and carry you to the first aid room, okay?"

"Why are you talking to me like I'm a child?"

Aaron snorts beside her and wipes his hand down his face, looking at the ceiling in a mixture of amusement and despair. The guy is a jackass, but there's no denying right now that he does care about her. He looks worried sick and he's not even fighting me about checking her over.

"I'm glad that bump to the head didn't get rid of your charming personality," I say playfully. "I'm going to carry you because you haven't got guards on. Plus, I'm scared if you walk and you collapse, when I catch you, I'm going to hurt you where that big-ass bruise is going to be. Can I pick you up?"

She grumbles expletives under her breath and gives me a half-hearted nod, paired with an eye roll. "I'm heavy," she mutters as my arms scoop under her legs and around her waist.

We leave Brady and Shithead behind us as I start the walk toward the locker rooms, where the first aid room is. "Shut up, Anastasia. You're not even half my warm-up weight."

She wiggles in my arms, and I realize she's trying to elbow me in the ribs. I'm too preoccupied trying to open the door with my ass to be worried about her being annoyed. Setting her on the medical bed, I take a step back and as soon as our bodies are apart, she punches me straight in the arm. "You can't tell me to shut up, I'm injured."

"*I'm* fucking injured now." I moan, gripping my bicep. "*Jesus Christ*. Who taught you how to throw a punch?"

"Lola's dad. He teaches boxing."

I collect the supplies I need from the cupboard—saline solution, gauze, and an ice pack—enough until she goes to the hospital. I wash my hands thoroughly, dry them, and reach for some gloves. "You're not allergic to latex, are you?"

Her eyes narrow, lips pulling into a tight line. "No, Nathan. I'm not allergic to latex."

Suppressing a snort, I brush off the obvious latex connotations that have her glaring at me. "Glad to hear it. We don't want to add a swollen face to your list of injuries."

I think I get a smile, but I might have imagined it.

I start on the semi-dried blood on her face, cleaning the area thoroughly, while working into her hairline. I must reach the cut because she winces, and her hand shoots out to grip my sweatshirt. "I'm sorry," I coo, trying to work as quickly and light-handedly as possible.

The blood is soaked into her hair and every time I dab, the gauze picks up more. Her hand is still gripping me, foot moving up and down in the air, and it's clear she doesn't like being tended to like this.

I need to distract her, but I can't think of anything to say that won't make her remember she's avoiding me. "You're a phenomenal skater, Stas. I couldn't stop watching you."

"Until I bowling balled across the rink and tried to take down a board with my body, you mean?"

Her eyes look up to meet mine, a 100 percent confirmed smile on her face, definitely not imagining this one. "Yeah, until the human bowling bit, you were breathtaking."

"Thanks," she mutters, looking back at her hands. "Why are you here so early?"

I round up the used gauzes now her wound is as clean as I can get it and throw them into the medical waste container. I don't know how to answer her question without ruining this nice, semi-normal moment we're having right now.

"I wanted to see you. You've been avoiding me, and I wanted to check you were okay. Can you raise your left arm for me? That's the side that took the impact, right?"

"Right," she repeats back, ignoring everything else I said. She grimaces slightly, but overall the movement is fine, nothing's broken from what I can tell. I strap the ice pack to her shoulder, where the majority of the inflammation is, and give her one last look-over.

"Ice pack for no more than ten-minute intervals, okay? You feel dizzy?" She shakes her head. "Sick? Headache? Dazed and or confused?" She shakes her head again, this time with a skeptical eyebrow raised.

I reach down to unlace her skates, pulling each one off her feet and placing them behind her. "I want you to go to the hospital. They need to check you over to be on the safe side, and you need to rest this weekend."

She snorts loudly, hand flying to her mouth to smother it. "Sorry, that was rude. It's just that I'm competing tomorrow, I can't rest."

"Anastasia . . ."

"It'll be fine. Are you done, Dr. Hawkins?" she says, releasing me and attempting to jump down from the bed. My hands instinctively grip her hips to keep her in place, but I let her go like she's made of lava. Her eyes meet mine, something uncertain swimming in them. "Nate, I—"

The door opens behind us, and Shithead walks in, carrying a pink gym bag. Like I didn't already have enough of a reason to want to strangle him. He places her bag behind her, handing her some sneakers, which she pulls on. He examines her head like he's got a clue what he's looking at.

Dick. I think he studies history or something.

For Stassie's sake, I temporarily put our differences aside and am polite. "Can you take her to the hospital?"

Nodding and mumbling an uninterested *mhmm,* he doesn't bother to look at me as he reaches into her bag again, pulling out a UCMH sweatshirt for her. "Don't let her fall asleep before the hospital and you need to tell Lola to check on her when she's sleeping later."

"I'll check on her," he says nonchalantly, throwing her skates into the bag and zipping it shut.

"No, I mean at night when she goes to bed."

"Yeah," he says, drawing out the word like I'm not understanding him. "I'll check on her. You know we live together, right? My bedroom is just as close to hers as Lo's is."

What the fucking fuck?

"Okay." I try to keep any sign of shock out of my voice. "Feel better, Stas. Good luck tomorrow, guys."

"You, too," Shithead says back.

Weird.

Anastasia looks over her shoulder and takes me in one last time before she leaves. When I've cleaned up the room and headed out to where the guys are waiting, they've clearly heard what happened and are all giving me fake-sympathetic looks.

"Poor girl would rather give herself a concussion than speak to you, Hawkins. That's rough, buddy," Robbie says, earning a chorus of snickers from the rest of the team.

"Hey, funny guy," I bite back. "Did you know your girl's dad is a boxer?"

His face pales. "Please tell me you're joking."

"Oh, I wouldn't joke about something as funny as this."

Chapter Eleven

ANASTASIA

IF THERE'S ONE DAY I'M exceptionally grateful for Aaron, it's on competition days.

In contrast to my fidgeting, panicking self, Aaron is calm and relaxed, gently reassuring me that it will be okay. Meanwhile, I'm throwing up from anxiety.

Unsurprisingly, according to him, it was okay, and we're going to sectionals. Brady even joked that I skated better than usual, crediting my serious head injury.

Go figure.

I'm like this every time; the older I get, the more there is at stake, and the worse the anxiety becomes. Aaron is as calm as, if not calmer than, he was when we started skating together freshman year. I think the difference is Aaron hasn't not qualified before, he's never fallen and gone flying across a rink, and thankfully, he's never dropped me.

He's never given himself a reason not to be confident.

We got through today, but the pressure is on even more for sectionals next month. If we get through that, we're off to nationals in January.

Brady has been annoyed with me from day one for not going further in my younger years. She says I have the talent, and she doesn't understand why I haven't been to international competitions before. The honest answer is that my partner at the time, James, wasn't up to it, and I didn't want to find someone new because I loved him.

"Absurd" is her favorite way to describe it.

"You were amazing today," Aaron says, looking at me from the driver's seat. We usually travel with Aubrey, but Aaron drove today since the competition was close. "I can't wait for Lo to see the video."

After something like this, Lola is always subjected to a play-by-play of our routines. She'd previously said she would watch us in action, since it was so close by, but Robbie asked her to watch the Titans play their first home game of the season.

I was expecting Aaron to be a bitch about it when she floated the idea this morning, but he was surprisingly positive and said she could always come to the next one.

"You, too. I couldn't have done it without you."

"We're a good team, Stas. We argue sometimes, but we can't do what we do with other people. It wouldn't be the same."

Annoyingly, he isn't wrong. "I know."

"We're going all the way. I can feel it. If we keep up what we're doing, and you stick to your meal plan. We can smash it."

"Do you wanna grab dinner or something? I doubt Lola will be back from the Titans game yet."

"I can't, sorry. I've got plans with Cory and Davey; we're going for drinks."

My phone buzzes in the cup holder, and I reach for it, seeing Lola's name flash up.

LOLS

Your man is fine as hell, jeeeeeeeeez.

        He isn't my man.

He should be. He just slammed someone into the wall and I swear I got a flutter.

        What's happening?

Dunno. Still don't understand hockey. Robbie is wearing a 3 piece suit and shouting at people though

Omg. Are they winning?

Yeah! Nate keeps sliding them in so easy, just like he did with your kitty cat.

I hate u

Let him puck your mouth, Stassie

Deleting your number

Wanna go out tonight to celebrate?

Not if it's with the hockey team.

I look forward to you changing your mind 😏

I know Lola well enough to know there's no point in trying to avoid the guys tonight. It might be fun because, unfortunately, I like a lot of them.

I told her under no circumstances was I going with her to Robbie's birthday party last week, and then I had to sit there, staring at her smug smile, while she did my makeup for the party I definitely wasn't going to.

If she's going out, and so is Aaron, there is no point in me staying home alone, right?

"That's okay. Lo messaged to say she wants to go out anyway," I tell him, stuffing my phone back into the cup holder.

"Trust Lola to get involved with a hockey guy, of all people," he tuts, checking his mirrors before turning onto our road. "At least Rothwell isn't a total jackass."

I make a mental note to remember that. Ryan will be thrilled he's only a bit of a jackass, not a total one.

Regardless of what feelings I have or have had about the hockey players, Robbie is great with Lola. He's thoughtful and kind, but most importantly, he treats her with the respect she deserves. And even his parents were very sweet to her during her impromptu meeting with them, proving Robbie has been raised right.

Unlike some people I know.

"He makes her happy and it's none of our business."

"It will be when she gets knocked up and ghosted."

"That's not—" This argument isn't worth it. "I'm sure it'll be fine."

"You should stay away from them, Stassie. They're bad news. You don't always have to go where Lola tells you to, y'know."

The words are on the tip of my tongue, but I swallow them down, desperate to not ruin what's otherwise been a great day. "Okay."

I don't bother telling him I'll be spending the evening with the exact people he wants me to avoid. Despite not wanting to spend time with me himself, he won't want others to, either.

"I'm trying to look out for you, Stassie. I care about you. We're partners, that goes beyond skating. I know you'd do the same for me."

I make allowances for Aaron, desperate to cling to those lovely moments we share. He does care about me, and he does care about Lola. But sometimes, like now, he says something that makes me question his real motives.

There are times when the idea he'd say anything bad about either of us feels impossible. When he's fiercely loyal and protective, without being toxic, and when the three of us are tucked up together in our living room, watching movies and laughing.

Then there are times like now when the nasty streak he has seeps through the cracks. Sometimes it comes so out of nowhere it feels like whiplash, making me wonder if I know him at all.

I wait for the car to stop outside our building before leaning over to hug him. "I care about you, too, Aaron."

I'M HALF READY BY THE time Lola bulldozes her way into my bedroom, hopped up on beer and Jolly Ranchers.

"I love hockey!" She looks the part in her Mitchell jersey and Titans beanie, and I'm a little jealous I didn't get to go. "Not as much as I love figure skating, obviously. But hockey has more drama; it was like an opera, but with sticks. I'm obsessed." She looks around, realizing I'm the only one home. "Where's the ice princess?"

"Drinks with friends. I asked him if he wanted to grab dinner with me, but he said no. Oh, and hockey guys suck, and I don't have to go where you tell me to, which is great news."

She groans, throwing herself on the couch beside me. "I swear, that boy is so dramatic. We're going to The Honeypot, we're not getting married."

The Honeypot is the most popular nightclub in Los Angeles. It's super exclusive; we only get in because Briar, our neighbor, works there. Lola made it her mission to befriend her when she found out we live in the same building.

Lo hates working out. No, that's an understatement. Lo despises working out with her entire being, but she went to the gym every day until she'd charmed Briar.

She was candid about her motivations from the beginning, and luckily, Briar thought it was funny. Every time we're at the club, Lo makes me buy her a drink to thank her for her sacrifice.

"No wedding? So, I shouldn't wear my bridesmaid dress?" I tease, poking her in the ribs where she's ticklish.

"Don't!" she begs, rolling away from me. "I'm too full of beer to be prodded." Stretching out, she kicks off her sneakers and reaches for the blanket draped over the back of the couch. "As soon as I've had a micronap, I'll start getting ready. I swear."

Lola's micronap turned into a real nap, and I've been listening to her run around the apartment cursing, frantically trying to get ready, for the past forty-five minutes.

She's blaming me, but she doesn't remember the abuse she hurled my way each of the five times I tried to wake her up.

I'm alone with my thoughts while I wait, and I can't escape the realization that I'm nervous about seeing Nate. He had Robbie text Lola this morning to pass on a good luck message, which was sweet of him.

It's time for us to bury the hatchet. He's clearly a good guy, like everyone has told me he is. Now I've had a week to process it, I don't feel embarrassed about my lack of willpower last week.

We're both adults. Sometimes adults let other adults prove they don't need navigation tools to find a G-spot. It's normal.

"Okay, I'm ready!"

Lola looks unreal in a black, strapless, corseted Max Morgan midi dress. It's her go-to when she doesn't know what to wear; she says she needs to get her money's worth since it costs so much. She bought it last year during a rare trip to Rodeo Drive. It's beautiful, but her dad was not pleased when he received her credit card bill.

Her hair is pin straight down her back, a contrast to her normal curls, and she's framed her eyes with a perfect winged eyeliner. Looking up at me, she smiles. "I know I'm hot, but we need to leave. Steve has already been waiting five minutes."

Walking across the lobby to our waiting Uber, Lola giggles to herself, which is always suspicious. "What?"

"Nothing."

"Lola . . ."

"Just wondering if you're going to keep it in your pants tonight, but I realized you're not wearing any anyway."

"You're so childish."

"Sorry?"

"You're not even a little bit sorry."

She winks, holding open the car door for me as I climb in. "Do you want me to get on my knees and beg for forgiveness?"

"I hate you."

"Sure you do. Just like you hated Hawkins when you came all over his face."

Steve the Uber driver begins to choke on air, but he doesn't say anything, which is enough for me to give him five stars when he drops us off.

The Honeypot is as busy as you'd expect on a Saturday night. We chat with Briar for a couple of minutes before someone tells her in her headset about an issue, and she runs off to deal with it.

The guys have reserved one of the booths in the VIP area, ready to celebrate their first win of the season. I'm most excited to see Henry; at this point, I don't feel like that statement requires explanation.

It seems we aren't the only ones who get perks from Briar. When Lola told me about the booth earlier, she also said Nate had pulled a favor so Henry wouldn't get carded. Nate knew Henry wouldn't want to go to a campus party without them, and he didn't want Henry to be home alone.

I'm trying not to obsess about how sweet it is.

I buy Lo her drink, thanking her for the millionth time for the six weeks that she did cardio. Making our way over to the booth, my stomach is full of nervous energy.

Bobby spots us first, crushing us both with an oxygen-stealing hug. "I'm so glad you came," he shouts over the music.

Mattie's next, proudly showing me his swollen eye, which appears to be going dark purple. He shouts the details of his fight, looking to Lola for confirmation it was cool like he says it was.

Most of them are sitting in the booth; the rest are talking to people, obviously trying not to go home alone tonight. One person is missing, though, not that I care. The only person I'm going home with tonight is Lola—I told her as much in the Uber. She gave me a sarcastic "Okay" and went back to texting Robbie.

I'm in a quieter part of the club with Joe and Kris, watching Henry talk to two women. The only way to describe how I'm feeling right now is astonished. They're both hot as hell, flicking their hair around, throwing their heads back to laugh at everything he says. *What's he saying to them? Where is the quiet and shy Henry I know and love?*

Joe laughs at my bewildered expression. "It's like this everywhere we take him. Women freaking love him."

No shit.

Kris huffs, gulping down his Jack and Coke. "I just wanna know how he does it so I can do it, too."

I'm busy listening to them discuss theories when hands land on my waist from behind, and I feel breath on my neck. "You shouldn't be drinking. You have a head injury."

Spinning around to face him as he straightens up, I immediately spot the angry-looking cut on his cheek. Moving closer, I reach up, rubbing my thumb beneath it gently. "Did you try to do a quad Lutz, too?"

Nate chuckles, his body vibrating against mine. "Yeah, you made it look super easy. Thought I'd try."

My body is buzzing from the proximity. No, it's the alcohol. Definitely the alcohol. I'm unbothered by the proximity. The same way I'm unbothered by how he's smiling down at me.

Anastasia Unbothered Allen.

"What happened?" I ask, keeping the conversation moving so I don't have time to spiral.

He brings his glass to his lips, smirking as he sips. "It turns out people from Washington aren't very friendly."

"A vicious lie, Hawkins. We're famously very friendly."

He shrugs, still smirking. "I will need you to show me because I'm struggling to believe you."

"Prepare to be amazed."

"I'm already amazed by you, Anastasia," he says, winking. With that, he steps around me and heads over to the booth.

What just happened?

Chapter Twelve

NATHAN

THERE'S NOTHING LIKE WINNING THE first home game of the season to put you in a great fucking mood.

We played phenomenally. It felt good to get back out there with my guys and lead them to a victory. Even Faulkner was happy, and he's never happy, so we must have played as well as I know we did.

We were all desperate to prove to him, despite the bullshit of the last few weeks, that we all deserve a spot on this team.

Coach and Robbie immediately had us sit around the table, analyzing the game while it was fresh in our heads. That's the bit I usually hate, especially after a win when I want to celebrate with a beer or ten.

The adrenaline pumping around my body doesn't want to revisit every pass and score while confined to a room. That's how the guys felt the moment they took a seat; I could tell by their tapping and shuffling and compliance with every word from Coach's mouth.

For once, I was perfectly calm.

I don't get to make mistakes this year; every move must be perfect.

Robbie wanted to wrap things up early, his eyes floating to his smartwatch every time it lit up. I knew Lola was somewhere in the building, proudly wearing the jersey I sent her.

Postgame nights out have always been the crème de la crème of nights out. We start at a party on frat row, not my favorite place to be, but since half the team isn't twenty-one and can't go to a club, it's nice to have a few drinks together before we part ways for the night.

Then we head to The Honeypot, which is, in my humble opinion, the best club in West Hollywood. B, Summer's roommate, and the worst drink mixer ever, works there and arranges tables for us.

Now that Henry lives with us, B made a secret arrangement with me to let him in without carding him, since he isn't twenty-one. I had to promise never to tell anyone so she didn't end up with half of UCMH on her doorstep, and in return, I get her, Summer, and Cami the best seats for our home games.

It's an easy promise to keep, because if the rest of the team knew I was pulling strings for Henry, I'd never know peace again.

Within minutes of our arrival, the booth was covered in bottles and unsurprisingly, several drinks in, half the team is wasted.

JJ and Robbie are having what looks like a very intense heart-to-heart, full of back-slapping and digging each other in the arm affectionately. They keep tapping their drinks together to cheers, although I have no idea what they're celebrating.

Joe and Kris are still watching Henry like he's the Discovery Channel, desperately trying to learn his ways.

Bobby, Mattie, and some of the other guys have disappeared to make friends with a bachelorette party on the other side of the dance floor.

JJ and Robbie finally break apart to look over at me as I continue to people-watch while sipping on my drink. JJ laughs, nodding in the direction of where Anastasia and Lola are dancing. "You fucked it with her already?"

"Probably."

I don't bother mentioning my plan to win her over or how surprised she looked when I stepped around her earlier, leaving her with my friends. From now on, she's going to come to me.

· · ·

IT'S BEEN HOURS, AND ALL I can think about is smooth, tanned, glowy skin. She's in a lilac dress that's so fucking tight, melting over every inch of her so perfectly it looks like a second skin.

It plunges between her breasts, and that's where my ability to describe what she's wearing ends, because as soon as my eyes travel over the strained material covering her tits, all the blood in my body rushes straight to my dick.

Her light brown hair is wavy, flowing down her back to just above the curve of her ass, an ass I know feels fucking amazing. She rolls her hips in time to the beat, smiling and bringing the drink in her hand to her mouth.

The song finally merges into the next one; I see her tap Lo and point in the direction of the booth, meaning I can finally stop watching her like a fucking creep. I would have joined her dancing, but I didn't want to be the guy who gets in a woman's space when she's trying to have a good time with her friend. I've got to stick to the plan and not get sidetracked. Not to mention I can't dance.

When the guys realized most of the bachelorette party were married, they retreated to the booth with their tails between their legs, and now the bottles are emptying much quicker.

Lola bursts into the booth first, cheeks flushed and a drunk, soppy smile on her face. She looks at Robbie like he's the best thing she's ever seen in her life, lunging forward to press her mouth against him, dropping herself into his lap.

He runs his hand up and down her shin gently, muttering something to her that makes her bury her head into his neck.

Anastasia is right behind her, and she's even more beautiful close-up. Her eyes scan the booth looking for a spot to sit, scowling when she finds it full of two-hundred-pound hockey players, but then her eyes land on me, and she shamelessly checks me out.

Her teeth sink into her bottom lip, fingers tapping on the glass in her hand as she scans the booth one more time. I'm about to tell her to sit with me, but she bends over, whispering into JJ's ear.

I shoot Kris a glare that tells him I will fucking kill him after I catch him patting Mattie's chest to get his attention, then pointing in her direction.

Her dress hardly covers her ass, and I'm about 0.1 seconds away from covering her with my jacket. Standing up straight, laughing at whatever Jaiden said, she tucks her hair behind her ears, casting me a look over her shoulder.

JJ spreads his legs wide, letting her step between them and sit on his knee. Her arm circles around his neck, and I'm surprised the glass in my hand doesn't shatter; I'm gripping it that tight.

Fuck the plan. The jealousy is suffocating me. I throw back the rest of my drink, letting the cold liquor soothe the burning in my chest.

I'm on my feet and brushing past the legs of my teammates before I even have time to consider this reckless, drunken display of envy. She is either trying to get under my skin or doesn't give a fuck about me, but either way, she's reaching distance from me now.

I bend down, my mouth millimeters from her ear. "Dance with me?"

Heat spreads through my body when she shudders because I love how she reacts to me. I move back, giving her room to stand. Instead, she looks over her shoulder, tongue flicking out to wet her bottom lip, blue eyes glossy, staring up at me. "We can make that happen. Just ask me nicely."

She grins as a shocked laugh rumbles in my throat. I hold out my hand, which she links with hers, letting me tug her to her feet.

I know the team is watching us like a soap opera, but I don't give a shit. Her body molds to mine, face much closer with the five inches added to her height by her stilettos. I'm sure they're the heels that left red marks on my back, and when my dick twitches, I realize now isn't the right time to remember that.

"This is me asking you very nicely. Will you dance with me?"

"Only because you won today," she shoots back, a mischievous glint in her eyes.

She takes our joined hands and rests them right above the swell of her ass, navigating us through the crowd to the dance floor.

I don't even know how to fucking dance. I just know I want the feel of her body on mine, and if I had to watch her touching JJ for a minute longer, I was going to rip his head from his body.

We reach the middle of the dance floor, where the lights are flashing, but she keeps going, dragging me through the drunk, sloppy clubgoers to an area of the dance floor the lights don't quite reach. "Our audience will have to find someone else to watch."

Despite all the alcohol flowing through my bloodstream right now, I'm painfully aware of the feel of her body pressed against mine. "I don't know how to dance."

"I'll show you."

The song changes to something slower, darker, dirtier. Her body turns in my arms, ass pressed up to me so tightly there isn't any space between us. Her head falls back to my shoulder, and she drags my hands down her body until my fingers are digging into her hips.

Rocking us side to side to the music, her ass rolls and grinds until I'm so painfully hard there's no fucking way she can't feel it. My head falls to her shoulder, immediately inhaling her sweet scent. "You're fucking killing me, Stas," I groan into her neck. Her hands reach behind until they're linked behind my head, and when I look down her body, I can see the stiff peaks of her nipples protruding through the flimsy material of her dress.

I wish we weren't in a crowded nightclub. I wish we were at home so I could roll her nipples between my fingers or dip my hand between her thighs, hopefully finding her wearing no underwear again.

I'm practically panting, heart hammering, body on fire. I didn't think I could feel better after today's win, but hearing Stas's satisfied sighs as I run my hands over her waist, whispering how fucking good her body feels against mine into her ear, it's definitely better.

I'm acting like I've never had a woman rub up against me before, like I haven't been the guy in the dark corner of the club with the beautiful girl in his arms. Still, Anastasia's attention feels like a reward.

The song ends and she unwinds her body from mine. When she turns around, her cheeks are flushed red, chest heaving, skin shimmering. I run my finger across her cheekbone, feeling the heat sear my finger, and watch her eyes widen as they lock with mine.

My hand cups the side of her throat, fingers gripping the back of her neck, thumb rubbing against her erratic pulse. I'm addicted to her when she's like this. When she forgets about this game we're playing, when her eyes drink me in, and her hands grip the front of my shirt like she's scared I'm going to slip away.

Our faces are dangerously close; I feel her breath against my lips.

"Hey, lovebirds. You two ready to go?" Lo shouts from behind me. My forehead falls against Stassie's, the regret of not seizing the moment hanging in the air.

She releases my shirt, stepping backward, fingers tapping against her lips. "Yeah, let's go."

If feeling Anastasia's body grinding against mine in a nightclub was my reward, having her sitting in my lap in the Uber on the way home is my punishment.

I slipped our driver an extra fifty bucks to let the girls get in with us. Otherwise, we would have had to get another ride for only two people. Henry and Bobby are on the front bench with the driver; JJ, Kris, and Robbie are in the middle row, with Lola across them; I'm in the backseat with Stas on my knee.

She wanted to sit on Henry's knee, but he politely said no. So now, she's wiggling about, leaning forward to talk to Lola in the row in front of us, and I'm stuck looking at the way her waist slopes in from her ass, trying not to think about how well my hands would fit there if I was p—never mind.

"Stassie, you need to lean back. You need to let me put this seat belt around you," I say softly, pulling her shoulders back slowly.

She doesn't fight me; she leans back against my chest and lets me pull the seat belt across her. I don't know where to put my hands, so they're gripping the seat in an attempt not to make this more challenging than it already is.

"What are you doing?" she asks, head tilting upward until her nose is brushing the underside of my jaw.

"What do you mean?" Even though the car is full of the others shouting and laughing, for some reason, we're whispering.

She nudges me again with her nose. "You're not touching me . . ." Her hands grip my forearms and travel down to where my fingers are digging into the seat, pulling them away and wrapping them around her body instead. An evil giggle slips from her lips. "You're hard."

I can't even stop the embarrassing groan that seeps out. "Yeah, my dick's having a hard time realizing the wriggling around you're doing isn't for our benefit."

If it's even possible, she relaxes her body farther into mine and intertwines our hands, placing them both in a comfortable position on her thighs. This feels manageable. No wiggling or squirming; I can get back to Maple Hills like this. Hand-holding and relaxed bodies. Nice, nothing to stress about.

"If it makes you feel any less embarrassed," she whispers, moving our right hands along her inner thigh until I can feel the heat radiating from between her legs, "I'm so fucking wet." Widening her knees, she moves our joined hands closer. "And I'm not wearing any panties."

Chapter Thirteen

ANASTASIA

THE DARKNESS IN THE BACK of this Uber is giving me more confidence than it should.

Maybe it's the alcohol, maybe it's the post-qualifying high, maybe it's the way Nathan's body responds to mine, and how he's practically dicking down my ego by telling me I'm the hottest thing he's ever seen in his life.

His hand is about an inch away from making this journey home more interesting, but I tried to avoid this, in my defense. I tried to sit with Henry, who I knew would go entirely out of his way to ensure our bodies touched as little as possible.

Shit, he probably would have forced me to sit on the floor of the passenger seat, and I'd have been good with it. But now, I find myself dealing with the consequences of my actions, with no one to blame for my aching, wet vagina but myself.

My traitorous hips are moving of their own accord, a desperate whimper slipping from my parted lips as Nate slowly and deliberately rolls his hips forward, hand still interlocked with mine between my legs.

His other hand leaves my thigh, and my arm instinctively raises to sink my fingers into his thick, dark hair. My breathing slows as he presses his palm flat to my body and travels across my stomach, over the curve of my breast, circling my nipple but not quite adding enough pressure for me to be satisfied.

"Nathan . . ." I whimper impatiently. His chuckle is dark and devious, telling me with no words that he does not give one fuck about doing what I want. His hand moves across to my other breast, the same frustrating light touch that has me arching into his hand just to feel more. "Nathan, please . . ."

I tug with the hand still gripping his hair, trying to ignore the goose bumps spreading across my skin every time his hot breath dances across my neck.

His fingers finally pinch my taut nipples, nose nudging my head to the side, the stubble covering his jaw scraping over my hammering pulse, teeth nipping the lobe of my ear. "You only like me when you're drunk and horny," he whispers.

"Not true." I finally let go of the hand settled between my legs, leaving his there as he strokes against the inside of my thigh gently. I twist to watch him over my shoulder, his eyes dark and heavy as they meet mine. "I don't like you at any time."

Lips crash into mine and his hand moves to grip the front of my throat. It's rough and passionate, overwhelming and heated, and a whole host of other words my brain can't even process right now. He squeezes my throat as his tongue explores my mouth, moaning when my teeth sink into his lip.

It's not enough; I want him closer, need him closer. He loosens his grip, trailing his mouth across my jaw, kissing and sucking my neck, voice rough as I roll my hips against him. "Don't tell me you don't like me when I can feel how wet you are all over your thighs, Anastasia."

"It'd be all over your hand instead if you did *something*."

I'm incredibly close to taking matters into my own hands, although I'm unsure where masturbating in his lap would put us on the frenemy-ship scale. A normal person would be worried about their audience, but I could scream until the windows shattered and our exceptionally drunk friends wouldn't notice. Drunkenness aside, Taylor Swift's "Cruel Summer" came on the radio, and Kris turned it to full volume.

We're in our own little world back here; the temperature is hotter, the air thicker, tension stealing every last bit of oxygen from my lungs.

I couldn't even tell you how far away from Maple Hills we are or how many minutes have passed since I climbed in here and settled on Nate's lap. His knees nudge mine farther apart, mouth descending on mine again, more possessive, more dominant. His nose brushes mine. "Can you be a good girl and be quiet?"

I nod, prepared to finally feel his long, thick fingers easing the throbbing between my legs. Instead, he drags one finger gently over my swollen clit, and I can't help the huff of frustration that escapes me. "I'm so close to doing it myself. Tell me if you don't know what you're doing, Nathan."

The last time I goaded him about not being able to pleasure a woman, he proved me very, very wrong.

His free hand sinks into the hair at the bottom of my neck, tugging so I look up at him. He increases the pressure on my clit and a satisfied moan grumbles in my throat, jaw slacking as the pleasure rolls through my very tense and sexually frustrated body.

Swapping to the heel of his palm, his other hand tightens in my hair. "One day, I'm going to fuck your pretty little mouth, and you're not going to be able to be such a bossy, impatient little brat."

He covers my mouth with his, absorbing my satisfied moan as two fingers slide into me, deliciously stretching me.

I shouldn't have promised to be quiet.

The slick, wet noise of Nate's fingers pumping in and out of me would be enough for everyone to know without me even saying a word. The music is still blasting, our friends paying attention to anything but us, and the familiar red-hot pleasure shoots up my spine.

"Your pussy is so perfect," he rasps into my ear. "So wet and tight."

My hips are bucking against his hand, incoherent pleas and moans slipping from my lips. My knees try to close, my body trying to shy away from the building feeling in my core.

He pins my legs open with his, and I'm about to fall headfirst into oblivion. "You gonna come for me? Come all over my fingers, Anastasia, show me what it's gonna feel like when I've got my dick buried inside of you."

Releasing my hair, his hand clamps over my mouth to smother my cries as the orgasm rips through me, and I give being so loud the windows shatter my best attempt.

Every bit of me is physically shaking, pleasure spreading through my entire body until my eyes roll back in my head and my back arches off him. He keeps pumping his fingers until the spasming stops, and I slump into a sticky, satisfied mess on his chest.

He gently pulls out his fingers and presses his lips against my damp forehead. "Open your mouth," he tells me, a curious glint in his eyes as I look up at him, confused.

I do as I'm told, too content to argue, and wait with an open mouth. He presses his two wet fingers against my tongue, and I immediately taste the heady, salty-sweet taste. "Suck. See how fucking good you taste," he whispers.

"Na—"

The music cuts off abruptly, and my entire body freezes, eyes widening as Nathan quickly pulls his fingers from my mouth and unpins my legs so I can close them.

"Does anyone want McDonald's?"

I PROMISE MYSELF THE REMAINING ten minutes in the car back to Maple Hills will be uneventful.

Lola shoots me a suspicious glare over her shoulder as she drops the window. "It's, uh, too hot. Need fresh air."

Looking up at Nathan, feeling a mixture of drunk, sleepy, sated,

I wait until he looks down at me before whispering, "Does it smell like sex?"

He snorts and presses his lips to my nose affectionately. "All I can smell is your shampoo. I'm going to be getting hard over honey and strawberry because it'll remind me of this. Very impractical, Allen."

Nate is right; it is very impractical, but right now I don't mind. He holds me close, keeping me chatting and laughing until we pull up in front of his house.

Everyone charges toward the door, some carrying full McDonald's bags and others attempting to carry each other.

I follow Lola into the house while Nate helps grab Robbie and JJ, who are so drunk they're fast asleep. As soon as we're out of earshot of the other guys, she tugs my arm and drags me to the kitchen corner. "Did you have sex in the Uber?"

Her voice says outrage, but her face says pride. So, so, so much pride.

"No, I did not!" Technically not lying.

"You did something, Anastasia Allen."

Large arms wrap around my waist from behind, and I feel his mouth kiss my shoulder. "Lo, Robbie said to tell you to go and get your chicken nuggets."

Her eyes widen and she probably forgot all about them, knowing Lola. When she runs off in the direction of the living room, Nate turns me in his arms so we're facing each other, a pleased smirk on his face. He pushes my hair behind my ears. "Do you want to go to bed?"

"So badly."

Grabbing a couple of water bottles from the fridge, he threads his fingers through mine, navigating us toward the staircase through his drunk teammates littering the living area.

He lets me go first, his hand gripping my waist tightly to ensure I don't lose my balance in these ridiculously tall heels. "Stop looking at my ass, Hawkins."

"Stop having an ass that looks like that."

We finally reach his door and I press in the code, frowning when the keypad flashes red instead of green. I do it again. Red. "Your door is broken," I grumble, trying one more time.

"It worked a few hours ago. Are you putting in the right code?"

"Yeah!" I punch in the numbers again. "Two-five-three-nine . . . It's red."

"That isn't my code," he says, shuffling me out of the way to put in four different digits. The keypad immediately flashes green.

"What do you mean it isn't your code? Have you changed it?" He shakes his head, ushering me through the door. I'm adamant I'm right, until the tequila fog clears for a split second, and I realize I'm not right. "No, sorry, tequila brain. It's the code for Ryan's room."

It's like the room temperature chills as I watch almost every emotion sweep across his face at once. Uncapping one of the water bottles, he takes a large swig, nodding to himself like he's having a conversation I'm not invited to.

He kicks off his shoes, pulls off his socks, and unbuttons his jeans, dragging them down over his muscular thighs, reaching over his shoulder to pull his T-shirt off his body.

It feels unfair to witness this for the first time not stone-cold sober. I'm scared I've missed a muscle or an ab, perhaps a freckle somewhere on his chest. He's unbelievable, and he's not even reacting as I shamelessly stare at him while he walks around his room in tight gray boxers.

He grabs a black T-shirt from a drawer, the Titans logo visible near the neck, and hands it to me. He sighs, finally saying something. "Ryan, yeah, I forgot about Ryan somehow. The guy you're fucking."

I should have seen this conversation coming. "We're not hooking up."

Following him with my eyes, I watch as he sits on the bed, shoulder muscles tense. "You told Henry you're fucking him. I even got to see him in your bed."

He doesn't sound mad. He sounds, I don't know. I don't know how he sounds; I don't know what's going through his head.

"We've had a friends-with-benefits thing for a while. He wants to date Olivia, so we've stopped." I shrug, hoping my brief explanation is enough, but I can tell by his face it's not. "We didn't even do anything the other night; we watched a movie and went to sleep. He's my best friend, Nate, and it isn't any of your business. Why are you jealous?"

He ignores my questions, tugging my hips until I'm directly in front of him. I expect him to say something now, but again, he doesn't.

Reaching to my feet, he unbuckles each heel and instructs me to step out of them. The relief of pressing my feet against the flat, hard floor after hours of torture is arguably better than the orgasm Nate gave me earlier, but I don't feel like now is the right time to bring that up.

He runs his hands up the back of my thighs gently. "I'm jealous because I want you all to myself, Stassie, and I'm jealous of any guy you freely give your attention to. I'm even jealous of Henry, for fuck's sake, and I love that kid."

"Ryan and I worked so well because we didn't get jealous. We didn't care what the other did outside of our arrangement . . ."

"That's swell," he says sarcastically. "But I'm not Ryan."

He grips the back of my thighs and pulls them forward so my knees fall on either side of his hips, straddling him. I'm painfully aware of the no-panty situation when my dress begins to ride up, stopping only when his large hands squeeze my ass, and he uses his grip to grind my pussy against him.

"I don't wanna share you with some other guys. You know I can keep you perfectly satisfied all on my own, in every way you need."

This feels dangerously close to exclusive territory, something I do not want. I brush his hair back from his face and press my lips against the corner of his mouth gently. "Stop overthinking and fuck me. It's not that serious."

Rolling me onto my back, Nate climbs between my legs, applying pressure exactly where I want it. My fingers sink into his back to pull his body on top of mine so I can feel every breath. I need more friction, more pressure, more him. "Do you have a condom?"

His nose brushes against mine, once, twice. A garbled moan rumbles in his throat when I roll my hips against where he's straining against his boxers. "I fucking hate myself right now, but we're not having sex."

Of all the things I was expecting him to say, that was somewhere right near the bottom. "What?"

"I don't want to have sex with you. No. Shit, I do, but not right now." He presses his forehead against mine, lowering his voice. "I want you to want me when you're sober, Anastasia. I can't do another week of you avoiding me. I fucking hate it."

The sting of rejection sinks to my stomach, and it's like I can't breathe. "Oh, okay. That's fine. C-could you get off me, please?"

"I didn't mean it the way it came out; I'm sorry. I just don't want to be another drunken hookup. Put the T-shirt on; we can talk or sleep, whatever you wanna do."

What he's saying makes sense, but somehow it doesn't soothe the embarrassment I'm feeling. My lip wobbles, despite my attempts to concentrate on him saying he does want me. It sounds like he only wants me if I offer him more, which I can't do. The need to please him and escape him are battling against each other in my brain, suffocating me.

"Stassie, please don't cry, fuck. I want you so badly; I just don't want the first time we have sex to be something you regret."

Saying nothing further, I reach for the Titans T-shirt and head toward the bathroom. When I've changed out of my dress, cheeks still pink and eyes threatening to water, he's already in the bed, so I climb in beside him.

He leans over and presses his lips to my temple, kissing repeatedly.

"Do you want to cuddle?"

I rest my head against the pillow. "I'm not a cuddler."

He chuckles, kissing me one more time. "Good night."

I wait until he's fast asleep before requesting the Uber.

Chapter Fourteen

NATHAN

SOMETIMES I DON'T USE THE brain I've been given.

It's embarrassing, and I'm going to own up and say I deserve the round of silent treatment coming my way.

I'm a fucking douchebag. Possibly the biggest douchebag that's ever existed. What kind of person has a woman under them, a woman they've been dreaming about for weeks, and tells them that they don't want to fuck them when she's asking for a condom?

I couldn't have picked a more vulnerable time to reject her; I didn't even mean to. I hope she understands that. Even if she does, I still hurt her, even with the best of intentions.

I was just drunk and jealous after she tried to get into my bedroom with Ryan's code. I've fucked everything up because I was petty.

Great work, Hawkins.

I wanted to show her I don't only want her when I'm drunk, I want her all the time. I like her spark, and I want to get to know her, but I well and truly fumbled the bag.

I only realized she wasn't there when I rolled over, half asleep, to wrap my arms around her. She'd obviously waited until I'd fallen asleep, not that I blame her.

Since I woke up, I've been calling her, but her phone is going straight to her voice mail. She only gave me her number last night and I practically died of shock. After she came, she was cute and sleepy and docile, curled up on my lap, babbling nonsense, asking me lots of questions, and looking up at me with her big blue eyes.

I grabbed my phone from my pocket to check the time, and she muttered about not putting it in her eye line so she didn't see all the nudes I get sent. I unlocked it and handed it to her, telling her to enjoy herself, and she went to contacts and typed in her number.

"What should I save me as?"

"Your name is usually a good place to start," I teased.

She giggled away, tapping her nails on the back of my phone. "Mhmm. That's boring . . . I want to be . . . slut from the Uber . . . No, that's a little long. Uber Slut. Perfect."

I couldn't help the snort. "You can't be serious, Anastasia," I challenged, but she was already tapping away happily.

So now, I'm stuck trying to get hold of Uber Slut.

UBER SLUT

Answer your phone Stas

Please

Answer your phone or I'm
changing your name

You'll have to be something boring
like Stassie or Anastasia

No more Uber Slut

I hope you were sober enough
to remember that conversation.

The last thing I fucking need is her thinking I'm calling her a slut.

After staring at my bedroom ceiling for an hour and receiving zero calls and texts, I finally drag myself out of bed.

JJ, Robbie, and Lola are eating in the kitchen when I finally make it downstairs; they look like hungover pieces of shit, but they're all laughing. Well, until I appear and then Lola's eyes narrow. "Bed cold, Hawkins?"

Dragging my hand down my face, I awkwardly shuffle toward them. I lean my elbows across the kitchen island and prepare myself for the torture. "I know, Lols, I know. How do you know so quickly? You haven't even been home yet."

"Because we saw her trying to sneak out of here in your T-shirt an hour after you two snuck upstairs."

For once, JJ and Robbie aren't saying a word; they're staring into the cereal bowls like it's the most exciting thing they've ever seen. "I've been calling her, but she's not answering. What's your apartment number? I'll drive over there."

"Have you taken too many hits to the head, hockey boy? She's upstairs." She picks up her mug of coffee and brings it to her lips, still glowering at me over the rim. "I wasn't going to let her get into an Uber drunk and sad wearing just a T-shirt. She slept in Henry's room."

"And where did Henry sleep?" I ask as calmly as I can manage.

"I dunno, probably snuggled up next to her." Her smile is huge, borderline sinister. "They haven't come down yet. You know what they say about men in the morning being glorious. He's so sweet and kind; it's always the quiet ones, y'know? Henry will treat her real good."

I can still hear her cackling laugh when I'm halfway up the stairs, definitely too hungover to be running anywhere. "You're not funny, Lola!"

Henry's room is next to mine, so the fact I haven't heard a peep is a good sign. I knock on the door and wait for someone to tell me to come in. Now that I'm standing outside the door, I can hear her laughing. I knock again, but nobody answers.

Fuck it.

Four zeros because Henry is too scared of being locked out of his room and not being able to get any of his things.

She's under the covers, bare face, wet hair, with a coffee mug between her hands. She's chuckling away at something Henry was saying, but when she spots me, her face drops a little before forcing a smile.

Much to my delight, Henry is sitting on a half-inflated air mattress on the floor. He looks between the two of us and stands. "I'm going to get some breakfast."

He shuffles past me awkwardly, and when I can hear him on the stairs, I step into the room and sit at the bottom of the bed. She sits up and rests against the headboard. She's still wearing my T-shirt, and fuck me, she's beautiful. "Stassie, I'm sorry."

She gives the same forced smile. "You don't need to apologize to me, Nathan. You're allowed to withdraw consent at any time. I'd never, ever be mad at you for changing your mind." She takes a deep breath, leaning to put her mug on the bedside table. "I jus—"

"Stas, stop," I interrupt, inching closer to her. "I'm so glad you know that, and you're right, but it's not the case here. I wasn't withdrawing anything, I was just jealous." God, I feel like shit admitting this. "I thought if we had sex, you'd wake up this morning and disappear. I hate you being mad at me, and every time I seem to break into the icy fucking fortress you put up, something happens, and I'm back to square one."

She listens to everything I say: no arguing, no eye rolls, no sass. "I struggle with rejection," she says softly. "I've never been any good at it, even as a little kid. I felt rejected and overwhelmed last night. I only wanted to hook up, and you started talking about not sharing me."

She shuffles on the bed, fiddling with the ends of her hair, and I can tell this is uncomfortable for her. "I feel like you want a relationship or something more than I'm offering. I'm really attracted to you, Nate, but we hardly know each other. I'm sorry for leaving. I just didn't like it, and it made me want to get away from the situation."

She's right. I like her and I haven't even considered what she wants. "I like that you know how to share your feelings."

She snorts and brings her knees to her chest, pulling my T-shirt over them to hug herself tightly. "I've had so much fucking therapy. It's taken years for me to say, 'I struggle with rejection.' Dr. Andrews will be so happy I managed to apply it to real-life situations."

"You can be his star patient. Listen, I'm sorry you felt rejected. That wasn't my intention."

"This is so fucking awkward. I wanted to ride your dick, Nathan, not cause drama. I need to be honest, I'm not into the whole exclusive thing. I don't like the commitment. I don't have the time. My schedule is full as it is."

She couldn't be more direct and clear. I don't like any of it, other than the bit where she said she wanted to ride my dick because I'd like that, but I can't fault her for not communicating. "I hear you, Allen, loud and clear. Commitmentphobe, gotcha. For the record, now we're on the same page, you can ride my dick anytime you want."

"Oh, Nate," she coos in the cutest and most patronizing way possible, shooting me a smile that goes ear to ear. "I'm not drunk anymore. You're back on my shit list, buddy. I'll consider taking you off it when you give me my rink back."

"I thought it was probation. When did it become a shit list? Am I at least at the top of the list? Am I number one?"

"You're definitely number one."

BEING NUMBER ONE ON STASSIE'S shit list is the easiest job I've ever had.

We've trained before her and Aaron every day this week because of some shit Brady's got them doing to *learn from their mistakes at regionals.*

The problem is that every day this week, we've started late and finished late because of some rant Faulkner has been on. She's been standing silently seething with her arms crossed tightly across her chest, trying to murder me with her eyes.

"Stassie . . ." I'd try as I got off the ice and would have to walk past her.

"Don't even start, Nathan, not unless you want me to beat you with your hockey stick." She'd say it so calmly, it was even more terrifying than if she were screaming, and goose bumps would spread all over my body.

Yesterday, we were busy winning our game in San Diego, so she had the rink to herself, but today I don't think I will get out of here in one piece. I can see her in my peripheral vision as I move up and down the rink. She's wearing a baby blue outfit today; the soft and delicate color feels weirdly unsuitable for someone so full of rage.

While I can't see her body, I'd put money on it clinging to her every curve, so at least it'll be the last thing I see when she murders me.

I spot her arguing with Aaron, which pleases me more than it should but distracts me enough for JJ to bash into me, sending me flying into the boards. "Pay attention, dickhead."

Looking up at the clock, I know we're a good fifteen minutes over. Faulkner has said we don't stop until he says so, and as long as Brady isn't standing there tapping her foot impatiently, he's prepared to push his luck.

Every muscle is aching since he's working us like we're navy fucking seals and w—

What the fuck is she doing?

She's skating into the middle of the rink with a look of sheer determination on her face, and she looks li— *Is she starting her fucking routine?* She's going to get flattened.

Where the fuck is Aaron or Brady?

"Stassie, get off the ice!" She doesn't even look at me, she just holds up her middle finger and carries on as the guys skate around her.

Bobby skates up beside me. "She's going to get hurt, Cap. You gotta do something."

She's floating around the rink between the guys, and I feel like

I'm trying to catch a fucking butterfly. A vision in blue spinning and gliding, unfazed by the danger she's in. Half the guys haven't even spotted her, so they haven't slowed down, and embarrassingly, I'm struggling to catch up to her.

Captain of the hockey team and I can't keep up with a five-foot-four figure skater—I'm never going to live this down.

She finally slows down to do some fancy spinning shit, and I close the gap, scooping her up over my shoulder, ignoring her squeal of horror. Her fists bang against my back, and it's a good day to be wearing protective equipment.

I haven't even said a word, but she knows it's me. "Nate Hawkins, put me down, now!"

My hand is gripping the back of her thigh to keep her in place; I give it a squeeze. "Shut up, Anastasia. Are you trying to get yourself another head injury?"

She's trying to wriggle off, but my grip is too tight, so all she can do is hit at me, and frankly, I've had worse. "Stop. Telling. Me. To. Shut. Up! Put me down, Nathan!" The anger is seeping through into every syllable, and I know I'm in for it as soon as I put her down.

There are practically flames in her eyes when I place her back on the ground behind the boards where she'll be safe, her cheeks are flushed red, fists clutching at her sides.

Her hands fly to her hair, fingers linking together as she shakes her head exasperated, chest heaving. I'm trying to concentrate on her anger, not her tits, but it's hard. "Anas—"

"If you ever"—her eyes lock with mine, and I'm frozen on the spot, her voice dangerously low—"ever, touch me again, Nathan Hawkins, I will make sure the only job you can ever get on ice is a Zamboni driver. Understood?"

I bite my tongue because, fuck, I want to kiss her so bad right now. Her hands have moved to her hips, and she's so fucking hot when she's mad at me. "Understood."

"You're overrunning and you're fucking up my schedule. I have plans tonight, and I'm going to be late if you don't get off the freaking ice and let me practice!"

"What are your plans?"

She huffs, crossing her arms across her chest. "Nothing you need to be involved in."

"Hawkins!" Coach shouts, pulling my attention back to the ice. "Finish up!"

I take one last look at her. "You look beautiful today."

Her mouth opens and closes, most definitely not expecting that. The anger in her face begins to dissolve, her eyes soften, and almost like magic, a split second passes, and it all disappears. "Oh fuck off, Nathan!" she shouts, stomping away from me.

I FEEL LIKE A DETECTIVE trying to work out where she's going tonight.

"*Stalker* is the word the cops would use, Nate," Henry informs me from the other side of the room. I wouldn't even put it past him to know where she's going; he probably asked, and she told him. That's how shit works with them two, isn't it?

I pull out my phone and hope she takes pity on me now she's tired from practice.

UBER SLUT

Where are you going tonight?

Who is this?

You know who it is.

I think you have the wrong number, sorry.

Hmm.

Don't think I do. Are you going to a party?

Meeting some bikers.

Big ones.

Full of sperm.

Great choice of film to reference.

Such a brat.

Tell you what, Hawkins. You
find me before midnight, and
you can finally fuck this "pretty
little mouth" of mine.

That way I won't be able to be such
an "impatient, bossy, little brat." Deal?

You're going to look
so good with my
cock in your mouth.

Happy hunting!

Anastasia has an affinity for using my own words against me, but
now she's given me the perfect incentive to find her.

Shit.

Henry is right; I sound like a stalker.

Chapter Fifteen

ANASTASIA

I'M INCREDIBLY PLEASED WITH MYSELF right now.

Nate is ten minutes away from my location, with only fifteen minutes to midnight. He's been blowing up my phone all night, begging for clues. I haven't budged, nor has anyone else after being sworn to secrecy.

Every party he fails to find me at, he gets more pissed at himself. He spent too long checking frat parties, which hindered his chances, and now I'm waiting for the minutes to pass.

Twelve minutes.

Accepting his incoming video call, I smile as his grumpy face fills my screen. "You're still in LA, right?"

"Tick tock, Hawkins. Your time is running out."

He drags a hand through his hair and blows out a defeated sigh. "This is punishment, isn't it? For playing late all week? You're still angry, aren't you?"

Standing from the bed, I stroll around the room, keeping my eyes on his face while holding the phone out from my body. "What do you think?"

"Of course you're still angry." He sighs. "I know that."

I walk around the room's perimeter, watching the realization settle over his face. "You should know not to fuck with my ice time, Nathan."

Nine minutes.

"You're in my fucking bedroom," he says flatly. "Why do you have me running all over Maple Hills when you're in my bedroom?"

"Did nobody tell you there is a party happening at your house? That's strange."

"I'm going to kill them."

"It's a shame you're so far away and won't be back by midnight." I sigh dramatically, enjoying every second of this. "I think I'll go downstairs and find someone else to be bratty with. Safe travels, Hawkins."

"Anastasia, wa—"

Convincing Nate's friends to mess with him was easy.

JJ

> I need a favor.
> It'll ruin Nathan's night.

You have my attention.

> Might have told him he can do
> some stuff to some parts of me
> Parts he really wants to do stuff to
> But only if he can find me on
> campus before midnight.

And where do I come into this?

> How do you feel about
> throwing a party after he's left?
> One he doesn't find out
> about until after midnight

You're evil.

I'm in

He's texting our group chat asking
if anyone wants to go out tonight lmao

JJ and I have developed an unlikely partnership rooted in the mutual enjoyment of annoying Nathan. It started last week when there was nowhere to sit. Nate was looking over, practically undressing me with his eyes, so I decided to mess with him a little.

Jaiden let me sit on his knee, joking that if Nate wasn't beside me within ninety seconds, he would pick up the whole bar tab. It was twenty-seven seconds.

He was also the person who stopped me from leaving after jealousy-gate, putting me in Henry's room to sleep it off. According to him, Nate wouldn't stop to use his brain if he found me in his room, but he'd give the kid the chance to explain.

It's because JJ is such an exceptional lover—his explanation, not mine—that makes him a threat to Nathan.

It was fun staying in Henry's room. There's a box of essentials like shampoo, wipes, hair ties, and tampons in his bathroom. I asked if an ex had left them, but he said he'd bought them for if a woman ever stayed over. He wanted to ensure she had everything she might need, especially because women never have their own socks.

I wish I had a sister so I could make her marry Henry because he makes my heart burst.

Making my way to the kitchen to join everyone else, it's clear the spirits are high. It's a miracle they managed to keep the party a secret. Mattie appears, holding a bottle of champagne. "Three minutes!" Robbie passes out the plastic cups while Mattie pops the bottle.

"One minute to midnight," Henry says, looking at his watch.

Despite being October, it feels like New Year's Eve because of the unexplainable excitement and clock watching.

There is a buzzing atmosphere in the kitchen, and anyone outside of our little group has no idea what's going on. I'm glad because it's so fucking silly, but the guys love it. From what I can tell, they're sick of Nate being able to get any girl he wants.

Three.

Two.

One.

The guys erupt into cheering, throwing back their champagne and high-fiving each other. A heavy arm drops onto my shoulder, and I look up at JJ's smiling face. "We make a great team, Allen. He's about thirty seconds away. Are you ready for the fun?"

Bobby and Kris have been on "Hawkins Watch" all night, secretly sending updates on where they're going and his frustration levels. He supposedly doesn't care about my proposal; he doesn't want to lose to me because I'd be unbearable.

Which might be the only thing we've ever agreed on.

There is a clear line of sight from the front door to the kitchen island where we're all congregating. When he walks through the door, the first thing he does is shake his head, scanning the room full of people.

"He looks pissed." Lola giggles.

"Yeah, that's for me," JJ says, downing the cup in one go, and he can't shake the smile he's wearing. "If he didn't react the way he does, I wouldn't do it. He makes it so freaking easy."

I decide to meet him halfway, partially scared that if he reaches the kitchen, he'll kill Jaiden, when a girl steps in front of him, wrapping her arms around his waist.

He looks surprised, even more so than the rest of us. Lola leans forward, squinting. "Is that Summer Castillo-West?"

Summer lives in our building with our friend from The Honeypot, and right now, she's on her tiptoes whispering into Nate's ear. His eyes find me, and after smirking at me, he winks.

I down the rest of my drink. "Yeah, it's Summer."

An uncomfortable, poker-hot feeling creeps up my spine, although it isn't one I recognize. I have no desire to feel it again; it spreads to my stomach, which churns when I see Nathan take Summer's hand and lead her toward the stairs.

It's not anger, it's deeper than that. Agonizing and maddening, igniting me like fire. I think it's jealousy. *Shit.*

JJ reaches up to scratch the back of his head, confusion etched into the soft lines of his face. He looks to the guys for support, but they're all examining their cups, avoiding eye contact. He clears his throat and looks back at me. "Nate's been chasing her since freshman year, but she's never taken him on. I, uh, I don't know what's happening right now."

That makes two of us.

I don't think I blink the entire time Nate and Summer are upstairs together. After about ten minutes, I finally spot her on the stairs, but she's alone. Rejoining her group to carry on drinking, she doesn't look like she just hooked up with someone.

Heading toward the stairs, I consider maybe this isn't a good idea. I'm fueled by alcohol, jealousy, and perhaps some disbelief. What's the worst that could happen?

Part of me expects to bump into him coming down the stairs, pulling up his fly or something equally gross, but I don't. Pressing the code into the pad, the right one this time, I watch it flash green.

Nate's sitting on the bed in the same spot I was earlier on the video call with him. He looks significantly happier than he did when he walked through the front door, which instantly makes me irritated.

"What the fuck was that?" I ask as calmly as I can, which, upon hearing myself speak, I realize isn't calm.

"Are you jealous, Anastasia?"

"I'm annoyed." He sits up straight, smirking as I approach him. "You made me look like a fool in front of our friends!"

He scoffs. "You had me running all over campus when you were quite literally where I've wanted you the whole time. Imagine how foolish I feel."

"You fucked another girl upstairs at a party I'm at!"

He stands; his body immediately towers over mine, the sweet smell of his cologne driving all my senses wild. He reaches out and tucks my hair behind my ear, ignoring me when I try to bat his hand away.

"I never touched her. She got her period and needed to use the bathroom urgently. I've been sitting up here waiting for you to come and get angry at me." He grips my chin softly, running his thumb across my bottom lip. "I've been interested to see how this no-jealousy thing you were talking about works."

"I—" *Fuck.* "Well, I am angry at you, Nathan."

"Good."

"So fucking angry."

"Perfect."

Our mouths smash into each other in a crazed, drunk, and desperate display of built-up sexual frustration. Gripping the back of my thighs, he lifts me, letting my legs wind around his waist. My hands sink into his hair as our bodies work in unison to get as close to each other as possible.

There's nothing romantic about what's happening. My body is sandwiched between his and the door, our tongues fight for dominance, and his hands sink into my ass cheeks. A tortured whimper escapes me when he grinds his pelvis into me, and I feel how hard he is.

Trailing his mouth along my jawline, he nibbles at the spot beneath my ear, making my whole body quiver. "Tell me you want me to fuck you, Anastasia."

"You tell *me.*" My hard words lose their impact when he sucks on my neck, and I literally moan them. Before I know what's happening, he sets me down on the edge of the bed and crouches to my feet, taking off my shoes.

It amazes me how he can switch from rough to gentle in seconds. When my shoes are off, I tuck my feet beneath my ass and watch him stand. There's a small moment of quiet where we just look at each other. My heart is still hammering, blood burning beneath my skin, everything hypersensitive.

His eyes are pouring into mine, so I don't miss the flash of surprise when my hands reach for his belt. "Can I?"

"Fuck yes."

He helps me strip him down until he's standing in front of me in only his boxers, which is the moment I realize there is absolutely no way it will fit in my mouth, or anywhere else for that matter.

Nate is smirking as I sit gobsmacked. I shake it off because I'm not a quitter, and I'm certainly not giving him the satisfaction of telling him how big it is.

"I've been tested recently and there's nothing to report, but I can put on a condom if you want me to?" he asks as I run my hands up the front of his thighs.

I shake my head and watch as he takes himself out, tightening his fist around the base and pumping a few times. He bends down and kisses me on the forehead. "Tell me to stop if I'm too rough, okay?"

One hand holds the back of my neck, and the other guides his hard dick toward me. "Stick your tongue out, baby." I do as I'm told, much to his immediate delight, swirling it against the head, tasting the heady-salty taste on my tongue. "That's a good girl."

I wrap my lips around the tip and suck gently. His hand leaves my neck and immediately sinks into my hair. "Fuuuck, Stas."

He moans loudly, and just like that, I lose my ability to wait for orders.

Placing my hands on the front of his thighs, I lean forward, taking him until he hits the back of my throat, and I splutter.

A series of expletives echo around the room. His other hand sinks into my hair on the other side as I take control. I wrap my hand around the base and move it in rhythm with my mouth, moaning and gagging, looking up at him with watery eyes.

His head falls back, stomach muscles flexing, deep, satisfied grunts as his hips drive forward, nudging deeper. "So fucking good, baby. You are so fucking good."

His thrusts get harder and sloppy, telling me how close he is, and when I cup his balls gently with my free hand, he's a goner.

"Oh, shitting fuck, Stassie." His hands tighten in my hair as he spasms, and I swallow everything he gives me, eyes still watering and throat raw.

I clean up the corner of my mouth with my thumb, licking it clean. "I still feel bratty," I tease. "And impatient."

His laugh is deep, spearing me in a way I'm not used to. A content, post-orgasm glow has flushed his cheeks, his eyes are glossy and wild, and he looks beautiful. "You're unbelievable."

Nathan lifts under my arms to pull me to my feet, tugging at the strap of my dress. "This needs to come off."

"Who's the bossy one now?" I spin on the spot so he can pull down the zip. His lips drop to my shoulder, kissing me all over while he pulls down the straps, and the material falls to my feet.

My entire body feels like it's filled with frantic, untamed energy. He's being so controlled and slow, purposely torturing me, dragging out the inevitable pleasure. When his hand palms my breasts from behind and his fingers roll my nipples, my ass instinctively rubs against him.

"Ask me nicely," he whispers into my ear. "I'll fuck you so good."

The more Nate tells me to ask nicely, the closer I get to telling him to fuck himself. I brush his hands off from where they're exploring my body and crawl into the middle of the bed, propping myself up on the cushions. His knee drops onto the bed to follow, but I press against his chest with my foot to stop him from getting any farther. "Stand at the end of the bed."

He looks confused but curious, eyes narrowing as he walks to the end of the bed. My fingers slip below the material of my panties, shimmying them down my legs.

His eyes widen when he realizes what I'm doing, and he leans forward to grip the bed frame. I spread my legs as wide as they'll go, giving him the perfect view of how dripping wet my pussy is—that way, he'll have no problem watching me plunge two fingers into myself. "Mhmm, Nathan . . ."

The slick, wet sound is the only noise in the room, other than my cries and moans and the occasional "Jesus Christ" from him.

His dick is already hard again, protruding proudly from his pelvis with cum glistening on the end. I take turns circling my fingers against my swollen clit and pumping them in and out of me while Nate looks like he's combusting.

I think it's the moaning of his name that's doing it and how my back arches and I grind into my hand. "Ask nicely," I tease. "And I'll let you fuck me."

"You're an evil woman," he grumbles, hand rubbing over his face. "Let me make you feel good, Stas."

He moves to the drawer and pulls out a condom, tearing the packet and rolling it onto himself. Crawling slowly toward me, he settles between my thighs and reaches for a spare pillow, instructing me to lift my hips so he can put it under the bottom of my back.

I can't concentrate on what I'm supposed to be doing to myself because he's on his knees between my legs, body looking like it's been sculpted by the actual gods and a thick, long, hard dick. "Do you want me to fuck you, Anastasia?"

"Yes." Yes, I do.

Nathan leans his body over mine, one arm supporting his weight and the other gently cradling my head. I reach between us, rub the head over my clit, making us both shudder, and line him up.

"I'll be gentle," he murmurs, affectionately nudging his nose against mine.

I sink my teeth into his bottom lip, immediately running my tongue over the same spot. "Don't be gentle. Fuck me like you hate me."

Chapter Sixteen

NATHAN

Is THIS GOING TO BE what happens every time I get her alone in my room?

I mean, I'm good with that, but it feels too good to be true. I've been thinking about how it'd feel to have Stassie naked beneath me for weeks.

I thought about what it'd be like to fuck her when she called me "rich-kid hockey star" and proceeded to tell me how much she didn't give a shit about hockey.

I should have known the trouble that was coming my way then.

I have no idea how I will make it out of this alive because my imagination hasn't done her justice, not even a little bit. I'd say she's going to ruin all other women for me, but I don't think about anyone but her.

As soon as Summer stepped in front of me, I knew Anastasia would be unhappy. She rightfully called me out for being jealous in the past, so when the opportunity to give her a dose of her own medicine, without actually rejecting her, landed in my lap, I couldn't turn it down.

I know what it looked like from the kitchen. I watched all their faces sink into horror. The guys know how long I've been after Summer, but for the first time, I wasn't interested. Yeah, I was shocked, too. I got her some tampons from the box of shit under Henry's sink and sent her back downstairs.

I was expecting Anastasia to hold out longer. Summer would

have only just reached the bottom of the stairs before Stassie was storming up them.

Maybe she didn't like Rothwell as much as she likes me, and she does like me, even when she says she doesn't.

It's ideal she was here the whole time. Now I can keep her up here all night and fuck the jealousy out of her. I affectionately nudge my nose against hers. "I'll be gentle."

Her teeth sink into my bottom lip, catching me off guard, her tongue sweeping over the same area. "Don't be gentle. Fuck me like you hate me."

Jesus Christ. "I'm not going to act like I hate you, Anastasia."

Her body squirms, desperately searching for something to dull the ache. Her eyes narrow, and she leans forward so we're nose to nose. "Why?"

"Because I could never hate you." I hold the back of her head to keep her mouth next to mine, absorbing her loud, satisfied cry when I slide into her, stretching her slowly. "I'm going to fuck you like this tight little pussy is mine. You'll take it like a good girl, won't you?"

I've stunned us both to silence, except for our matched pants and her soft moan when I roll my hips. She's soaking wet and is gripping me so fucking good, it's hard to believe I'm expected to do anything else ever again.

It's taking every shred of self-control to stay still and let her adjust, knowing her bossy ass will let me know when she's ready. It's not until I'm hovering over her that I realize how much bigger than her I am.

"You just had to give me all of it, didn't you? Fucking show-off." Her fingertips travel across the planes of my back as her hips begin to wriggle, the sign I need to pull back and thrust forward again.

"I'm only giving you half." Her hooded eyes snap wide open, and she sits up to look down at where our bodies join. "But I think you can take more."

Pulling back, I thrust forward as far as I can until I meet resis-

tance. Her nails sink into my shoulders, her arching back pushing
her stomach into mine. "Oh my *God*."

"You feel so fucking good, Anastasia, such a perfect pussy." Her
legs wrap around my hips, ankles crossing at the bottom of my back,
tightening to keep me there when I'm deep inside her.

"Nate," she whispers like a prayer, "it's so big. Full. *Ah*."

She's trying to finish me just with her words, and fuck, she might
manage it if she carries on. My head falls to her shoulder; I press my
lips against her collarbone, then up her neck until our mouths are
crushed together, a desperate thrashing of tongues and lips.

One hand tugs my hair, and the other claws at my back. She's
close; I can tell by the way she's writhing below me, by the way her
breath hitches when the end of my cock brushes against her G-spot,
by the way her face twists with ecstasy when I get deeper.

I remove the hand cradling her head and slip it between us, thumb
rubbing against her swollen bundle of nerves until her whole body is
arching and her jaw drops. "Come all over my cock, Stas. Give it to me."

Her entire body tightens as she cries my name into my shoulder,
nails sinking so deep I'd be surprised if she hasn't drawn blood. With
her pussy pulsing around me as I slow down, I press my lips against
her forehead and roll us over so I'm on my back, her body soft and
limp on my chest, my cock still buried inside her.

"That was . . . ," she pants. "You are . . . Did you come?"

"Not yet. I wanna watch you ride me."

Stassie on top of me has been the star thought of every shower
I've had for the past week. Ever since she said it out loud, it's all I've
thought about. The way her eyes glimmer as she looks at my face, a
coy smirk on her lips, I know I'm fucking in for it.

She sits up straight, sliding down on my dick slowly until she's
taken every inch. I look at the space between her legs where we're
joining, and there isn't a slither of space.

Jeeeeeeez.

"Like this?" she asks gently, brushing her hair from her face. I nod, hands sinking into her hips, unable to formulate any actual words. Her hips swirl and grind down, and my breath catches in my throat. "Or like this?"

"Yeah, baby, just like that," I tell her, voice strained.

I know Stassie is flexible from watching her skate. So I don't know why I'm so surprised when she stretches her legs out to each side, doing the splits. "What about like this?"

Can't talk or think. I go deeper; I don't fucking know how or where it's coming from or where it's going. She places her hands on my stomach, lifting herself up and down. The bolt of pleasure crashes into me hard, and I'm gripping her hips so tight she'll have marks for days. "You're incredible, fucking incredible."

Every rock of her hips is the perfect rhythm, and I'm losing my mind. I snap my hips up as she comes down, and her head falls back. "Right there, yeah, right there . . ."

Collapsing onto my chest, her fingers reach up to grip my hair. Still rocking back against my thrust, the satisfying sound of slapping skin echoes around the room, and I'm suddenly glad there's a loud party on the other side of my door.

Stassie's body is perfect; strong and flexible, with a round, fleshy ass and full tits. None of that even matters when it comes to how fucking good it is feeling an orgasm rip through her.

"You gonna come for me again, Anastasia?" I tease as her legs tremble and her fingers dig into my skin.

She mumbles something incoherent under her breath, her tanned skin shimmering under my bedroom light, baby hairs stuck to her forehead, an exhausted, satiated look on her face while she takes every inch like a fucking champion.

I wrap my arm around her waist to keep my hold on her and slip my other between our joined bodies. I apply light pressure to her clit and she shatters.

I deserve a medal for not busting right now because her entire body tightens, which seconds ago I would have said was impossible. She's trembling, hips bucking as she rides out her orgasm, crying my name.

"You're a demon." She reaches up, pressing her lips to mine, our bodies still stuck together in the best way. "Real-life freaking demon."

"I never had you down as a quitter, Allen." I tuck the hair hanging over her face behind her ears, cupping her face in my hand. I take a second to look at her. Flushed cheeks and a lazy smile as she turns her head to kiss the palm of my hand. "You are so goddamn beautiful, y'know?"

"You're already fucking me, Hawkins. You don't have to blow my ego, too."

There she is.

My post-coming docile, affectionate girl is gone, her typical bratty attitude restored. I slap my hand against her ass cheek, rolling her onto her back again. Pulling out of her, I chuckle at her whimper of disappointment and her squeak of surprise when I flip her onto her stomach. "I can't go again." She moans. "I can't."

I tug her hips until her ass is in the air and this view is what I'm going to dream about every night. "You wanna stop?" She looks at me over her shoulder and shakes her head. "Good, hold on to the bed."

Her hands reach out and grip the bars of my bed frame, head resting against a pillow trying to watch me as I position myself behind her.

I genuinely don't think I've ever been this hard.

I rub my cock up and down, taking extra time to circle her oversensitive clit, making her body shudder. When she's impatiently whimpering, I finally line myself up and sink into her again.

She meets every thrust forward by pushing back onto me, her ass bouncing off me and letting me go even harder. My hands fit perfectly in the curve of her waist, and the noises she's making aren't going to let me last long like this. "I told you I was going to fuck this pussy like it's mine, Anastasia, 'cause it *is* fucking mine."

"Nathan . . ." She's moaning but still manages to sass me. "In your dreams."

"Let go of the bed." Satisfaction bubbles under my skin when she immediately listens to me, doing what she's told for once. Pulling her back to my front—I want her closer, need her closer—I run my tongue along her shoulder to her neck, tasting the salty sheen on her skin.

One of my hands snakes up her body to her tits, and the other cups between her legs, feeling my dick move in and out as she bounces on it in a fervent rhythm. Her entire body is trembling, chest heaving, pussy throbbing around me. "It's too much, Nate. It's too good, I can't."

"Don't be a quitter, Anastasia." My fingers slowly tease her clit, deliberate and controlled, and she's almost there. Her mouth tilts toward me, hips bucking and grinding, eyes rolling back. I crash my mouth into hers as she screams, squeezing me so fucking tight I can't hold back, spilling into the condom.

It's like fire spreading across my entire body, consuming and engulfing me, suffocating me in the flames. I'm twitching and spasming inside her well after we've stopped moving, the pleasure flooding through me.

"Was that better than hate sex?" I grumble, forehead falling to her shoulder.

She starts laughing, her body wiggling in my arms. "Oh. My. God. Shut up, Nathan."

THE DOWNSIDE OF HAVING A house full of people, other than having a house full of people, is trying to sneak around.

After finally convincing myself to slip out of her, I dispose of the condom and pull on some sweatpants. She looks over from the bed, nose scrunching when she realizes I'm a man on a mission.

"You've melted all my bones," Anastasia says. She's naked on my bed, her stomach flexing as she takes controlled breaths. She looks incredible. Unbelievably, after all that, my dick twitches, but if I suggest going again right now, she'll murder me. She watches me cross the room toward the bedroom door. "Where are you going?"

I kiss her forehead and pull a blanket over her, ignoring her frown. "I'm about to open this door. Do you want to risk whoever might be standing outside of it seeing you butt-ass naked?" She shrugs. "I'm going to steal shit from Henry. I'll be back in a minute."

Henry is the MVP tonight and I think I'll be going to Target tomorrow to buy a box of girl shit. I punch in all the zeros and stroll through, getting the shock of my life when Henry is in his boxers making out with a half-naked girl on his bed.

"Oh shit!" I shout, covering my eyes. "I'm sorry, buddy, fuck, I need to get that box of stuff from your bathroom. I'm sorry . . ."

"Daisy," the mystery girl says.

I keep my hand over my eyes and head toward the bathroom, closing the door behind me, immediately finding what I need. I've stolen shower gel, shampoo, conditioner, a hair tie, and a brush. I take one last look, deciding to grab some socks, too. I balance them on one arm and use my other to shield my eyes as I venture back out into what should be classed as no-man's-land.

"She's gone. You can move your hand," Henry says flatly.

"I'm sorry, kiddo. I didn't think you'd be up here. Who's the girl?"

"Someone I know. She's Briar's younger sister." He sighs and I feel so guilty. "Next time you've got a girl, Cap, don't leave her alone, or I'm taking her."

Great. "You probably could, bud. I won't come back, I promise. Go find your girl."

Anastasia is where I left her when I let myself back into my room. "Just cockblocked Henry by accident. No more talking to him, Allen. He said if I leave you alone, he's taking you."

She's still laughing after I've put the supplies in the bathroom and walked back to my bed to scoop her up.

"He could, y'know. He's got that mysterious-but-sweet thing going on."

Don't I know it. Women love Henry. I turn the shower on to the correct pressure and temperature and step us in, gently putting her back on her feet. I reach for the shampoo and she huffs. "Nathan, I can do this myself."

"Why would you do that when I'm here to do it for you?" She doesn't fight me as I methodically move my fingers through her hair, coating every strand in suds and washing them away.

My fingers sink into her shoulders, her body lulls, and she leans back into my chest, sighing contently. It's quiet and peaceful here, a stark contrast from earlier—well, until I pick up the conditioner bottle, squinting at the tiny instructions. "Where the fuck does this go?"

She folds over laughing. "The ends."

I scrub her from head to toe and when we're done, I wrap her in the biggest, fluffiest towel I've got. Stassie flips from tame and passive to irritated quicker than anyone I know, but by the way she's snuggled into my chest, you wouldn't know it.

I grab her a Titans T-shirt from my drawer and pull it over her head, pulling on some boxers myself before laying her down on the bed and climbing in beside her.

I couldn't care less about the loud party outside my door. I flick off the lights and lie down beside her, wrapping my arms around her, when she immediately shuffles toward me. She drapes her body over mine and immediately falls asleep, soft snores tickling against my chest.

Instead of going to sleep myself, I lie in the dark, listening to her breathing and trying to devise a plan to make her not want to do this with anyone else.

And I come up with absolutely nothing.

Chapter Seventeen

ANASTASIA

It's hard to be happy about having the best sex of your life when the guy you did it with is impossibly annoying.

"Look at my neck, Nathan!" I fume, catching my reflection in the mirror when we step out of the shower. I didn't even think to look last night, but the hickeys are incredibly bold and angry-looking this morning, standing out against my neck. "I look like leeches have attacked me! Who are you? Fucking Dracula?"

"I'll buy you a scarf when I go to Target," he says nonchalantly, examining his handiwork. I watch him in the mirror, the unmistakable look of pride on his face. "Stop being dramatic."

"Stop being dramatic? If you hand me a scarf, I will strangle you with it," I shoot back, unraveling my towel to dry myself. "I have to teach kids this morning. Do you know what kids notice? Absolutely everything."

"You are so full of rage for someone so small and cute," he teases, kissing the ugly marks on my neck.

"I hate you."

"No you don't." His hand travels across my bare stomach, and he pulls my body close to his. The towel hanging on his hips does nothing to hide how eager he is for me not to go to work. His voice is low and dark as he whispers into my ear. "I want you again."

"Mhmm. I can tell."

"Quit your job so we can go back to bed."

Why am I getting wet from four words?

Why did I consider quitting my job for a split second?

Is this what being dicknotized feels like?

"We don't all have a trust fund, Hawkins," I say, snapping out of it and wiggling out of his grip, muttering expletives under my breath.

I'm still muttering threats about covering him in hickeys when he ushers me into his car, and he's still smiling like a fool.

Last night was something else. I don't know whether it was all the built-up sexual frustration or the excitement of the game, but the man knows how to use his dick for the greater good.

I don't think I slept. I might have passed out from the exhaustion of being railed so well. This morning when I mentioned the dull ache between my legs as we climbed into the shower together, he asked me could he kiss it better.

And he did. Twice.

"Want me to come up?" he asks as we pull up to my apartment building so I can get changed before work.

I shake my head. "You'll distract me. I won't take long."

The real reason is I don't have the energy to deal with how Aaron will react if I show up with Nate covered in hickeys.

Thankfully, Aaron is still in bed when I let myself into the apartment. Once I'm in my bedroom, I decide the only appropriate outfit today is something involving a turtleneck. Once my neck monstrosities are suitably covered, I head back down to Nate.

"I wouldn't be able to concentrate if you were my skating teacher." Nate reaches over the center console to rest his hand on my thigh, fingers tracing patterns the entire journey to Simone's. When we finally pull up outside the rink, he turns to me with a hopeful look on his face. "Can I watch you teach?"

"Absolutely not," I say, hopping out and grabbing my bag. "Thanks for the ride."

"Stassie," he yells as I start to close the door. "Can I see you later?"

I reach into my bag and pull out my planner, flicking to October 23. Work, study, gym, dinner. "No, sorry, I'm busy. Bye, Nate."

"Stas!" he shouts again, stopping me in my tracks. "What about tomorrow?"

My eyes scan over October 24. "Nope, busy. I gotta go, and if you shout at me again, I will kick your car. I can't be late, bye!"

I'm not even through the entrance doors before my phone buzzes in my pocket.

NATE

Monday?

> Busy.

Tuesday?

> Busy 👎

Wednesday? You're killing me here, Allen.

> You have a game in Arizona.

Fuck's sake.

How do you know that?

> Lola—the hockey expert—Mitchell

Thursday? You have training after us. I'll wait for you?

> I have to go to the mall on Thursday to get a Halloween costume.

Same.

Weird coincidence.

Let's go together.

> ☹ Sure.

Weird coincidence, my ass.

The kids seem to be full of extra energy today, so by the time I'm sitting for my lunch break I'm exhausted. I'm trying to decide what to eat when my phone buzzes on the table, and Nate's name flashes up.

NATE

Can I pick you up from
work?

> No need I'll get an Uber

That's makes no sense.
Let me pick you up.

> You make no sense.

Only because you fucked
my brains out.

> Ffs

3?

> Yeah. Don't be late! You've
> gotta take me straight home.

No shenanigans.
Scout's honor.

> There's no way you
> were a Boy Scout.

I was but I got kicked out.

> Why?

I accidentally set Robbie on fire
when we were 8 🔥

As promised, he's waiting for me in the parking lot when I walk
out of work at three p.m. on the dot.

"Hey, firestarter," I tease, climbing into the passenger seat. He
leans over and cups my face with his hand, greeting me with a
toe-curling kiss that sends a shiver through my entire body.

I'm trying not to overthink it. I wouldn't think anything if Ryan
kissed me, and this man did filthy things to my body last night . . .
and this morning. I probably shouldn't be concerned about a little
kiss.

"Hi," he chirps, putting the car into drive and pulling away from
the parking spot. "Speaking of starting fires, gimme your planner
right now, Allen."

I clutch my bag to my chest and bat his incoming hand away. "No. Why would you even joke?"

"Because that thing is ruining my week. Why are you so busy?" His hand settles on my thigh, momentarily distracting me. "What could you possibly be doing that means you don't have any time for me?"

The thigh-holding I can deal with. I can't deal with the patterns and the occasional squeeze. That shit is making my vagina scream and I'm not sure she's ready for the consequences of being a horny little slut . . . again.

"I don't know, Nate. Maybe getting an education? Training so I get to fulfill my dream of being on the Olympic skating team? Chores? Meal prep? Working?" His fingers dig into my thigh playfully and I squirm in my seat. "You'll see me before or after practice and I have Thursday evening free, that's when I usually hoo—have time for friends."

Don't say 'hook up,' Stassie.

"I suppose if it's to support your lifelong dreams, I could probably find a way to be okay with it. When did you start having such a meticulously planned lifestyle?"

"When I was about nine."

"Nine?!" he splutters. "You were a nine-year-old with a color-coded planner?"

"Not quite." It's hard to know when to start dropping the details of your life in a friendship. It's not a secret, and it isn't something I'm ashamed of, but still. "I can explain if you want me to, but it's maybe a little deep for a Saturday afternoon."

He squeezes my thigh again, looking over as we roll to a stop sign. He nods, encouraging me. "I'm good with deep." His eyes press shut. "Not like that."

Trust me, I know, but that's a very, very different conversation.

Focus, Anastasia.

"Okay, so I've always known I was adopted. My parents are super-loving people. They've always wanted the best for me." *Good start.* "They put me in every extracurricular activity because they wanted to give me the best opportunities. I started skating and I was advanced, and I kept being more advanced until someone realized, okay, she's a figure skater."

I stare at my hands, picking at the corner of my nails. "They told me how proud they were every single day. How I was going to be a star, a famous skater, an Olympian."

Nate's hand rubs up and down my thigh gently. "That sounds like a lot for a little kid."

"I felt this crushing pressure, which now as an adult I realize was severe anxiety, but I loved skating so much, and I wanted to be the best for them." His fingers thread between mine. "I thought they wouldn't want me anymore if I failed."

"Oh, Stas." He sighs.

"Looking at it as an adult, it's ridiculous because they love me so much. But I was so scared they'd reject me if I didn't do well for them, and it spiraled into this intense obsession."

He doesn't say anything, which I appreciate.

"I couldn't explain how I was feeling, and I'd become upset and frustrated, so they put me in therapy. For a good reason: I was becoming a nightmare. Dr. Andrews taught me how to communicate my emotions."

"And the planner?"

"It started as a therapy activity. I felt out of control, which seems unbelievable for such a young kid. I had to sit with my parents on a Sunday night and write out what I had to do that week."

"Smart."

"Three categories. What I had to do, what I'd like to do if I had time, and what I was going to do for me that had nothing to do with school and skating."

I shuffle in my seat, uncomfortable because I'm undoubtedly oversharing at this point, but he looks over and nods, urging me to continue.

"It was a shiny sticker chart thing when I was younger. It made me feel like I could do everything without spiraling, and as time passed and I got older, it morphed into a planner."

"So d—"

"Please don't ask me if I know my birth parents," I interrupt. "I'm perfectly happy with my parents, and I've got no desire to go digging up my past."

"I wasn't going to ask that, Stassie." He brings the back of my hand to his mouth, planting a kiss right on my knuckles. "I was going to ask if those ridiculously optimistic quotes you post are something to do with therapy, or if you just like catfishing people into thinking you're not the most temperamental, bossy, and terrifying woman they may ever meet."

"Excuse you. I'm not temperamental or bossy."

Laughing at my shocked face, he kisses my knuckles again. "I feel like the evidence weighs heavily in my favor." We finally reach my building and he finds a spot away from the normal drop-off area. "Thank you for sharing."

"Thanks for listening. I know it was . . . a lot."

"I can handle a lot. Besides, I like hearing what makes you tick. It's important for me to be able to be there for my friends, knowing stuff helps, I guess." My mouth opens to respond, and it's immediately covered with a large hand. "Do not tell me we're not friends. We are."

I nip his palm, causing him to whip his hand away, laughing. "That isn't what I was going to say." He pins me with a skeptical glare. "Okay, it wasn't the *only* thing I was going to say. I was going to say your friends spent a lot of time convincing me you're a good person, so whatever you're doing is working."

A shit-eating grin spreads across his face. "Did you just admit you think I'm a good person? Did you . . . *compliment* me?"

"Oh my God. I'm leaving. Thanks for the ride."

Nate doesn't let me leave; instead, he leans over and kisses the life out of me.

Which I let him do. For twenty minutes.

I spend the short ride in the elevator up to my floor trying to regain control of my facial expressions, because I never look this happy after work. Stepping into the apartment, Aaron and Lola are both home, bickering about nonsense like normal.

Anxiety spikes in my body when Aaron spots me, immediately looking at me with a strange expression. I drop my bag on the floor and reach for a glass to get a drink. "Hey."

Ignoring my greeting, he moves toward me and uses his finger to move the fabric covering my neck slightly. It's that small action that makes me realize it's slid down. *Fuck.*

"You need to tell Rothwell to eat a decent meal before letting him near you, Stas." He scoffs. "It looks cheap as hell. I'm not skating with you at sectionals if you have those."

"Get off her dick, Ice Princess," Lo shouts at him from the couch. "Don't be a little bitch because you're not getting laid and Stassie finally gets the hockey hype."

"Hockey hype?" He looks between us frantically and my heart sinks. "You're fucking Nate Hawkins, aren't you?"

Lola's eyes widen, realizing her mistake.

"It's none of your business." It *isn't* his business. I'm an adult woman and I can do what I want, but it doesn't stop me from knowing I'm about to get shit from Aaron, which fills me with dread. Over the years, I've learned which battles with Aaron I can win. The ones where he's already decided to hate someone are definitely battles I can't win. "Drop it."

"Why do you make such horrible fucking choices? Jesus Christ. It's like you don't respe—"

"Finish that sentence," Lo snarls, storming toward us. "I fucking dare you, Carlisle. Finish that sentence and see what choices *I* make."

He huffs and rolls his eyes, stomping away from us in the direction of his bedroom, muttering something about living with women under his breath.

When his door slams shut, Lola flings herself at me, suffocating me with a tight hug. "Sorrysorrysorrysorry."

"Mhm. You will be, Mitchell."

THURSDAY ARRIVES AND FIVE DAYS after Aaron started sulking, I can confirm he is still sulking. He's hardly said two words to me since I arrived home from work on Saturday, which works for me, but makes for a chilly living situation.

I've kept myself busy and after what I'm calling "planner wizardry," I've somehow managed to get myself ahead of schedule and free up my time until Sunday.

"Phone away." Henry doesn't even look up from his sketchbook as he barks his order at me. "Or I take it again."

I reluctantly do as he says, tucking my phone back into my pocket. Henry has been my study buddy all week, keeping me company in the library and confiscating my phone when I get distracted by messages from pesky hockey players. Plural, because JJ blows up my phone more than anyone else.

So far, Henry hasn't done any studying himself, claiming he prefers to procrastinate until the last minute, then study under duress and the feeling of impending doom, but he did draw me as a giraffe, which was nice.

I'm nearly finished with my assignment when I hear Henry's pencil knock against the library table we're working at. "You know Nathan wouldn't abandon you, right?"

"Huh?"

"Yesterday. You said you would be happy to fall in love because I wouldn't abandon you. Nathan wouldn't, either."

Like most conversations with Henry, his words catch me off guard, evidenced by the garbled laugh that sounds a bit like choking that escapes my lips. "It was just a joke, Hen."

In exchange for a hot chocolate with marshmallows, yesterday Henry gave me a very detailed account of how he would make me fall in love with him if Nate were to ever ruin the chances of him getting laid again. Naturally, my immediate reaction was to tell him I was totally okay with falling in love with him, foolishly adding that there was absolutely no way he'd ever abandon me, so to let me know when the time came. It's clearly been on his mind.

"You don't need to lie to me, Anastasia. A nice girl like you isn't single without a reason—you don't need to tell me about it, but I wanted you to know he wouldn't abandon you." He looks so genuine when he says it that I want to cry. "He's never abandoned me, and I'm only his friend. He gets to see you naked and that's ultimately more appealing. Before you say he doesn't, my bedroom is right next to his, and you are incredibly loud when you climax."

I can feel the blood drain from my face. "That's . . . good to know. And on that enlightening note, it's time for us to head to the rink."

Henry and I pack up our things and head across campus toward the arena. We chat casually, thankfully about topics not involving how I sound when I orgasm. Being friends with Henry is easy; you know what he says is the truth, and there is no sneakiness or back-handedness. This week, that kind of unfiltered honesty has been a huge comfort in the face of tension with Aaron, and I'm more than a little gutted when we arrive at the rink and he immediately ditches me.

Why couldn't he have been a figure skater?

I try to concentrate on my warm-up and not how hot Nathan

looks shouting instructions at his team. By the time I'm stepping onto the ice myself, I'm more than a little flushed, but Aaron immediately puts a stop to that, because his shitty attitude is like being swept up in a blizzard.

"He's distracting you, Anastasia. You're being sloppy. Stop wasting my time if you're not going to put the effort in," Aaron complains, gesturing toward Nate, who is watching from the stands. Today is the day Nate and I are heading to the mall, and I said he could watch me skate. I knew it was a mistake when I said yes, anticipating Aaron being a dick, but he asked so nicely that I couldn't say no.

"I'm not distracted!"

The only distracting thing right now is Aaron's attitude. His movements are tight and sharp, we feel out of sync, and when he moves to lift me, his hands grip me a little tighter than he usually does. It's frustrating and disorientating, and by the time we're done, I feel like I need to lock myself away and cry.

The second we finish, he storms off toward the locker rooms, and Nate slowly walks over to me. I don't even need to tell him; that disastrous session was evident to everyone. We were terrible.

"I'll kick his ass if you want me to." His hand cups my cheek and I nuzzle into its warmth.

"If you hurt him I can't compete at sectionals in two weeks."

"Noted."

"But if we don't qualify and you happen to hit him with your car, that's not my concern."

"Also noted." He chuckles, leaning forward to kiss my forehead. I'm sure Brady is lurking somewhere judging me, too, but as I wrap my arms around him and let his calm wash over me, I can't find it in me to care what she might think.

I mirror his deep breaths, instantly feeling less like I need to sob. "Thank you for waiting for me."

"Can I make a suggestion about our plans?" he says carefully, tilting my face up to his. "I don't wanna fuck with the planner, but I feel like the way you feel right now justifies some amendments."

He's being so careful with me, so gentle, like I might break. Leaning forward, he hovers an inch from my face, waiting for me to close the gap. "I'm not kissing you until I know the proposal."

His smile is so beautiful it almost ends me, but I hang on in there, concentrating on putting air in and out of my lungs so I look like a normal human in front of this painfully attractive man.

"Instead of going to the mall, we get your favorite takeout and order a costume online. You can stay over because I bought loads of girly shit from Target on Saturday after I took you to work, and I think a bit of space from Aaron might be what you need right now."

"You presumed you'd be able to convince another person to sleep with you?" I tease, instantly feeling lighter.

"You haven't seen how good this stuff is. It makes Henry's box look like amateur hour. You'll be begging me to let you stay over."

"It's a well-thought-out plan, Hawkins."

"It's a great plan. I'll even take you home in the morning for a change of clothes and take you to class. Might be my best plan yet."

I close the gap, pressing my lips to his. It's hard to remember we're in public when his tongue rolls against mine. He breaks us apart. "Is that a yes?"

"Yes."

Chapter Eighteen

NATHAN

WE PULLED UP IN FRONT of my house three minutes ago, and so far, she's made no attempt to get out of the car, so we're sitting in a semi-comfortable silence.

Her hands are gripping the straps of her bag, she's staring into the distance, and her body is visibly rigid. I know she's lost in her head, overthinking, so I let her stew for a little while longer, not wanting to intrude.

Another few minutes pass and her lips are still pulled into a tight line, so I reach out and brush my fingers against her cheek lightly, clearing my throat to capture her attention. I curl a strand of her hair around my finger, and she turns her head to listen to me speak. "Do you want to play house?"

"Huh?" She sounds confused, which I can't blame her for. Faint crease lines appear beside her eyes as she shoots me a funny look. "House?"

"Like what you played as a kid."

Her frown slowly fades, the corners of her lips tug up slightly. "And what does playing house entail? We gonna pretend to be Mom and Dad to the guys?"

"We forget about the outside world until tomorrow. I mean, if JJ calls you Mommy, I will hurt him, but other than that—what do you call it when you're catfishing?—positive vibes only."

"I do not catfish people! I *am* a positive person," she insists, lying to both of us. She huffs, crossing her arms defiantly, but she can't keep it up and her pretend-annoyed expression softens. "Have you always been so soft? You're not at all like I expected."

"Yep, just how my momma raised me. If I like you, I like you. I'm an all-or-nothing person, always have been."

A tiny shred of panic rushes through me when I consider that she might take my words the wrong way after we've previously talked about what she's looking for, but thankfully she laughs.

"I would have guessed with your status on campus that you'd have dicked half of Maple Hills by now. A captain title guarantees getting laid, right?"

"I have, and yeah, it kinda does."

I'm not sure it's the answer she's expecting because her eyes widen, and she just looks at me. "Oh."

"Are you slut-shaming me, Anastasia Allen? The queen of non-commitment?" Her jaw drops, and she begins spluttering to argue back, but I don't give her a chance, enjoying seeing her speechless. "Hooking up with people and liking people is very different. If I like someone, I want to be around them and get to know them. It's not often I want something more with someone, so when I do, I make them a priority."

"God, so clingy," she grumbles, cheeks flushed red. Her hand reaches over to the door handle, the other secured around her bag. "Let's go in the house before the kids start a riot."

It feels great when your best friends like the girl you like, but we're barely through the front door before they spot Anastasia behind me and turn back into golden retrievers. If I wasn't seeing it firsthand, I would never believe it. I've known these guys for years, and I've never seen them act the way they do when Stas and Lola are around.

Henry is the first to start. "What are you doing here? Do you want to watch a movie with us? Are you staying over?"

Winding her arm around my waist and leaning into me, she grins up at me before looking back at Henry. "Nathan kidnapped me because he wants to play house."

"You can call me Daddy anytime, Stassie," JJ shouts at her from the couch.

"Up." I hip bump her gently in the direction of the stairs. "Stop being a menace, Johal. She doesn't want you."

JJ scoffs loudly. "I don't believe that. Everyone wants me."

Henry frowns as Stassie heads toward the stairs, muttering under his breath. "I don't want you, JJ."

BEING WITH STASSIE COMPLETELY SOBER might be my new favorite thing.

I love talking to her. It sounds obvious, and it is, but I love listening to her dive headfirst into a story. The way she has to hold back a laugh when she tells me something Lo said, or the sad smile she has when talking about Seattle. Her Brady impression with a terrible Russian accent still makes me cackle laughing, even after I've heard it twenty times.

She has opinions and interests, and beneath her obsessively organized and competitive nature, she's a woman who just wants to do well. It makes me feel like shit that I labeled her as dramatic because, don't get me wrong, she has her moments, but ultimately, she's committed and she was just scared.

Another fun discovery I've made about sober Stassie is that for someone so opposed to clingy behavior, she's being pretty goddamn clingy.

As in, literally clinging to me.

Like a koala.

Or a sloth.

Her entire body is wrapped around me. Face buried in my neck, hair repeatedly tickling my nose, legs straddling my waist, leaving me no choice but to balance my laptop on her ass, one hand scrolling through a costume website and the other tickling up and down her back.

As much as I wish she didn't feel like shit, especially since it's because of me Aaron is annoyed, I'm glad she's with me instead of pushing me away.

"Do you have any body fat?" she huffs, wiggling down my body until she's straddling my hips, sitting up a little so we're face-to-face. "It's like lying on a pavement. You're absolutely solid."

Closing my laptop and putting it on the floor, I turn all my attention to the beautiful woman on top of me.

My T-shirt is drowning her, which is another thing I love. Weird, I know. It makes me wonder if there's a psychological reason why her wearing my clothes makes me horny.

"I'm sorry the body I work so hard for doesn't make a good mattress for you." I run my thumb across her bottom lip, and when she nips her teeth against the pad, a devilish look on her face, all the blood in my body rushes straight to my dick. "I'm pretty sure you like my body for other reasons, though."

Her hips roll against the erection fighting to get out of my boxers and I swear to God, one tiny movement and this girl has me ready to lose my damn mind.

"You know what I want?" she muses, finger outlining each ab as her hand trails toward my belly button.

"Tell me, Anastasia, what do you want?"

"Food." She giggles, lying back down on my chest, propped by her forearms. "I'm starving."

I've been trying to get her to choose something to eat since we got home. It's been an impossible and frustrating task, possibly the most infuriating one of my life.

I offered to get takeout. I offered to cook. I offered to just choose for us, but everything was met with a grumble and a head shake. So

I try again, leaning forward first to kiss the tip of her nose since she looks so fucking cute right now. "Burgers?"

"Too many calories."

"Pizza?"

"Calories."

When I'm about to suggest Thai food for the millionth time, her phone rings beside us. "Sorry, lemme just grab this . . . Hey, Ry." She holds her phone away from her body as his face fills the screen.

Great.

"What's up?" she adds cheerfully.

"Hey, I've just picked Liv up from rehearsal and saw Lo. She said Aaron upset you, just wanted to check in." I'm trying not to look at her phone over my shoulder because I'm not sure if I'm in the shot based on the angle. "We're going to Kenny's for wings if you wanna join us?"

There's a quieter mumbling in the background, and he chuckles. "Liv says hi—apparently, I'm too tall and I'm cutting her out of view."

"Hey, Olivia! Yeah, he's just being his usual charming self, but it's fine. He's just stressed because he thinks I'm being irresponsible about . . . stuff."

Me. I'm stuff.

"And he's always in a bad mood right before we compete, but he'll be fine on the day, which is all I need. I'd kill for Kenny's, but I can't. Thanks for the offer, though."

"I suggested wings, and you said no," I mumble quietly.

She rolls her eyes at me, lowering her voice. "Calories."

"Did you just say 'calories'?" Ryan says harshly. "Is he trying to control what you're eating again? Wait . . . Who are you with?"

"I'm with Nathan," she says, holding her phone out to the side so he can see her lying on my bare chest. "And nobody is controlling anything, so don't start. I have sectionals in two weeks, Ryan. We can't all live on a diet of saturated fat and carbs."

To my absolute surprise, when I look over at her phone and give a polite nod, he's got the biggest grin on his face. "Nice to see you took my advice, Allen. I won't intrude on your evening any longer. Bye, guys! Let me know if you wanna join us."

Stassie disconnects the call and puts the phone down beside us, saying nothing.

"What advice did you take?"

"Huh? Oh, he, uh, Ryan said I should stop being so hard on you and give you a chance. Said you were a good guy and I should stop being stubborn."

I've famously always said how much I like Ryan. I've always said he's a really good guy, a wise guy who should be listened to. I take back all the other shit I said.

"And then he said I should fuck you, for science, and Lo agreed."

I like Anastasia's friends. They're good people.

"Is this you giving me a chance?"

I'm prepared for whatever answer comes my way. She's still here in my bed, whatever she says. I understand where her line is and I'm happy on the side of it I'm on right now.

"Yeah, I suppose I am. Although if I don't get some food in me soon, I'm going to get hangry and who knows what I'll say or do to you."

"I'm ordering Kenny's. You want wings, so you're getting wings." She buries her head into my chest and groans, mumbling some bullshit about putting on weight.

"Oh shut up, Anastasia." I laugh, flinching when she digs me in the ribs for telling her to shut up again. "Calories don't exist in pretend realities anyway. It's one meal and you burn hundreds of extra calories a day. Okay?"

She fiddles with the ends of her hair, anxiously rolling a strand between her fingers. Eventually, she nods. "Okay."

"We don't have to talk about it now, but I wanna know what Ryan meant about Aaron controlling what you eat. Now, what do you want me to order for you?"

About an hour later, I have a much happier girl on my hands.

One big-ass bowl of boneless wings and cheese fries, and she's got a massive smile on her face, looking at me like I created the sun. All I did was place the order and collect it from the front door, but it's enough for her to be ecstatic.

Henry didn't know where to look when she breezed past him toward the kitchen in my T-shirt. Nobody knew where to look when she physically moaned while biting into the first wing. JJ's mouth opened, but even he thought better of it, which was a relief because we have a game on Saturday, and I'd rather not be down a defenseman.

But nothing can stop Henry and his concerned face. He's been trying hard to not blurt out the first thing that comes into his head, but he doesn't always succeed.

Stassie bites into another wing and his frown deepens. "I know I will have to listen to you making that noise later, Stassie. It doesn't seem fair that I have to listen to it over dinner."

"Fucking hell, Hen," JJ splutters, spraying his drink all over the kitchen island.

Her mouth hangs open and even I'm unsure how she should respond. That's my cue to get her away from my friends. When she's finished eating and has washed her hands, I drag her back up the stairs.

The second I close my bedroom door, she pushes my body against it and wraps her arms around my neck, dragging my face down to hers.

Stassie's soft body molds itself against mine and her fingers sink into my hair. "What's the rush?" I ask, tugging down my sweatpants anyway because I'm not foolish enough to ask too many questions when she's kissing me like that.

"Henry told me I'm loud when I come, so now I want to do it before he goes to bed."

Jesus Christ.

All the reasons I thought she'd give me, that one wasn't even on the list.

My hand slips beneath the flimsy material of my T-shirt she's still wearing, dipping between her legs, and dragging my finger across the outside of her panties. She grinds into my hand, looking for pressure, fingers gripping my biceps as her tongue moves against mine.

Her little noises and movements are driving me wild. Moaning and squirming, her breathing heavy when I move my mouth down her neck and grip under her thighs to pull her up around my hips, pushing her farther against the door.

I'm fucking desperate to be inside of her. It's all I've thought about since Saturday night. Her hips wiggle against mine, and goose bumps spread across my whole body. "What if I like it when you're loud?"

"Do something to make me scream, then, Hawkins."

I drop her to her feet and grip each side of her panties, pulling them to her ankles when she gives me a nod. The T-shirt goes next, leaving her naked, thighs rubbing together, rosy cheeked and glossy eyed. She's the sexiest woman I've ever seen, and I don't even think she realizes it. I leave her standing there, throwing myself down on my bed and lying back.

"What are you doing?" Her hands settle on her hips, and she tilts her head to the side, equal parts confused and unimpressed.

"I'm waiting for you to move your ass over here and sit on my face, Anastasia. What does it look like I'm doing?"

I love playing house.

Chapter Nineteen

ANASTASIA

I FREAKING LOVE HALLOWEEN WHEN I'm happy with my costume.

Even though Nate and I didn't manage to order anything, I knew what I wanted to be when I woke up yesterday morning in his bed.

When I opened my eyes, Henry was sitting at the end of Nate's bed, looking guilty. Nate was standing beside him in only his boxers, his arms folded across his muscular chest, scowling like an unimpressed parent.

"Say it," Nate grunted.

Henry shuffled awkwardly, spinning his phone around in his hands. "I'm sorry, Anastasia."

"What for?" I looked over to Nate, who was still giving angry-dad vibes, which were low-key turning me on.

"I'm sorry if I made you feel embarrassed about your sexual endeavors and how you eat Kenny's. Volume is relative, I suppose, and you're much quieter than Kitt—"

"Okay, okay, shut up, you're done," Nate interrupted, pulling him from the bed and pushing him toward the door. "Get out."

Out of the three of us, I was the most mortified, which made me want revenge on the overprotective man who did this.

Nate looked unbothered and climbed back into the bed, his colossal frame covering mine as he settled between my legs. I was still thinking about how annoyed I was with him when he started to roll himself against me and kiss my neck.

"How can you be thinking about sex when you've just embarrassed me in front of your best friend?"

His body stopped straightaway, head moving so I could see his puzzled face. "First, I'm always thinking about sex with you—ow," he whines. "Don't pinch me. I'm sorry if you feel embarrassed, that wasn't my intention. I didn't like what he said to you. I want you to feel comfortable when you're here."

"I do feel comfortable when I'm here . . . Not right now. Right now, I want to hide forever."

His grin went ear to ear. "That makes me happy, other than the hiding thing. I'm sorry you're embarrassed, but he doesn't get a free pass because he's cute."

"He is cute." I nodded in agreement. "I love him, Nathan, like, it's becoming a problem. I just wanna squish him. I don't want him to think I got him in trouble."

"He's very lovable." He kissed the tip of my nose gently, momentarily distracting me. "But if he doesn't learn, he will upset someone one day properly. I worry about how he will get on when we've all graduated, so I have to teach him."

"As much as I don't like waking up to Henry's guilty face, I like this sexy-but-caring-dad thing you've got going on."

"Don't even joke, Anastasia." His whole demeanor changed, and the grinding against me resumed instantly. "Because I will put a baby in you right now, and you'll be stuck teaching bratty little skaters like Brady."

"Get off," I said playfully, pushing my hands against his chest, ignoring his groan. "I need to take my birth control."

He laughed, climbing off me, sitting back on the heels of his feet, all six feet four inches of thick thighs and protruding muscles. I should be given an award for knowing how good Nathan looks without any clothes on and still managing to leave his bedroom. Having the motivation to push him off me was beyond difficult. Even my ovaries were screaming.

• • •

LOLA IS BUTT-ASS NAKED IN my room, rummaging through my closet when I walk in from my Saturday shift.

"Hey, hot stuff," she chirps. "How was work?"

I throw my purse down on the floor and sit down at the end of my bed. "Good, thanks. Not that I don't like seeing your peachy tush, but why are you naked in my room?"

"I'm stealing from your closet. I need something to wear tonight."

The Honeypot is throwing a big Halloween party and, thanks to our favorite neighbor, we all have tickets to it.

Wanting their costumes to be a surprise, the guys have asked to meet us at the club, which works for me, because mine is a surprise, too. I check the time on my phone and spot a message from JJ telling me he's on his way. "JJ is dropping off my costume soon."

"You should probably wait by the door," she says, plucking an emerald-colored dress from the rack and holding it against her body. "If Aaron finds a hockey player in this apartment, he might burn down the building."

She isn't wrong. "He isn't here. I don't know where he is. He isn't answering my calls."

Things with Aaron suck more than they've ever sucked. This far into our friendship, I'm used to his mood swings. He eventually snaps out of it, apologizes, and spends a few weeks making it up to me and Lola.

It's been a week since he found out I hooked up with Nathan, and he's still mad, but I can't work out why for the life of me. Nate dropped me off at the rink yesterday morning, but Aaron showed up late and didn't even talk to me. By our afternoon practice, when he realized that I wasn't leaving with Nathan, he seemed to warm up a little.

I feel like screaming every time someone suggests that it's because he's in love with me, but they won't be convinced despite my objections. When I say "someone," I mean everyone on Nate's hockey team, including Nate.

My theory is Aaron never learned to share, and this might only get worse.

FINDING OUR FRIENDS IN A nightclub packed full of people should be impossible.

Well, it would be if when we looked out over the balcony, there wasn't a cluster of yellow bodies where the private tables are.

JJ is the first to spot me and Lo making our way through the crowd. Judging by the overexcited look in his eyes, he's more than ready for what's about to happen. He hits the guy next to him, who hits the next guy until we have a dozen guys in minion onesies staring at us.

The last minion has his hood down, so I can see that it's Bobby. He pats Nate on the shoulder, interrupting his conversation with Robbie.

Nate's wearing dark trousers, a zip-up jacket, and a striped scarf around his neck. He grabs at Robbie's chest, never taking his eyes off me. Robbie's wearing a white lab coat, a yellow T-shirt, and thick-rimmed glasses, and by my astute, vodka-influenced powers of deduction, I'd say that these boys are the cast of *Despicable Me*.

Nathan's eyes are glued to me as we cover the final few feet to the booth, stopping right outside the entrance. His eyes start at my feet, running up my black thigh-high boots. I know he's reached the exposed section of skin by the way his Adam's apple bobs as he swallows, and his tongue flicks out to wet his lips.

His eyes keep going beyond my thighs, past the hem of the Titans jersey and the belt sinching it in at my waist, over my breasts until his eyes lock with mine. He blows out a breath, running his hand down his face.

It's a fucking intimidating experience having all these guys staring at me, but it's too late to back out now. JJ is still smiling wider than any of the other guys and begins to whoop over the sound of the music. "Give us a spin, Stassie!"

Dragging my hair over my shoulder, I slowly turn, pausing for two seconds when my back faces the team. It's long enough for the laughter and cheering to start, and when I finish my spin, Nathan's face is frozen.

His knuckles are white from gripping his glass tightly. He hasn't said anything, so I don't have confirmation, but I'd imagine it's because he wasn't expecting me to be JJ for Halloween.

"You were right, this is fun. He looks super mad," Lola says gleefully, taking a step into the booth.

Just as I'm about to follow her, I hit a six-foot-four wall of muscle. "Come with me."

I'm not sure I can classify what I'm doing as walking because my feet aren't always touching the ground.

Nate is—very nicely—dragging me through the crowd, but he hasn't said where we're going. He hasn't said anything. Even in his anger, his grip on my wrist is still tender, and he's using his body as a human shield as he pushes through the sea of drunken Jokers and Playboy Bunnies, making it a lot easier to follow.

At least my costume is original.

Nate murmurs a "Thanks" in the direction of a scary-looking security guard as he takes us down a dark hallway. Stopping outside a black door, he nods in its direction. "In."

Maybe this is where he murders me and I'll be on true crime podcasts forever. I cross my arms, shaking my head. "Make me."

"Your choice."

I'm upside down over his shoulder before I've even had a chance to think about my final words. He walks through a door, then another door, before finally setting me back on my feet.

Looking around as he locks the door, I quickly realize we're in a very fancy bathroom.

"Do you not like peeing alone? You could have just asked me nicely," I tease.

"Take it off, Anastasia."

It's hard not to smile like a Cheshire cat right now. I love getting under his skin; I understand why the guys do it because it's so easy and *so* satisfying. "Take what off?"

Nathan stalks toward me and with every step he takes forward, I take one back until my back hits the wall. The excitement begins to build as I concentrate on his furious face and for some masochistic reason, there is nowhere more excited than the spot between my legs that's freaking pulsing.

A hand settles on either side of my head and he leans down to my eye level. "Take off Jaiden's jersey, or I will rip it from your body."

"You seem angry, Nathan," I tease, running my finger up and down his scarf. With his face an inch away from mine, I rub my nose against his, enjoying how his breathing slows when I whisper. "I think you need to find a way to channel your rage into something rewarding."

"I'm so fucking angry with you," he rasps, capturing my mouth with his. He picks me up, pressing me harshly into the wall, and if I wasn't dripping wet before, I am now.

I don't know what to concentrate on as his hands roam my body and his hips press into me. He's finding this as hot as I am. He's solid, straining against the zipper of his pants, and when I roll my hips, a groan rumbles in his throat.

I'm supposed to have the upper hand in this situation. I don't, not even a little bit. I'm needy and desperate, whimpering when his teeth scrape across my hammering pulse.

"Last chance, baby. Which one of us is taking it off?"

"But JJ is my favorite hockey pla—"

I don't get to finish my sentence before he's snapped the clasp of my belt, letting it fall to the floor. He pulls the jersey over my head with one swift movement, throwing it across the room away from us.

Every single inch of my body feels blistering; it's suffocating, maddening. I'm not even drunk, but I feel intoxicated by him, his touch, his smell. It's unbelievable; the man is dressed as Gru, for fuck's sake, but I swear one touch, and I'm going to combust.

He looks down at my body and scoffs. The tiny Titans cheerleader outfit I'm wearing is now visible since he's abruptly stripped me of outfit number one. He pinches my chin between his thumb and finger, tilting my head back. "How much do you like being able to walk straight?"

I tighten my legs around his waist, the anticipation near boiling point. "Never been a fan."

"Good."

The sounds that follow are a mixture of moaning and rustling, belt clanging and foil ripping until he's protected and teasing me with the head of his dick.

I know what he's doing; he wants me to beg him for it, but the joke's on him because I don't beg for anything. "Let me put the jersey back on so you can look at JJ's name while you fuc—"

I don't get to finish my goading because he sticks the whole fucking thing in with one hard thrust, robbing every single slither of oxygen from my lungs when I gasp.

Nate's fingers sink into my ass cheeks, using his grip to fuck me even harder, and all I can do is cling on for dear life.

Every thrust is as delicious and as punishing as the last. The sound of slapping skin echoes around us, and his teeth sink into my lip as he grunts and moans, driving me harder into the wall.

The orgasm comes out of nowhere and hits me like a freight train, but he doesn't pause; he doesn't even slow down.

He lets me cry into his chest and claw at his shoulders, and when

I finally stop spasming, his arm hooks under one leg and navigates it up to his shoulder, then repeats on the other side.

He's folded me, supporting my entire weight in his two hands. *Where did this man come from?* The only thing I can think of right now is, *Thank God I'm flexible, and he is strong.*

"Such a tight little pussy, Anastasia. All for me." He pants against my mouth. "You think you can get under my skin, mhmm? Do you think I don't see the little game you're playing? It's my cock you come all over. Even when you wanna put another guy's name on your back . . . It's my name you fucking scream."

Every word makes me grip him tighter, the angle, the frustration, the control, he's destroying me. I'm bucking and wiggling against him. Every single cell in my body is wound tight and is ready for him to make me disintegrate.

I'm trying to hold off, not give him the satisfaction of thinking his little speech has any impact on me, but then he groans my name into my neck, and it's so fucking erotic that my entire body betrays me.

I swear I'm seeing stars. My body tenses and melts and fucking bursts into flames because it feels so goddamn good; I don't even know what I'm feeling.

His thrusts get sloppier, moans louder, and when his mouth crashes into mine, he slows, shuddering and cursing as he throbs inside of me, spilling into the condom.

His forehead falls to mine, and he releases my legs, lowering me back to my very, very wobbly feet. Our breathing is labored, his lips press to my forehead, and he inhales. "I like your cheerleader outfit."

"Mhm." It's not even a response. It's just a vague noise that sounds a bit like acknowledgment. He wasn't joking when he asked about not being able to walk straight, but he didn't say anything about not being able to formulate words.

Nathan's arm is wrapped tightly around my waist, and when I look up at him, he's got an annoyingly smug smirk on his face. When we reach the booth, Nate throws JJ's jersey back at him, smacking him straight in his face. "I hope you like bag skating, you little shit."

I smell like sex and I have sex hair, but I don't have it in me to care. I tried to sort it out in the bathroom, but after a couple of minutes of trying to drag my fingers through it, I gave up.

The guys are shooting each other knowing looks when we reach for drinks.

All but one.

"You should have been a minion like us," Henry says, looking my outfit up and down, total disinterest on his face. "You'd be much comfier right now, and there would be no risk of us seeing your ass."

He's right and next year I'm wearing a minion onesie to the club. Nathan tugs me into his lap, pushing a drink into my hand, kissing my shoulder affectionately.

"Nobody is seeing your ass, Allen," he whispers below my ear, making my entire body shiver. "I'm pretty sure there's an indent of my hands on both cheeks."

I see Lo walk into the booth out of the corner of my eye, and when I turn to face her, Aaron is right behind her, clutching his arm. Her eyes widen when she spots me and she gives me a look that, after more than two years of friendship, I know says that shit is about to hit the fan.

I look at Aaron, giving him a welcoming smile, but he doesn't return it. "Hey! I'm so glad you're here. Are you okay?" My eyes flick back to the arm he's clutching, and I feel physically sick when I realize it's not a costume. "Aaron, what happened to your arm?"

His eyes narrow and he looks at me with so much hatred that I can't breathe. "Ask your boyfriend, Anastasia."

Chapter Twenty

NATHAN

I'VE HAD A MIGRAINE FOR well over twenty-four hours.

It started when Aaron Carlisle stood in front of me with a busted arm and bruised hip and blamed me for it. That's when I felt the twinge at the base of my skull, shortly followed by blistering heat spreading through my head until it was so painful, I could feel it at the back of my eyes.

The whole mess descended into chaos. Lola shouted at Robbie, JJ called Aaron a fucking liar, and I frantically gripped Anastasia, trying to promise her I never touched him.

She flew to his side, not caring about anyone else, examining his arm carefully, and said his name with the most broken, heart-shattering voice. "We're not going to be able to compete at sectionals."

I couldn't see her face, but I could tell. We could all tell. The anguish, the realization, the hurt. She was stunned, and when she sank into his chest and began to sob, I had no idea how things could go wrong so quickly.

I didn't know what to say to her. I never touched him, despite joking about it and her telling me off. I'd never jeopardize her dreams.

Aaron's hand stroked her head, soothing her. I wanted to drag her away from him and promise her I didn't do it, but he ushered her out of the booth, Lo close behind them, and I let them leave.

The team was just as confused as me, each promising it had nothing to do with them. No pranks, no misbehaving, they'd all stayed away from him like I told them to. Nothing was making sense.

I called Anastasia the minute we got home from the club, but she didn't answer. Not the first time nor the second time. The third time, Lola answered and told me she was asleep. I tried to explain I didn't do anything, but she said she wasn't the one I needed to convince.

On Sunday, Stassie texted me saying she needed some space because she didn't know what to think. She was stuck between her partner and me, both promising we were telling the truth, and she needed to process the fact she'd have to pull out of her competition.

I told her I'd miss her, but she didn't reply.

I spent all day Sunday bouncing from house to house to grill each of the guys who weren't there last night, and they all swear it wasn't them. Call me naïve, but I believe them.

I was sitting on a disgustingly sticky couch in a frat house with three underclassmen in front of me. Their eyes were bloodshot, and they collectively looked like they'd had five minutes of sleep. How I was supposed to be looking if my Saturday night out hadn't been fucking hijacked in the worst possible way.

"We didn't do anything, Cap. Johal said no messing with the skaters—even when they were being dicks. He said we couldn't upset your girl, or you and Robbie would bench us."

Your girl. She couldn't be further from being my girl than she is now. She felt closer to being my girl the other night, but now I'm not even back to square one. I'm not even on the board.

Now that the weekend is over, I've been trying to psych myself up for college for an hour, but even the darkness of my room isn't helping soothe the stabbing pain in my head.

My phone starts to vibrate, but instead of Stassie, I find messages from the team.

PUCKBUNNIES

ROBBIE HAMLET
Email from Faulkner: Award room at 7:30 a.m.

BOBBY HUGHES
Welp. Was nice knowing you guys. Fly high.

MATTIE LIU
Should have played fucking basketball.

HENRY TURNER
You haven't got the hand-eye coordination for basketball, Liu.

NATE HAWKINS
My brain feels like it's trying to turn itself into goo while simultaneously set itself alight.

JAIDEN JOHAL
You need Tylenol, buddy?

NATE HAWKINS
I need a shovel to the head.

KRIS HUDSON
I'm sure you won't need to ask Faulkner twice.

This was always coming, so I can't act surprised. Aaron told his coach something was on the floor outside only his locker, and he slipped. *The hockey team is playing pranks again*, he told her.

He told Anastasia someone saw me do it and told him afterward. But he claims he doesn't know the witness's name, and he's not told Brady it was me. No, he saved that bit for Anastasia, claiming he doesn't want to get me into trouble because he's looking out for *her*.

I only know because of Robbie, who has a distraught Lola on his hands. She's stuck in the middle, unable to take sides or do anything to make things better. Her friends are all hurting.

She knows I'd never do anything to hurt Anastasia.

It's all bullshit.

Seven thirty sneaks up on me quickly, and I've somehow managed to drag myself to Faulkner's impromptu meeting. The room is in total silence as Faulkner sits and stares us all down, and for the first time, I can't read his mood.

I don't know what he's waiting for. An admission of guilt? A look that says it was me?

"Did everyone have an enjoyable weekend?" Faulkner drawls.

I've been in enough of these meetings over the years to know he does not give a shit about our weekend, and it is not a question that needs answering.

Henry looks at me for guidance and I give him a slight shake of my head.

"Mine was great," Faulkner continues. "I spent Saturday at my daughter's volleyball game, filled with pride. They won and I couldn't have been in a better mood. Even planned a family day on Sunday to celebrate together."

If there's one thing I've learned in the three-plus years I've played on this team: you don't mess with Faulkner and his family time.

He traveled a lot when he was pro, the nature of the job, but he struggled with being away from his wife and his then newborn daughter, Imogen. The accident forced him to slow down, and now there is nothing he values more than time with his girls.

"On Sunday, I got a phone call from the dean." He brings his coffee thermos up to his lips, watching people shuffle awkwardly over the brim. "Oh yeah, you can all look fucking uncomfortable. Not Director Skinner, oh, no, it was above him. The dean wanted to know why my team of highly skilled, Division One athletes had purposely injured another student."

"Coach, we—"

"Shut your mouth, Johal," he barks, slamming the thermos down on the table. "The dean received a phone call from the student's mother, who threatened to pull her sizable donation to the new Arts building. She's understandably very upset, not only because her child was hurt on college property, but also because he has a competition in two weeks."

He doesn't need to tell us. We all know about sectionals. It's all Anastasia shouts at us when she's trying to get us off the ice.

Kris had told her he would take a shot every time she said the word *sectionals*, earning snickers from the guys around him. I had been ready to step in, but she pinned him with a glare so cold a chill ran down my spine, and she wasn't even looking at me.

She had looked him up and down slowly, and I saw him shuffle on the spot, but then, she gave him a dazzling smile and patted him on the arm. "I'd take a shot every time you miss the goal, but I don't have time to get alcohol poisoning this week."

That's why the guys love her, even if she does spend most of her time calling us the bane of her existence and telling us to learn how to tell the time. She can hold her own and she's funny when she's grumpy.

"Am I boring you, Hawkins?" I hear faintly, only fully registering he's talking to me when Mattie elbows me in the ribs.

"No, sir. I have a migraine, but I am listening."

His eyes narrow as he assesses if I'm lying, but I'm white as a sheet with huge bags under my eyes. He'd struggle to claim I'm not ill right now.

I would get migraines when I lived at home from the stress of spending so much time with my dad. They were unbearable, which is how I know if I keep on top of the painkillers, I can just about function. If I let it spiral out of control, I'll be vomiting and hiding from the light like a vampire before I know it.

"So, you can see we're in quite the predicament here. Now tell me, who did it?"

The room is still silent because, as I said, everyone has said it wasn't them. The normal thing to do would be to speak up, tell Faulkner he's got it wrong, and work together to find out the truth.

But that isn't the Titans way.

He's decided we're guilty because we've given him no reason to believe he can trust us to tell the truth.

He's had years of petty, exhausting bullshit where it's turned out to be a guy on the team to blame every single time. He won't give us the benefit of the doubt because we've never earned it.

"You're all off the team until someone comes forward and admits the truth."

The silent room erupts into chaos as every person tries to reason with him. The volume increases and my head aches until he eventually bellows, and everyone stops talking instantly. "I don't give a fuck about forfeiting your games. I will make this team finish last if you boys don't start behaving like men!"

I've said before he's a scary guy. His anger is bubbling up so blatantly it's unmissable, but he's disappointed when you look beyond the flushed face and the loud voice. Robbie has been pinching the bridge of his nose and staring into his lap for the last five minutes, disappointed, too, because he can't coach a team that doesn't exist.

"Hockey is a privilege! College is a privilege!" Faulkner shouts. "When I have my answer, you can play again."

I clear my throat and avoid eye contact with my teammates. "It was me, Coach."

I KNOW THE TYLENOL IS wearing off the moment nausea hits me like a bus.

Coach is on the phone to the dean, uhming and yessing, not giving too much away. I've already received about twenty messages calling me a whole host of creative insults, which is deserved, I'd say.

Faulkner doesn't believe me. I can tell by how he's watching me as he mumbles into the phone, but his hands are tied, and I gave him an out he desperately needed.

He could lose his team for God knows how long because nobody would ever say it was them. Alternatively, he can lose me temporarily and have me back before the season is in full swing. It was a risk on my part, I'll admit, since I don't know what the punishment is, but the longer we drag it out, the more my team suffers, and the more I want to beat the shit out of Aaron.

At least if I knock Aaron out I'd have something to be guilty of.

He puts the phone back in its cradle. "You don't play until he can skate again. That's what the dean said. You can come to games in your suit, but you sit and watch. You don't train with the team, and you can't be part of any team-related activities other than traveling."

"Do you know how long he's out for?"

"No. He's seeing a specialist this evening and we should know then. It will be two weeks minimum based on the bruising on his wrist and hip. He hasn't broken anything, so rest and a few mobility actions should be enough, but his parents are demanding he gets a second opinion to be on the safe side." He drags a hand down his face, and when I take a second to look at him properly, he seems about as ill and exhausted as I do. "He obviously lifts his girlfriend when they skate, so they don't want to put her at risk if he's not going to be strong enough in two weeks."

"She's not his girlfriend." The words fly out of my mouth before I can even stop them and his eyes instantly close in on me. *Fuck.*

"If I find out this is over a woman, Hawkins, so help me God, I'll kill you myself. I'm not totally clueless. I know this doesn't add up, but what am I supposed to do when you tell me you did it?"

Faulkner pinches the bridge of his nose and I wish I had something to offer him in the way of an explanation. "I don't have the energy to scream at you right now; I'm too disappointed. I suggest you tell your guardian about this shit show because I do not want angry emails when you're not playing. Now get the hell out of my office—I'll call you later in the week."

The walk to my car feels like a marathon, but I eventually make it, immediately reaching for painkillers and a bottle of water I stored in the glove box.

My phone is still blowing up, and I finally force myself to look at it because the guys deserve answers.

PUCKBUNNIES

JOE CARTER
Hawkins, you fucking turnip. What the hell is happening?

BOBBY HUGHES
Not been this stressed since I found out condoms aren't 100% effective.

JAIDEN JOHAL
Excuse me? What was that now?

KRIS HUDSON
How are we supposed to play without a captain?

JAIDEN JOHAL
No let's not move past the condom thing?????????

NATE HAWKINS
Can't practice or play until Aaron can skate.

MATTIE LIU
How long is that?

NATE HAWKINS

Going to Stassie's place to try to talk to her.
See you all later.

My head is still throbbing, and I've never been as grateful for a car that drives itself as I am right now.

JJ texted me her apartment number since I've never been invited around and don't know it. He was here on Saturday to drop off his jersey, so I hedge my bets that she hasn't taken his name off the visitor list and give his name to the guy in the lobby. It works and thankfully he doesn't ask me to provide ID. He hands me a temporary code to make the elevator work and tells me it'll work for twenty-four hours.

It makes me happy that she lives in such a safe and secure building. When she's not angry with me, and I'm not essentially committing fraud to gain entry, I'm going to mention I managed to lie my way in here.

But now is not the time.

Maple Tower is said to be the best accommodations Maple Hills offers, and I can see why—the whole block is luxurious and beautiful. Part of me wonders how Stas can afford it because I doubt her Saturday teaching job pays enough, and I know her scholarship doesn't cover housing. But then I get to her door, apartment 6013, and right underneath the numbers, in cursive, it says, *The Carlisle Residence.*

I take a deep breath and knock on the door a few times, hard but not frantic. I don't want her to think I'm here for a fight because I'm not.

I can't tell if the cramping in my stomach is anxiety or because my body and my brain are giving up. But the urge to vomit intensifies when the door pulls back, and Aaron is on the other side of it, only wearing basketball shorts.

"I'm here to see Anastasia. Can you get her for me, please?" I ask calmly. I want to scream at him, call him a liar, pummel my fist into his obnoxious fucking face, but I don't.

He smiles at me. I swear I'm not imagining it, he smiles and moves to the side and opens the door wider, holding out his bandaged arm to indicate for me to come inside.

"She's in her room," he chirps, closing the door behind me.

"I don't know which one that is," I say, lifting an eyebrow. "I haven't been here before."

He shrugs and the fake smile drops. "Middle door. The one next to the table with flowers."

"Thanks," I murmur back, making my way toward it. He's being too nice, too calm, and it's putting my entire body on edge. I'm waiting for whatever he's so pleased about to show itself.

I tap lightly on the door, but I don't get an answer. So I try again, and this time I hear a sob. "Go away, Aaron!"

I take my chances and push the door open, and right before me is why Aaron was so happy to let me in. Ryan is propped up against her headboard, one arm wrapped around her and the other stroking her hair as she sits between his legs and sobs into his chest. This is what Aaron wanted me to see, but the only reason my heart fucking aches is because she looks broken.

They both look at me simultaneously, wildly different expressions on their faces, but hers is unmistakable.

Betrayal.

"Get out," she says, her voice cracking. She twists in Ryan's arms and uses the back of her hands to wipe the tears from her eyes. "You lied to me again! You promised you didn't do anything, and you lied, Nathan."

"Stassie, please. Can we talk? I promise I didn't do anything."

"Stop promising me things!" she screams, her entire body shaking as sobs rack her. Ryan buries his head into her hair, muttering something I can't hear, but her eyes are glued to me. "The dean told Aaron's parents, Nate! I know you've been dropped! I know it was you!"

I feel like I can't breathe. My head is throbbing and I desperately want to tell her everything that's happened today, but all I can concentrate on is the white stab of pain in my head and the burning behind my eyes.

Ryan lifts Stas and puts her on the bed beside him. "You good, Hawkins?" he asks, sliding off the bed. "You don't look so great right now, buddy. Do you need to sit down? You need water?"

My head begins to spin as I feel Ryan's arms on my shoulders, navigating me backward until my legs hit a chair and I sit down.

"What's wrong with him?" she asks, panic in her voice.

I bring my palms to my eyes and drop my head between my legs, taking deep breaths. I can't take any more painkillers, so it's pointless asking.

Ending up in Coach's office put too much of a gap between the last dose wearing off and the new dose kicking in, and now I'm paying for it while also embarrassing myself.

Great.

Her soft hands press against my forehead, and I can't help but lean into her touch. She's never going to let me near her again. I just wish the moment wasn't ruined by the hot twinge in my brain and my entire body feeling like it's being crushed bit by bit.

"Migraine. I'll drive home. Will come back when we can talk," I manage to whisper.

"He can't drive," is the last thing I hear.

Chapter Twenty-one

ANASTASIA

I'VE REPOSITIONED THE IPAD IN front of me ten times already, but I can't help but move it slightly to the right one more time.

Everything I need is in front of me, lined up in order of priority. My planner, water, and Kleenex—the biggest box they have.

I've done this hundreds of times, so I don't know why I'm nervous, but the uneasy feeling is prickling beneath the surface. Lola and Aaron went to Kenny's to get wings and give me privacy, and the silence of my apartment only adds to my unease.

Right on cue, Dr. Andrews's name appears on the screen as the iPad rings.

Pressing Accept, my heart sinks when the screen fills with the familiar Seattle backdrop and the muted décor of Dr. Andrews's office.

He's sitting at his desk, a journal balanced on his crossed legs, with a pen resting between his fingers. "Good afternoon, Anastasia. How are you feeling today?"

Homesick is the word on the tip of my tongue. For the first time since I left for college, I wish I were back in Washington.

I've seen Seattle in movies or shows countless times, and I've never been affected. Seeing it through a window I looked through for close to ten years makes me want to hop on the next flight out of LAX.

Wiping my sweating palms against my pants, I smile into the camera. "I'm good, thank you."

"Are you sure that's the answer you want me to write down?"

Dr. Andrews is in his early forties now, but he was fresh from collecting his PhD when I first became his patient. He hasn't aged; his face has the same soft lines around his eyes, and his hair has always been the same light brown with flecks of gray.

Med schools grays he called them when I asked what they were, probably very rudely, when I was around nine. In a way, I think him defying the signs of time is a comfort to me. That feels like something I should address with him at some point.

He doesn't say anything while I consider what to say next. It's not like I think keeping things from your therapist is good. I just don't know how to verbalize my feelings right now, which is why I'm back in therapy. "Your view is making me sad."

"Can you pinpoint what about the view is upsetting to you?"

The sound of pen scratching against paper begins, a noise I've grown accustomed to over the years. "I haven't been home in almost a year. I miss Seattle."

Sitting up straight in his chair, he rotates slightly, knowingly or unknowingly, partially blocking the view. I unclench my fists, something I didn't realize I was doing until my palms started to sting from the indent of my nails.

"Do your parents visit you in Los Angeles?"

"Never. They ask, but I'm always busy, and they don't like flying, so I don't like making them travel. I'm too busy to visit them."

"We've talked about your parents a lot, Anastasia. You've told me you feel overwhelmed by the need to succeed for them, more than yourself." He pushes his glasses up the bridge of his nose and looks into the camera. "Does the pressure, or the overwhelmed feeling you describe, diminish when you haven't seen them?"

"It never fully goes away. Skating is always the first thing they ask about when they call." A lump in my throat forms and I struggle to swallow it down. "When I don't hear from them, I feel, uh, I feel relief."

He nods, scribbling down notes on the page in front of him. "Does the relief make you feel guilty?"

Oh God. Why are my eyes watering? "Yeah."

"What are your interests outside of figure skating, Anastasia?"

I try to answer immediately, but when my mouth opens, I realize I don't have anything to say; skating is my entire life. "I don't have any."

"And if you were to lose a competition or decide you didn't want to skate anymore, do you think your parents would be mad? Take a moment to think about it."

I don't need a moment. As soon as he asked the question, the answer immediately dropped into my head. "No, I think they'd be confused at first, but they'd want me to be happy."

"From our joint sessions with your parents in the past, and the sessions we've had together, I know how highly you think of them. Would I be correct to say you still find them very supportive, whether it's therapy, school, or sports related?"

"Absolutely. They're great."

"Parents, well, good parents like yours, who have high-achieving children with very specific interests, sometimes struggle to know what to talk about outside of those interests." He clasps his hands together and rests them against his stomach, leaning back in his chair. "Your parents have said in our joint sessions they understand skating is your biggest priority. You might find that them asking you about it every time they speak to you is their way of showing you they still support you, despite not seeing you regularly."

My chest constricts—guilt. Guilt because I know my parents support me. Guilt because I haven't seen them. Guilt because I haven't appreciated them.

I keep my eyes stuck on the iPad screen, staring right at his tie pin; if I look at his face, I'll cry. "I know they only want the best for me."

"It's normal to understand something logically but emotionally feel something different. Loving someone but feeling relief not speaking to them, it's a huge conflict in a person's mind, but it doesn't make you bad in any way, it makes you human." *This is rough.* "Going back to the view, Anastasia. Do you think perhaps my view upsets you not because you miss Seattle, but because you miss your parents?"

I nod, my eyes not leaving the pin even as they line with tears. "Maybe."

"Like children, adults need boundaries. I'd like you to tell your parents you don't want to discuss skating. Even if it's just for one call, one visit, see how you feel, knowing it won't be brought up. Achievable?"

Blinking away the tears threatening to fall, I look back at his face and force a smile. "Sure."

I stopped having regular therapy sessions when I moved to LA two years ago. I was so immersed in the whole college experience I didn't need it. But something would happen, I'd have an ad-hoc session and promise myself I'd go regularly again, but I never did.

Nothing about therapy gets easier. You just learn to accept those hard conversations are worth it when your feelings become more manageable. Halfway through the session and I can breathe now, but from experience, I know that could all change again before the session is over.

"In our session last week, you explained how the uncertainty around your competition was causing severe anxiety. Can you tell me how you're feeling this week?"

"I feel good," I answer honestly. It's nice to have something positive to say for once. "Aaron was cleared by the doctor yesterday so we can compete tomorrow."

"I'm thrilled to hear that. It must be a huge weight off your mind." Aaron and I skipped class to practice, and thankfully, everything went smoothly. "And how's your relationship with Aaron? Last week you mentioned you were feeling smothered."

Smothered feels like an understatement. Aaron has barely left my side for two weeks, and it's been a lot. In many ways, I appreciate that despite being the injured one, he's made time for me to grieve. Because that's what the past two weeks have felt like: grief. Grieving the loss of things I could have had.

But even with the best of intentions, sometimes Aaron's kindness feels like control. My tears were understandable, but only if they were about skating. The anxiety I was feeling would get better, but only with him by my side to help me.

"Aaron has backed off," I explain. "I told him I needed to process on my own, especially now I have doubts about what happened. He was annoyed at first, but he seems to have forgotten all about it now he's been cleared to skate."

"Do you find he gets annoyed with you often?"

"Uh, Aaron would benefit from therapy is probably the nicest way I can say it." I fight the urge to nervous laugh because where do I even start. "Aaron's parents manipulate each other all the time; it's super unhealthy, and Aaron has grown up being shown it's how you get what you want. He wants to be better than them, and he does try. A lot of the time, he's a wonderful friend."

"But does he get annoyed with you often?"

"I definitely take the brunt of his bad moods, but I spend more time with him than anyone else. Sometimes it feels like everything's perfect, and suddenly it won't be, and I won't know what I did wrong."

"Sounds difficult."

"It is. He holds me to a different standard, like, I don't know how to explain it. Something Lola does is fine, but if I do the exact same thing, it might not be fine."

"You feel like the rules are different for you?"

"Yeah, exactly. When he's in a good mood, it doesn't matter, but if things are bad, he's tough to be around. But I wouldn't abandon Lola if she had issues; I don't want to abandon him."

"Very admirable, Anastasia." He jots something down, and sometimes, I wish I could read his notes. "I would encourage you to remember while everyone has progress to make, it's important for you to make sure you prioritize your well-being. Friendships are important, but so is living in a healthy environment."

"Gotcha."

"I'd like to talk about Nathan next if you're able to. I'd like to know about his impact on your life."

I knew it was coming, but I was still unprepared for it. Your therapist isn't going to forget about you ending a session early because you couldn't stop crying about a man you've only known for two months.

Last week, I gave Dr. Andrews a rundown of the events leading up to my unlikely friendship with Nathan. It was when I started talking about playing house that made me cry.

"I haven't heard from him in two weeks. I yelled at him really bad, and I think our, well, whatever we have, is over."

He flicks through the crisp pages and taps on the page. "You were angry because he had admitted he was responsible for Aaron's accident after promising you he wasn't."

"Yes."

"And he's made a promise before, which turned out to be a lie. To protect a teammate, right?"

"That's right."

"But you think he might be telling the truth, and that's why it upsets you to talk about him?"

Two weeks ago, after Ryan refused to let Nathan drive home, Bobby and Joe showed up to get him. Nate had passed out by that point after violently throwing up multiple times, and I wished *I* could pass out. Bobby took one look at my tear-soaked face and tried to convince me Nate didn't do it, even though he admitted to it. Joe was next to jump in to defend Nate, explaining Coach Faulkner wanted to cancel all their hockey games unless someone confessed.

They both promised Nathan would never do anything to hurt me, which was hard to hear and even harder to stomach.

Dr. Andrews has a finger pressed to his lips, patiently waiting for me to explain. All I want to do is end the call, but I push through. "Nate's a fixer. He looks out for his friends; I know how proud he feels to be trusted with the title of Captain. It makes sense to me that he'd take the fall if his team would suffer."

"It sounds like a difficult time for you all. What is it specifically that's upsetting you? Being lied to again?"

I have been asking myself the same thing. Sighing, louder than intended, I try to put it into words. "Kinda. I feel naïve more than anything. Nathan and Aaron can't both be telling the truth. Aaron hasn't gained anything; he has no reason to lie."

"And Nathan?"

"Nathan . . ." *Oh God. Why am I getting upset?* "Nathan makes me feel cared for when we're together. He makes me feel wanted. I don't think he'd jeopardize my competition, but I don't trust my judgment because I've started to get feelings for him."

"Have you told him this?"

Shaking my head, I finally admit defeat and reach for the Kleenex. "Like I said, I haven't heard from him. I've thought about calling him so many times, but I'm scared."

"What're you scared of?"

"That it's too late. He'll hear what I have to say and reject me anyway because I didn't believe him."

Admitting it out loud hurts. Wanting him when he might not want me back hurts. Not trusting myself to get things right hurts. Missing him hurts.

I've managed to avoid everyone by practicing at the rink at work.

Brady wasn't happy about it, but I didn't give her any choice. Mattie gave me a sad wave when he saw me in one of our shared lectures, but he didn't approach me. Lola's under strict instructions to not keep me updated.

"Rejection is scary, but so is living with never knowing what could have happened if you were honest. I think you need to communicate your feelings with him. Any relationship, friendship, or more, will not survive through all this dishonesty."

"It feels unfair that I have to be the honest one." I snort, dabbing at my cheeks with a tissue. "I'm not the one telling lies. It's everyone else. I'm stuck in the middle, looking like a fool."

Dr. Andrews smiles, smothering a laugh with his hand. "Yes, the irony isn't lost on me, but nobody thinks you're a fool, Anastasia. What's the saying? Be the change you want to see, or something. Lead with honesty. It sounds like you have good people around you, and it's important to remember people make mistakes."

"I'm fine with mistakes. I don't expect anyone to be perfect—"

"Other than yourself."

I roll my eyes because he's got me there, but there aren't enough minutes left in this session to tackle that one. It's been more than ten years, and it still hasn't been long enough yet.

"Other than myself, but not with my friends."

A timer beeps quietly, which is our reminder the session is coming to an end. It's not until I have a session that I remember how exhausting therapy is. It leaves you with a feelings hangover. I always need to sleep it off, but when I wake up, I feel better.

"We've covered a lot, but to recap: What are the things to take away from this conversation?"

It feels like we've covered so much, but in reality, I could probably fill another few hours obsessing over this. "I need to set boundaries with my mom and dad so I can enjoy spending time with them, not worrying."

"Good. What else?"

"I need to put myself first when Aaron is being difficult. I can be a good friend while also prioritizing my well-being."

"And?"

"I need to speak to Nathan. I need to be honest about how I feel."

"And finally?"

"People make mistakes."

Closing his journal, he gives me a crooked smile. "Top of the class, well done. Your competition is tomorrow, right?"

"Yeah, at lunchtime."

"I've seen you through many competitions, and I know the prospect of losing is not one you or any competitive athlete looks forward to. How do you feel mentally going into this? Are you prepared to potentially not qualify?"

"Yes," I lie. "Because I'll have tried my best, and I'd rather compete and lose than not compete."

"You give that line to me every time, Anastasia, and I must say, you are no more convincing now than you were when you were nine." He puts his journal and pen on his desk and straightens his tie, chuckling. "I honestly hope you get the outcome you've been working so hard for, especially after all of this unhappiness."

"Me, too, Doc."

Chapter Twenty-two

NATHAN

THE PAST FOURTEEN DAYS HAVE been the longest of my life.

For two weeks, I've sulked and moped around, desperately jealous of my teammates, pining after a girl who hates me.

In a nutshell, I've been a loser for two weeks.

I genuinely nearly cried with happiness when Robbie called to tell me to get my ass ready for practice because Shithead had been cleared to skate.

Not playing with the team has made me realize how much I love hockey. I know it sounds outrageous because you'd think I'd know, right? I thought I did. But having time away has given me a new focus and clarity.

My next thought was Anastasia and the fact her dreams were back in reach. *Jesus*, I want to see her so fucking bad.

My bathroom is full of bottles that smell good, just like she does. I've never liked the smell of honey and strawberry as much as I do now that I haven't seen her.

But she doesn't want me near her. I saw it in her face when she thought I'd lied to her again. I want to call her; I've thought about calling her dozens of times, but I'm scared I'll make everything worse.

Mattie told me how sad she looked when he saw her in class, and I hate being the reason for it. She must care for me a little, even if she doesn't realize it. When I felt like I was at death's door with my migraine and I violently and very unattractively vomited multiple times, she was beside me, rubbing my back.

When I passed out on her bed, and she climbed on to check my temperature, I pushed my luck and buried my head in her lap. I wanted to hide from the light that was making my brain fry, but she stroked my hair for what felt like forever. I tried to stay awake to appreciate it, but I couldn't.

Lola is sick of me asking how her best friend is. Every time I even mention Stassie, she tells me LAPD has tons of unsolved crimes I can confess to and to annoy them instead of her.

It's wordy, so you'd think she'd shorten it after two weeks, but no, she's very committed to her craft. As much as she likes giving me a hard time, I know she's stuck in the middle and is super upset. Robbie told me Anastasia forbids Lola from even mentioning any of us, which only makes me feel worse.

I wanted to text her to say good luck for sectionals but chickened out when I thought it might stress her out. I want things to go back to normal more than I've ever wanted anything.

Getting away from Maple Hills and smashing UT Austin 8–3 was an excellent way to put my drama to the back of my mind.

I was worried I'd be rusty, but everything was perfect other than Joe and JJ living in the penalty box like they were paying rent. I'll let Robbie deal with them because I'm in too good of a mood.

For now, anyway—it might not last long since I'm sneaking across the hotel lobby with two bags from the liquor store.

Technically, it's not illegal because I'm twenty-one, but Faulkner won't see it that way if he catches me passing around bottles of Jägermeister. I was picked to take the risk; the guys say I owe them because they had to take all the shit Robbie normally gives me when I wasn't there.

Pressing my key card against the door, I push the handle down when the light flashes green. Most of the guys are already in the room I'm sharing with Robbie and Henry, putting their sweaty feet all over my bed.

It feels more like walking into a funeral than the room of a team that just won a game. "Who died?" They all turn to look at me, identical somber faces. "I was joking, but now I'm not sure. Why are you all looking at me like that?"

They look between each other, and Kris is the first to clear his throat. "Faulkner is looking for you, dude."

"I haven't even opened a bottle yet." I laugh, putting the bag on the desk. "How can I be in trouble already?"

"It's not that," Robbie says, running a hand down his face. "Aaron can't skate again, Nathan. You're back on the bench."

"What the fuck do you mean he can't skate?" I yell. *I'm going to get another fucking migraine.* "Did they compete?" Silence. "Can someone please tell me what the hell is going on?"

"He dropped her," Henry says flatly, walking over to the bags and pulling out a bottle. "His wrist gave out when they performed, and he dropped her."

I'VE BEEN SITTING OUTSIDE OF Maple Tower for thirty minutes, and I still haven't managed to make it inside yet.

Fifteen of those minutes were me on the phone with Lola, trying to convince her to give my name to the concierge so I could get a code for the elevator. The other fifteen have been mentally preparing for Anastasia to kick me out.

Faulkner confirmed what the guys said when I found him. Aaron's injury gave out while they were on the ice; he tried to catch her on the way down, injuring himself further.

"I'm sorry, Hawkins," Faulkner said, handing me a beer from the minifridge. "We'll know more Monday, but Skinner wants you benched from what's been said so far."

I don't care about myself right now. I'm thinking of my team like I always am, but mainly I'm thinking about her. I won't be able to stop thinking about her until I see with my own eyes that she's okay.

There's an ache in my stomach the whole elevator ride. Thankfully, Lo didn't ask for me to be forcefully removed, and I was let into the building. Knocking my knuckles against the door three times, I step back. The ache intensifies, and my heart feels like it's beating in the wrong rhythm.

The distinct Brooklyn harshness I'm used to being thrown in my direction echoes on the other side of the door. The door swings open and Lola leans against the frame. "If you make her cry, Nathan, I swear, your dick will live in a jar in my room, and I'll make it my life's mission to ensure you are never happy again."

"Noted."

Dragging me in by my sweatshirt, she huffs as she closes the door behind me. "She's in her room and she doesn't know you're here. Be patient with her; she's tough, but she's vulnerable at the moment." Behind her, Aaron peeks out of his bedroom, then slams the door shut when he spots me. "Everything is out of her control, Nate. She's not a girl who likes being out of control."

"I got it. I want to see her because I've missed her, and I'm worried about her."

She gives me a cautious nod and moves out of my way. "She's missed you, too."

I have no right to want anything right now; I'm grateful to have made it this far. But a tiny, selfish part of me hopes I don't find Ryan Rothwell on the other side of this door.

Tapping my fingers lightly, I listen for her quiet "Come in" before pushing it open.

She does a double take and sits up straight in her bed, wincing at her quick movement.

She's wearing my T-shirt.

"Hey."

Great start, Hawkins.

She blinks at me, then again like she can't comprehend it's me. I step into her bedroom and close the door behind me, keeping my distance from her. "Hi," she whispers back.

"I know you don't want me here, but I heard what happened. Even if you rip my head off, I had to see you, Anastasia. I needed to see with my own eyes that you're okay."

Bringing her knees to her chest, she pulls the T-shirt over her bare legs and nods. She looks anything but okay right now. "You look better than the last time you were here. I didn't know you get migraines; it was scary."

I take a step closer to her bed and she doesn't react badly, so I take another. "I didn't mean to scare you, and, uh, I'm sorry for the vomit. And I'm sorry about everything else. I've fucked up so badly, but it's not in the way you think."

"I know."

"You know?"

She rests her chin on top of her knees and sighs. "I know, Nathan."

She looks broken. Pale and puffy face, eyes red from crying or rubbing, or both. Her hair, ordinarily shiny and flowing down her back, is tied into a ball on the top of her head, and her entire demeanor feels deflated.

"Stassie, can I hug you? You look like you need one, and I, well, I've missed you a lot."

"I'd like that," she says, so quietly that I hardly hear her.

Kicking off my sneakers, I climb toward her. She stretches out her legs and I immediately see the fresh bruises from yesterday. Not knowing where to put myself, I sit beside her, propped up on her millions of pillows, just close enough so our legs are touching.

It's like two weeks apart has made us forget how to be near each other, but when I put my arm around her, she climbs between my legs, and sinks her face into my chest.

My body knows what to do better than my brain. I pull her closer gently, wrapping my arms around her. All the tension in my body fades and I can breathe properly again. Until her shoulders shake and her fingers cling to my sweatshirt. I press my lips to her forehead as her cry becomes audible, getting louder and louder. "Shh, baby. It's okay."

"Everything is a"—her voice cracks between sobs—"total mess."

Cupping her neck with my hand, I brush my thumb across her cheek until the cries stop, and she stills against my chest.

I keep my arms around her, saying nothing, holding her until she's ready to talk. I'm listening to the gentle sound of her breathing when she finally speaks. "I'm sorry about the crying."

"Hey, I chucked up and passed out on you, Stas. I can deal with a bit of crying. You wanna talk about what happened?"

She releases my body, and for a second, I think she's making a run for it, but instead, she straddles my lap and sits facing me.

I rub my hands up and down the front of her bare thighs while she rubs her palms against her eyes, getting rid of the stray tears. "You ever been dropped from a great height in front of hundreds of people?"

"Fell out of a ski lift once."

She snorts and shakes her head. "Of course you did." She plays with the string of my sweatpants, not looking at my face. "Everything was fine. We'd practiced and practiced, and he was fine. We were near the end of our routine, doing the lift, and his wrist just *went*."

The way her voice shakes when she says it is like a punch to the gut. Her eyes finally meet mine, tears brimming.

"I th-thought I was going to crack my head open. It all happened so quickly; Aaron caught me on the way down, but I bashed his leg as he swung me around. He has these hideous cuts and bruises; I feel so guilty."

I circle a particularly angry-looking bruise on the inside of her thigh lightly with my finger. "You hardly got off lightly."

"I landed on my feet instead of my head, Nate. It could have been so much worse." Her entire body is shaking on top of me and I don't know how to fix it. "He got my feet on the ground, told me to keep skating, and we managed to finish."

"Then what happened?"

"I threw up and cried." She scoffs. "We waited for our score and by some miracle, we just managed to qualify. We'd been perfection until that moment, and I don't know." She laughs, but it's humorless. Bit by bit, it morphs into tears until she's half laughing, half crying. She shrugs at me because I don't think she knows what's happening, either.

Tugging her body to mine, I rub her back as she sobs again. She wraps her arms around my neck and rests her head on my shoulders. Her sniffs and sighs tickle my neck, and I feel so out of my depth.

Her cheek presses against mine, and her breathing deepens. Then she presses her nose to my nose, and her hands settle at each side of my face, where they stay until she presses her lips against mine.

Everything is so much slower than usual. There isn't the usual urgent, sexually frustrated rush or the drunken, horny haze. It's just me and her, sober, her soft body underneath my hands and her tongue gently moving against mine.

She breaks us apart, hand brushing across my stubble affectionately as I watch a thousand questions swirl around her pretty blue eyes. "Nathan, will you play house with me?"

"Always."

I suspect washing women's hair usually doesn't take this long, but I don't have the heart to stop.

I tried not to gasp or stare when she pulled her T-shirt off and stepped under the running water. I could see deep purple bruises across her ribs and stomach from the impact of Aaron catching her, making me feel sick.

I'm used to seeing people battered and bruised. It comes with the territory of being both a hockey player and having a friendship group filled with clowns. But never this. She gave me a sad smile, holding out her hand for me to step into the shower with her. "It's not as bad as it looks, I promise."

Playing house, essentially forgetting real life for a few hours, was the best thing she could have come up with. Thinking back to what Lola said about control, I asked Anastasia what she wanted to do. Immediately she wanted to wash her hair, claiming she couldn't face the tangles herself.

I'm good at massaging the stuff into her scalp. At first, I was a little rough, but I've got it right now, and I get all the suds out.

Being in her shower is fascinating; there's tons more smelly stuff than I knew existed. Found out body exfoliator is a thing and it's blown my mind. "Is that why you're always so soft?"

It feels really fucking good to hear her laugh. "Uh, yeah, maybe."

After we were both under the spray, her body relaxed into mine, where it's stayed. There's nothing sexual about this shower and I don't want there to be. I want to look after her and I feel grateful she wants me to.

Spinning around to face me, she creeps onto her tiptoes and rubs my head. "Can I wash your hair?"

Her eyes are brighter now, cheeks flushed, bringing the color back to her face. I've been trying to get her hair to stand up straight for the past five minutes, determined to give her a punk rock hairstyle. It's too long, and every time I get enough shampoo foam into it, it flops over and smacks her in the face. I get an elbow in the stomach and she gets a mouthful of shampoo.

"You can't even reach my head properly," I tease, linking my fingers with her grabby hands. "Do you want some help?"

She looks like she's about to be stubborn, but she must realize she doesn't have another choice because she nods.

Lifting her as gently as I can, she winds her legs around my waist. I keep my hands under her to keep her supported; well, it's actually to keep her away from my boner. My dick doesn't understand the naked, wet woman wrapped around us giggling doesn't want to sit on him.

She lathers the shampoo between her hands and sinks them both into my hair, and I swear I moan.

"Thank you, Nathan. I needed this."

"I needed it, too."

Chapter Twenty-three

ANASTASIA

WHEN I WOKE UP THIS morning, I promised myself I would not cry this week.

I meant it, too. It felt achievable at the time; I even posted *new week, new start.* That's how positive I was things were going to be great. I've cried so much over the past two weeks I'm surprised our building didn't flood. But last night was the mark of the end of all the crying.

So I thought, anyway.

I wasn't off to a great start when I had to drag myself from my bed. Nate's head was buried in my neck, his warm body clinging to mine. The idea of having to detach myself from him was cry-worthy.

He was so caring last night. No, he *is* so caring. Settling into bed with him after he washed and brushed my hair for me was the most calming experience of my life. In that moment, it was easy for us to talk about everything that's happened.

"I can't believe you think I could ever reject you, Anastasia," he said in shock. "You have no idea, do you? The lengths I'd go to if you'd let me. What I'd do to make you happy."

My heart did a weird thing I've only read about. A mix between a thud and a flutter, the kind that made me question whether it would continue to function properly.

Being with Nate brings an overwhelming sense of safety, like whatever problem I throw at him, he'd cope with. In a world where I feel like I could be swept away by the waves at any moment, he anchors me. I value that, value him.

"I'm sorry for yelling at you," I mumbled into his chest, where my head was resting.

"I deserved it," he admitted, kissing the crown of my head. "I could have done more. I could have called you before Aaron's parents did and explained. I could've not admitted to something I didn't do." He laughed. "I'm sorry you had to spend one second thinking I would do something to hurt your dreams."

"I like you, Nathan," I said, peering up at his face. "And it hurts me on multiple different levels that I'm now a person who likes a hockey player. But I do. It's so hard because Aaron is so convinced it was you, but I'm trusting my gut."

"I like you, too. The last two weeks have sucked so bad."

Our conversation was interrupted by the sound of Aaron banging around our apartment, presumably unhappy Nate was around.

Aaron's hurting, too, both physically and mentally, but he hasn't found a healthy way to communicate it with me. He dropped me and it's making him fucking hate himself. Apologizing more times than I can count, he's obsessing over one little mistake that wasn't his fault, and I can't get him to snap out of it.

I don't blame him; it was an accident neither of us saw coming. Other than a few marks, I'm safe. I've told him how grateful I am that he caught me, but it's not enough for him.

I'm scared of how that will affect us when he's back since the idea of being picked up right now freaking terrifies me. Even in the shower with Nathan, when he started to lift me to get closer to his head, for a moment, my heart wanted to stop.

I'm surprised I didn't crush him; my legs were so tight around him that he probably has an indent. He didn't seem to care. I think he was concentrating on not accidentally poking me with his penis.

Worrying about Aaron is something I'm used to, but you can only properly help someone who tells you what's wrong with them.

The banging of doors—undoubtedly Aaron again—woke me up this morning, and I opted to lie awake, listening to Nate's breathing instead of going back to sleep.

"I can hear the cogs in your brain turning, Stassie. Tell me, what could you be thinking about this early in the morning?" He yawned, kissing my shoulder affectionately.

By that point, I'd already declared a cry-free week, so I didn't want to launch into my Aaron issue.

"I'm trying to decide whether you put a hockey stick in bed between us or if you're really happy to be waking up beside me."

He rubbed himself against my ass, groaning next to the shell of my hair. He's a vocal guy and it does *something* to me. It's like he flicks a switch somewhere and suddenly it's Niagara Falls between my legs. "If I say it's a hockey stick, will you play with it?"

"Oh my *God*. You are so cringe. I hate hockey, would you believe?"

"I could make you fall in love with hockey, Anastasia," he whispered, sending goose bumps across my entire body. "With the right educational tools, of course, and the appropriate amount of practice."

I don't think he was talking about his dick.

Trailing a line of kisses down my neck, his hand traveled below the band of my panties, lightly brushing his finger across the material between my thighs.

I wanted to pant like a dog. Embarrassing but totally justified. In the back of my head, I knew I needed to get out of bed and not roll around it with him. "I'm a very hands-on learner . . . but I'm afraid we don't have the time to practice, *Captain*."

"Oh *fuck*." His hand tilted my head back, immediately capturing my mouth with his. "Call me Captain again."

Breaking away from him, my eyes narrowed. "I think that might be something we need to explore."

"I'm one hundred percent for exploring it."

"I mean in a psychological way."

He grinned. "Kinky. I like it."

That's the moment I should have canceled Monday and stayed in bed. I could have let Nathan climb on top of me, show how much we've missed each other, and hide from the day together.

But I was unwise and naïve, thinking Monday couldn't royally fuck me.

"Could I get another vodka and diet coke, please?"

When you're not allowed to cry to deal with your issues, alcohol is the next best thing. I never thought I'd be a person who wanted to get drunk alone but having no skating partner for eight weeks will do that to a girl.

The bartender puts a new coaster in front of me and places my drink on top of it. Muttering a quiet "Thank you," I bring the straw to my lips, eyes shutting tight when I get a mouthful of unmixed vodka.

Eight weeks. The worst bit? I'm not even worried about how good he'll be in eight weeks; I'm concerned about myself. I'm worried about my new aversion to lifts and my ability to keep up with him. Aaron could take a year out; I can't imagine him being anything short of spectacular when he gets back.

Nationals is eight weeks from now and I have no idea if we'll be good enough to compete, and it fucking terrifies me. Aaron isn't picking up my calls and he didn't show up to practice, even just to talk, so that's *great*.

Nate calling to say he's not allowed to play until Aaron could skate was the final straw, and the second the call ended, I requested an Uber.

I told Lo I was going to Simone's for extra practice, but what I did was go to the dive bar two blocks away from Simone's.

I've been minding my own business for about an hour, and I've had no problems, but the group of guys a few seats away have been getting louder and more obnoxious, sip by sip.

Each time they get up to go to the bathroom, they take a seat closer to me when they return. Bit by bit, they've ended up right next to me.

Smelling their desperation, I throw back the rest of my drink and request my bill.

"Lemme buy you a drink, darlin'," the one closest slurs, leaning toward me. "You look lonely."

"No, thank you." I'm not too nice, not too rude. Like every women-blaming propaganda piece has ever told me about dealing with intrusive drunk men. "I'm leaving now."

"Don't go yet. The fun is just star—"

"You ready to go, baby?" I recognize the voice before I see him, and the relief I feel when Russ's baby face is looking back at me when I look up is overwhelming. Bending to grab my duffel bag from the floor, he slings it over his shoulder, holding out a hand to me. "I'm sorry I'm late."

". . . That's okay . . . muffin," I say, accepting his hand. Putting some bills on the bar, I jump down from my stool, not realizing how drunk I am until my feet hit the floor.

Unsurprisingly, the drunk guys don't utter another word. Russ's size is intimidating; I imagine he'd have no issues if they were causing trouble.

Holding open the door, the cool November breeze hits me as I walk under his arm, out into the street. "Well, that was weird."

"Sorry, I'm Russ. We met a few weeks ago at the icebreaker thing. I'm on the hockey team."

"I know who you are, Russ."

The tips of his ears go pink. "Those guys are awful. They're always in there, drinking and harassing people. I heard you say you were leaving and I didn't want them to give you any trouble."

"I appreciate it, honestly, I do."

The tips of his ears go from pink to red as he mumbles, "You're welcome," quietly.

"I need to request my ride."

"There's a coffee shop right around the corner. I can wait with you if you like? I'd offer you a ride, but I usually run home."

"You're welcome to join me, but don't feel like you have to."

Turning the corner, Café Kiley is quiet, with only a few people eating and drinking. We take a seat at one of the outdoor tables and order two coffees.

"So, Russ. What motivated you to spend your Monday evening in a bar alone when you're underage and live miles away?" I clasp my hands together, leaning forward to rest my elbows on the table like I'm interrogating him.

He scratches the back of his neck, squirming in his seat.

The server puts down our coffee and makes himself scarce; we probably look like a couple on the verge of a breakup—my eyes are glassy, and he seems mega-uncomfortable.

Russ takes a sip of his coffee, prolonging the silence until he can't take it anymore. "I work there in the evenings. I work in the kitchen or whatever," he says, looking embarrassed.

"I work in Simone's a couple of blocks away." As far as I know, the other hockey guys don't have jobs. Like every college in America, the economic divide runs pretty deep. "I'm not rich but have rich friends, so I need the cash. They like to eat expensive shit and working helps me pay my share. I'm super lucky my parents pay for my skating stuff, but the rest I need to earn."

The tenseness in his shoulders dissolves as they drop, and the reluctance I was sensing fades slightly. "Yeah, the guys in my frat have trust funds. My scholarship pays for most stuff, but working helps me pay my share, or whatever. Sorta like you said."

"I get it," I tell him honestly.

"Why are *you* in a bar alone on a Monday?"

"I take it you know Nate is on the bench?" He nods. "My skating partner won't pick up my calls, and I've had to ban myself from crying. Alcohol is the next best thing, right?"

"I don't often drink. A few sips of beer now and then, but my d—" He stops himself, immediately reaching for his coffee, using the long sip he takes to silence himself. When his mug is empty, he looks back at me. "I'm sorry about your partner, even if he is a dick to you. What will you do now?"

"He isn't a dick to m—" My eyes narrow. "You don't like talking about yourself, do you? You did this at the icebreaker. You kept me talking about myself and I learned nothing about you."

"There isn't anything interesting about me, Anastasia." The way he says it breaks my heart. Confidently, well-practiced. Like he's said it a million times.

"I refuse to believe that. I'm interested in what you have to share."

"Did you request your Uber?" he asks, totally changing the conversation.

Shit. "No, I forgot." He looks uncomfortable again and when his eyes flick to his phone screen, I understand why. "You told Nathan, didn't you?"

"I texted him when I saw you at the bar. I'm sorry."

"He's on his way, isn't he?"

"In my defense, I didn't tell him where we were. He makes the team use a location app, says it's in case we get into trouble, and he needs to try to find us."

"Oh, Russ. I was beginning to like you. You just *had* to rat me out."

His cheeks flush again and he sinks back into his chair. "You're less scary than Cap." Nathan's white Tesla pulls up beside us and Russ puts some bills on the table. "I think."

It takes a lot of effort to convince Russ to let Nathan give him a

ride home, but once he's finally in the car, Nathan stays quiet while I
try hard to get Russ to share about himself. When we pull up outside
the frat house he lives in, he awkwardly smiles at Nate. "Thanks for
the ride, Cap."

"No problem," Nate says coolly.

Leaning into the back of the car, I hug Russ. "Bye, muffin. I'm sad
our relationship has come to an end."

He laughs nervously, eyes flicking to Nate quickly, then back to
me, shaking his head. "Bye, Stassie."

When Russ has climbed out and I'm back in my seat, I realize
Nathan has the most confused face. 'Muffin'? 'Relationship'? I swear
if you wear Russ's jersey next, I'm transferring to UCLA."

"Our love was short but meaningful." I sigh. "The connection
Russ and I have will outlive us, but I'm happy it happened, instead of
being sad it's over, y'know?"

"You're drunk." He grins, brushing my hair from my face. "Why
did you get drunk on your own, baby?"

"I'm on a crying ban."

He nods, pulls away from the curb, and rests his hand on my
thigh. "I don't understand how those two things are related, but
okay. You wanna talk about it?"

"I should be asking you that," I mumble, tracing the outline of his
hand. "I know you said you're okay, but are you?"

"It's the consequences of my own actions, Anastasia. Skinner is
using me as an example. It's fine. The team still plays without me; I'll
be back in a couple of months. Come on, tell me what's happening in
that big brain of yours."

"Aaron's avoiding me. You can't play hockey. I can't practice and
I'm scared of being lifted." I chew the inside of my cheek, reminding
myself not to cry. "Nobody can fill in for Aaron because everyone
has commitments or partners already, and I ju—"

"I'll be your partner."

I'm choking on my words, literally. He pats my back gently as I struggle to make my lungs work. "I mean this in the most respectful way, huh?"

The drive from Russ's place to mine is short and Nathan pulls into the drop-off zone. Twisting in his seat to look at me, his face is serious. "I said I'll be your partner. I have to skate and work out anyway, I'll just do it with you. I'll be gone for away games, but you can have me the rest of the time."

Dragging my hand through my hair, I can't help but shake my head, immediately thinking of every reason it would be a horrendous idea. "Figure skating isn't like hockey; you can't just switch. It'd never work, Nate."

"It's eight weeks, Stas. I might not be able to leap about like Aaron, but I can help you practice and do your lifts."

"You can't lift me. You're not trained."

Resting his hand on my neck, his thumb rubs tenderly against my cheek. "You'll have to show me what to do, but I'm more than capable of safely lifting you." He sighs and the weird heart thud-flutter thing returns. "I'm an excellent skater and I'm strong. I'm much stronger than Aaron. I'd use myself as a human mat before I'd ever let you hit the ice."

I gnaw on my lip, thinking about what he's said. "It's kind of you, but it'd never work."

"Give me one good reason why it wouldn't work." He brings my hand to his mouth, kissing it gently, and gives me the real reason. "Just one."

"Because of that," I respond quietly. "I can't mix skating and whatever we are. I like you, which pains me greatly to say out loud, but you've wormed your way in and made me enjoy spending time with you. I'm nice to you now. It's a true representation of how far I've fallen. A disaster, some people would say."

He chuckles, staring at me with adoration that steals my breath away. "You're saying a lot of words, drunk girl, but you're not saying anything that makes sense."

That seems fair. "I need to focus, Nate. I can't do that if I'm in your bed every night."

"What about every other night?"

I roll my eyes, smothering the grin trying to betray me. "Nathan . . ."

"If you think I can't keep my dick in my pants, you're wrong. Two months ago, I thought you would rip it off and feed it to me. Look how far we've come."

My eyes are watering. Traitors.

"You fucking love bossing me around. Think how good it's going to be teaching me to figure skate. Please say yes."

"I don't think this is a good idea . . ."

"But say yes anyway."

Blowing out an exhausted, tension-riddled sigh, I nod. "Okay. Let's be partners. Yes."

Chapter Twenty-four

NATHAN

WHEN I WOKE UP THIS morning, picking Stassie and Russ up from a cute little coffee shop date seemed about as likely as me becoming a figure skater, yet here I am.

It takes thirty seconds for the panic to set in. The little line between her eyebrows appears, like it does every time she's deep in thought. "I can be hard work, Nate," she blurts out with a shaky voice. "I know you think Aaron walks all over me, but he doesn't. Sometimes we full-on argue in the middle of the rink."

Reaching toward her, I tuck her hair behind her ear, cupping her cheek gently. "Why are you telling me you're hard work like I don't already know?"

The line deepens, but a small laugh slips out. For me, Monday started great, went shitty, and now it sort of seems to be ending great. I don't know where my offer came from; I think I've just reached my limit of seeing her upset.

I'm not convinced I'll be any good, but I won't drop her, and that's what she needs.

"You don't understand what you're signing yourself up for." She nuzzles into my hand and lets out a sigh. "What if you can't stand me when we're done?"

"Anastasia, me not liking you in eight weeks is not a concern you need to have. But just know, if I'm ever down a guy I'll be expecting you to step up to play hockey. I think your hostility would be a great addition to the team."

I manage to catch the arm that flings in my direction and give it a gentle tug until Stas is climbing over the console to straddle my lap. "When you get out of this car, we're partners, and I'm not going to be able to touch you until January," I explain, "if I'd known this morning would be the last time I could kiss you, I'd have done it better. One last kiss?"

"You can't be serious."

"Of course I'm serious. If you hadn't been drinking, I'd be asking to fuck you in the backseat. So, a kiss is mild."

Rolling her eyes, she leans in, stopping an inch from my lips. "Your charm is endless, Hawkins."

Sinking my hands into her hair, I kiss her with everything I've got. It's a weird moment, where it feels like both the start and end of something, and when her hips roll against me, I don't know whether to cry or rejoice.

"I'm still allowed to think about you when I jerk off, right?" I ask quickly as she moves back to climb out of the car. "Or is that against the rules?" *Please don't be against the rules.*

She actually snorts. Like a little piglet. "I'm fair game if you're fair game. You're my go-to. Deal?"

Fuck my life. I nod, unable to speak while my brain paints a very inappropriate image.

The next eight weeks are going to be hell.

By the time I reach home, everyone already knows what is happening because Stassie has texted Lola. I called Faulkner from the car; he said he thinks it will work in my favor reputation-wise, and he will design me a regime to stay fit. Figure skating will help contribute to my ice time, so I *think* he might be pleased with my plan. Only think, not know, because then he called me the most bizarre kid he's ever had to tolerate and told me to enjoy wearing leggings.

Lo has all the guys around the table in the den, folding pamphlets for the theater society's rendition of *Hamilton*. It makes it easier to tell everyone the whole story simultaneously but makes the laughter at my expense ten times louder.

"Since you're so good at helping other people with their stuff, take a seat." She hands me a huge pile of papers to fold and points to the chair beside Mattie. "Can't wait to see your ass in tights, Hawkins."

"I'm more worried about him getting a boner," Henry adds, concentrating on getting his pamphlet edges straight. "He's like a horny little dog around Stassie."

"Gee, thanks. Nah, there will be no funny business. She wants to make sure she's not distracted. Just friends."

The laughing starts again; I imagine there's going to be a lot of laughing at my expense for the next two months.

THE FIRST DISCOVERY OF THIS little figure skating experience is that my Tuesday class schedule aligns with Anastasia's and we both finish at two p.m. We're both supposed to be studying, but we've just arrived at Maple Hills Mall.

You know in a movie when there's a red button, but nobody is allowed to touch it, and you scream at the TV when someone inevitably does? Anastasia is my red button. I know I shouldn't touch her, but I want to, and she'll scream at me if I do.

She looks so pretty right now, passionately explaining the importance of skating in the right outfit. "Stop staring at my lips and pay attention," she drawls.

"I am paying attention. I still don't see why I can't wear sweatpants."

"You just can't, okay? We're buying *leggings*."

So pretty. "Yes, Ma'am."

The first store doesn't have anything for men, the second doesn't have anything that goes over my thighs, but the third is perfect.

"What about these?" she asks, holding up a pair in my size.

"They're leopard print, Anastasia."

"I can see that. What about them?"

Quirking my eyebrow, I lean against the rack. "I mean, is them being leopard print not enough of an answer? Why don't we rule out all animal print to save time."

As she's about to argue, we're interrupted by my ringing phone. *Dad.* Reject.

Putting my phone back in my pocket, she holds up another pair when I look at her. "So that's a no to the zebra print?"

"Correct."

"Are you *absolutely* sure? These will make your thighs look great."

"If you want to see my thighs, I'll skate in my Calvins. Problem solved. Food?" She doesn't even bother responding. "I'll take that as a no, then."

Searching through a sea of black, non–animal print options, I find a handful in my size. She's all grumbles and scowls as I pay for my "boring" outfits, and we exit the store.

I reach for her hand, immediately stopping myself and styling it into a stretch. Walking in silence toward the food court, I can see something bothering her by the unsettled look on her face. Just as I'm about to ask her, my phone rings again.

Dad. Reject.

We grab a table away from other people, where it's quieter, and she still has the same look.

"What's on your mind, grumpy?" I tease.

"The NHL."

Unexpected. "I'm all for diversity in sport, Stas, but I think you're a bit small to be a hockey player," I tease. "Why are you thinking about the NHL?"

"I'm just thinking about how peaceful my senior year will be, since you're going to Canada to fight moose or whatever." She shrugs and forces a smile. "It's silly; forget it."

"I'm impressed you think I can fight a moose, but I'm not sure they tend to frequent downtown Vancouver." I laugh. "I'm not sure you know this, but there are flights to Vancouver from LA. If you ever wanted to disturb your peace a little and visit."

She's about to answer and my fucking phone starts ringing again. *Dad* again. I reject it, *again*. She drags a hand through her hair and sighs. "You can answer your phone in front of me."

"I know."

"I'm not going to freak out if you have a conversation with another girl." She puts her elbows on the table and rests her head in her hands. "Just because you can't fuck me doesn't mean you can't fuck anyone."

Rolling my eyes, I push my phone across the table. "Three-nine-nine-three."

Immediately shaking her head, she tries to push the phone back to me. "Nathan, I don't nee—"

I type the numbers myself, since she apparently wants to respect my privacy. I watch her fight herself before her eyes finally look at my phone screen, and she sees the word *Dad* littering my call log over and over. "It's complicated."

"Oh, okay, well, uh," she splutters. "I do mean it, by the way. Like, I don't expect you to be celibate for two months."

Snorting, I watch her eyes widen, uncertain. "We're going to be spending so much time together, Anastasia. I'm about to cockblock you at every available opportunity. You can do what you want, *obviously*. But good luck trying to fuck someone that's not me."

Her eyes brighten, heat flushing her cheeks instantly. "Is that supposed to be endearing? Feels a little possessive and toxic."

The corner of my mouth tugs up, loving that this is my day now. "Don't give me that shit. I've seen what you have on your smutty bookshelf." Her mouth falls open. "Now, what do you want to eat?"

"I'm good. I'll eat when I get home, but you get whatever."

"You got something against eating out?"

"No, but I need to stick to my diet."

"Diet?" It's clear to anyone who spends time with Anastasia that she has a complicated relationship with food. I swear half the time her bad moods are because she's hungry.

"Aaron and I have a food plan. I do the food prep and stuff through the week; we have to be organized with it."

"It's cool you're so disciplined," I say carefully. "Nutrition is part of my course, so I do a lot of this kinda stuff. I'd love to look at your food plan if you're cool with that?"

Reaching into her bag, she pulls out my enemy: her planner. She flicks through the pages until she finds a piece of paper, handing it to me. "Knock yourself out."

Oh *fuck*. Vegetables. Vegetables. A small amount of protein. Vegetables. I get my phone and bring up the calculator, roughly working out the numbers. "Who designed this meal plan?"

"Aaron."

The answer's an unsurprising yet still disappointing one. For once, I'm speechless. My feelings about Aaron Carlisle are understandably not great and I feel like I've earned that. But this is fucking weird. He either has no idea what he's doing when it comes to nutrition or does this on purpose. "Anastasia, you are *massively* undereating. You're not eating enough, not even close."

I'm trying not to seem like I'm telling her off or belittling her; this isn't her fault. She takes the paper back, running her eyes across the page. "What do you mean?"

"Your body burns calories just by you being alive. So you need to fuel your body to live. Someone who burns as many calories as you do, through skating and strength training, needs to eat even more to make sure your muscles recover."

"I'm fine."

"Not eating enough makes you more prone to injury and serious health problems. Have you always bruised as badly as you do now?"

Her mind must be going a mile a minute. She's frozen on the spot, clearly trying to take in what I'm saying. "Maybe? I don't know."

I noticed a while ago she's always covered in bruises. I assumed it was down to falls and stuff, but now that I've seen them up close, I know how bad they are.

"Bruising badly can be a sign of nutrient deficiency. Are you tired a lot? Anxious? Irritable for no reason? Changes to your menstrual cycle?"

"Jesus Christ, Nate." She fumes, looking around us to make sure no one is listening. She lowers her voice. "I'm tired, anxious, and irritable because I work hard. Surely you know better than anyone that it comes with the job."

"Stas . . ."

"And as far as my menstrual cycle is concerned, which is none of your fucking business, I'm on birth control that fully stops it. I haven't had one in years."

She folds her arms across her chest and sits back in her seat. Defiance, annoyance, a sliver of uncertainty. It isn't my intention to upset her, but I'm also not going to let her eat like this.

"There are hardly any carbs in this plan."

"So?"

"You need carbs, Stassie. I'm not asking you to fill yourself on junk food, but you need to eat more calories, baby. I can write you a new plan; we'll give them both to Brady and see which she prefers."

"Fine." She shrugs. "Whatever."

"Did Ryan look at your meal plan?"

Her eyebrows furrow together. "What? No. Why?"

Thinking back to the video call a month ago, I've been meaning to bring up what Ryan said but haven't had a chance after everything that's happened. "Ryan said once that Aaron was trying to control what you ate."

She rolls her eyes. "Ignore Ryan. He'd make me eat KFC every night, which is not realistic. I don't have his superhuman metabolism. Aaron says he struggles to lift me sometimes; it makes Ryan cranky."

What the fuck. "He said he *struggles* to lift you?"

"If I don't stick to the plan, yeah. Sometimes my weight fluctuates a little."

Dragging my hand down my face, I suppress the anger brewing. The arena sharing situation doesn't mean only the rink, it also means the gym. I've seen Aaron comfortably lift twice Anastasia's weight. He might not be a big guy, but he is strong. "He's fucking unhinged, Stas."

"You're being dramatic."

"I don't want to argue about this because it's not your fault. But the guy is controlling you and showing this to Brady will prove it."

She huffs, rubbing her temples with her eyes closed. "You're giving me a headache."

"It's because I care."

"Can you care in a way that isn't going to cause me tons of problems?"

"We'll fix it together, I promise."

Reaching across the table, her hand lands on top of mine, and she squeezes it. "I'm going to get us some food. I'll be back."

I try not to focus on the crack in her voice when she says it.

Chapter Twenty-five

ANASTASIA

"What's taking so long?"

I can hear him stomping around on the other side of the locker room door, but he hasn't materialized yet. It's our first session, and we're going to be getting on the ice late, which doesn't bode well for the next two months, or for Nathan retaining his life.

"Nathan!" I yell, banging on the door.

"I can't come out."

I'm scowling at the door, knowing I look ridiculous, but I can't scowl at him since he won't come out. "Why?"

"The leggings. They're too tight. You can see *everything*."

"If you don't come out, I'm coming in!"

His head pops out, body shielded by the door. "I'm being serious. They're, uh . . . You can see *everything*."

"Yes, we all get it. You've got a big dick. *Blahblahblah*, ego fed? We're late. Come on, let's get started." Brady approaches as Nate pulls back the door, wearing what are quite possibly the most revealing leggings I've ever seen. They look like they've been painted on, and you can see outlines. Very, very detailed outlines. "Oh my *God*."

Brady surveys him head to toe, then once more for good measure. Her hands land on her hips and she shakes her head. "I'm sorry, Mr. Hawkins, but I cannot let you wear those." Nate looks like a rabbit in headlights, hiding behind the door again. "Do you have anything else with you?"

"I have shorts in my locker I could put on over the top?"

"I think that would be a wise choice." Nate disappears back into the locker room and I feel Coach hovering behind me. Turning to face her, she shakes her head. "It's a slippery slope, Anastasia."

"Don't know what you're talking about." Lie. Big lie. *Huge* lie. "Should I get warmed up?"

"Use protection. Ask Prishi. Your bladder is never the same."

"We aren't d—"

She interrupts me with a flippant wave of her hand. "We're both adults. Don't insult my intelligence; I see how that man looks at you. I want to see my best skater on a podium, not a birthing ball. Clear?"

"Couldn't be clearer, Coach."

What she didn't consider with her little speech is the probability of her *best skater* dying of embarrassment.

And why does she only call me her best skater when I don't have witnesses?

Finally emerging from the locker room, Nate lightly nudges me in the ribs. "You ready to do this, Allen?"

"Nope, don't crash into me."

"No crashing into you, no birthing balls . . . So many rules, Anastasia."

My eyes widen as I look up to meet his, his smug grin smiling down at me. His happiness is a comfort and it's proof he isn't feeling nervous like I am. Proof that he doesn't realize that if this little experiment fails, I might finally break.

I'm lost in my thoughts when fingers weave through mine. "It's going to be okay," he whispers as we approach the warm-up area. "It might even be fun."

I tut loudly. "If it's fun, you're not working hard enough."

He laughs, earning a hiss from Brady. "Spoken like a true tyrant."

After warming up, it's finally time to find out if this was a horrible idea.

"If this is going to work, I need you to remember the routine, Nathan." Coach tightens her faux fur, wrapping her arms around herself tightly. It never occurred to me that it might not be me that Nate can't cope with. "I'm not sure what *shenanigans* Coach Faulkner lets you get away with, but you do what I tell you in my arena."

He nods, his smug grin from earlier a distant memory. "Got it."

"Both of you give me a lap." She concentrates on Nate. "Concentrate on being graceful, not fast, but keep up with Stassie."

"Graceful. Slow. Got it . . . Ow! Why do you always pinch me?" He groans, rubbing his stomach.

"I am not slow! I've already proven I'm faster than you are once. Do I need to do it again?"

Nate's mouth opens, but before he can fire back, Brady claps her hands. "What part of 'graceful' made you two think I want to watch a race? Do as I ask, now!"

Setting off, Nate manages to keep pace. When we're far enough away to feel safe, he moves closer. "What's with the clapping?"

It's fun having other people experience Brady's antics for the first time. After over two years of working with her, I don't even notice anymore. "I like to imagine she was a dog trainer in a past life."

We make it back to where we started, and I recognize Coach's distaste immediately. It's very easy to recognize something you see six days a week. Poor Nate looks pleased with himself, and to his credit, he did match my pace.

"How was that?" He grins.

She kisses her teeth. "Like a drunk deer, misguidedly stepping onto a frozen lake."

"Do they have a lot of drunk deer in Montana, Coach?" I ask, remembering to say Montana and not Russia at the last second.

"Do not sass me, Anastasia. The pair of you, do it again. *Grace-*

fully." I've done more laps than leaps before Brady is finally satisfied with Nate's version of graceful. "Much better, Nathan. You're not playing hockey now. Nobody is going to attack you on the ice."

"Respectfully, Coach"—his eyes flick to me quickly—"I don't think you can promise me that."

Once we get into the swing of things, I'm thoroughly enjoying my training session for the first time in forever, and I *think* Brady might be, too.

Moving to the center of the ice, I move to Nate's side to introduce the simpler jumps. He doesn't need to do anything complex to help me but ensuring he's in the right spot and facing the right direction is essential when I do the real technical part.

More than anything, I need him to recognize the names of things so he knows what I'm doing, and doesn't accidentally get in my way.

"I'm going to make it easy for you. Just pay attention to my feet."

"Stassie," he drawls. "I'm pretty sure I skated before I walked. You don't need to make it easy for me. I probably know far more than you expect me to."

Arrogance. My favorite thing to deal with.

"Okay, brainiac. What edge do you take off from when you're doing a Lutz?" He moves in front of me, and I can see on his face that he hasn't got a clue. "Joke's on you, you've proved you need to shut up and listen to me."

"Joke's on you." He scoffs. "I don't even know what a Lutz is."

"You are the most annoying man I've ever met."

"I don't care what you call me as long as I'm at the top of the list."

How the hell am I supposed to get through this six days a week?

Even when he's annoying, I still want to jump his bones. The long-sleeved T-shirt we bought earlier is clinging to every muscle, his cheeks are flushed, and every time he looks at me, and the corner of his mouth tugs up, I forget every thought.

I've been totally and utterly unhinged by a man. I'm disgusted with myself, for being distracted, for knowingly letting every sliver of feminism shrivel up and die over dimples and thick thighs.

"Why do you look like you're having a crisis?"

Because I am? "Pay attention. I'm not explaining this again."

"Hey, I'm not the one daydreaming."

"There are six types of jumps in figure skating: toe loop, flip, Lutz, Salchow, loop, and Axel. They fall under two categories, which are toe jumps and edge jumps. Can you guess what toe jumps are?"

"Is it jumps that use this useless fucking pick thing?"

The only thing Nate's been unhappy about is his new skates. Unlike his hockey skates, the skates we use have toe picks. We did a quick practice skate at Simone's after we finished at the mall, and I lost track of how many times he went flying. Not to mention that breaking in new skates can fucking suck.

"It isn't useless; you're going to need it. But yeah, you take off by hitting the ice with the 'useless fucking pick thing.' Edge jumps take off from the inner or outer edge. Simple, right?"

He grunts something that roughly resembles "Yes," closely watching my feet as I turn, stretching my left leg back and striking the pick against the ice. "Single toe loop."

Replicating my movements and, to his credit, getting it reasonably accurate, with the exception of his wobbly landing, we move on.

"What move were you doing when you bowling balled a couple of weeks ago?" he asks, standing and brushing the ice from his ass.

"I was trying to do a quadruple Lutz." *Trying* being the operative word. "Lutz is a toe jump."

"It looked hard."

"It *is* hard."

"I sense you don't want to talk about this."

"There's nothing to say." I sigh. "Brady made us take it out after I hit my head. It's not common in women's figure skating and virtually unheard of in pairs. She felt it was an unnecessary risk."

"So why do it?" He isn't being rude; I think he's genuinely interested. "I'm only trying to understand your mentality, Stas. Not make you feel bad."

I don't know how to explain it. It feels like a topic for therapy, not part of an impromptu chat in the middle of a training session. But I owe him honesty.

"I wasted years skating with someone who couldn't match my skill because he was my boyfriend." *Classic.* "Don't get me wrong, we were very good, we just weren't great. With a different partner, I might have achieved more. I don't want to be that for Aaron."

"And Aaron can do it, right?"

"Of course he can." I snort. "He's spent hours and hours trying to help me nail it, even though he never thought I'd be able to. There's a reason it's not common, but I'm stubborn. I'll keep trying, but it's not going to be this season."

"I like how determined you are," he says softly.

"If you two want to look lovingly at each other, do it on your own time!" Coach shouts across the rink, reminding us both we're supposed to be skating, not sharing.

He sighs heavily, putting his hands on his hips. "She scares the shit out of me. What's with the coat? Does she know we're in California?"

"Her aesthetic is Cruella de Vil. You'll get used to it."

Nathan groans and winces loudly as we climb into his car.

"You're so dramatic." I laugh, throwing my bag at my feet. "It wasn't that bad."

"I'm not built for ballet and yoga, Stas," he mumbles, putting the car into reverse. "My legs are on fire."

"You're not bendy at all, are you? It was like watching a tree trunk."

Looking over from the driver's seat, he quirks his eyebrow. "I don't need to be bendy because *you're* bendy, which makes us perfectly matched."

"You did good, Nathan. Seriously, I'm grateful. Thank you."

"I spent half the time on my knees or face-planting. I've never concentrated as hard as I did doing those fucking laps. I was terrified I was going to trip. Are you sure I can't wear my own skates?"

"I promise you'll get used to them."

"Or you'll get used to seeing me on my knees." He frowns. "Not like that. Or like that, if you want. That way is my preference."

"A day." I huff. "You lasted a day."

Nate keeps me laughing all the way back to my apartment, mainly at his expense, but it still counts. Climbing out of the car and grabbing my bag, I lean in. "See you in the morning."

"Bring coffee!" he yells as I close the door.

I've secretly been dreading coming home, and now that I'm watching the elevator numbers rise, I wish I were anywhere but here. I haven't told Nathan, but Aaron has been ignoring me since I told him about my new skating arrangement when I got home last night.

If that wasn't enough, what Nathan said about my meal plan has been on my mind since this afternoon. Blame where it's due, I've never shown any interest in learning about nutrition. When I lived at home, my mom dealt with it, and at college, I let Aaron deal with it and trusted he knew what he was doing.

I know Lola is at rehearsals, which means Aaron should be alone, hopefully giving me the perfect opportunity to talk to him. Emphasis on the *hopefully*.

Letting myself into the apartment, I immediately spot him on the living room couch, watching a movie.

"Hey." He turns his head, looking at me, but doesn't answer my greeting. I swallow the lump forming and wipe my sweating palms against my stomach as I approach him. "Can we talk?"

Again, he doesn't respond, but he pauses his movie and looks at me when I sit on the couch, dropping my gym bag at my feet.

"Uh, I was just wondering . . . Do you think my meal plan has enough calories? And is, like, I dunno, varied enough and stuff for me to be healthy?"

"Why the fuck are you asking me that?" he snaps.

Taking a deep breath, I shrug. "It just came up today, and it was sorta suggested that I'm undereating. I wanted to run it by you, so we cou—"

"Suggested by who? Hawkins?" The way he says Nathan's name is borderline poisonous. "You suck his dick a couple of times and suddenly he knows what you need better than I do?"

His words knock the wind out of me. I splutter and choke on what I want to say, surprised. *Astounded* is a better word for what I'm feeling right now. As that feeling dissipates, the hurt sets in.

"What? No! Why are you being so mean? I only wanted to check with you, so we cou—"

Interrupting me again, he stands from the couch, dragging a hand down his face. "You know what, Anastasia? Fuck off. If Nate Hawkins is so fucking smart, go rely on him for everything." His hands are shaking, eyes burning into me. "But when he gets bored of you, don't come crying to me because you're the one who drops your panties for anyone in a jersey!"

My heart bangs in my chest as he storms toward his room, slamming the door so harshly it's like the whole building shakes. Sinking to the couch, I reach into my bag, pulling out my phone.

"Miss me already?" He laughs when the call connects.

Wiping the tears away with the back of my hand, I clear my throat. "Can you pick me up?"

Chapter Twenty-six

NATHAN

"PINCH OF SALT. *No*, A pinch. A pinch, Robbie! That isn't a pinch!" Anastasia takes a deep breath, forcing a smile as she fishes out the mountain of salt Robbie just added.

"My bad," he mumbles, taking a real pinch this time.

"It's okay. Sorry for shouting."

Stassie is teaching Rob how to cook. Actually, attempting to teach is slightly more accurate. I bet Stas ten bucks she'd lose her cool with him before the pan was hot. She claimed it would be easy, but I think he's sweating from the stress, and every time she's about to say something, her eyes flick to me first, and she says it calmly.

"You've got to let it all get to know each other in the pot," Stassie explains semi-patiently. "But you can't let it burn."

"No burning. Friends in the pot. Got it."

Walking around the counter, Stassie slides into the seat beside where I'm working, reaches for her textbook, and resumes studying.

Weirdly—now I'm forced to bow to the planner—I'm on top of all my schoolwork for the first time since I started at Maple Hills. We train together, brush our teeth side by side, and cook the same meals. I have no clue what we are, but I like it. We've taken playing house to the next level.

She doesn't say anything about my ten bucks as she sits next to me, concentrating on her work; she just lets her leg gently rest against mine.

This is where I'm at right now—grateful for leg touching. Having her here all the time but not being able to touch her has been difficult, continues to be difficult, and will likely only increase in fucking difficulty.

It's been two weeks since Aaron reacted in the most Aaron way possible by swearing at her and insinuating she's a slut. She was a wreck when I picked her up that day, sobbing as she stood outside her building clutching an overnight bag.

Promising it would only be one night, we built a pillow barricade to respect our agreement not to overstep our friendship. That was two weeks ago and I'm still sleeping on the other side of the pillow barricade. On the bright side, we're getting to know each other properly. When we're lying on either side of our barricade at night, we talk about anything and everything until one of us falls asleep first. It's always her; I'll never get tired of hearing her talk about herself.

In a weird, twisted way, I'm glad. If things were different, I'd have spent the past two weeks buried inside her instead of getting to learn what makes her tick. We'd have achieved nothing. I might have even dropped out of college to stay home and find out exactly how many ways there are to make her scream my name . . .

But I can't think about it because we're friends now, and the only time she screams my name these days is on the ice.

"Stassie?" Robbie calls. "I think they're buddies now. What do I do?"

Hopping off her stool, her fingers trail across the bottom of my back as she walks past, sending a jolt up my spine. She looks at the dish, nodding proudly. "Looks good. Nailed it."

"What are *we* having, chef?" I ask her playfully, closing my textbook, officially bored.

My calculations were correct, and she was undereating by following Aaron's plan. It's one of the only times in my life I've hated being right. Brady approved the plan I designed, perplexed why Anastasia would ever eat so little in the first place. Stas didn't want to drag Aaron into it, pointing out that she's still going to have to skate with him, and ratting him out to her coach would only make her life difficult in the future.

Anastasia and Lo don't believe Aaron would be so messed up as to do it on purpose, arguing he's just too stubborn to admit when he doesn't know what he's doing, but that's a debate for a different day.

Part of the changes to Stassie's eating plan is giving her more exciting food to eat than salad and chicken. We've all taken turns teaching her different dishes, or she finds something online she likes the look of, and I adapt it to meet her macros. I don't think either of us anticipated the fear she's developed through this disordered way of eating.

She can rationalize having what she calls a 'cheat' meal to a certain extent, but understandably, changing 99 percent of what she eats has been highly overwhelming for her to process. I tried to plan things slowly, but she said she doesn't have time for slow, and she'll just get on with it. I know warning signs when I hear them, but she's promised to talk to her therapist about it, so there isn't more I can say.

It's not that she doesn't like the food she's eating; she has this unwavering fear of gaining weight and being too heavy to lift or not fitting into her skating outfits. It's scary—practically conditioning—making me question how many times she's heard it.

"JJ wants to teach me how to make an authentic Indian curry. I accidentally told him I've never made one that didn't originate from a jar, and he said something about offending his ancestors." She takes her phone from her pocket, and without even looking I know she's checking her calorie app. She looks up at me for reassurance. "We can make it work, right?"

"Traditional Indian food is good for you. It's basically vegetables, spices, meat, lentils, or whatever you're putting in. Nutritionally, it's very well-rounded," I explain, emphasizing the most important benefits first. "It's the westernized convenience version that's pumped full of crap. Somewhere along the line, the whole cuisine has been demonized. We can definitely make it work."

"Okay, he should be home from the gym soon." She tucks her phone away and holds out her hand to me. "Let's stretch you out, my little figure skater."

I groan, putting my hand in hers and letting her drag me to the living room.

It's been two weeks of sore thighs, toe picks, and fucking ballet. Two weeks of her proving she's a better skater than I am. Two weeks of Brady staring at me like she's staring into my soul and learning all my secrets. Everything fucking aches: my ass, my thighs, my calves. I might be strong, but I've learned I am not supple.

Lying down on the floor, I raise both of my legs. Using the weight of her body, she holds my legs against herself and leans forward, stretching my hamstrings.

Me moaning with my legs in the air is always the perfect time for JJ and Henry to get home. It's hard to judge their expressions from my position on the floor, but I hear JJ laughing to himself. "Me next, Stassie."

Henry stands beside us, head tilted as he assesses what we're doing. "Does it feel weird to be on this side of the body bending, Anastasia?"

She presses down a bit more, making my hamstrings scream. I love it and hate it in equal measure, but the discomfort means I don't register what Henry says until she answers him. "You know what, Hen? It does feel weird, yeah."

As much as their shit is usually at my expense, I'm glad the guys keep Stas distracted enough to not obsess over Aaron. He's been blowing up her phone with apology after apology. *It was a moment of anger*, he wrote, he didn't mean to shout at her. But she's hurt, and she's questioning her judgment.

"Friendships are important, but so is living in a healthy environment," I overheard her say to herself when she rejected his tenth call. "Everyone has progress to make."

I tell her every day she can stay as long as she wants to. Selfishly, I love having her around all the time, and so do the guys. They're as on board with her staying as I am and told me to stop being a dipshit when I offered to book the two of us into a hotel. They don't want her going back to Aaron any more than I do.

After Lola gets home and inhales the food Robbie made, she and Anastasia claim that being surrounded by so much testosterone is rotting their brains, so I drop them both off at the movies for some girl time.

Not to make things uncomfortable with the planner slander, but Stassie has been filling her time with unnecessary stuff. Living here has been a culture shock for her because nothing gets done when it's supposed to.

I can see how uncomfortable it makes her when she feels behind, so I do my best to stick to her timeline while still reminding her that sometimes a change of plan is good—like an impromptu trip to watch some romance movie.

Pulling into the driveway back home after dropping them off, I notice a car I don't recognize parked in my spot. My phone rings as my keys twist in the door, and when it swings open, I don't need to ask who is calling me or why.

"Nathaniel," my dad says curtly. "It's nice to confirm you're alive."

"What the hell are you doing here?" I blurt out.

"You mean in the house that I paid for, where my only son lives? Or in California?"

The superiority in his tone has bile rising in my throat. I truly don't know how Sasha and I have been raised by someone so fucking obnoxious and not turned out like him.

Visually, it's like looking in a mirror that shows your future. Same hair, same eyes, same face basically. There's unfortunately no doubt whose son I am. But his personality, *Jesus Christ*. It would be like if I had Aaron's personality or something.

"Both."

"You haven't been answering my calls."

"You flew one thousand miles because I've been too busy to answer your calls? Are you for real?"

I haven't even noticed the guys are also here until I spot them all shuffle into the den in my peripheral vision. It's always been awkward for me because all their parents are nice. Henry's moms live in Maple Hills and even they don't drop in on us unannounced.

"I traveled because I have business in California. I'm here because I wanted to see you." The caring-father act has always been a favorite; if you don't know him, it's almost convincing. "As I said, you haven't been answering my calls."

I sit on the couch, mirroring his seated position on the chair across from me. It's all suspicious; my gut is yelling at me that something is off.

"What business could you have in LA? You know it doesn't snow here, right?"

"Don't pretend to know anything about our family's business." His façade slips. "You don't mind spending family money on your tuition, or your house, or that hundred grand car you drive. You just don't like contributing anything."

Leaning forward to rest my elbows on my knees, I sigh, refusing to engage in the same conversation we've been having since I graduated from high school and told him I wasn't going to study business at Colorado State. "Why are you here, Dad?"

"Your sister is unhappy." *No shit.* "I need you to talk to her. She says she wants to quit skiing."

Sasha doesn't want to quit skiing. It's the only thing she can say to him to get him to listen to her. "What else is she saying?"

Eyebrows furrowed, his hand rubs against his jaw. *Fuck*, even our movements look the same. "What do you mean?"

"She didn't just come to you and say she's quitting. What is she asking for that you're ignoring? What does she want? *God*, I shouldn't have to teach you to parent your sixteen-year-old."

"Watch your tone, Nathaniel."

"Do you even listen to her?" My voice gets louder, the anger bubbling in my chest. "She's not a freaking racehorse, she's a little girl. She doesn't exist to win trophies for you. She has needs! You're lucky she hasn't filed for emancipation."

I want him to shout back, for us to argue this out, but he just stares at me with a blank expression.

"She loves skiing, you know she does. She wouldn't be as good as she is if she didn't love it. But she needs breaks, Dad. She needs care and attention, and to know that how much you love her doesn't depend on how clean her runs are."

"She wants to go on vacation for Christmas."

I knew he'd know; I wouldn't be surprised if she's been asking for months, and he's ignored it. "See? Easy. Take her to St. Barts or something. Let her lie on a beach, read a book, chug a virgin piña colada or two."

Without missing a beat, he ignores what I said and nods toward the stairs. "There appears to be a woman living in your bedroom. Where is she?"

He catches me off guard, clearly his intention. His *only* intention usually, as demonstrated by turning up here uninvited. When the initial shock subsides, the realization hits, and for the first time, I'm glad Anastasia isn't here.

"How did you get into my room?"

Standing from the chair, he straightens his suit jacket. "Because I remember my own wife's birthday." The air changes. Cools. Suffocates me. I don't even know. "Well, you're clearly busy and don't want me here. I'm staying at The Huntington if you decide you can tolerate the man who has given you everything you've ever wanted for the length of one meal. I fly home in two days."

And with that final fake-self-pity act, having gotten what he came here for, I watch him leave.

Chapter Twenty-seven

ANASTASIA

FOR SOMETHING DESIGNED TO MAKE you feel better, positive affirmations fucking suck. They aren't working. I don't feel any more positive. I don't feel any more affirmed. Why do I bother?

Moving behind me so his body looms over mine, Nate's hands hold my waist tightly, the heat of his fingers searing the skin of my exposed stomach. Keeping his body close to mine, his mouth finds my ear, whispering. "You ready for this, Allen?"

My heart is ready to beat out of my chest, thoughts in irreparable chaos. It's been weeks, and I don't know if I'm ready. No. I know I'm not. I don't want to.

"Three, two, one . . ."

"No!" Gripping his wrists, it doesn't take much to pull him off me. "No, I can't!"

Letting me go, he allows me to skate away, shaking off the uncomfortable prickling tension at the bottom of my neck. This is getting ridiculous, and I know that. I can feel his frustration when I stop him before he lifts me. He never takes it out on me, he never says anything, but I know it's there.

Nate skates off in the opposite direction, hands on his hips, catching his breath. "Nate, I'm sorry!" I shout for what feels like the millionth time.

He glides toward me, and I want to cave to my instincts. Let him scoop me up, carry me away, and shower me in affection. I want to wrap myself around him and let him whisper promises into my skin about how he'll never let me down.

Two hands capture my face, lightly tilting my head back. I want him to bend down and kiss me, but he won't because I've told him he can't.

Another thing to be angry with myself over.

"Why don't you trust me?" His tone is soft, which only makes this harder. "Stas, I'm not going to drop you."

"I . . ." I don't have an answer for him. Every time the anxiety swirls in the pit of my stomach, I can't breathe. We've been practicing in the gym and I know he can pick me up, but for some reason, being out here doing it for real is just too much. "I do trust you. I don't know what's wrong with me."

Moving toward Brady, she's wearing her signature look of irritation. "You two need to work this out. Anastasia, if you want to be a pair skater, you need to be able to work with a pair."

She's saying it like that knowledge isn't my current obsession. "I know, Coach."

"The longer you let this fear rule you, the more you suffer. Work it out and work it out quickly."

Holding back the tears, Nate and I step off the ice and put our guards on. The worst bit is I'm having so much fun training with Nathan, and now that he's used to his skates, he's learning quickly.

Even though he's here to help me, I'm weirdly proud when he nails a jump. Don't get me wrong, he's landed on his ass a hundred times, each time funnier than the last, but now if he's on the floor, he knocks my legs out from under me when I try to help him up, catching me in his lap.

My love for skating has been revitalized and he's a massive part of that. He drapes an arm across my shoulders as we walk toward the locker rooms. "We're going to do it. I'll make a plan. We'll get through it together."

Stopping in his tracks, I follow his eye line to the last person I was expecting to see. "Aaron, what're you doing here?"

"Can we talk?" His eyes float to Nate, and his posture stiffens. "Alone."

"Absolutely not," Nate snaps.

"Nathan . . ." The last thing I need is a brawl. "I don't have anything to say to you, Aaron."

"Don't say anything, then," he says softly. "Just listen and then I'll go."

Nate's arm tightens around me, and I dislike the feeling of being stuck between them. This is the longest Aaron and I haven't talked; it's not because I'm not desperate to hear him say something that helps me make sense of this, it's because I'm sick of being his verbal punching bag.

"Let me get changed first," I tell him. "I'll meet you in the office in a couple of minutes."

"Anastasia," Nathan says firmly, and I can sense his anxiety, but I can't avoid Aaron forever.

Squeezing the hand resting on my shoulder, I attempt to reassure him. "I'll be fine, and it won't take long."

Heading into the locker room, my mood immediately improves when I can hear a few of the younger skaters gossiping before their practice.

"He's so freaking hot."

"He's the captain of the hockey team."

"What a lucky bitch."

"They're *so* hooking up behind Aubrey's back."

"I heard he's the one who messed up Aaron."

"I thought she was with the basketball guy."

"Good, Aaron's a creep."

"No, I follow him, and he's always posting about a blond girl called Olivia."

"They definitely are. I bet Aubrey has already guessed."

"I'd risk her wrath if he looked at me like that. Did you hear he had to put on shorts because of how big his d—?"

"Girls?" I say, trying not to laugh. "Coach Brady is waiting for you all."

It's so quiet you'd be able to hear a pin drop. There isn't another peep out of them as they all walk past me looking horrified.

Part of me is in no rush to get changed, dreading facing Aaron. The other part of me wants to get it over with. Nathan is waiting for me when I finally drag myself from the locker room.

"I don't like this," is the first thing he says. His hand cups my cheek softly, and I can't stop myself from leaning into its warmth. "I want you to make your own choices, but please remember you don't owe him anything. Don't let him guilt you."

"Wait for me in the car?"

He nods, leaning forward, changing his mind again and leaning back, then finally committing and kissing my forehead quickly before heading toward the exit.

The walk to the office feels twice as long, knowing who's waiting, but I face the music anyway, pushing the door open.

Aaron's sitting at the table, his bad wrist strapped to his chest, making it look extra serious. Closing the door behind me, I take a seat opposite him, concentrating on my breathing.

"I've wanted to come here for weeks," he says quietly, staring at his free hand resting on the table. "But I was angry at you, and it wouldn't have been good for either of us."

I'm surprised my jaw doesn't hit the floor. Aaron has practically hounded me, begging me to move back home, but apparently, he was angry at me? "What could you possibly be angry at me about?"

"Are you kidding me? You move out without telling me, and you move in with the guy responsible for me not being able to skate?"

My jaw tics as I fight to stay calm. "He says he had nothing to do with it."

"You'd believe anything he tells you. That's your problem, Stassie." He scoffs, looking me dead in the face. "You're naïve. You make out that you're Ms. Positive, and you want to communicate, but it's all bullshit. You're just a liar."

Is this a fever dream? There's no way I'm hearing this right. I don't know what to address first. I should walk out and never talk to him again, but unfortunately, I can't. "If you're going to sit and attack me, I will leave."

"I'm not attacking you. I want to talk. I want to sort things out between us."

"How can you not hear you're attacking me? You're mad at me for moving out, but you told me to fuck off." I'm trying not to let him get under my skin, but my brain wants to scream, and my heart wants to cry. "I've been undereating, Aaron. I've been at a higher risk of injury for *months*, and you're the one with the problem? I trusted you!"

"You are so fucking dramatic. Why are you acting like I've been starving you?" He groans loudly, looking to the ceiling, then back to me. "I thought it was fine! You've never complained and you're an adult, Anastasia. You can eat more if you're hungry! How is it my fault you don't listen to your own body?"

"Oh, and have you remind me I have an outfit to fit into? Or have you groan when you lift me?"

"So, I'm a bad guy because I keep you accountable?"

"It isn't accountability, Aaron, it's obsession! You care too much about what I'm doing and whom I'm doing it with." My voice breaks, and I hate it. I hate that he can tell what he's doing to me. "You want to control me, and you're destroying our friendship, our partnership!"

"When are you coming home?" he says abruptly. "I miss you."

His change of direction gives me whiplash and it reminds me

that deep down, Aaron's lost. "I can't come home until you properly understand what you've done, and I believe you will change." Standing from my seat, I sling my purse over my shoulder. "I can't trust you right now, Aaron. But we're paired together whether we like it or not, so I'm going to need to be able to navigate this somehow."

He nods, face blank. "I know you believe anything he tells you, but why would I purposely put you at a greater risk of injury, Anastasia?" Sighing, he lets his shoulder sag. "If you don't believe I care about you, fine. But you know I care about myself, so why would I risk my own goals if you ended up with an injury?"

If this wasn't such a miserable situation, what he said might be funny. He isn't wrong; the number one thing Aaron Carlisle cares about is himself. "I don't know why you do a lot of the things you do. But it doesn't mean you don't do them."

"I didn't like watching you skating with someone else. I do want to fix this, Stas. I promise."

"I believe you, but right now your promise isn't enough."

WHEN I CLIMBED INTO NATHAN'S car earlier, bursting with too much adrenaline, I asked him if he felt like doing something irresponsible.

Throwing a party the week before finals start is my version of irresponsible, as is playing drinking games with a man a foot taller and a hundred pounds heavier than me. To even our odds, Nate's drink is twice as strong as mine, not that he's noticed. Luckily for me, the game of choice is Never Have I Ever, and it turns out Nate has spent quite a lot of his time at college gaining new experiences.

Mattie clears his throat to get everyone's attention for his turn. "Never have I ever . . . accidentally called Faulkner while I was having sex."

"Oh for fuck's sake," Nate mutters, lifting his drink to his lips. He doesn't bother looking at me. "You don't wanna know."

"Okay, okay." JJ rubs his hands together. "Never have I ever . . . left the club with an older woman"—several of the guys lift their cups, stopping when JJ asks them to wait—"then found out I'd also hooked up with her daughter when I saw the family pictures on the wall the next morning."

Nathan curses under his breath, shaking his head at his best friend as he lifts his cup to his mouth again.

"Oh my God!" My jaw might as well be on the floor, Lola is cackling beside me, and Jaiden looks incredibly happy with himself. It's my turn, and I can't think of anything as outrageous as the guys have, but I have one thing that I know will make him drink. "Never have I ever . . . fallen out of a ski lift."

Nate snorts, lifting his cup straightaway. Beside him, Robbie drinks, too.

"You as well?" I laugh when he nods, wincing as he swallows his drink. Lola made that one, so God knows how strong it is.

"Yeah, the little shit dragged me with him."

The game continues, and naturally, the guys use it as a way to air each other's indiscretions. Lola and I move away to catch up on the day's events, and after an hour of us swapping theories and basically straight-up bitching about Aaron, I track Nate down.

I find him in the den, totally ignoring two girls trying to talk to him. As soon as I approach, he pulls me into his lap and buries his head in my neck. "Where have you been? I've missed you."

"With Lo. How can you miss me? You see me every day."

Not bothering to answer my question, I feel him nibble my ear. "I can't remember why I'm not allowed to kiss you anymore, but I really, *really* want to." He's so drunk his words are slurring, but I can't remember, either. "You're so pretty, Stassie."

Spinning in his lap to face him, his groan lets me know that wasn't the best decision. He places his hand on my face and pouts. "We do sex so well. Come on, I'll remind you."

I'm taking him to bed, but it's certainly not going to be for that. "Come on, drunk boy."

It's like trying to control a very rowdy toddler as I navigate him up the stairs. Crashing into his room, Nathan instantly strips, throwing his clothes around haphazardly. While I'm picking up his clothes, I hear the shower start, and moments later, a very loud, off-key rendition of "Last Christmas" echoes over the sound of running water.

He appears minutes later, smelling strongly of honey and strawberry, so I know he's used my shampoo. The towel is hanging loosely from his hips, droplets of water running down his solid chest.

Jesus Christ.

Not caring that he's dripping wet, he stomps across the room, stopping in front of me. "Wanna do the no-pants dance with me?"

"No. I want you to get into bed and go to sleep."

He looks genuinely shocked. "Why not?"

Pushing him to the bed, he flops down, not landing anywhere that even resembles a normal sleeping position. "Why do you think?"

Thinking on it, the realization kicks in. "You're drunk, and I'm sober, so that means . . . ," he sings, making an X with his arms. "No naked sleepover."

Not fully accurate, but the important parts are right. "Bingo. Lie properly, please."

Ignoring me, he yawns and closes his eyes. "Drunk people can't give consent, Stas."

"That's right, bub," I pant, lifting his alarmingly heavy legs to try to maneuver him. "Nate, can you he— Okay, you're asleep. Great."

Lo's nose scrunches when I rejoin her downstairs. "Why do you look so sweaty?"

"Nathan's drunk and heavy."

"Have you realized you're falling in love with him yet?"

"I've known him two minutes, Lols. I'm not falling in love, we're not even dating," I say back, looking over my shoulder to make sure nobody is around listening.

"It's been nearly three months and you've lived together for nearly one of them. I think that sorta makes the dating thing redundant."

It's been an hour of Lola giving me shit and making wedding suggestions, and she suddenly squeaks, making me jump. "I forgot to tell you because I was rushing! Aaron is hooking up with Kitty Vincent!"

I feel like one of those cartoon characters when their eyes spring out of their head. "Say you're joking right now."

"I would never joke about something so horrific. I saw it with my own eyes. Unrelated, but when you move home, we need to burn the couch. Rosie is still the sweetest, but Kitty is worse. So, so much worse."

Kitty was our friend freshman year, and we were getting to know Rosie, her roommate, too. Rosie is the daughter of Simone, my boss, and it was Rosie who recommended me for the job.

As Lola said, Rosie was sweet, but Kitty was a nasty, conceited bitch, and that's not something I call another woman lightly. Scientists should study their friendship because it's been two years and I *still* don't understand it.

Annoyingly, they live in our building, so we see them sometimes, and we can't get to know Rosie better and avoid Kitty because they're inseparable.

Before I can process the information thrown at me by Lo, cheers erupt around us. Lola's eyes widen, and her hand flies to her mouth as she does what can only be described as a scoff-snort hybrid.

Turning to search out the source of the chaos, I immediately spot Nathan pushing through the crowd in his boxers. His friends appear from the den, also searching for the cause of the noise, and all reach for their phones.

Nate is stomping across the room with purpose and I wish he were headed toward his friends.

I really, really wish he were going to them.

But he doesn't; he stops right in front of me, lip pouting with sleepy, half-lidded eyes. "You weren't there when I woke up."

"Oh my God. Where are your clothes?"

"Come back to bed," he whines loud enough for other people to hear. "No funny business. Just cuddle with me."

"This is gold," Lola says behind me and when I look over my shoulder, she has her phone out, too.

The guys are all watching, and several are bent over laughing. One of them looks like they're hyperventilating. Reluctantly letting Nathan drag me toward the stairs, I shoot them all the evils. "Thanks for your help, guys."

"But you're doing such a good job," Robbie shouts back.

When we reach his room, Nate flops onto the bed, and I can see that he has decided to demolish our pillow barricade. He's already snoring when I'm ready to crawl in beside him, but he still senses me there and pulls me closer to him.

After three weeks of pillow separation, being flush against him feels so freaking good. I don't bother fighting to keep my eyes open.

Chapter Twenty-eight

NATHAN

My phone is full of messages, and I don't need to open them because I opened one, and the rest of them are guaranteed to be the same.

They'll all be of me, strolling through my living room drunk and practically naked, trying to drag Anastasia upstairs with me like a needy, inebriated baby.

She's still curled up beside me, her soft breath tickling against my chest, brown locks decorating my bicep. I can see the remains of our pillow barricade strewn across my bedroom floor.

I can't remember, but I'd imagine I'm probably to blame for that.

I'd say the fact that we're cuddling right now is probably me, too, but judging by the content look on her face as she sleeps peacefully, I'd guess she's about as happy about this closeness as I am.

I never usually get super drunk because my friends are too irresponsible to be around other people and not have some real adult supervision. But last night, I was goaded into a drinking game by a woman who I assume was cheating.

She was looking after me and not the other way around, and that alone practically confirms my suspicions. I decide to brave the worst while she's still asleep and open the team group chat.

PUCKBUNNIES

JAIDEN JOHAL

Nate when Stassie dares to talk to someone that isn't him.

JOE CARTER

When she's not there when you wake up.

KRIS HUDSON

When he says no banging, just cuddling.

The next message is from my sister, Sasha.

SASH HAWKINS

God you're embarrassing.

I'll take UCMH off my potential school list.

> How do you even know

Saw it on the UCMH gossip page

Need therapy now, thanks.

> Great.

Already annoyed at you for abandoning me at Christmas.

> Oh, it must be so terrible for you.

> How will you ever cope on the beach in St. Barts.

> You're welcome, btw.

Oh well.

Enjoy Christmas alone, weirdo.

My dad took my advice and offered to take us on vacation to St. Barts for Christmas. I don't know who was more shocked: Sasha for getting what she wanted or me because he listened to my advice.

I'd love to spend Christmas with Sasha, but I'd genuinely rather swim in shark-infested waters wearing a seal suit than spend two weeks with Dad in another country.

My phone buzzes with another message from the team.

Oh great. I'm a meme now.

Sometimes I make it too easy for them, but this is next-level too easy for them. I haven't had a girlfriend the whole time we've been at college. Not that she's my girlfriend. *Why am I panicking like she can hear my thoughts?* When I told her I was an all-or-nothing person I was mainly joking. I sure as hell wasn't expecting her to move in.

The idea of her not living with me and the guys is weird to me now, and I'm worried about where we go from here. She says once she sorts things out with Aaron, she wants to move back. It's hard to understand, especially since she calls this house *home*.

Anastasia thinks starting our relationship—yes, she said "relationship"—off in such an intense way might set us up for failure. Then she reminds me at the end of the school year I'll be moving to Canada, and she'll be here alone. She isn't wrong, but it still doesn't convince me she should live with Aaron again.

She stirs in my arms, which feels like about the right time to start fake snoring, but her eyes snap open, and she immediately looks unimpressed. "Why are you staring at me, you big creep?" She doesn't give me a chance to respond. "Don't even try telling me I look beautiful. I can feel dry drool on my cheek."

"I love it when you talk dirty to me."

"You are in such big trouble, mister," she says with a yawn, stretching out all her limbs. I'm not sure if it's the hangover or anxiety from waiting to be shouted at that's making my stomach churn, but I'm queasy. "How's your head? Do you want me to make you some pancakes?"

Well, shit. I wasn't expecting that. "I embarrassed you and you want to make me pancakes?"

"You embarrassed yourself." She chuckles. "And I know for a *fact* your friends are going to terrorize you today. Potentially for the rest of your life, thinking about it. You could say they're pity pancakes more than anything. You want choc chip?"

She sits up beside me, wild hair like a lion's mane and sleepy but warm eyes. I can't help but reach up and cup her face, brushing my thumb carefully where her cheeks are flushed. "What did I do to deserve you?"

She kisses the palm of my hand quickly and climbs over me to get out of bed. "You're very kind and you're very pretty."

"What if I get attacked by a mountain lion and it eats off my face, will you still like me then?"

I can see her trying to suppress a laugh as her lips pull into a tight line. "You spend too much time with JJ. He's always asking me shit like this. Uh, will you still be kind when you're faceless?"

I think about it. "Yes."

"I'll still like you."

We pick up this conversation in the kitchen, where everyone is now impatiently waiting around for the pancakes Stassie is making.

"What if he gets bitten by a shark but survives and has a cool scar, but every full moon he becomes a shark. Will you like him then?" JJ asks, flinching when he tries to steal a pancake from the pile Stassie is adding to, and she slaps his hand away.

"When he's a shark, does he live in the sea or is he in a bathtub that I have to refill and stuff?"

Without hesitation, JJ fires back. "Sea. You just have to drop him off at Venice Beach before the sun sets."

"Yeah, I'll still like him."

Plating up the pancakes and passing them around, she covers her own plate in strawberries and syrup. Protein pancakes are her new obsession because it means she no longer has to tolerate the disgusting taste of protein shakes.

Henry's been oddly quiet listening to Robbie, JJ, and Lola round off scenario after scenario to see where the line is. Henry doesn't tend to stay quiet for long. "So, what I'm hearing, Stassie, is that as long as Nathan is nice to you, there isn't anything that would make you not like him?"

She shrugs. "Uh, I suppose? I don't know. I'm not too worried about him joining the Mafia or having to only wear a clown suit for the rest of his life, so I mean, it's not real, is it?"

"That sounds like you're in love with him to me." Everyone's eyes widen and heads turn to face him at the same time. With a mouthful of pancakes, he looks between us all, confused. "Ww-hhott?"

Does it feel good that Stas would still like me if I had crab hands? Of course. Do I want Henry putting her on the spot over pancakes when we're trying to wait this out until January? No.

Taking a sip of his water, he clears his throat. "Judging by the way everyone's staring at me, I feel like that might be one of those things I'm not supposed to say."

"These pancakes are amazing, Stassie," JJ says loudly.

"The best," I mumble, sticking another forkful in my mouth.

She's concentrating hard on her strawberries, but she can't hide her pink cheeks.

Interesting.

"NATE, THIS ISN'T THE WAY to the rink."

"We're not going to the rink."

Brady said we needed to work through our trust issues, so that's what we're going to do. *Trust issues* is what we're calling them because we're a team. Saying it's Stassie's fear puts the blame on her and gives her something else to punish herself for.

"We can't skip practice because you're hungover," she drawls.

"I had three doughnuts with JJ earlier, I'm not hungover anymore. And we're not skipping. Brady approves."

"And what're we doing?"

"We're going to learn to trust each other."

The rest of the car journey is quiet as she sits and sulks because I won't tell her where we're going. Joke's on her—I like her pouty lips and the way her nose scrunches when she's annoyed.

Pulling into the UCMH pool parking lot, I immediately feel her eyes on me. "Swimming? You're joking, right?"

"The whole swim team are in Philadelphia at some comp. We have the pool to ourselves; I'm going to prove to you I can handle whatever you throw at me."

It's a good plan in principle, but the way her face sinks makes my heart ache.

"I don't even have a suit."

"I took Lola home at lunch and she got me all your things. You have everything you need and it's all going to be okay."

"If you say so," she grumbles, unbuckling her seat belt.

I've been waiting outside the locker rooms for fifteen minutes and there's no sign of her. I have considered she might have requested an Uber, but finally, her head appears.

"Did you give Lola any requirements when you asked her to get me a swimsuit?"

"I asked for her to get something that you can go in the pool in, why?"

She huffs and rolls her eyes. "Well, just know that this bikini was last worn during spring break in Palm Springs."

Her head disappears, then all of her steps out, and I choke on nothing. Air? My own saliva? I don't know, but I'm struggling for oxygen.

Calling what she's wearing a bikini is a massive exaggeration. What she's wearing is tiny scraps of material that do absolutely nothing to cover anything. She spins around, and yep, her whole ass is out, the tiniest bit of pink string resting between her cheeks. "You honestly thought Lo was going to give me something practical?"

My mouth is like a desert and I'm struggling to swallow. She's been getting undressed in the bathroom since the start of our agreement, so I haven't seen this much skin since we last showered. She was genuinely wearing more than this the last time we had sex.

"Uh." *Smooth.* "Uh, should we get in the pool?"

She's trying not to laugh and I'm trying not to blatantly ogle her, and neither of us is doing very well. I'm so fucking glad the swim team isn't here right now. I'm not sure I could punch every single guy who looked in her direction, although I'd give it a good go.

The swim center has a couple of different pools, so we're working in the most shallow one. The aim is for Stassie to believe I won't drop her while she has the security of a mouthful of chlorine being the worst-case scenario.

"Oh great." She groans after hearing the plan, lowering herself into the water from the side. "So not only do I have to worry about you dropping me, now I have to worry about drowning."

"I'm not going to drop you and I'd never let you drown. Repeat it back to me so I know you're listening," I say, moving beside her.

"You're not going to drop me."

"What else?"

"You'd never let me drown."

"Good. Now, what are we doing first?"

I've never concentrated on something so hard in my life. Even with the added element of the water, every move so far, which we've practiced at least ten times each, has been very easy.

The depth of the pool is enough to give her that security she needs, while still allowing us to work with our height difference. She told me we're starting the hard ones now and immediately her enthusiasm has changed.

"I lean forward and push my body up from your hips," she says, putting both her hands on my hip bones. "My cheek is going on your shoulder like this. Sort of lock your arms under my rib cage and lean back. It's almost like a counterweight situation."

I do exactly what she says, slowly leaning back as her body rises out of the water, legs extended perfectly. I have a great view of her ass right now, but I'm happy about the lift, too.

Her body lowers down, and I stay in position until she tells me I can stop. Her smile is practically infectious and I'm so relieved this seems to be working. We do it another handful of times until she's happy.

"What are we doing next, Coach?"

Pressing her fingers to her lips, her cheeks blush and she shakes her head. "I don't want to show you."

"I promise I won't drop you."

She splashes her hands against the water, looking anywhere but at me. "It's not only that. Uh, I'm kind of concerned you're going to get an eyeful of what's between my legs. I have to spread my legs wide while I'm above your head."

I've seen her do this one; I'd say her concerns are valid, given the size of her piece of string. "You can't show me anything I haven't already seen. You've used my face as a seat, Anastasia. I'm a big fan of your work—arguably your biggest fan."

She mutters, "For fuck's sake," under her breath and turns around to face away from me. "Ready?" She links her fingers with mine and counts down from three. I push her up in the air, locking my arms as her legs spread out. She's wobbling a little and her hands are gripping me tighter.

"Don't panic, I've got you. I'd catch you before you even hit the water, baby. Concentrate." I can hear her muttering to herself, but I can't work out what she's saying and after a few seconds the wobbling stops, and she begins to laugh. Her legs drop down and I slowly lower her back into the water. "Well done, you're doing so well."

We practice a handful more times until she's happy we've nailed it, and each time I lower her back into the water, I can feel the fear slipping away.

"You're really strong, you know," she says, almost like she's surprised. I'm not getting into it with her because I know that she probably weighed herself this morning and now isn't the time.

"Why don't we do the lift you were doing when you were dropped. Is that the one worrying you the most?"

She floats in front of me in the water explaining the ins and outs of the move but doesn't let me touch her. I sink down so my shoulders are submerged, too, and listen to her tell me where our hands need to go. I can hear the anxiety in her voice, and I can't imagine how much worse it'd be if she had hit the ice.

"Anastasia, listen to me. I'm not going to drop you, and even if I did, you're going in the water. That's the absolute worst thing that could happen. You get wet hair and a mouthful of gross Maple Hills pool water."

"I know I'm being silly, I'm sorry. I trust you, I promise."

"Come on, no more talking. Let's do it." We get into position, and before she has time to change her mind, she's above my head, balancing on one of my hands. Even with my hand only on her hip, I can feel the way her body is shaking and can hear her erratic breathing. "Deep breaths."

"Let me down, I don't like it."

"Try to make yourself fall, Stas. Wiggle about. Move as much as you can."

"You're being ridiculous!"

"Just do it!"

She mutters some expletives as she begins to thrash about above my head. It takes me all of one second to get my other hand on her other hip and it doesn't matter how much she moves, she's not going anywhere. I give her another ten seconds of moving around, trying to get free, before I slowly lower her back into the water in front of me, hands still secured on her hips.

"See? You're safe."

Her stomach is flat against mine, arms tight around my neck, breathing labored. "What did I do to deserve you?"

I press my lips against her forehead, thinking about the best way to answer that question. There isn't one, so I'll have to settle. "I don't know, but I'd like you if you had crab hands, too."

Chapter Twenty-nine

ANASTASIA

I HAVE NEVER BEEN SO happy to say good-bye to studying and exams.

The boys' house is currently undergoing a transformation to turn it into Maple Hills' best Santa's grotto, which is Robbie's dream. For someone so normally chilled out, he's incredibly stressed about the whole grotto situation . . . that he is solely responsible for starting.

JJ says he's an old man trapped in a young man's body and is allowed to be grumpy by default. Henry says that Robbie needs an excuse to boss them around outside of hockey. Lola says he's rocking a dominant personality, and it's hot as fuck.

I'm not sure which of them is correct, but when enough mistletoe to fill the entire house arrived this morning, I decided to stay out of the way when it comes to putting it somewhere.

Lola and I have been dancing to Christmas music while scratching our heads, trying to work out where to put everything. Eventually, I had to give up because there was too much. I decide to go back to my other task, staring at my laptop and deciding whether to book a flight to Seattle for Christmas.

Stepping through the front door, Henry stops and takes in the new and improved living room. "You're both slow. Me and JJ would have been done by now."

He manages to narrowly avoid the ornament Lo launches at him, stepping out of the way, so it hits Robbie in the chest as he rolls through the doorway. He throws it back at her. "Thanks, babe. I've missed you, too."

"Honey, I'm home!" JJ shouts as he struts through the front door in his suit.

They've all been in Utah for a game, so they had to stay there overnight. Even though Nathan isn't allowed to play, he's still allowed to travel and watch. Although he ended up sharing a room with Mattie and Bobby, so I think he wishes he hadn't gone. They tried to sneak women back into the room, and Nate got woken up by the sound of Faulkner tearing them a new one.

Nate flashes me a beautiful smile as he walks in, duffel bag slung over his shoulder. *I miss my legs being slung over his shoulder.* He has broad shoulders, and they look good in his suit. All of him looks good in his suit. I'm thinking about how tight it is around his thighs when he lands on the couch next to me, mouth tugged up in the corner. "Stop eye-fucking me, Allen."

He's right, I'm practically drooling and I'm not even being discreet about it. "I'm sorry, you just look exceptionally good in your suit. I'm having a moment in my head."

"We can have a moment in real life if you want," he teases, picking me up and putting me on his lap. He takes a look at my laptop screen and gives me a sympathetic look. "Still can't take the plunge?"

"I've been trying for an hour." His hand gently runs up and down my shin as I explain for probably the millionth time how I *do* want to go home. He knows how I feel because we've talked about it at length, and he understands that I'm stalling but thankfully he's not calling me out on it.

"Why don't you come to Colorado with me?" he asks when I'm listing off my excuses again. "My family won't be there; we can skate on the lake in my backyard and use the spa at the ski resort as much as you want. Tell your parents it's competition prep."

"Why are you searching for flights from Seattle?"

"I thought maybe we could go to your parents' for a couple of days then fly to Eagle County via Denver. Or you could go, then fly to meet me or whatever. I think you should see your mom and dad. I honestly think you'll be upset when New Year rolls around and you haven't seen them."

The prospect of staying at my parents' house with Nate feels super serious, but in a way, makes the anxiety I'm feeling slip away. "Let me speak to my mom first, okay?"

"Okay, but be quick. Santa is coming, after all."

ON THE LIST OF ALL the reasons my planner is wonderful, being organized for Christmas is up there near the top.

I make notes all year round of things people mention liking and at Christmas, I narrow it down. Well, everyone but one person.

"What do you want for Christmas?"

"Nothing."

"Nate," I snap. "Tell me what you want for Christmas or you're getting coal."

"I don't want anything."

"Nathan!"

This argument has been going on for days, but I'm running out of time to buy him something. Everyone else was so easy, but Nate never gives anything away, so I never have anything to write down.

I bought Henry new sketching pencils and paints, and I bought Robbie some hockey merch. JJ doesn't celebrate Christmas, so I bought us a Vietnamese cooking class for two to continue our food education in the new year, since we enjoy cooking together so much.

But Nathan has nothing.

Our pillow barricade was never reinstated, so it's not that hard to climb on top of him and demand his full attention. "Please, tell me what you want. I want to get you something that will make you happy."

"You already make me happy. Just let me have you."

"But you already have me," I whine. "And you can't unwrap me."

"I could unwrap you if you'd let me . . . ," he rasps, hand slipping under my T-shirt to tickle across my stomach.

I can feel him growing hard between my thighs and every thought about distractions and conflict of interest instantly leaves my head.

Four weeks doesn't seem long in the grand scheme of things, but the more I've gotten to know him, the more I've wanted to climb him like a tree. There is something about learning the tough, muscular hockey player's favorite movie is *Coco*.

It does funny things to your insides.

When I hold my arms up in the air, he sits up and pulls the T-shirt over my head. His brown eyes darken and the heat of his gaze travels over me, sending a jolt of anticipation up my spine. My bra goes next, his tongue immediately flicking over my already taut nipple. Traveling up my chest, he kisses his way to my mouth, grasping my face between his hands.

"We breaking all the rules?" he asks against my mouth. There's hardly any room between us and I swear this is the most content I've felt in weeks.

"Definitely."

Finally, his mouth meets mine, tongue exploring fervently as my hips develop a mind of their own and grind against him. Each swirl of my hips sends the most addictive wave of pleasure through me.

"God, I've missed you." His teeth nip at my bottom lip, voice low and strained. "I'm not going to last if you keep doing that to me."

"Tell me what you want for Christmas or I won't let you come at all," I tease, reaching between us to grip him through his boxers. His shocked chuckle is instantly replaced with a low, throaty moan as I rub up and down. "Come on, Hawkins, just one little Christmas present."

"I don't know!" My back hits the mattress as he flips us over, his hard body hovering over mine. He works his way down my body, stopping to lick and kiss every spot until his mouth is hovering right over the damp spot on my panties. He frowns as he looks up from the spot between my thighs, tugging at the lace. "These are in the way."

The second his mouth is on me I'm climbing, back arching from the bed, grinding into his face. Desperate, needy cries that he doesn't seem to give a shit about ring out as he takes his time, sucking my throbbing clit into his mouth. I can't take it. The pleasure rolls through me; a pleased grumble vibrates in his throat as his tongue pierces me, sending me tumbling over the edge, crying his name.

You'd think that'd be enough for him to relent, but it's not. He locks his arms around my legs, pinning me in position, gripping me tighter when the oversensitive and overstimulated aching has me trying to squirm away. The sensation is too much, and if my back arches off the bed any more, I swear I will snap. It's been weeks of just me and the showerhead, so watching him bury his head between my legs and devour me, moaning happily, is more than I can handle.

"One more, baby."

And of course my body does whatever he says.

"Clever girl," he coos, climbing back up my body, brushing the hair from my damp forehead. I push his boxers down, letting his dick spring free, and move my hand up and down it, watching his eyes roll back in his head.

"Tell me what you want for Christmas, Nathan."

He thrusts into my hand slowly. "How can you still think about Christmas when I just made you come twice?"

"Because it's important to me to do something nice for you."

"I only want you, Anastasia. Nothing you can buy me is better than the past four weeks with you. Give me more of that, and I'll be happy."

I pull his mouth to mine, tasting myself on his tongue. I'm lost for words. How could I not be? This man blows every negative thought I've ever had about exclusivity away. Why would I ever want to share myself, share him?

He kisses me, cradles my face, and gives me every sliver of his care and attention. His arm reaches toward the bedside drawer, and the words spill out of my mouth. "We don't have to use a condom . . . unless you want to. I'm on birth control, and I'm not having sex with anyone else. I trust you," I take a deep breath, "and I hope you trust me."

I don't think I've ever seen him speechless. He finally clears his throat after staring at me with a slack jaw for thirty seconds. "You're serious?"

"Yeah. I've never done it without before but don't feel pressured."

"Neither have I. Oh my—*fuck*." He lines himself up and the anticipation is killing me. "You're sure?"

"*Please,* we've waited long enough."

Nate sinking into me bare is like nothing I've ever experienced; everything is ten times more intense, and I can feel every bit of him. He's panting into my shoulder, letting me adjust after filling me.

"Oh my God. So *fucking* good, Anastasia. Jesus Christ, you're so wet and ready for me."

He pulls back his hips and snaps them forward, skin slapping echoing around the room. My skin feels ready to burst into flames and every nerve is on edge. I want more.

"Hard and fast," I whisper, wrapping my legs around him and crossing my feet at the bottom of his back.

"I won't last." He groans. "You feel too good. It's taking every ounce of self-control not to go right now."

Using my feet to lift my hips and slide up and down him, rolling my hips when I get back to the tip.

I want him to pound me into the bed and see him lose his mind, but Mr. Generous is too concerned about turning me into a quivering wreck. *Again.*

"I don't care," I tell him honestly. "Give me everything you've got."

Sliding his hands under me, his fingers wrap around to cling to my shoulders. I'm trying to hide the giddy expression on my face, but he spots it, and his lips tug into a smirk. "Wrap your arms around me and remember you asked for it."

Nobody can ever say Nathan Hawkins doesn't know how to take instructions.

His hands pull me down as he drives forward, every thrust has me crying into his mouth, and digging my nails into his shoulders. My legs are shaking, and every time he goes deep, my back arches, and my legs tighten around him.

"*Nathan . . .*"

"I know, baby. I know." His forehead falls to mine, noses brushing against each other, and our mouths crash together desperately. "Look at you taking it all like a good fucking girl."

"I'm so close," I cry, gripping the back of his neck tightly with one hand and rubbing frantically between my legs with the other.

"Whose pussy is this, Anastasia?" he gasps, his thrusts getting rougher and sloppier.

"*Oh my God.* Yours. It's yours."

"Come for me. Let me feel you."

"Nathan, *oh fuck—*"

My entire body thrashes, tightens, stills, and melts simultaneously. I don't know which sensation to run with, so I settle for disintegrating. His body collapses on top of mine, chest heaving, body shaking as I feel him throb and jerk inside of me. "*Fuuuuuuck.*"

We lie there for minutes, stunned to silence, him still hard inside me, lazily kissing. I'm not sure how anything is supposed to feel better than this, how I could ever be expected to settle for less.

When I eventually get my breath back, and the post-orgasm fogginess begins to clear, I rake my fingers through his hair. "I didn't make you tell me what you want as a Christmas present," I grumble, disappointed in myself for getting dicknotized and forgetting.

He snorts, his breath tickling against my neck where his head is currently resting. "I think you just gave me my Christmas present."

Merry Christmas, I suppose.

Chapter Thirty

NATHAN

"I'm not buying her fucking lingerie," I say for what feels like the millionth time.

"Hi, can I offer you any help?"

We all turn in search of the polite voice that just interrupted the world's most pointless argument. The sales assistant looks like she's seen a ghost, and I suppose we are all a bit intimidating when we're staring.

Her cheeks are flushed, but she's doing her best to maintain eye contact, a friendly smile on her lips. I don't envy anyone who has to work in customer service at this time of year.

"Yeah, you can. Help settle this argument, please," JJ says, nudging me out of the way. "Is buying your sometimes fuck buddy pajamas a terrible fucking idea?" Her eyes widen slightly but she recovers quickly. "Don't you think she'd prefer something like this?" He holds up the lace corset we've been arguing over for fifteen minutes and stares at her, waiting for her to take his side.

I punch him in the bicep as hard as I can. "Don't call her a fuck buddy. That isn't what she is."

"He's right, Jaiden," Henry says, with an obnoxious smirk that tells me he's about to make me pissed. "You can't call her his fuck buddy when she hasn't let him anywhere near her in a month. She's his buddy at this point."

I obviously haven't told anybody about last night. Or this morning. Clamping my hand over her mouth to stop her from waking everyone up and feeling her squeeze the shit out of me bare is how I spent my morning. Based on the fact that Henry thinks I'm chilling in the friend zone proves that we're getting better at being discreet.

After spending all last night—and this morning—making up for the weeks we behaved, I'm surprised I even have the energy to walk around this mall.

The girl snorts loudly, and her hand flies to her mouth in horror. She recovers quickly, though, and puts her customer service smile back on. "I'm sorry, uh, underwear is quite an intimate gift, so maybe if you're unsure, I would say pajamas might be the safest option for you."

"What if I buy her lingerie? What then?" JJ teases, picking up the matching panties and holding them against Hen's body.

Henry has been checking out the salesgirl since she floated over here, and now I think she'll struggle to shake the look of him with lingerie pressed up against him from her memory. He blushes and pushes JJ away, calling him something not very Christmassy under his breath.

I scratch at the stubble on my jaw and huff, mainly because I could be in bed balls deep in Stassie right now, but I'm here, in Maple Hills Mall, with these two jackasses. "I think Faulkner will be even more pissed at me if I rip off all your limbs."

I look back at the rack of pajamas beside us, and I think the ones I have are the nicest. She specifically said she wanted some nice pajamas that she could wear around the guys. She feels comfortable around the boys in my house, but sometimes when she heads downstairs to get a drink in a T-shirt, some of the other hockey guys she doesn't know as well are around playing video games, and she feels a little bit awkward.

Plus, if I were going to buy her lingerie, I wouldn't be doing it with fucking JJ and Henry.

I can hear Henry terrorizing the poor girl, accusing her of flinching or something. "Leave her alone, Hen," I grumble, picking up some floral pajamas and holding them against the ones I'd already picked.

I leave them all to it as I explore the other nearby options. When I circle back, I hear Henry telling her about our big red door bow and saying his roommates are attention seekers, which makes me snort, but Jaiden looks offended, which makes it even funnier.

She breathes out a heavy sigh. "Okay."

"Okay, like, see you later?" Henry says in a weirdly cheerful voice. I discreetly look at JJ, who is already looking at me with a surprised expression. Normally we don't see the magic happen, or even better, we have to sit and watch women throw themselves at Henry.

This girl is pretty, so I can see why he's interested; tall and lean, long silky brown hair, big brown eyes, full lips, and glowy brown skin. I'd say she's Henry's type but I'm not even sure what that is because I've never seen him with the same girl twice and they all look different.

"What's your name?" he shouts as she tries to escape.

"Uh." *Poor girl is probably making it up.* "Gen."

"Bye, Gen!" JJ and I shout, ignoring the weird stares from the other people in the store.

After another ten minutes, I decide I can't decide so I'm going to buy both, much to JJ's annoyance. I make the two of them stand outside while I head to the cash register to pay, and as soon as we're done I'm going home. I've already bought her main presents, so I think I'm all set. I step up to the counter and put the items down, immediately getting a shock when Summer is the person serving me.

"Hey, stranger," she says politely, pulling the pajamas closer to her and scanning the tags. "Sister?"

"No." *What is she?* "Anastasia."

"Oh. I saw that video but I didn't realize you were together . . . ," she says, tapping away on the register.

"We're . . . uh, she's amazing." I hand over my credit card, still not sure what I'm supposed to call her to people. "Are you coming to the party later? I think Henry just bullied one of your staff into coming."

"Not tonight, sorry." She puts the pajamas in the bag and holds out the handle to me, and it all feels awkward. Not like the Summer I know at all. "We're going to a service at Cami's church with her family, and Briar flies to New York tomorrow for Christmas. She's got an early flight, so we're not drinking."

"I thought B was from England?"

"She is. Her parents relocated to New York last year. Two of her siblings go to school there. Her sister Daisy is at Maple Hills, though."

"Wow. I never realized her family was so big."

She nods, forcing a smile. "I've put your receipt in the bag, I hope she likes them. Have a good Christmas, Nate."

"You, too, Summer."

Well, that was unnecessarily awkward.

By the time we get back to the house, it looks like Santa threw up on it.

I think Lola extra spiked the eggnog because Stassie is extra bouncy as she dances around the den in her elf outfit. She's calling it an elf outfit but what she's actually wearing is a tiny green dress with elf shoes she got from a costume store.

Robbie's had me putting random shot glasses and cups on a *Twister* mat, and instead of helping, Henry has been chatting away to Stas and Lo. Earlier, I made what I'm now considering a mistake: I told the girls that Henry had hit on a girl while we were Christmas shopping; now they're obsessed.

Anastasia immediately started asking about someone called Daisy, whom I apparently stopped Hen hooking up with. This was the second time this afternoon I was hearing the name Daisy. *Did Henry have a thing with Briar's sister?* I didn't remember meeting her if he had. Then it hit me that it happened months ago, when Henry threatened to take my girl off me.

JJ appears with the new girl in question, plus a friend, and I can see Stassie trying not to be too obvious with her staring. Rob maneuvers himself to the top of the mat and clears his throat in a very Robbie-esque way to capture everyone's attention.

Taking a sip of my beer, I kind of love watching him in his element of being the center of attention. "Welcome to the first official drunk *Twister* game. The rules of the game are very simple: you touch it, you drink."

Bobby digs me in the ribs and shouts, "Name of your sex tape," earning a middle finger from Rob.

"The game ends when someone falls, takes their hand or foot off the mat, or they refuse to drink. Stassie, JJ, Joe are playing, we need two more," Robbie continues.

Henry moves to put his cup on the windowsill beside me. "I'll do it."

Stassie points at me and mouths, *You*, but before I can volunteer myself, JJ shouts up. "Gen is playing!"

The poor girl looks mortified when everyone turns to look at her. I can hear Mattie and Kris whispering about her being hot, but her eyes are on one person, and he's looking right back at her. I can't decide if JJ is playing matchmaker or he's hoping Gen ends up intertwined with him so he can piss off Henry.

Robbie claps his hands and fucking hell, it's like being at practice with Brady. I'd never noticed until I'd spent some time away from Faulkner, but Robbie is a mini version of him. He clearly has a little bit of Brady in him, too. "Stas, Joe, you two stand at this end. Henry, go over there with JJ and Gen. Everyone take their shoes off and, uh, maybe stretch? I don't know."

Stassie bounces over to me with a big drunk grin. She kicks off her elf shoes and wraps her arms around my neck, pressing her mouth to mine and giggling to herself. "Guard my shoes with your life."

She doesn't even let me respond before she's bouncing back over

and high-fiving Joe. If anyone didn't know what was going on between us, they do after tonight. From the minute the party started
we've been glued to each other one way or another. Our friends don't
care, although I think some money has changed hands paying bets.

I turn my attention back to Robbie. "Do you know how to not
be bossy?"

"Shut the fuck up, Hawkins," he snaps back, rolling his eyes.
Winding Robbie up has been my main source of entertainment for
about fifteen years, and I have no plans to stop now.

He eventually stops arguing with me and starts the game. The
girls only get feet moves, but Joe and JJ are very, very intertwined.

"Stas, right hand yellow," Robbie shouts over JJ and Joe arguing
with each other. The second she bends over I realize why all my
friends started looking at me the second Robbie called out her move.

Henry huffs as soon as her hand lands on yellow. "Anastasia,
please get your ass out of my face."

"It isn't even in your face!"

Her ass is definitely in his face. To make it worse, her dress is only
just covering her ass; if it rises any more, the whole hockey team,
plus anyone else watching, is going to see all the hickeys I've left on
the inside of her thighs.

"Nathan," he shouts, twisting his neck to find me in the crowd of
onlookers. "What's your blood pressure like right now?"

Yeah, the kid knows me. "Pretty high, buddy."

"See! Because your ass is in my face. You're going to kill him."

The game goes on until Henry lifts his hand off the mat to flirt
with Gen, and Anastasia immediately bounces back over to me, reclaiming her shoes.

She creeps onto her tiptoes, brushing her lips against mine lightly
and lowering her voice. "Between my legs is aching, but I want you
so badly."

Yeah, Henry's right. She's going to kill me.

. . .

I'VE LOST MY ELF.

While I was in the bathroom, the guys snooped on Henry, who had mysteriously disappeared into our laundry room with Gen. Their indiscreet lurking scared the poor girl off and ruined Henry's chances, and he has vowed to get revenge on them all. I've never been so relieved to not be involved.

I haven't got what it takes to go head to head with Henry over Anastasia. If I had been there when they cockblocked him taking Gen upstairs and I now couldn't find Stas, the first place I'd be checking is Henry's room.

There is nothing sexual about their relationship, but I genuinely think Anastasia would be perfectly happy having a platonic marriage with him.

Catching up with some people whom I haven't seen in a while, I try my best to fend off the questions about me not playing, all while keeping an eye out for my girl.

She eventually appears on the bottom step of the stairs, her eyes scanning around the room. Her green dress isn't visible anymore because she's wearing a Titans T-shirt that drowns her body.

I feel weird watching her from across the room, but she's so fucking beautiful, I couldn't take my eyes off her even if I wanted to. She eventually spots me in the kitchen, cracking a breathtaking smile, and the satisfaction I feel when I realize she was looking for me is unmatched.

She's halfway across the living room when arms wrap around her, stopping her in her tracks, and an uncomfortable feeling settles in my stomach.

He buries his head in her neck, and my blood pressure is back up. Do I have a right to be jealous? I mean, she's not my girlfriend, but she's my something. Will I always be a bit jealous of Ryan Rothwell? Maybe, but I hope not.

I know Olivia broke things off with him. Anastasia had a coffee date with him yesterday, and he told her Olivia has baggage and always had one foot out of the door. Does he think that he's going to get Anastasia back now?

I'm trying not to interrupt but it's hard to stay put. Fighting my instincts is hard, but nothing good has ever come from me trying to force exclusivity on her. I think he was talking in her ear, because she unravels his arms and takes a big step away from him.

I can't hear because of the music but I can see that he's drunk as hell, touching her at every chance he can get. She gives him a friendly hug, hopefully because she's ending the conversation, and he bends down to kiss the crown of her head. When she takes another step back, he looks up to see me staring right at them; his hand scratches at his jaw awkwardly and he gives me a sheepish smile.

I'm still watching Ryan shuffle about, looking uncomfortable, when I feel her arms wrap around my waist. "So you *could* see me, then. Why didn't you save me?" she grumbles, creeping onto her tiptoes to kiss the corner of my mouth.

"I didn't know you needed saving." Her big blue eyes are staring up at me, and her eyebrows pinch together. "I know he's a good friend. I didn't want you to think I was interfering."

"Uh, okay, Mr. Diplomatic." Her arms link around my neck. "Next time, save me. I love Ryan, he's a great friend, but the only man I want wrapped around me is you."

Shit. "Noted."

"He's a touchy person and he's drunk, but I put him straight. Don't hold it against him; I think he's sad about Liv."

I feel relieved right now. I could have stormed off the second he touched her, or worse, stormed over there and started some drama. I could have jumped to conclusions and fucked everything up. Brushing the hair away from her face, I tuck it behind her ears, resting my hands on each side of her neck, rubbing gently as she looks up at me. "What did you say to him?"

"I told him I'm with you and he couldn't be all over me because I don't want you to get the wrong idea. Is that okay? I'm sorry, I didn't know what to say."

She bounces about nervously, the elf shoes still on her feet. I lean down to press my lips against hers, savoring the way her tongue moves against mine. "Sounds perfect to me."

Chapter Thirty-one

ANASTASIA

BEING AROUND A CAMPFIRE REMINDS me of camping when I was younger.

My parents plowed every spare dollar they had into skating, so we couldn't afford to go on exotic or luxurious holidays when I was a kid. But every summer we would camp at Snoqualmie Pass for a few nights, and I loved it.

I'd help Dad build a campfire, and Mom would prepare the stuff for s'mores, then we'd sit in front of the fire all night, playing cards.

A campfire in the backyard of a big-ass house in Maple Hills isn't quite the same as the Washington wilderness, but the company is good. The party started to naturally get louder the more drunk people got, so the guys thought it would be a great time to head outside and sit on huge comfy camping chairs, drink beer, and talk nonsense like old women.

I've started to sober up after my excessive shot taking from earlier. Now I'm just left feeling sleepy and needy. Robbie is extremely pleased with his new game but has decided that next time, he's going to take away the cups of soda to make it worse and put another person on the mat. I didn't even know there was soda on offer because all I got was tequila.

I'm grateful that Henry threw the game because I was seriously going to vomit. When I managed to grab him after Gen-gate, he said he took his hand off the mat on purpose because he was worried she was going to accidentally expose herself. I said what about me and the risk of me exposing myself? He said it was only a matter of time until that happened anyway, and I should probably invest in some pants.

He's in a bad mood now because when he tried to find his mistletoe girl, she and her friend were nowhere to be found. He didn't think to get her number or, you know, her full name.

The crackle of the fire is relaxing, to the point where I might fall asleep outside. It doesn't help that I'm curled up on Nathan's lap under a blanket, his hand tickling up and down my leg and his other arm cradling me like I'm a baby. It sounds strange, but I'm ridiculously comfortable. He's laughing away with his friends, talking about sports, and sipping on a beer. He keeps name-dropping sportspeople I've never heard of, which is helping me stay zoned out.

Every so often he looks down and kisses me on the forehead, checking that I'm comfortable enough and I'm warm enough. Then he wraps the blanket around me tighter and makes sure none of me is exposed.

There's a warm, full feeling in my heart when I'm around this team. It's unfamiliar but familiar at the same time; a contradiction, I know, but so specific that it feels like it was specifically designed for me. It's the feeling I didn't know I needed until these guys crashed their way into my life three months ago.

Every second that passes makes it harder to keep my eyes open; his heartbeat drums softly against where my cheek is resting like a lullaby, and eventually, I can't fight it anymore and my eyes flutter closed.

I'm not sure how long I've been out when the shouting shakes me from my deep sleep, but it's Nate springing to his feet that properly wakes me up.

It's like when you're dreaming, and you feel yourself falling so you jerk awake and adrenaline soars through your system. My skin feels like it's buzzing as Nate harshly lowers me onto the seat he just vacated. One quick look around the campfire shows all the guys jumping up and running toward the house.

"Stay here and don't move," Nate says, before running toward the house, too.

I unravel the blanket wrapped around my body and stand to follow, but as he reaches the back door, Nate turns to look at me. "Sit the fuck down, Anastasia."

I'm frozen on the spot, half ready to run in and half unwilling to ignore Nathan, both because I know something bad is clearly happening. My phone starts ringing and I scramble to find it, finally grabbing it from underneath the seat.

"Where are you?" Lola shouts over the noise on her end.

"The backyard. What's going on?" I ask, jogging toward the back door.

"There's a fight. Stay outside, I'll find you when they stop."

"Who's fighting?" *Please don't say Nathan.*

"I don't know! I'm in Robbie's room, I can just hear it."

There is no one hanging out in the den when I walk through the door from the backyard; they're all huddled in the archway to the kitchen and living room.

The crashing and shouting are making me feel sick, and so is the fact that I can't see any of the boys, which means that they're on the other side of the crowd. Being five foot four has some advantages, but right now, pushing through a crowd of drunk people, it has zero.

I'm panting by the time I make my way through the gathering. When I finally get to the source of the noise, my heart sinks to my stomach.

Kris and Joe are pulling Bobby off some guy in one corner, and Mattie and JJ are pulling Henry off someone else in another. My blood feels corrosive, rushing around my body as my heart pumps erratically.

Scanning the room frantically, I spot Nathan, pinning someone to the wall by their throat. Blood is pouring out of both of their faces, Nate's face hard as he says something to the guy through gritted teeth. It's not until JJ leaves Henry to pull Nathan off the guy that I realize the guy Nathan is pinning is Aaron.

I can't move.

Aaron's face is swollen and cut; he doesn't even spot me as the guy Henry was fighting with drags him out of the door.

"Everybody out!" JJ shouts, when someone turns off the music. "Get the fuck out now!"

I feel like Mufasa getting stampeded as everyone starts pushing past me to leave. I need to move but I can't. *How the fuck did this happen? Why is Aaron even here?*

Feeling a tug on my hand, I follow, letting Lola drag me out of the way to where Robbie is sitting with his head in his hands.

I've never seen a party empty so quickly. The last person leaves, and the door slams shut, which seems to give Robbie the privacy he wants. "What the fuck were you thinking?" he bellows. "You're all lucky the fucking cops aren't here!"

JJ shrugs as he drops onto the couch, wiping the blood from his lip with the back of his hand. "Had it coming."

I'm too busy staring at their busted faces and hands to notice Nathan step in front of me. "I told you to wait outside," he says angrily.

"I was worried." As far as Christmas grottos go, this one now looks like one from nightmares. There's a tree on its side with ornaments decorating the floor instead of its branches, and half of the fairy lights on the walls have been pulled down. Joe appears with an armful of beer bottles and starts handing them out, which annoys me because beer shouldn't be the priority here.

"Do you guys have a first aid kit?"

"You could have been hurt, Anastasia!" Nate yells, making me jump.

"Me? I'm not the one with the bleeding face! Will someone please tell me what the fuck is going on?" I yell back.

"Aaron was drunk and mouthing off with some guys I don't know," Nate says, taking the cold beer from Joe and holding it against his jaw. "Typical Aaron bull."

"So you beat the shit out of him? Really, Nathan? With Skinner on your ass you thought, *Let's make this whole situation so much worse*?" Robbie moves next to me, passing the first aid kit into my shaking hands. "Sit down!" I snap at Nate, apparently in a scary enough way that he does it without a fight.

It looks like they're prepared for this situation because Robbie gives a different first aid kit to Lo and she begins to wipe the blood from Bobby's face. He's wincing with every touch, and she just tuts loudly. "Oh shut up, you big baby."

"You're shouting at the wrong man, Stas," Nathan says, hissing when I wipe the alcohol solution across the cut on his cheek. "I was stopping the fight. Which is why you should have stayed outside where I left you."

"You don't get to be mad at me right now!"

"I do when you ignore me and put yourself in harm's way!"

I want to kiss him and strangle him. Scream at him and take care of him. Careless, reckless man. He grips my wrists lightly with each hand, slowly lowering them. It's not until his steady hands are on me that I realize mine are shaking.

"I hit Aaron. You can shout at me, Stassie."

Perhaps the one person I wasn't expecting to hear that from is Henry, but here he is, sipping a beer and pressing an ice pack to the side of his head. He doesn't look guilty, there is no hint of remorse in his voice. He was just simply informing me that he hit Aaron.

"What the fuck, Henry?" I squeak, brushing Nate's hands off me when he moves up my arms and tries to squeeze my shoulders.

I'm still mad at him and he doesn't get a free pass just because Henry wants to be Muhammad Ali.

"I'm not going to apologize."

"I got a busted face splitting up the bullshit you caused," Nate shouts at him, pressing a Band-Aid to his cheek. "You're gonna fucking apologize to her if she wants an apology."

"You want me to repeat the things he says about her? So she understands why he deserved it?" Henry says, looking straight at Nathan, face emotionless. "He's a piece of shit and I'm not sorry. You're only pissed at me because you should have done it months ago."

"Watch it, kid," Nate snaps, and my stomach sinks.

"At least your ban would have been worth it. He came here looking to start shit. He succeeded. End of story."

"What do you mean what he says about me? Can you stop talking about me like I'm not here?"

Everyone's eyes are on me, but no one is saying anything. It feels like screaming into a void. It's like there's a huge secret and I'm the only one who wasn't clued in.

"It doesn't matter, Stassie," Robbie mutters. "You can't just fucking fight people for talking shit, Hen."

"I happen to disagree," JJ says, standing from the couch to grab another beer. "Just give me the heads-up next time, yeah, Hen? I was about to score and your little dramatics cockblocked me. Consider us even for the Gen thing."

"Can someone please explain to me what the fuck is being said about me!" I shout over them chatting like somehow this situation is normal.

Lola is totally unfazed as she examines each of them for injuries, moving on to the next when she's cleaned all the cuts.

"Lols, how are you so calm?" The adrenaline has officially worn off; I feel exhausted, and I haven't even done anything other than get more and more confused and shout.

She shrugs and kicks at Nathan with her foot until he gets the message and shuffles along enough for her to sit down beside me. "I have brothers. Our house looked like this most days—this is tame." She looks at Nathan and scowls. "Make yourself useful and go get her a drink, Rocky."

She wraps an arm around me and kisses me on the forehead. "Sometimes it's better not to know what people say behind your back, honey. I think we both know Aaron is a snakey little shit, and when you get back from Colorado it might be time for us to talk about our living situation." I tilt my head to rest it on her shoulder. "Don't be too hard on him," she whispers. "He was protecting Henry."

Nathan reappears with two bottles of water in one hand, holding out his other to me. "Let's go to bed." He's not asking, he's telling, and as much as I want to stay down here, I feel like I'm more likely to get answers from him alone.

Lo kisses me on the head again. "Go, I'll see you in the morning."

Chapter Thirty-two

NATHAN

How the fuck am I in more trouble than Henry?

She's stomping around naked getting ready for bed, ignoring my existence. I can only imagine how she must be feeling, knowing once again Aaron is in the center of another fucking disaster.

I don't even know what he said this time. Henry's right, though, I'm pissed because I should have done something weeks ago. I see why Anastasia wants to give him the benefit of the doubt, allow him room to grow and be the friend she believes he can be.

From the stories she's shared about their friendship and the good times with him, I can understand her reluctance to cut him off. The problem I have is I know what he says behind her back, and she doesn't. I made a choice, rightly or wrongly, and I've kept it to myself.

I'm selfish; I don't want to be the one she associates with the hurt she's going to feel. I don't want to see her face drop when she realizes just how much of a prick the guy is.

Stassie was fast asleep in my lap when I heard the signature sound of shit going down. Fighting isn't normally something we have to deal with at our parties; we all have enough of it during games, we don't need that kind of shit in our downtime, too.

Now that we have Anastasia and Lola around all the time, the urge to keep the peace is much bigger. When I finally made it inside, Henry was pounding his fist into Aaron's face, and Bobby and JJ were pulling two guys off him. I don't even think Henry noticed they were there on him, and the second I got him off Aaron, he started on some other guy like a fucking douchebag.

I picked Aaron off the floor, not starting anything, just wanting him to leave, and he swung for me. He punches like a kid who's never had a fight before in his life, but he got a good shot at my face and managed to split my cheek a little.

I've been hit harder by Lola when I've eaten the last of her favorite cereal.

Pinning him to the wall by his throat, the temptation to take out all my hatred was unbelievable. Feeling his pulse hammer beneath my fingers, my grip tightened, and his eyes locked with mine. He struggled against me as I threatened him, telling him if he ever came back here, I'd do something he'd finally have a reason to get me in trouble over.

Even in the heat of the moment, I'm not reckless enough to not see the trap Aaron was laying out. Skinner is itching to blame me for everything; I can't give him ammunition.

Stas huffs as she roots around my desk, moving books out of the way. Her routine is very specific, so I know she's looking for her hairbrush, because brushing her hair comes after brushing her teeth. It's amazing having the most predictable girl on the planet.

"I don't mind if you're ignoring me, Anastasia," I tell her, watching her cute butt swish about. "Because I'm ignoring you."

I hear a scoff, but she doesn't bite.

"And I know where your hairbrush is, but I can't tell you because I'm ignoring you."

I expect her to run over here and jump on me, pin me down and demand the information. Maybe kiss it out of me? I don't know. A guy can wish. She doesn't, though, not even close; she throws up her middle finger and keeps searching.

Her frustration is growing, so I'm biding my time, patiently waiting for her to cave. She looks over at me sprawled out on the bed, and I think she's cracking, but instead, she works out where her hairbrush is and comes storming over.

Her hands land on her waist and her hip snaps to the side. "Stop staring at my breasts and show me your hands."

"Hi, baby. Nice to hear your voice again."

"I know you're hiding it from me, and you've been watching me search for fifteen minutes knowing you've got it," she grumbles, fighting hard to keep the smirk from her lips. She's fighting her amusement with her frustration because she knows I've outsmarted her. "I hate you."

"I can neither confirm nor deny because I'm currently ignoring you."

She takes a step closer to me; close enough for me to grab and give her a tug, causing her body to tumble into mine with an *oompf.*

"It's behind the pillow, isn't it?" My fingers dig into her sides until she's squirming, squealing, and laughing, and I know I've got her back. "You're *so* annoying."

Her body is warm and soft against mine. She peers up at me with flushed cheeks and a relaxed smile. I brush the stray hairs from her face, kissing the tip of her nose.

She sighs and gently brushes underneath the Band-Aid on my cheek. "I don't need you to defend me," she whispers.

Her sassy, stubborn nature is what I've come to expect, but sometimes she stuns me with her vulnerability.

"I know you don't, but you're worth defending. Every cut, bruise, every single pang of anger or frustration. It's all worth it. I'd throw my last punch defending you because you deserve to have someone be that person for you, and there's no one more qualified for the job than me."

Tears line the rim of her eyes, threatening to fall, but she blinks them away, sucking in a shaky breath. "Kiss me."

I don't need to be told twice, and when my lips meet hers, things don't feel so bad. There's something different about us, something deeper, something real. I can't imagine how she's feeling right now, knowing someone she cares about is betraying her trust.

"I promise I'll tell you everything in the morning, okay?"

"Okay, bub."

She's already awake when I open my eyes, and I wonder how long she's been overthinking.

Promising to tell her everything is one of the things on my mind, too. Her head is buried in my chest, legs intertwined with mine, and I'm not sure how I'm ever expected to wake up alone again.

"Whatcha thinking about?"

"The showerhead in your bathroom."

My eyebrow raises. "Why?"

"High pressure. It's my favorite."

Finally realizing what she's talking about, I climb out of bed, dragging her with me. Laughing loudly, I slap my hand down on her ass as she giggles away. She didn't bother putting on clothes last night, so I dump her straight in the shower, under the warm spray, while I take off my boxers, stepping in beside her.

"Leg," I say, tapping below my chest. She leans against the wall and looks up at me, a mischievous glint in her eyes, effortlessly lifting her leg. I grab the showerhead from the wall and turn it on, making sure the stream is on the most powerful setting. "Ready?"

She nods, teeth sinking into her bottom lip, hands running down my chest. I point the spray between her thighs, my own chest heaving with anticipation as her eyes roll back.

"*Oh.*" She moans, her fingers sinking into my skin. It doesn't take long because the pressure is so intense. Her back begins to arch and she grips me tighter; I know she's there, so I move the showerhead away and watch her face drop as her orgasm dwindles away.

She doesn't say anything after a whine leaves her lips, which I'm pretty sure was involuntary, so I put the showerhead back, a bit farther away this time, and move it in tiny circles. *"Nathan . . ."*

"Yes, baby?"

Her nails scrape below my belly button, sending a shudder up my spine. Her head is tilted back, mouth searching for mine. I grip her throat with my free hand and tug at her bottom lip with my teeth. She's almost there again, her leg is shaking against my chest, voice desperate. "Please let me come."

"Uh." I move the showerhead away again. "No."

"You're torturing me," she whines as I once again point the stream of water toward her clit and let her orgasm build. Finally tired of the anticipation, I let her leg drop to the floor and she whimpers. "Nate, please fuck me."

"But I thought it was your favorite?"

Her arms link around my neck as she creeps onto her tiptoes. "I don't like anything more than I like you. You're my favorite."

I scoop her up and turn off the shower, reaching for a towel to wrap around her as I step out. The second I lower her onto the bed, she rolls onto her front and sticks her ass in the air, cheek resting against the bed, head turned to watch me. *How did I get so fucking lucky?*

"I'm about ten seconds from getting back in the shower, Hawkins. Alone." She hums, ass swaying side to side impatiently.

I slowly crawl toward her on the bed, taking my time, ignoring the arm that reaches out to make me move quicker.

"Such a pretty pussy, Anastasia," I praise, running my cock between her folds, watching the goose bumps spread across her back when the tip nudges her.

"Hurry up and fuck it, then." She sighs when I line myself up. *"Please."*

"So impatient," I coo, holding on to her hips tightly as I plunge into her, gasping at how wet she is.

My eyes roll to the back of my head as she grips me so fucking tight. She starts backing up on me, her plump ass slapping off my hips as she fucks herself, breathy moans as she cries out.

"Shit, you're perfect." I groan, head falling back.

I sit back onto the heels of my feet and pull her body flush against mine, letting her sink down onto every inch.

"You're too big."

"You can take it, though."

I'm close. I'm so fucking close. The sound of her skin slapping against mine is second only to hearing her moan my name and seeing her play with her tits. I slip my hand between her legs and rub her swollen clit, using my other hand to tilt her head toward me. "Are you going to come for me?"

"Ahh."

"Whose girl are you?"

Her eyes lock with mine, taking my breath away. "Yours."

"That's right, baby," I coo proudly. "I'm almost there . . ."

She must see it as a challenge, because her movements become sloppy and rough as she slams herself down hard over and over. Her body is shaking, arms reaching behind her to sink into my hair and tug tightly. Then every inch of her tightens and she practically screams, "*Nathan,* oh my, oh *fuck—*"

That's all I needed for her to tip me over the edge; my balls tighten and I fucking explode inside her, sweaty forehead falling to her shoulder.

I don't want to let her go, but I have to because, as unbelievable as coming inside of her is, it's messy and kind of ruins the moment.

"You gonna get me a warm cloth like they do in romance novels?" she teases.

"I can offer you some toilet paper and maybe a wet wipe if I have any."

Tutting playfully, she awkwardly stands from the bed and waddles toward the bathroom as my cum runs down the inside of her thigh. "I'm going to start making you wear condoms again. You're getting too big for your boots."

"Stop telling me I have a big dick if you don't want me to have a big ego!" I shout after her, smiling at the laughter that comes out of the bathroom. After she'd cleaned herself up, Stassie wanted to get back into bed and cuddle. Who am I to say no to that?

"So what does being your girl entail?" she asks carefully, finger tracing patterns on my chest.

I think about it for a minute, knowing how carefully I need to play this without fucking it all up. "It's basically everything you already are and do, I just get to call you my girl without fear of scaring you off."

"And what do I call you? I can't call you my boy, that's just weird."

"You could call me that . . . or your boyfriend. Or whatever you want, whatever makes your little commitmentphobe heart feel comfortable."

She's quiet for a little longer than I'd like.

"It doesn't matter what you call me, Stassie. Titles don't matter because I get you regardless. I know I'm a bit full-on and I joke, but I want you to know I've never done this before, either. I've never had a girlfriend and I've never committed to anyone. Three months doesn't seem like a long time, but I'm a guy who knows when he's sure. I'm sure about you."

"I'm sure about you, too," she whispers, running her thumb across the cut on my cheek. "I know things have been messy and chaotic, and I'm grateful you've stuck with me through it all."

I scratch at my stubble awkwardly. "I, uh, I think I've been to blame for a lot of the mess and the chaos, to be honest, baby. So I'm grateful you've stuck with me through it all."

She's quiet and pensive, but I just let her, giving her time with her thoughts. I'm starting to doze off when she clears her throat. "I'm ready to hear what's been said about me. Can we get Henry?"

I've been dreading this, which is why I was willing to fool around earlier. She was clearly looking for a distraction, too, but maybe knowing will do her good. "Of course, I'll go get him. Maybe put some pants on so he can, y'know, cope."

She hits me softly on the arm and laughs. "I think we're all underestimating Henry."

I think she's right.

Chapter Thirty-three

ANASTASIA

CONSIDERING HENRY STARTED A FIGHT with three guys last night, he's surprisingly chipper, and from what I can see, he doesn't have a scratch on him.

Henry flounces into the room, shoveling cereal into his mouth, and throws himself at the bottom of the bed. His face twists as he looks between me and Nate. "It smells like sex in here."

"You're on thin ice, Turner," Nate gruffs, climbing back onto the bed beside me.

"You'd think sex would chill you out but apparently not, grumpy," he mutters, spooning in another mouthful of Lucky Charms.

"I assume you know why I asked Nathan to get you," I say, interrupting what will most likely escalate into a nonsensical argument.

He puts his now empty bowl beside him and crosses his legs, leaning back against the bed frame. "I hope it's not for a threesome because you're not my type."

Nate's head falls back, his hand rubbing his forehead as he stares at the ceiling, groaning. I hope it's not a migraine, but if anyone is going to induce one today, it'll be Henry. Nate looks back at him. "*Dude.*"

"What do you mean I'm not your type?" I hiss.

"You're too short," he says bluntly. "You're, like, what? Five three? Five four? Gotta be five-nine or above to ride."

A lot of bad stuff has happened recently, and this is by far the absolute worst. I mean, technically I sort of have a boyfriend now, although that word currently makes me feel a little unwell.

"I want to file a complaint. This is discrimination," I snap.

"Baby, I'm right here?" Nate says, raising an eyebrow.

Henry chuckles, winking at Nate. "Yeah, thankfully. I think Anastasia wants me."

"Remember when you were quiet?" Nate drawls. "I miss those times."

Rolling my eyes, I nudge my shoulder into Nate. "We're off topic. Hen, you have to tell me what the hell started last night."

My palms are sweating, stomach twisting with anticipation. I want to know and at the same time, I don't want to know.

"I don't want to tell you, Anastasia," Henry says. "Not because I want to lie to you, but because I don't see what you gain from knowing. He was talking shit, I hit him, and he left. You don't need to ever live with him again; even next year when Nate and JJ are gone, I'll still be here to look out for you."

I feel like the Grinch when his heart grew three sizes; the love I have for Henry is overwhelming. I don't think he even realizes how sweet he is. But sweet or not, my brain is going to carry on creating situations in my head until I know.

"I'd still like to know, Hen." I sigh heavily. "I mean, you took on three guys; it must have been bad. I didn't even know you knew how to fight."

He looks at me like I've got two heads, face scrunching. "I'm a hockey player, study art, and I have two moms. You think I've never had to hit someone before?"

"All right, tough guy," Nate drawls. "Let's not pretend you didn't grow up in the cushy Maple Hills suburbs. Tell her, she has a right to know."

Henry sighs and nods. "I was looking for Gen when I noticed

him come in with two guys. They were clearly drunk. Aaron asked where you were, so I told him to leave. He said he wouldn't, so I punched him."

My eyes narrow as he looks everywhere but at me. "You're lying to me."

"I don't lie, Anastasia."

"I know you don't, so why are you lying now? Tell me what he said."

Nathan sighs and tugs my body closer to his side, pressing his lips to my temple. "It started at the beginning of October. It was right after I asked you to bring Lola to Robbie's birthday party. Said he'd enjoy watching you drop me like you do with everyone else."

"And then what?"

His fingers gently stroke up and down my back. Henry sits silently opposite us. "Every time we had practice after you and you'd go into the locker room, he'd hang around Brady telling her you're distracted, you're out of control at parties, drinking and hooking up with strangers. It went on for weeks until one day, Brady fucking lost it with him."

"We didn't hear what he said," Henry interjects. "But she said if he had such an issue with how you skate, he should look for a new partner. This was right before he got hurt."

Coach Brady has been a lot nicer to me this year, but I assumed it was pity after all the shit we've been through. She's still scary as hell, but I've noticed she's not been as quick to pick me apart like she had been previously. It never occurred to me she didn't want to give Aaron ammunition.

"Okay, so he was talking shit up to Halloween. He spent two weeks glued to my side, I made up with Nate, and I started staying here. It's nearly Christmas, so what are you leaving out?"

Henry sighs, rubbing his jaw with his hand. "Tim, a guy from the team, was at a Titans basketball game and was sitting behind

Aaron. Tim didn't think the two guys he was with were from Maple Hills."

"All of Aaron's friends go to UCLA, so he never bothered making friends here," I explain. "He was supposed to go there with them, but he got accepted here. It's how we ended up together, we were both pair skaters whose partners didn't get an offer from UCMH."

"It might have been them, I don't know. But Tim could hear him talking about you. He said Ryan ghosted you because he realized you're just a jersey chaser."

"Original," I scoff. "What else?"

Henry's eyes dart to Nathan, looking for guidance. Out of the corner of my eye I see him give Henry a nod. Henry shuffles on the bed and my palms sting from my nails sinking into them.

"Tim heard him say your parents are broke, so you're latching on to guys going pro. He called you a slut, said you'd always been one, and you're trying the same thing with Nate."

Don't cry. "Okay. Is there more?"

Henry nods and my heart pounds in my chest. "He said you would trap Nate with a baby. You didn't have the talent to go all the way in skating, and it'd give you an excuse without having to admit that you're not good enough. Said that's probably what Coach Brady did."

My words get caught in my throat. I don't even think what I'm feeling is hurt; Aaron has said worse to me himself. It's the embarrassment. The knowledge that these people, Nate's friends, people who respect him, have had to listen to how I'm this awful person who wants to trap him. "Are we up to last night yet?"

"Last night, he said he was coming to take you home where you belonged. I said you weren't going anywhere, and he said, 'So you're fucking her, too?' I told him to get out, but he carried on." Henry looks to Nate again, looking uncomfortable.

"Go on," I urge. Nate's hand slips into mine, his thumb rubbing over the nail marks gently.

"He said you're using us for a place to live, just like you did with him. That Nate was deluded if he thought you actually liked him, because you're fake. Then he said . . . *Fuck*." Henry drags his hand down his face and stares at the bedding. "I'm sorry, Stassie. I'm sorry I have to repeat this . . . He said no one will ever be able to love you, because how could they when your own parents couldn't, and the ones who bought you only want you to fill up their trophy cabinet."

"Fuck," Nate snaps.

"And that's when I punched him."

"Nathan, you're hurting me," I whisper, looking at my pink fingers where he's gripping me too tight.

"Thanks for telling me, Hen," I say, steadying my voice. "And thanks for defending me. I'm sorry I brought this drama to your door."

He looks uncomfortable and I feel it, too. "Lola said I'm not allowed to talk about whether you two love each other or not, but I love you, Anastasia. I was serious when I said I want you to live here. Whether you two are together or not, if you get tired of Nathan you can sleep in my room. I'll get the air mattress again."

There's a loud, dramatic sob threatening to rip out of me but I push it down, nodding my head instead. "I love you, too, Henry."

He grabs his empty cereal bowl and leaves the room, and when the door closes, Nathan pulls me on top of him and leans back, cradling my head on his chest as I wrap myself around him. "Let it all out. You're safe. I'm here."

So, I let the dam break and hold him tight, while every emotion I've been suppressing hits me all at once.

Nathan lets me cry until I wear myself out, and when I'm finally silent, he tells me what he's been patiently waiting for me to be ready to hear.

"I know you're not using me. I know you're not trying to trap me. I fucking love living with you. The guys love living with you, we *all* want you here. I know you like me, even though you definitely hate it," he adds, chuckling as he presses his lips to my forehead.

"Really, really hate it."

"I don't know how much you care about my opinion on this, but you're an incredibly talented skater. I have every faith you're going to achieve all your goals. I would not be forcing my tree trunk body into fucking yoga positions if I didn't think you and your talent were worth it."

"Nate . . ."

"I'm not done. You're a good person, Anastasia. I'm sorry I don't tell you every day. You make me feel cared for, feel listened to, and the other stuff I don't even know how to put into words properly. You make me feel valued, for who I am as me, not who I am as team captain or whatever."

"I do value you."

"That isn't a feeling I've had in a long time. Not since my mom was alive. I love the guys, but it's not the same thing. I can't think how to describe it . . . It's like there's a spot in your life you keep just for me. One I don't have to share, one where you don't expect anything from me. Do you know how amazing it is? How lucky I feel to know you? You make me want to be the best I can be."

"Oh . . ."

"You're smart and determined, and you are so fucking worthy of love, Anastasia. *So* worthy. You're surrounded by people who love you, and we're all on your team. Aaron isn't, and it's why he's trying to hurt you. I'm sorry you had to listen to it."

"Thank you for saying, well, everything. You make me feel valued, too."

"It's the truth, and I wish I'd told you before this. Look, I don't feel like it's my place to talk about your parents, but from what you've told me about them, it sounds like you're the best thing to ever happen to them."

I nod, saying nothing more. He's answered every question or doubt in my mind. It's not enough to stop the noise, but it has turned the volume down a little bit.

We lie on the bed in silence for a while, and when I promise I'm feeling a little better, Nate gives me the space I'm craving to process. He heads to the gym with Robbie and Henry, leaving me home with JJ and Lola, who claim that *working out is for losers*. In their ultimate wisdom, they've both decided to keep me distracted by furthering my culinary education.

Lola has been feeling guilty about the whole meal plan disaster, scolding herself for not paying closer attention. Like me, she doesn't think Aaron did it on purpose, but she thinks she could have weighed in more and prevented the whole mess.

Since then, she's been trying to teach me some more of her favorite dishes. Well, she was, until JJ banished her from the kitchen and told her to sit on the other side of the kitchen island when she started criticizing how I cut chicken. JJ told her if she wasn't going to play nicely, she wasn't allowed to play.

We're making butter chicken because—quoting JJ—"basic white girls love butter chicken." JJ has already told me it might suck because we haven't marinated the chicken long enough, but we're sticking to it anyway because Johal-Mitchell-Allens aren't quitters.

He watched me add baking soda to the dry ingredients for our naans, checking I remember after he taught me last week. Now that I'm flipping the fifth one on the tawa, he's lost interest and is swiping on a dating app.

Learning to cook new recipes is healing my relationship with food. I'd be lying if I said looking at the cream we put into the chicken dish didn't have my fingers twitching to open my calorie app, but I'm trying hard to enjoy the moment.

Putting on seven pounds in the past month was a huge blow; obviously, I cried, because all I do these days is cry it seems, but Nate was quick to point out it's muscle. I'm leaner and I'm beating all my personal bests every workout as I get stronger. I'm fueling my body properly for the first time in so long, and as hard as it is, I'm trying to forget about the numbers. I never realized before how toxic my view of food was, but I'm trying to be better every day, feeding my body what it needs, not what I think it needs.

JJ finally looks up from his phone as I put the last naan on the plate. "Are you two moving in here?" he asks bluntly.

"Where's your filter, Johal? Didn't wanna ease into it?" Lo laughs.

"I'm a busy man. Gotta cut to the chase."

"I don't know what we're doing." I sigh. "We're going to talk about it when I get home from Colorado."

"Well, I'm sure Hawkins has given you a full speech and promised to lay down his life for you or whatever, but so you know, I'm cool with you both living here. My instincts about men are impeccable and I'm telling you, Aaron is a walking, talking red flag."

The front door opens, and the guys come in, all looking sweaty and tired. "God, that smells good," Robbie praises, joining us in the kitchen and immediately reaching for a naan.

I swat his hand away before he even gets to the plate. "Patience."

After what feels like forever slapping hands away of hungry boys trying to sneak a taste, I finally plate up the food and make everyone sit at the table.

"This looks good, Stassie," Henry says, not even one hint of something backhanded coming my way.

"I'm so proud of you," Nate says, leaning over to kiss my temple. "It smells amazing."

Fuck you, calorie app.

Chapter Thirty-four

NATHAN

AM I SURPRISED MY GIRLFRIEND—yes, I'm allowed to call her that now—is the most annoying person to travel with, ever? No.

She's so fucking awake right now that it's making me feel sick. We're getting the first flight to Washington, meaning it's not even light, yet she's bouncing around the place.

On the one hand, it's so good to see her happy after the post-Aaron slump she's been in. On the other hand, we wake up together every day, and I've never seen her act like this before lunchtime, so I'm freaking confused. I'm currently sipping my second coffee, and I still have the nauseous feeling you get when you wake up too early.

It isn't flying to Seattle she's happy about, we could be going anywhere. She likes getting organized to travel, it turns out. Bossy Anastasia is my favorite; she's determined and sassy, fucking hilarious when I don't listen, and she starts scowling. In bed when she takes control, *Jesus*, I'm a lucky man. I would happily deal with Bossy Anastasia every day.

Travel Anastasia is the worst. Lists. So many fucking lists. Nothing I do is trusted; all the bags had to be rechecked by her because my checks aren't as good as her checks.

Travel Anastasia forced me to use packing cubes, meaning I spent an hour playing freaking *Tetris* with my case. When I was on my third go of making it all fit, failing once again, I launched the pointless cubes across the room. Sensing I was feeling a little frustrated, she sank to her knees in front of me, reached for my belt, and showed me how much she loves traveling. It was the only thing that stopped me from canceling the flights.

Downing the last of my coffee, I lean back in the rickety airport seat, immediately feeling eyes on me. "You're a grumpy gills this morning," she chirps, tucking into the fruit salad she paid about fifteen bucks for in the airport shop.

"Early. Tired," I grunt.

"Poor baby," she says sarcastically, giggling and pinching my cheek. "Want to sleep on my boobs on the plane?"

"I obviously wanna sleep on your boobs," I mumble, leaning to steal the piece of pineapple on her fork. "How are you so awake? And happy?"

"I love airports. People-watching, organizing, shopping and stuff, it's great. Plus, I'm about to spend nearly two weeks with your undivided attention, how can I not be happy?"

Oh man. It's like she knows what to say to make me want to propose. She holds out her fork to me, letting me steal another piece of pineapple. Sighing, I tuck a loose strand of hair behind her ear. "You're annoying, but you're cute."

"Oh, I think our gate is up!" she squeaks. "Let's go!"

Springing to her feet, she frantically tries to collect her bags with one hand and balance her fruit cup with the other. It's a disaster waiting to happen.

"Stand still," I tell her, taking the bags from her hand and slinging them over my shoulder. She watches me round up our things, grinning ear to ear. "Okay, let's go."

"Aye, aye, Captain."

The second the plane took off I fell asleep in the middle of Stassie's chest. After three peaceful hours, we land in Washington to much cooler temperatures than LA. Hopping into a cab, Stassie gives her address, and we head off.

We're only staying here two nights before heading to Colorado, where we're spending Christmas and New Year's. It's an understatement to say I'm fucking terrified to meet her parents. She speaks so highly of them and I only get to make a first impression once.

She turns her phone back on and all their excited messages start coming through. Threading her fingers through mine, she brings the back of my hand to her mouth and covers it in kisses. "You okay, bub?"

"What if they don't like me?"

"They already like you, Nathan. And if somehow you make a terrible first impression, I see them once a year, so it doesn't matter anyway. I like you enough for everyone."

"Remember a month ago when you said sleeping in my bed every night would be distracting?"

"I do."

"I'm glad you let me distract you. Thank you for not letting me spend the holidays alone."

She gives me the smile I love. It's a soft one, one that makes her eyes shine, and it's one I think she saves for me. "I think you've probably improved me more than you've distracted me."

We sit in comfortable silence for the rest of the journey, and I feel calm until the cab turns into a cul-de-sac and stops in front of the house. Stassie gives my hand one final squeeze, then starts to climb out. No turning back now.

AFTER FEELING LIKE I'M GOING to pass out with nerves for the first fifteen minutes of being here, I can honestly say Julia and Colin Allen are the most welcoming people I've ever met.

It's been overwhelming but in a nice way. I already know a bit about them from Anastasia, but it's been nice to hear from them about their family. One thing they would never need to tell me is how much they love Anastasia, because it's clear from the way they looked at her when they opened the door to watch us climb the porch. Julia wouldn't let her go for five minutes.

They quickly gave me a tour, before letting us put our bags away, and the whole place is covered in pictures of Stas. Birthdays, camping, Christmas, all with the same mischievous face on them.

God, our kids will be adorable.

Julia hands me my third gingerbread cookie, then turns to Stassie and clears her throat. "You didn't get back to me about booking time at the rink, honey. I didn't know what to do . . ."

The atmosphere in the room instantly changes, it gets cooler, or maybe it's my imagination because I know skating is both the sunshine and the black cloud over this family.

I slip my cookie-free hand into Anastasia's, giving it an encouraging squeeze. She clings tightly. "I'm not planning to skate, and, uh, if it's okay, I'd like it if we don't talk about skating while I'm here. I had some sessions with Dr. Andrews last month; he thinks it would be good for me to find other things to talk about."

Colin leans forward, looking genuinely shocked. "Really?"

She nods, looking between both her parents. Julia is trying hard not to show her shock, but she's not quite managing it.

"It helps with the pressure. He thinks it's good to rest physically *and* mentally. So you not asking about it helps me. I can let you guys know if anything new or interesting happens in the future."

"Of course, Annie. We only ask because we know how important it is to you. We only care about your happiness, honey. We won't bring it up, will we, Col? Not unless you want us to."

I feel the tension in Anastasia's body ease, her grip loosens, and she relaxes. I change the subject to move on from this one, questioning a nickname I've never heard. "'Annie'?"

Stas looks at me, her expression serious. "Yeah, they call me Annie because I was an orphan."

Colin bursts out laughing as Julia gasps, crossing her arms over her chest. "Anastasia Rebecca Allen!" she squeaks. "We call you Annie because you couldn't spell *Anastasia* until you were eight!" Looking at me, she shakes her head. "Please don't listen to my daughter."

I can't help but laugh. "I have to, ma'am. She's pretty scary when she wants to be; she even has my whole hockey team terrified of her."

"She's always been like that," Colin says proudly. "When she was thirteen, a boy in her class was being bullied by a few older boys. We got called in to see the principal because Anastasia made them all cry."

"Mhmm," Julia hums. "What you seem to be missing is she ended up in detention for two whole weeks because she told the principal if he needed a teenage girl to do his job for him, he wasn't fit to be head of the school."

Stassie's cheeks flush a little, but she brushes it off. "Was I wrong, though? And they never bullied him again."

"Brady has been bullying me for weeks and you haven't stood up for me once," I tease.

She nudges me playfully, laughing. "I'm brave, but I'm not *that* brave."

A couple of hours after we arrived, Julia produced two Christmas onesies—a reindeer for me and a snowman for Stas—and it's the comfiest thing I've ever worn. I feel like I know Anastasia so much better now that I've heard every embarrassing story in her parents' repertoire.

Since today has been so low-key, Anastasia suggested we go out for dinner this evening, so nobody had to cook. She's been getting ready since forever, so I've made myself comfortable on her bed with a massive bag of chips Julia gave me. My stomach rumbled once earlier, and she's made it her personal mission to feed me everything in the house.

I love watching Stassie get ready; she's curling her hair strand by strand, concentrating on every single piece. Her teeth are piercing her bottom lip as she focuses, studying every curl. Every now and then, she leans toward the mirror and the light catches her tanned skin; I can't help but let my eyes travel across the slope of her waist, the curve of her hips . . .

"You're so hot."

She looks at me through the mirror, smirking. "Are you talking to me or your chips?"

"You. Chips are good, but you're obviously better. Can you help me off the bed?"

Her eyes narrow, rightfully suspicious. "Why? So you can pull me onto the bed as soon as I give you my hand?"

"No," I lie. Turning off the hot stick thing, she slowly walks to the side of the bed. "Why are you so far away? Come closer."

Her lips tug up at the sides as she takes a small step toward me, but it's enough for me to lunge toward her and pull her onto the bed. She squeals as my fingers dig into her sides, tickling her until she can hardly breathe.

She leans against my chest, her perfect curls decorating my skin. "You need to get ready."

I know I do, but she looks so content I don't want to miss a minute of it. "Can we spend the next week like this? Naked, though." I add, "Well, you naked. I like this onesie, my balls are super toasty."

"As long as your balls are toasty, *obviously*."

"Can we fool around for ten minutes? Then I'll get ready," I ask, wrapping one of her curls around my finger.

"No."

"Five minutes?"

Huffing, she rolls her eyes. "Second base for three minutes, but then you have to get ready."

"Deal."

I MADE A MISTAKE NEGOTIATING for fooling around time earlier. What I should have been negotiating was wearing my reindeer outfit to the restaurant. After an afternoon of comfort, this shirt feels suffocating.

Its only redeeming quality is the fact Anastasia is looking at me like she's picturing more than second base in her head.

"Stop looking at me like you want me to fuck you," I mutter as her parents walk ahead of us, following the host to our table.

"But I want you to. I think it's the rolled-up sleeves. You look so hot."

A laugh rumbles in my throat, but I don't say anything. Rolled-up sleeves are a JJ classic. He insists it's the sluttiest thing a guy can do, and it has a 100 percent success rate. I fucking hate it when he's right.

Anastasia and I don't eat out a lot when we're at home because we're working so hard with her new plan, it seems a little counter-productive when learning new recipes makes her happy.

Tonight is obviously a special occasion since it's Stas's first time home in a year, so it's nice to see what type of restaurant makes it on her favorites list.

It's too fancy for my onesie, I'll say that much. Quiet atmosphere, low lighting, intimate. Taking a peek at the menu, I pretend to look at it for the first time, not revealing to Julia and Colin that Stassie made me study it in detail fifteen minutes before we left the house.

All that prep work and she still won't know what she wants. I lean in, looking at her menu with her. "What are you getting?"

"I don't know," she says, confirming my suspicions, chewing on the inside of her cheek as she flips the menu to study the other side.

"What are the choices?"

She flips it back over. "Crab ravioli or the chicken pizza. I sort of want the ravioli on the pizza, is that weird?"

Her parents overhear her, both looking at us over the top of their menus, nodding in unison. "Yeah."

"Why don't I order the pizza and you order the ravioli. We can switch if the food comes and you get buyer's regret."

Placing the menu on the table, she looks at me, eyes swimming with *something*. "Have I told you you're my favorite human today?"

"Good even— Oh, hey guys."

Turning away from Stassie, I look at the waiter who just approached our table. He looks oddly familiar, despite the fact I've never been here before.

Looking to Stas for guidance, it's clear she definitely knows him by how awkward she looks. Julia stands from the table, leaning in to kiss the guy on the cheek. "James!" she says cheerfully. "How nice to see you, honey. I didn't know you were working here."

It's funny to see Julia force a smile, because it's exactly the same as Stassie's forced smile—terrible. As soon as she says "James," I realize who he is. I've been looking at pictures of him all afternoon, younger but still the same face and sandy-blond hair.

James was Stassie's skating partner before she started college. He was also her first boyfriend, first love, first everything.

Great. So glad he's here.

Colin shakes James's hand, and they both look as awkward as I feel. "Here for a few weeks while I'm home for the holidays." His eyes travel past me and land on the woman beside me who hasn't said a word. "It's good to see you, Stassie."

Hearing her name seems to knock her out of whatever weird moment she's having. "You, too, James. This is Nathan, my boyfriend. Nate, this is James. He was my skating partner until I moved to Maple Hills."

Boyfriend.

It's the first time I've heard her say it, and she said it so confidently. I definitely didn't imagine it.

This isn't the time to have an internal meltdown, Hawkins.

I hold out my hand to shake his, weirdly formal, but it's what Colin did, so I'm doing it, too. "Nice to meet you."

"Likewise," he says, doing an awful job of not looking awkward. "What can I get you guys to eat?"

After taking our orders, my new buddy James disappears, and when our drinks come, it's a totally different person.

The food is delicious, the conversation is easy, and I can't believe how different this would be if it were Stas meeting my dad. Which makes me so fucking glad we're flying back to LA before he gets home from vacation.

Wiping my mouth with my napkin, I summon the courage I've been looking for for the past five minutes. "I'd like it if you'd let me pay for dinner, as a thank-you for you welcoming me into your home." Colin's mouth opens, but I carry on before he can say anything. "And I know you're going to say no, but just know, I'm not above pretending to go to the bathroom and paying sneakily. I've had a great day with you guys, I'd like to say thank you by paying the bill."

"Oh, Dad, let him." Anastasia groans. "Honestly, he's so stubborn he'll argue with you about it for hours."

We all look at her, our heads moving in slow motion, the same identical baffled look on our faces. "Wait, *I'm* the stubborn one?"

Her fingers thread through my hand resting on the table and her laugh is soft and musical. Her eyes are shining as she tries to hide her smile. She's mesmerizing. "Uh, obviously."

Fuck. I am so in love with this woman.

Chapter Thirty-five

ANASTASIA

"ARE WE THERE YET?"

"I swear to God I will leave you in this airport," Nate grumbles, slapping my ass, laughing when the noise causes an elderly couple to turn around and look at us, making my cheeks blush.

We're currently rushing to our connecting flight at Denver, and Nate is as cheerful as ever after our early-morning flight from Seattle. I wasn't expecting to be sad leaving Seattle, but I was. I still am.

The way my mom and dad reacted to me wanting to go out for dinner, not skate, and cook for them, shows me how militant I've been during my previous trips. Letting go of those issues, even for the two days we were there, has done more for my well-being than any therapy session. When we left this morning, I promised I'd be back soon, and I genuinely meant it.

Yesterday I spent the entire day being a tour guide, showing Nate everything the city has to offer until our noses were frozen, and we couldn't possibly stomach any more hot chocolate.

I've been living in LA too long because I could feel the drop in temperature. Nathan joked I was in for a nasty shock when we reached his house, and I'd learn what cold truly feels like. He's promised that at least 90 percent of our time can be spent in front of the fire, so I think I'll learn to cope with that other 10 percent.

I loved playing tour guide, and we were seriously tired by the

time we got home. Watching Nathan being the charming and caring man that he is, watching my parents learn that, too, has been a
dream. Not to mention, watching him stuff his six-foot-four frame
in a onesie has been the highlight of my year.

This trip has been a lot of Nathan-watching—which is very easy
because he's so pretty.

He spent hours last night talking about hockey with my dad, telling him all about joining Vancouver in the summer when he graduates, and Dad was understandably impressed.

"I can't wait to watch you play. Now, I'm not promising to switch
teams, but you win the Stanley Cup and I might consider it," he joked.

It was a weird mix of emotions for Nathan, I think. All he's ever
wanted was for his own dad to take even the slightest bit of interest
in his career, and yet someone who was essentially a stranger forty-
eight hours earlier is so genuinely excited for him.

Hockey aside, my mom might be in love with my boyfriend,
which makes me happy but also a little scared for my dad. I offered
to cook biryani for dinner to help out, but also to show off my new
cooking skills a little. She sat staring at me, teary-eyed.

"What's wrong?" I asked, a skeptical eyebrow raised.

"Nothing's wrong, honey," she murmured, seemingly holding
back the tears. "I'm proud of you. You're home, happy, and healthy.
You have a wonderful boyfriend. I'm your mom, so I'm allowed to be
emotional when I see my daughter thriving."

She wanted to know everything, how we met, how we got together, and I, uh, had to get creative with the truth. Unfortunately,
it's impossible to talk about me and Nate without also talking about
Aaron.

"That little shit," she fumed, aggressively chopping cilantro. "Wait
until I see him."

His accident and our argument weren't the difficult part; she tutted and rolled her eyes at some bits, knowing exactly how Aaron can

sometimes be. It was when I reached his fight with Henry that things became awkward.

"He said . . ." I paused, wondering if it was something I could stomach repeating out loud. Sighing, I reached over and took the kitchen knife off her. "He said nobody would ever be able to love me because my birth parents couldn't."

Her eyes widened, face rapidly paling as she gripped the kitchen counter.

"And if that wasn't bad enough, he said you guys only want me to fill up the trophy cabinet."

There was no emotion to my words as I said them; I used them all crying into Nate's chest a week ago. But watching my mom's face sink into horror made me want to weep.

"He didn't," she said, voice hardly above a whisper. I nodded, letting her tackle me with an oxygen-stealing hug. Burying her face into my hair, she choked on her words. "How could anyone think that? How? Why? What? What the hell is wrong with him?"

"He hurts people when he's hurting," I explained with a sigh, detaching her with great difficulty. She took my head in her hands, kissing my forehead affectionately. "Don't say it. You don't need to."

"I do need to. You are the best thing that ever happened to us, Anastasia. The absolute best. How talented you are adds to what makes you so special, but I loved you long before you put on a pair of ice skates."

"I know." It wasn't a lie. Beneath the insecurity and the self-induced pressure, I know my parents love me. They didn't jump through the hoops of the American public adoption system hoping that they might get a sporty kid. They wanted to complete their family.

"What are you going to do about him?" she asked.

The impossible question I wish I had an answer to.

Understandably, Nate wants to lock me away and refuse to let

Aaron even look in my direction ever again; Lola isn't far behind him with that plan. But the reality of the situation is I don't have much choice when he's my partner.

I was expecting to hear from him after the fight, but there's been nothing. Lola told me he left for Chicago and wouldn't be back until the new year, and I know spending the holidays with his fighting parents will only put him in a worse mood.

I'm slowly making my peace with the fact that my friendship with Aaron has taken all the strain it can handle. I can no longer be a doormat for a broken man to dump his emotional baggage on when he refuses to even attempt to help himself.

Aaron is incredibly privileged and has every resource available to him. I'm desperate for him to use those resources, to be the man I know he is deep down beneath all the insecurity and the anger, but it feels like he's constantly taking steps further away.

It hurts to admit all of this—that I'm *giving up* on him.

Or at least that'll be the way he sees it.

His snappy moods and his subtle attempts at control I could cope with. But the time we spent laughing at home or grinning ear to ear when we nailed something on the ice isn't enough to cancel out the bad anymore. It could never be enough when I can't even trust him not to say vile things about me if I'm not there.

Even with all those emotions rampaging through my body, the voice in my head shouting *Clean break*, I can't be a pair skater without a pair. I need to start thinking about it as strictly a professional partnership.

Colleagues.

Nathan hates it, *obviously*, but this isn't about him or what makes him feel comfortable. I get it, I honestly do. The way Nathan cares for me incites a weird, fuzzy feeling in my stomach—the kind I thought people made up.

He treats me with respect and with kindness, and he roots for me in every way. I'm calling him my boyfriend, for God's sake, a word that previously sent a wave of horror through my body but now makes me feel content. We're inseparable and we're both happy with it like that.

But what he forgets is he's leaving in the summer and moving to a different country, so he needs to get on board with the idea that I can handle Aaron alone.

It isn't normal that Nate and I live together, even though we both love it. I've always loved living with Lo and Aaron, and I'd like to get back to the point where Aaron and I can exist in the same space, even if we're not best friends anymore. I don't even bring that bit up anymore because Nathan hates the idea of me moving back to Maple Tower.

Basically, if it's about Aaron, Nathan hates it, but it's nice of him to be so consistent. He doesn't have the same fears as me; he doesn't question if we only work because we're together twenty-four seven, and if when he moves, and we have to spend time apart, we'll last.

I hope we last. I need us to last. Going from frenemies to lovers in three months wasn't something I ever thought would happen. But despite my best efforts, I'm so freaking in love with this man.

"ARE WE THERE YET?"

Nate pinches the bridge of his nose, sighing heavily. He doesn't find me funny right now, but the more irritated he gets, the funnier I find it.

Am I . . . JJ?

Lowering his head, his nose brushes against mine gently. I can feel his warm breath on my skin, lips an inch from mine, and momentarily, I lose all function. "As soon as we're alone"—he nods toward our driver, who's minding his own business in the front—"I'm going to spank you for every time you've asked me that."

My breath catches in my throat, somewhere between a giggle and a gasp, and he closes the gap, making me melt with a kiss. Breaking apart, he presses his forehead to mine. "Don't threaten me with a good time, Hawkins."

Leaning back to look at me, his brown eyes lock with mine and I just know. I know I made the right choice to spend the holidays here with him. "You're so naughty sometimes."

"Are we nearly there, though?"

His fingers weave between mine in my lap, and he peeks out of the window. "Two minutes. That still counts, by the way."

"I was hoping it would."

It's the longest two minutes of my life, but finally, we pull up to a large gate. I'm trying not to be impatient; I'm more trying not to reveal how nervous I am because I know it's silly. It's an empty house, how can I be nervous about an empty house?

Scratch that.

Mansion. A gigantic, snowy mansion with a massive driveway up to the front door. I don't realize my mouth is hanging open until Nate taps under my chin, chuckling, prompting me to close it.

"You're seriously rich," I whisper, not even necessarily talking to him, just processing.

I knew Nate's family has money, but it never occurred to me it would be *this* much money. The car stops outside the front door that's so big it may have been originally designed for giants.

"My *dad* is seriously rich."

It's all a bit of a blur as we get our bags, and he ushers me in. He nudges me toward the middle of the room. "Go snoop, you know you want to."

He's right.

"I'm scared I'm going to get lost, can you give me a tour?"

Dumping our bags by the door, he guides me through one doorway, revealing the kitchen. "This is the kitchen."

"Well, I didn't see the oven and think it was the bedroom." I haven't even finished rolling my eyes before he's trying to grab me. Darting to the other side of the kitchen island in a fit of laughter to avoid him, he scowls and shakes his head at me.

"You're so fucking annoying," he says with a groan.

"And you're slow. You should work on that."

The rest of my tour takes hardly any time because it's done by me running between rooms, cackling as Nathan tries to catch me. I know he's letting me get away, one of his steps is two of mine, but this way is more fun.

I vaguely take in the tall ceilings and natural light. *Blah blah.* All the things you're supposed to comment on when you're in a beautiful home. What I'm really thinking is these big archways are making it super easy to not get tackled to the ground.

Running up the mammoth staircase, a staircase that should be reserved for ball gown entrances, Nate sneakily guides me toward one room in particular.

Out of breath, overexcited, and ready to admit defeat, I open the door to what is—surprise, surprise—his bedroom. Stopping in the doorway, his arms wrap around me from behind, carrying me in and throwing me on his bed.

Throwing himself down next to me, he rolls me on top of him. "What did you think of the house tour?"

"I think I need to do more cardio."

I feel the laugh rumble in his chest beneath my body, and his hands brush the hair out of my face. "I've been nervous about bringing you here."

"Why?"

"It's nothing like your house. There aren't pictures, the only trophies you'll see are Sasha's, and it's all a bit . . . I dunno. Cold."

Even as I quickly moved between rooms, it was hard not to notice how clinical everything feels. There aren't even any Christmas decorations anywhere, for fuck's sake.

I know his dad is an asshole, Nate's made that perfectly clear. But knowing your son is going to be home alone and not even putting a Christmas tree up? What about Sasha, who lived here all month? What if I'd stayed in Washington or California? He'd be in this huge, empty house alone.

A lump forms in my throat and I try to swallow it down, but it's no use.

His eyes widen, body freezing. "What's wrong?"

"I'm sorry," I cry, pushing myself to a seated position. "I don't mean to be an emotional wreck all the time, I just . . . *Fuck*. I'm just thinking about what it would have been like for you to be here alone. I'm so happy I'm here with you."

"Me, too."

Chapter Thirty-six

NATHAN

WHEN IS THE RIGHT TIME to tell someone you love them?

Falling in love was not what I expected to do this year. I've never been in love, and I don't know how I'm supposed to tell her without her running. She only said the word *boyfriend* out loud to other people a couple of days ago, and now suddenly I'm thinking of hitting her with those three words? I must be losing it.

But I can't help it, they're on the tip of my tongue constantly.

My anxiety might come from knowing it's been a series of unfortunate events that's brought us to where we are now—an incredibly fortunate situation—which doesn't happen very often. I feel lucky. That's the only word that seems appropriate because things could have gone the complete opposite direction.

I could talk for hours about her beauty. Describe every freckle, every faint line, every inch of her body. Anastasia is like the sun, warm and blindingly beautiful. But to be honest, it's not what makes her my person.

I'm in love with her determination and her commitment, her soft side, the way she manages to tell me exactly how she's feeling and why, no matter how uncomfortable it might make her at first.

She's taught me communicating doesn't mean everything is perfect, it doesn't mean we don't disagree. It means we work through the imperfect bit together, and if we don't agree, we at least know why the other feels that way, even if it's not going to change our minds. We're still individuals, but we're individuals together, and I never knew relationships could be like this.

Above all else, she cares about me and my happiness. She makes me study, she encourages me to talk about my mom; I could lie here and list all the things she does that push me to be the version of myself I want to be. She's my best friend.

I need to stop waiting for shit to go wrong because I know things aren't supposed to be perfect, and we're both stubborn and determined enough to fix the bits that aren't working for us.

It feels too early to be able to make those kinds of statements. *Shit*, it feels too early to be in love. Three and a bit months isn't long, but when we've spent as much time together as we have, I think I can be forgiven for my confidence.

I should definitely just tell her.

Dragging myself from my thoughts, I brush her cheek with my thumb. "We can get Christmas decorations if it makes you sad. We can go right now."

"It's not that. I don't care. I just hate the idea that you'd have arrived alone, and your dad didn't even bother putting a Christmas tree up for you. Or Sasha! Poor Sasha."

"They're hardly ever here. They're always at the resort," I explain. "It's not a big deal to me, I swear. But we can go and buy a Christmas tree if you want to. I didn't think. I know it's not like your parents' house. I should have prewarned you. I'm sorry."

"No, no. Please don't apologize to me. *I'm* sorry. I'll cheer up, I swear." She shakes it off and forces a smile, laughing when my brow furrows. Stas climbs off me and throws herself back onto the mattress. *"Oh my God."* She moans and my dick twitches in my pants. "This bed is divine. It's warm! How the hell is it warm?"

"I asked Betty to put the heated blanket on when she dropped off food."

"Is Betty your other girlfriend?" Raising her foot into the air, she tugs at her boot and launches it over the side of the bed.

"Betty is our housekeeper. She's about a hundred and she's worked for my family for years," I say, watching Stassie attempt to remove her other boot with great difficulty. "She refuses to retire, and she makes the best mashed potatoes in the whole world. She's great, you'll like her. We won't see her, though; I told her to take time off and spend it with her fami— Do you need help?"

She stops trying to remove her sweatshirt, which is also tangled in her hair and stuck on her watch. Her eyes peer at me over her arm. "I was trying to get undressed to seduce you, but *God* getting undressed in this climate is tiring. I should have pulled my pants down a little and bent over."

Her thrashing continues until she's free, but it only reveals another layer. I kick off my own boots and tug at my zipper, unwilling to be left behind. The main downside of being in the mountains is how long it takes to get naked. I made Anastasia layer up this morning before our flight, thinking the first thing she'd want to do when we got here would be to check out the lake, but I don't think it's even crossed her mind.

"Done!" she shouts, breathless but sporting a smug grin. "I beat you."

Only Anastasia Allen could turn getting naked before sex into a competition, then declare herself the winner. Climbing up the bed, propping herself against the headboard, she watches me watching her with a mischievous smirk on her face.

Finally kicking off my boxers, I crawl toward her, stopping when her foot presses against the center of my chest. Sitting back onto the heels of my feet, I grip her foot, pressing my mouth against her ankle as she giggles. "What's your prize for winning?"

Jumping when my teeth graze her skin, her lips pinch together as she pretends to think. "Hmm. Can you be my prize?" she hums, eyes shining when I nod. "I want to watch you touch yourself."

I almost choke.

Pulling her foot from my grip, she plants it on the bed, giving me the perfect view of her pink, wet pussy. I could spend hours trying to predict what Anastasia is going to say and do next, but I'd never be right.

"Don't look at me like that," I say, leaning forward to hover over her body. "Staring at me with those big doe eyes like you didn't just say you want to watch me jerk off."

Her chin tilts up, mouth searching for mine. She smells so good. How the hell does she smell so fucking good all the time? Sweet and delicious and maddening. Pulling her body to mine, I roll us over so I'm on my back, and position her so she's straddling my thighs. I'm already rock hard; how could I not be after what she just said? She immediately reaches for it, but I grip her wrist. "Hands behind your back, Allen."

She doesn't know where to focus as her eyes bounce between my face, my flexing stomach, and the hand fisting my cock. I groan her name, enjoying the surprising flicker across her face, quickly morphing into something darker.

Her hips squirm, looking for friction she isn't going to find with her legs spread wide by my thighs, and she fidgets as her eyes follow my fist up and down.

"You're so fucking hot," she rasps, eyes dark. "Let me touch you, please."

"But I'm giving you what you wanted." Reaching up with my free hand, I tweak her nipple between my fingers, and the moan she lets out is a mix of satisfaction and frustration. As I pump my hand faster, the pleasure begins to lick up my spine, tingling and building.

My eyebrow quirks with curiosity as she wiggles farther away from me. Placing a tentative hand on the bed beside my hips, she leans down, eyes locked with mine. She leans forward, hovering so she's not touching me.

"What're you doing?" I ask, reducing my hand to an agonizingly slow pace.

"What about if I don't use my hands? Can I touch you then?"

"Open your mouth, baby."

You'd think I'm the one in control of this situation, but you'd be wrong. I watch her, fucking mesmerized, as she licks and kisses from the base to just before the tip, pausing to watch me hold my breath, desperately wanting her to slip me into her hot, wet mouth.

She doesn't. I feel her hot breath on the tip, she's that fucking close, but she kisses and licks her way down to my balls, sucking on them softly.

Letting the breath I'm holding go, I drag my hand through my hair when her tongue swirls around me. "Fuck, you look so good."

She carries on teasing me, touching everywhere but the tip that's throbbing and glistening with precum. I know she's going to keep going until I'm at the point where I'm ready to fucking beg her.

I'm ready to beg now.

One final look at my tortured expression and she smiles, looking genuinely pleased with herself, and I'm ready to fuck the smugness off her face.

She slowly—and I mean slowly—lowers her mouth onto me, and I can't help but lift my hips to speed up the process. A satisfied *mhmm* vibrates against my dick, and she hollows out her cheeks and tries to suck the soul from my body.

Holy fucking shit.

Scooping her hair, I wrap it around my fist in a makeshift pony-tail, holding it tight, moving with the controlled motion of her head as she bobs up and down.

Her nails scrape down the inside of my thigh, causing me to flinch forward, hitting the back of her throat. For a split second I worry it might be too much for her, until her watery eyes watch me through thick, dark lashes, and even when she's noisily gagging on my dick, she looks smug. So I keep thrusting, deep and precise, as she hums happily, meeting every movement perfectly.

Don't tell her you love her during a blow job, you fucking loser.

My entire body trembles. "Baby, I'm going to come."

Her moan of approval sends a jolt through my body and she speeds up, sloppy, crazed movements, until an intense fire ignites in my blood, disintegrating my entire body.

"Fuckkkkk," is the only word left in my vocabulary when I spill myself down her throat.

Dazed and slightly light-headed, I watch her sit up and clean up the corner of her mouth with her thumb, sucking it into her mouth. My stomach heaves as I struggle to come back down to earth. We have a lot of sex, but I'm always too desperate to be inside of her, but that . . . That was—

God. I might have to propose to her.

Tugging her body to mine, she lands on my chest with a squeak, before moving to my side with her leg draped across my stomach. I press my lips to her forehead, holding her close, then slap my hand down on her butt, eliciting another squeak.

"What was that for?"

"How many times did you ask 'Are we there yet?' Hmm? Actions have consequences, Anastasia."

"Is that so?"

"Yup," I chirp, bringing my hand down again.

She maneuvers herself to be on her stomach and sticks her ass in the air a little, the shape of my hand glowing lightly. Her head twists to watch me, the same light pink flushing her cheeks. "Are we there yet, Nathan?"

ONE OF THOSE NICE THINGS about having the house to ourselves is being able to walk around naked.

I leave Anastasia sleeping peacefully in my bed, while I search the fridge for something to feed us. Taking an orange juice carton, I stand at the floor-to-ceiling kitchen window, overlooking the now frozen lake at the back of the house.

The white goes for miles, bright and untouched, making it unclear where the lake ends and the ground starts. I know, though; I know out there like the back of my hand. I've spent enough time on it, in it, around it over the years.

A warm body wraps around mine from behind, lips pressing in the center of my back affectionately. She steps around me, taking the juice carton and bringing it to her lips, leaning against my body while we both stare out.

"It's beautiful," she whispers.

"Not as beautiful as you."

"You're cheesy."

"Maybe. But I'm not wrong."

Chapter Thirty-seven

ANASTASIA

I HAVE THE OVERWHELMING URGE to tell him I love him every time he looks at me, and I don't know how to make it stop.

I'm scared it's going to come out by accident and that somehow, I'll burst this bubble we're happily floating around in.

I'm sure every new relationship starts with you thinking your partner is perfect, but mine is. He's attentive and affectionate, he makes me feel valued, and he strives to make me happy. Not in a materialistic or a frivolous way, but in a way where he actively works beside me, hand in hand, to try to make my life better. I don't imagine there are many men, college men at that, that look at the ugliest parts of you and want you anyway.

The irony is, if I were to say this to him, he'd tell me I didn't have ugly bits.

But I do, and I feel like they've been on display for weeks, constantly thrown in my face as a way to bring me down. Being here with Nathan, miles away from everyone, I feel like I can finally breathe, knowing I'm not going to get blindsided. Part of me wishes we didn't have to go back to LA at all, but somehow, I think the bubble will probably pop as soon as Nate's dad—my new archnemesis—gets home.

I can't imagine growing up somewhere like this; staring at the sprawling estate through the kitchen window with Nate took my breath away. It's all covered in snow, but even so, you can tell how big it is.

As stunning as it is, everything feels so vacant, and I'd give anything for a baby Nathan picture. *Anything*.

The ski resort has been in his paternal family for generations, passed from father to son. Nate prefers Nate or Nathan, but his full name is Nathaniel, named after the great-times-something-grandfather who founded the resort.

Nate has no interest in taking over; he hates that it would go to him because he's a man, arguing why would he want a ski resort when his sister is a skiing prodigy? He grumbled something about fucking the patriarchy and went back to whatever he was doing at the time.

The resort is only fifteen minutes from here, and I can see the tips of the buildings from Nate's bedroom. Nathan said I'm not allowed to ski while I'm here, since I've never done it before. He doesn't want me to risk hurting myself when I *hopefully* have a competition next month. He said we can come back in the future, and he'll take me on the bunny slopes with the little kids.

It felt good hearing him make plans for the future, and I could pretend I don't know why, but denial is useless at this point. Everything he says makes me melt, and half the time I don't know how to react, so I kiss him, then things escalate, and before I know it, I'm screaming his name and seeing stars.

Nathan's dick deserves an honorable mention in the list of his positive attributes. His mouth, too, and his fingers. Have I mentioned his body yet? And his face.

God, I should probably tell him all this and then say *I love you* and find one of the million rooms in this ginormous house to hide in.

I could hide for at least two days before he finds me.

"How willing are you to get dressed?"

I don't answer him straightaway, pretending I'm thinking about it, and that I don't know the answer is *not willing at all*.

"It's not the getting dressed bit. It's knowing I have to get undressed later."

"If I promise to undress you later, will you put your clothes on and come somewhere with me?"

I link my pinky with his. "Only because you promised."

Getting dressed is a lot easier than getting undressed, and within ten minutes Nate is dragging me toward his backyard, skates in hand.

"I can't believe this is the first time you've done this."

When Nathan said we could skate on the frozen lake in his backyard I assumed he was exaggerating a little, and I'd be skating on a little pond, but I should probably never underestimate him because this is *not* a little pond.

I can't work out where it ends, since it branches off into what looks like smaller streams through the trees. Nate taps on his phone until "Clair de lune" begins to play, and he gives me a smile that makes me dissolve a little. "Dance with me?"

We practice my routine until my body is sore and I can't see anything but my breath in front of me. There is something different and refreshing about being outdoors while doing it, but something is missing. I rack my brain, trying to put my finger on what it is, then I realize.

Brady. Nobody is shouting at us.

"Wait here," he says, skating off toward the house again. Reappearing a minute later, he's holding two hockey sticks and a tiny net. "Let's put all that rage you have to good use, Allen."

Finding out I'm terrible at hockey was not what I wanted this holiday season, especially given my company.

I'm not used to being bad at anything—especially on ice.

"Stop pouting," he teases, burying his head into my neck, his warm mouth a contrast to the bitter wind.

I don't stop pouting, not even when he lets me score against him twice.

"You are such a sore loser, Stas."

"You're literally a Division One hockey player! And you're fucking huge, you take up the whole goal!" I shout over the sound of his laughter.

He skates out to me and plants his front to my back, reaching around me to grip my hands on the stick, cheek flush against mine. "Practice makes perfect, Anastasia," he whispers, hitting the puck straight into the back of the net.

Okay, that was hot.

"Let's go inside; it'll be dark soon and I can sense that you're getting hangry." He pecks a kiss against my temple and takes the stick out of my hand.

"I'm beginning to think you know me really well, Hawkins." I sigh, spinning to wrap my arms around his waist. "I think I'll stick to figure skating."

His cheeks are flushed with the cold, the tip of his nose bright red, eyes glossy. I love seeing him at his childhood home, smiling, teaching me something he loves.

He reaches down to kiss the top of my woolly hat–covered head. "Of course I know you really well, Anastasia. You're my favorite subject."

NATE INSISTED ON COOKING DINNER, which gave me nothing to do other than sit in front of the fire in my snowman onesie, drinking a fancy wine from the wine cellar.

By the time dinner is over and we're sitting on the couch in front of *Home Alone 2*, I'm a little bit tipsy. Tipsy is fine, tipsy is fun, tipsy means that my camera roll is full of candid pictures of Nathan strutting around in his reindeer onesie and I can't stop giggling.

When I reach drunk, that's when we're going to have a problem, because I'm feeling exceptionally mushy, and there is a real risk that drunk Stassie is going to confess all her feelings. The irony that I encourage people to communicate and share, but I can't tell my own boyfriend I love him, isn't lost on me.

Nathan brings his beer to his lips, tilting the bottle up slightly, and I watch him like a creep. He must feel my eyes on him because he looks over, eyebrow raised slightly, then goes back to watching the movie. His hair is a little long right now, and he's got the start of little brown ringlets at the nape of his neck. It's so cu—

"Why are you staring at me?" he grumbles, tugging me closer.

The proximity to him is more intoxicating than the wine. He smells great. Exceptionally and overwhelmingly great.

"Anastasia?"

I sigh and take a glug of my wine, prolonging the silence. How do I say what's in my head without sounding obsessed? I'm a bit obsessed, but I can't let him know that.

"You're just really fucking pretty, Nathan. It's super hard to concentrate sometimes, do you know that? Do you understand how difficult it is sometimes to focus on literally *anything* when you're around me looking effortlessly beautiful?"

His eyes widen at my confession, and his cheeks blush a little. *Oh my God*, I think I've embarrassed him. I should probably feel more embarrassed than I do but watching the blood rush to his cheeks and him avoiding eye contact, scratching nervously at his jaw, is too good.

"Uh," he mumbles, threading his fingers through the hand not clinging to my wineglass, bringing the back of it to his lips. "Right back atcha, Allen."

The movie finishes and he changes the channel to sports highlights, stretching out on the couch until he's horizontal, holding out his arm for me to curl up beside him. Butterflies flutter around in my stomach as I look down at him, so relaxed and settled. This feels like a sneak peek at my future, cuddling in front of a hockey game, drinking wine in a house surrounded by snow.

"Would you ever want to move back to Colorado?" I ask.

"Christ, no."

"Why do you hate your dad so much?" *God, I'm unstoppable this evening, what is wrong with me?* "I'm sorry, you don't have to answer that. I know you've told me some stuff, it just feels like there's more to it."

His arm reaches out and tucks a strand of my hair behind my ear, pausing to cup my cheek. "You can ask me anything, Stas. I'm not sure *hate* is the right word," he explains. "My mom was sick for a long time before she died, and he hired all these private nurses to look after her so she was very comfortable, but he hardly saw her. He buried himself in work. Betty made dinner and he'd show up to eat then disappear again. He saw Sasha on the slopes but other than that, it was like he was a ghost."

I put my hand over his and give it a squeeze. I already know that Nathan's mom, Mila, died of a rare blood disorder when he was in eighth grade.

"Long story short, he was cheating on his dying wife with a twenty-five-year-old ski instructor from the resort." I feel sick as I absorb his words, my heart instantly breaking for teenage Nate. "I suspect it'd been going on long before she got sick. Then a few years later, when Robbie had his accident, it was at the resort. His medical bills were astronomical, and the Hamlets are wealthy, with good insurance, but Dad wouldn't help, even though that's what the company insurance is for."

I already knew that Robbie was injured in a skiing accident, but it never occurred to me that it might be here. How do you even navigate that as a teenager?

"He was convinced they were going to sue and bankrupt him; he was acting so strange. He buried his head in the sand over it for weeks until Mr. H had no choice but to get a lawyer involved, which he'd never wanted to do. The Hamlets loved my mom, and they've always treated me like a son."

"That's so awful," I whisper, squeezing his hand even tighter.

"I won't forgive him for those things. I think he feels guilty now, all these years later. I think I've already told you Dad owns our house in Maple Hills—he bought it at the end of freshman year. He paid for our garage to be converted into a room for Robbie. Wheelchair-accessible bathroom and all the shit he needs. It was strange, we'd been struggling to find somewhere suitable to live, and suddenly I got a phone call to say he'd bought a house on Maple Avenue, and it'd be renovated in time for sophomore year."

"I'm sorry, Nathan. That's . . . a lot."

He gives me my favorite smile and pulls me to his warm body, tightening his arms around me and kissing my forehead. "It's okay, there are people that have it far worse than me. I'm not ignorant enough to think I'm not completely privileged, and it's the definition of first-world problems. But he's taught me everything not to do as a dad . . . so our kids will be fine. Wait no, wait, that didn't come out right. Oh God."

Now it's my turn to blush. He's stilled beneath me and neither of us is saying anything. What the fuck do you say to that exactly? Wine-drunk Stassie is not the person for this conversation because for some reason what's in my head is not what comes out of my mouth. "I want to adopt."

He clings to me a bit tighter. "Sounds good to me."

"I always wanted to anyway but pushing out your big-ass baby would absolutely wreck my vagina. Like, totally destroy it."

"Noted."

I'M STILL HALF ASLEEP WHEN I roll over and reach toward Nathan's side of the bed, finding a piece of paper instead of him.

Running a top-secret errand, but I won't be long.
Enjoy snooping.
N
PS I made you a smoothie, it's in the fridge

I have so many options of things to do I don't know what to do first. Starting with the smoothie, I stand in my new favorite spot, looking out at the back of the house. It looks like something out of a Christmas card it's that beautiful. It doesn't feel like real life.

It takes me all of ten seconds to realize what I want to do. Rushing to find my skates and jacket, I head out of the door toward my new favorite rink.

I'm not even dancing, I'm just enjoying the view, which is when I spot a deer watching me from the woods in the distance. Living in LA for the past few years has sucked after being spoiled by living in Washington my whole life.

The closest thing to wildlife in Maple Hills is frat row.

It walks across the frozen ground, running between the trees, so I skate a little closer. I forgot to ask Nathan where this part of the lake leads to, but it's straight out of a movie the way the trees are overhanging with tiny frozen drops hanging from each branch.

The deer is still watching me from the trees as I get to the edge of the woods, but then my phone rings and it races off. I pull off my glove and bring the phone to my ear, unimpressed. "Hello?"

"Hey, where are you?" Nate asks. "I just got back, and I can't find you."

"I'm trying to make friends with a deer, but your call scared it off," I grumble, scanning the trees.

"A deer? Where are you?"

"Skating by the edge of the woods. I was going to have a Snow White moment and everything."

"Anastasia, it isn't safe—"

But I don't hear the rest of what he has to say.

Because the ice cracks beneath my feet and the water paralyzes my entire body the second my head goes under.

Chapter Thirty-eight

NATHAN

I NEVER WANTED TO BE the man fighting his way through a store on Christmas Eve, but here I am.

I'm surrounded by panicked-looking men, frantically pointing at every surface, clearly buying things they were supposed to buy weeks ago.

I'd ordered Stassie's main present to be delivered to the house, so I didn't have to try to travel with it, but the delivery driver arrived when Sasha wasn't in, and Dad rejected the delivery, saying it was a mistake.

So it's been two weeks of arguing with various companies, but they finally emailed last night to say I could pick it up in the store, meaning I reluctantly dragged myself here.

I know she's going to lose her shit about how much iPads cost, but I have thought this through. And she can't be mad if I've thought it through, right?

She does therapy through video calls since her doctor is in Washington, but because she doesn't have her own, she has to borrow Lola's. I can't always let her borrow mine because I use it to take notes in class and it's got my entire schedule built into it.

That brings me to the second bonus: a digital planner. I already know that her planner evolved from a sticker chart, but I feel like it's time for it to evolve again. I think—no, I'm *convinced*—that if she can easily move around her plans—like she'd be able to with a iPad—she'll be more inclined to be flexible with herself.

It's some psychology shit, I know, but once she stops stressing about it and uses it, it'll be a gift she can benefit from.

I understand her worry. Our disposable income is not the same, they're not even close. She once said she couldn't skip work because "we don't all have trust funds," and she's right. I'm not expecting her to buy me something expensive, though. I'm not expecting her to buy me anything because her being here is more than enough.

She sobbed at the idea of me being alone on Christmas. I have a girlfriend who cries over my hypothetical unhappiness. How is this real life? She must care about me a lot, or that's what I've convinced myself, anyway, so I'm going to tell her I'm in love with her tomorrow. Christmas feels like the right time to be expressing feelings, right?

Right?

The drive back to the house takes far too long for my liking. There isn't any traffic, I'm just impatient and itching to get back to my girl. I wonder how much of the house she's snooped through while I've been gone. I'm fully expecting her to be in the living room with a collection of things she wants an explanation for when I get back. I know she's desperate to see some baby pictures, or at least some evidence that I was once a child, since there aren't any pictures of me in the house.

Luckily, she's nowhere to be found when I finally walk through the door, which gives me the chance to stash the bag under my bed, ready to be wrapped later.

I plod through the rest of the house, listening out for her, but each place I check, she's not there. Eventually, having lost all patience, I pull out my phone and tap her name.

"Hello?" she huffs.

"Hey, where are you?" I ask, trying to listen for a response over the sound of wind on her side of the phone. "I just got back, and I can't find you."

"I'm trying to make friends with a deer, but your call scared it off," she grumbles quietly.

"A deer? Where are you?"

"Skating by the edge of the woods," she says, making my heart sink to my stomach. "I was going to have a Snow White moment and everything."

I feel sick as I start rushing to the back of the house, heading toward the lake as quickly as my body will take me. "Anastasia, it isn't safe. Carefully move away from there."

But I don't think she hears me, because the phone goes dead and, in the distance, I hear a bloodcurdling scream.

THEY SAY THAT WHEN SOMETHING traumatic happens, time stands still, but I don't agree.

I can feel every single second fly by me as my boots crunch into the snow. Every thought in my head seems to be occurring at the exact same time and I can't concentrate through the chaos.

She's strong, she's so fucking strong, and she can swim; I've seen her swim with my own eyes. The luminous orange life ring catches my eye as I approach the lake. Mom made Dad install it when Sasha started walking; she was terrified that having this much water so close by was an accident waiting to happen. I tug it off its stand and carry on toward the woods.

I couldn't even say how long it's been since I heard her scream.

The life ring is bouncing off my hip and I'm sprinting faster than I ever have before, my breath in front of me clouding my view, but then I see it. A big gaping hole in the ice, fractured pieces floating around on the water. Every safety video, article, or presentation—

anyone with a bit of common sense—will tell you that you don't run on thin or uncertain ice. But I'm not uncertain, I know this water better than anyone, which is how I knew she was in danger.

I fall to my knees where I know the ice thins and crawl toward the hole; my heart is beating so hard it might beat right out of my chest. The only thing I can think is, *For fuck's sake*, please *be alive*.

I'm inches from where the ice has splintered when the water begins to ripple, and her head emerges, her terrified eyes locking with mine before her head submerges again. She's panicking. *I'm* fucking panicking as I reach my arm into the water, feeling for any part of her that I can latch on to.

Nothing.

I'm trying to keep my weight even, off my front, all the shit I'm supposed to do as I throw the ring onto the water, hoping that somehow she can find it. Going in after her isn't the smartest decision—my body could go into shock, too, but it's the only one I have right now, so not being weighed down by clothes is the best way for me to survive this.

For us both to survive this.

My jacket is off when the rope of the life ring starts to move beside me. I roll over, careful not to crack the ice beneath me, and gasp when I see her tiny hand clinging to the edge of the ring, skin blue against the bright orange surface. Her other hand joins it and I see the crown of her head, so I pull the rope and watch her travel to the edge.

"Stas, are you okay? Can you say something? You need to hold on, I'm going to pull you out," I tell her frantically, voice wobbling with every syllable.

Nothing.

I shuffle backward, moving myself closer to safer ground, ignoring the sting of the cold through my clothes, pulling the rope tightly until I feel the resistance of her body against the edge. I'm panting, swearing, close to tears, but I keep tugging and finally, *finally*, her body begins to slide across the ice. I keep going until I see her skates and I know her whole body is out. When we're far enough away from the danger, I stand and rip the ring off her, rolling her onto her back.

Her lips are blue, delicate features deathly pale with her eyes closed tight.

"Anastasia?" I cry, pressing my ear to her to listen for a murmur, a breath, anything.

She isn't breathing.

My body starts moving on its own, tilting her chin up and pinching her nose, lowering my mouth to hers, and blowing until her chest rises. I tug at the zip of her jacket, but it's frozen, so I pull until it splits apart, placing my linked hands on her sternum, pressing down rhythmically until it's time to blow again.

Her chest rises and falls, but then it rises again, and she begins to splutter, coughing and retching, choking out all the water.

"Oh my God. I thought I'd lost you," I whisper, scooping her up in my arms. Her eyes close again, but she's breathing on her own, which gives me enough time to cover her in the coat I'd pulled off earlier and run toward the house.

Taking two stairs at a time, I speed toward the bathroom, wanting more than anything to stop her violently shivering in my arms. She still hasn't said anything; I have no choice but to place her on the bath edge to pull off her skates. Ensuring she's stable, I turn toward the shower to turn it on at the right temperature.

"Nate," she whispers, lips a slightly more human shade compared to the blue.

"I'm here," I try to reassure her, desperately trying to keep the emotion from my voice. I usher her under the warm water, focusing on the center of her body, wincing when she hisses and begins to cry. "I know it stings. I'm so sorry, baby." The shower is only on a mildly warm setting, but to her, it'll be like standing under a boiled kettle.

Stripping off her coat and sweatshirt, I wish more than anything that we could go back in time to yesterday, when undressing her was fun and filled with laughter.

She lifts her arms slowly, allowing me to rid her of underlayers. "You're doing so good, Stas, so good. I'm so fucking proud of you; it's going to be okay. We will get you warmed up and I'll get you a doctor. You're okay."

I up the temperature a little and crouch to pull off her pants and socks until she's naked under the spray, her skin still freezing cold under my hands.

The adrenaline is subsiding, the reality of what happened kicking in as she stands before me sobbing, holding on to her body. I shed my own clothes until I'm naked, too, and step toward her, pulling her body to mine, cranking the temperature up a bit more, trying to soothe her as she cries.

Her head tilts up and her eyes meet mine properly for the first time—they're swimming in tears, but the terror from earlier is gone, replaced with confusion. "I thought I was going to die."

I can't stop my own eyes from streaming, because I thought she was going to die, too.

I press my lips against hers gently, letting my forehead rest against the crown of her head when we break apart. "I promised you I'd never drop you or let you drown, Anastasia. I will always be there to save you."

Her arms tighten around my waist and her breath hitches as I turn the shower up a little more. The color is returning to her cheeks and the tears are slowing down. She gnaws on her lip as I wipe beneath her eyes.

"I love you, Nathan." She coughs a few times, trying to clear the raw, gravelly sound. "And this isn't some, I don't know, trauma response. I'm in love with you, and that's what I thought when I fell through that ice. How I've known for so long and I hadn't even told you. How I was going to die and you weren't going to know, and I was so mad at myself. I love you and I'm sorry I didn't tell you when I realized."

Three times she said it and my brain still hasn't processed it.

"I love you, too," I finally manage to stammer out. "I'm so fucking in love with you, Anastasia."

I WAKE FROM MY NIGHTMARE with a jump, frantically looking around me. Stassie is fast asleep, hooked up to multiple machines that tell me she's okay, not dead like she was in my dream.

Vail Health Hospital is not where I was expecting to wake up on Christmas morning, but I wasn't expecting my girlfriend to drown, either, so I'll let the impromptu trip to the ER slide.

As soon as she stopped shivering, I re-dressed her with as many layers as her fragile body could support and bundled her into the car to take her to the hospital.

I was expecting to be yelled at for not calling an ambulance, which is what I should have done, but I imagine they took one look at my stressed face and thought better of it.

The doctor commended me for safely bringing her body temperature back up and gave her the all clear after checking her over.

She heard "all clear" and thought it was time to go home, not realizing that neither the medical staff nor I was letting her go anywhere. I haven't left her side since yesterday; I even resorted to waving my card around until the hospital upgraded her and provided me with a bed for her room so I didn't need to leave.

The bed is still perfectly made, because as soon as we were alone, I climbed in beside Stas. I pretended to be asleep when the nurse came in to check her vitals so she wouldn't make me get out.

"Merry Christmas," Stassie whispers.

"Good morning, baby," I say, kissing her temple. "How're you feeling?"

"Like I don't need to be attached to a fluid drip and I'd rather be at home with you in our onesies." Her fingers dig into my sides playfully. "I feel good, Nathan, I promise. It's Christmas, can we please get out of here?"

"Not until you've been looked over."

"I've been looked over. I'm a picture of health, let's go."

My eyes flit to the fluid line sticking out of her hand. "Oh yeah, you look it."

"At least I'm not dead." She giggles at my shocked face. "Too soon?"

"It's always going to be too soon."

Chapter Thirty-nine

ANASTASIA

THE PAST WEEK HAS BEEN the epitome of calm after the storm.

After my Christmas-morning debate with Nate about my health status, he threaded his fingers through mine and brought the back of my hand to his lips. "Shut up, Anastasia. Let me take care of you, please."

The hospital bed wasn't as comfortable as Nathan's huge heated one, and the poking and prodding weren't the types I'm used to. Everyone was very nice to me, not once judging me for the senseless decision I made to venture out onto unsafe ground alone.

I was physically and mentally exhausted but in good spirits under the circumstances. He practically forced the doctor to look over me one more time while the nurse removed my fluid line. "Protective, isn't he?" The nurse chuckled.

"Very." I nodded in agreement. "It's because he cares, though, so I don't mind."

"Ah, young love."

Even after the most traumatizing day and a night of shitty sleep, when he looked over from the desk where he was collecting my discharge papers, his smile made my entire body hum happily.

The drive back to the house was quiet, George Michael on the radio and Nate tapping along to the tune on my thigh. He looked over at me as we pulled up at a stoplight. "What're you smiling about?"

"Do you remember singing this drunk in the shower?" I said, thinking back to Nathan screeching "Last Christmas" at the top of his lungs two weeks before.

"Hey!" He squeezes my thigh. "As soon as the night is over you have to forget about drunk shenanigans. Those are the rules, Allen." He snuck a look over at me again, grinning wide. "I love you."

I place my hand over the one warming my thigh. "I love you, too."

We arrived back at the house late morning, both too tired to make an effort for Christmas, and that turned into the theme of the week. The relief of being back in Nate's bed didn't last as long as I'd hoped, and the reality of the seriousness of what happened started to hit me.

Calling my parents from Nate's phone was the starting point. I realized my phone was at the bottom of the lake, and they'd be trying to get hold of me to wish me Merry Christmas. Mom and Dad freaked the hell out, and I had to talk them out of flying here by convincing them I was fine.

The nightmares are intense, but when I wake up in a pool of sweat, terrified, Nathan is always there to lull me back to sleep. If hockey doesn't work out for him, he'd make a great nurse. Each day he's taken me to the resort spa, booking me for treatment after treatment, making sure that there isn't an inch of me that isn't relaxed.

Even now, a week later, every fire in the house is burning because he's worried I'm going to get sick. The benefit of that is he's already a human radiator, so the addition of the fire means he's had to strip down to his boxers to stay cool.

I'm enjoying the view, and being obsessed with watching Nate stroll about is helping me feel more like myself.

"Stop looking at my ass," he shouts from inside the fridge. His head is practically resting on the shelf, and he's pretending that he's searching for something to eat, but in reality, I think he's trying to cool down. He didn't think it through when he decided to turn this house into the inside of an oven, but he wouldn't listen to me when I said I'm fine, meaning it this time.

"The lake is pretty cold, if you want to cool off," I shout back at him.

The fridge door slams shut and he spins to face me, looking annoyed. His annoyed face is so cute. Is he supposed to be scary with his pouty lips and furrowed brow? If this is what he does during a game, he's not going to be putting the fear in anyone. "Not funny."

Stomping through the archway between the kitchen and living room, he throws himself down beside me on the couch. I crawl into his lap, brushing his hair back and planting a kiss lightly on his forehead. "Hey, grumpy. It's over, okay? I'm safe. You saved me and I'm perfectly healthy. I'm roasting alive in this heat, but I'm good."

"You promise?"

"I promise. Do you want to open the Christmas presents? We probably should before the year is over." Neither of us has been feeling particularly festive, so all our gifts are still in the suitcase.

"I thought you gave me my present already."

Rolling my eyes, I climb off him. "Coming inside of me is not a freaking Christmas present, Nathan."

"It makes me feel jolly when I do it."

He narrowly avoids the cushion I pick up and throw in his direction, muttering something about me not making the dodgeball team. With my hands on my hips, I huff, "Will you just get the present suitcase, please? I need to do something upstairs."

I ignore the strange look he's giving me and run toward the stairs, sprinting up each step until I'm pushing his bedroom door open and rummaging through his wardrobe for the bag that I hid when we got here.

I do what I need to do, pull on a robe, and rush back downstairs. He unpacked all the presents and put them into piles, and now he's patiently waiting by his pile with his legs crossed.

"You ready?"

We work in unison, ripping apart the rest of the presents, drowning in a pile of gifts from our loved ones until all that's left is the ones we bought for each other.

"I didn't buy you a lot," I preface, handing over the bag of gifts. "Start with that one with the blue ribbon, but, uh, yeah. You're super hard to buy for, has anyone ever told you that?"

He hands me an identical bag and leans over the pile of torn wrapping paper, pressing a kiss to my lips lightly. "You are my greatest gift, Anastasia."

I tear into the first present and find two pairs of the prettiest pajamas I've ever seen. "You said you wanted something to wear around the house and I couldn't choose . . ."

"I love them, Nathan. Thank you," I say, running my fingers across the satin. "Your turn." He pulls the paper apart until the leggings fall into his lap. He holds up the leopard and zebra leggings and raises an eyebrow. "I also couldn't choose . . ."

We go back and forth, unwrapping and laughing until he puts his hands behind his back. "I forgot about this, so I haven't had time to wrap it, so close your eyes and hold out both hands."

"If it's your dick, Na—"

"Shut up and do it, please," he grumbles, rustling around. I follow his instruction, holding out both hands as he places something heavy on my palms. "Okay, open your eyes."

My eyes widen immediately as I stare down at the iPad box. He's nervously nibbling on the corner of his thumb, his knee bobbing, staring at me expectantly. I don't know what to say, so I stare at it.

"Are you mad?"

Shaking my head quickly, my voice breaks as I speak. "No."

"Do you like it? It's so you always have it for therapy and there's this cool app I'm going to download for you. It's a digital planner and you can do school notes an—"

"Nate, I love it. I'm just shocked at how generous you are. I don't know what to say, thank you so much." He bought me a freaking iPad so I'd always be able to speak to my therapist—how is he real? "Seriously, thank you."

"You're welcome, baby. I'm so fucking relieved you like it," he admits, blowing out a sigh. "Okay, the last gift. Let's go."

For the last time, I watch him tear off the wrapping paper and remove the lid to the gift box. His mouth pulls into a straight line, and he looks at me inquisitively. "It's empty?"

I move onto my knees and slowly untie the robe I'm wearing until it falls off my shoulders and pools on the floor behind me.

"I kind of cheated, it's sort of more of a gift for me, but I thought you'd like it." The Titans jersey is a little big on me but only enough to cover the tops of my thighs. His eyes are practically black as they rake up and down me. "I haven't even shown you the best bit." Shuffling until my back is facing him, I pull my hair over my shoulder.

"Hawkins," he says, with a softness in his voice I haven't heard before. "You have my name on your jersey."

I lean forward so the jersey rides up my ass, just revealing enough to prompt him into action.

"You look so fucking good, Anastasia. *Jesus.*" After a week of being treated like I'm made of glass, feeling his body push up against mine is a *very* welcome change. His mouth runs up the side of my neck as his hand slips beneath the hem. "I wanna fuck you with this on, okay?"

"Yes, Captain." His hand palms my ass and the excitement floods me. "I have an idea. Can you lie down on the kitchen island?"

Chapter Forty

NATHAN

WHEN ANASTASIA POSTED A MOTIVATIONAL picture this morning saying *The day is only as good as you make it*, I thought it was going to be another example of my grumpy girl catfishing the internet with her pretend positivity.

But apparently, New Year's Eve makes her happy, and now I'm lying naked on the kitchen island, and my hands are tied above my head with a Christmas present ribbon.

To be totally honest, I'm not sure how I ended up in this position. My girlfriend is a creative visionary—she claims—so when she told me to drop my boxers and lie on the counter, I did it with zero hesitation.

What can I say? I'm a weak man.

I doubt there's a guy out there who would've stopped to question what was happening if their girl was wearing their jersey with no panties on. I'm basically putty in her very talented but very bossy hands.

I can hear her rummaging in the refrigerator. "Stassie, what are you doing?"

"Patience is a virtue, Hawkins," she chirps, clanging what sound like jars against each other.

"I'm not feeling very virtuous right now, Anastasia," I gruff, tugging against the ribbon. "Quite the opposite."

Her feet patter softly against the tiles. Placing whatever she's selected beside me out of my view, she climbs up onto the counter, then on top of me, straddling my hips. She hasn't even done anything and I'm hard, resting against the warmth of the apex of her thighs. Wiggling against it, she moans quietly, eyes fucking sparkling as she looks down at me. Her eyes rake down my body. "You're so fucking hot."

Stassie calls me beautiful all the time, even when I've just woken up. At first, I was a bit taken aback. I'm not sure what it was in the beginning; I sort of had it ingrained in my head I was supposed to be the one complimenting her, and trust me I do, but it turns out I like hearing it.

It's not just beautiful; she calls me kind and smart, among so many other things. Hearing her ramble about how much she likes me for me, how special I am to her, is beyond what I ever thought I should expect in a relationship.

But hearing her call me hot while she's got me tied up and my hard dick is rubbing between her legs is a whole other level of *I fucking love my girlfriend.*

Reaching out of my line of sight, I hear the signature sound of a lid pop. The excitement is practically buzzing in my blood when I spot the can of whipped cream in her hand. Bringing the nozzle to her mouth, her eyes roll back, and she squirts it onto her tongue. *"Mhmm."*

My hips flex forward, nudging against her wetness. Her mouth lowers to mine, the sweet residue of the cream on her tongue.

She sits back up, hand reaching back for the cream, immediately squirting it along the indent of my abs. Before I can even complain about how cold it is, her mouth descends and she licks her way up my body, smirking up at me when she feels my dick twitch.

Her hips move back and forth, sliding me between her folds. My hands strain against the ribbon and my body wiggles underneath her impatiently. "I need to be inside of you."

She tsks and picks up a new jar. "Not until you beg me, Hawkins."

As I'm about to snipe back, the alarm rings, telling me the front door was opened.

"Nate?" Sasha shouts, her voice ringing out loudly across the house.

Anastasia's eyes widen, all the blood draining from her face instantly. "What the fuck?"

Tugging at my hands until they're free, the pair of us scramble off to the floor, and I put my boxers back on.

"Wait a minute, Sash!" I shout, moving Stassie in front of me. The kitchen door flies open, and Sasha looks between me and Stassie frantically.

"Ew!" she squeals. "Were you two . . . Yuck! Nate! I cook in here. Oh my God!" Her nose scrunches, face twisting in disgust. With her head turned away, she shivers. "You must be Stassie. I'd hug you, but I think it'd be awkward for everyone."

Stas shuffles nervously, head hung low so her long hair hides her pink cheeks, but she nods and holds up a hand to wave.

This is not how I wanted the two most important women in my life to meet each other for the first time.

"What the fuck are you doing here, Sasha? You're supposed to be in St. Barts."

"I've been calling and texting you, jackass. You didn't answer," she huffs, folding her arms across her chest, still looking away. "Do you want me to bore you with the details of our father's latest betrayal, or would you prefer to let your girlfriend put on some pants, y'know, before Dad brings the bags in from the car?"

Betrayal? "Gimme five. We'll be right back," I promise, nudging a mortified Anastasia toward the staircase that isn't going to walk her straight into my Dad's line of sight.

"You're so rich you have two staircases," Stassie whispers.

"I'll humble myself for you and buy us a house with only one set of stairs. Will that make you happy?" I tease, squeezing her ass when it bounces in front of my face as we climb the stairs. "I'm so sorry about this, baby. I can't remember the last time I looked at my phone."

We reach my room, and she immediately finds her panties and a pair of jeans, tying her hair back up into a ponytail. I approach her from behind, wrapping my arms around her waist and burying my head into her neck, inhaling the smell of honey and strawberry I love.

She sighs and sinks back into my chest, tilting her face up to kiss me. "Your dad is going to hate me, isn't he?"

I can feel the anxiety rolling off her—it's written all over her face, it's in her posture, in the desperation of her kiss.

"Anastasia, listen to me. You do not need to worry about the opinion of that man. I love you and I will be counting the minutes until I get to get you away from him."

"So that's a yes, then," she says, shaking off my embrace. She waits on the bed and watches me get changed into jeans and a sweater. I hate that he's here, that he managed to burst our bubble. We're going back to Maple Hills tomorrow evening, and we were *so* close to having a perfect week. No drownings, no fighting, and no parent.

"You changing?" I ask, eyeing her jersey.

"Your dad ever watched one of your games?" She nods knowingly when I shake my head. "Then no, I'm not changing. Okay, let's get this over with. And Nate, I love you, too."

Sasha is snacking away on chips with *Criminal Minds* blasting from the TV when we return downstairs, entering the living room hand in hand.

"He went to the resort," she says, not looking away from her show. "He wants us to meet him for lunch in an hour."

Great.

"Anastasia, this is Sasha, my baby sister," I say, trying to make this less weird. "Sash, this is my girlfriend, Stassie."

I finally steal her attention from the TV, but I instantly regret it when she raises a perfectly sculpted eyebrow. "Why are you acting like we haven't met? I caught you two doing it in the kitchen, like, ten minutes ago . . ."

"Jesus, Sasha," I whine, raking a hand through my hair. "That's not what was happening. Can you be nice?"

"Tell that to the can of whipped cream, Nutella, and strawberry sundae sauce on the counter," she says with a snort.

As soon as she rhymes off the contents on the counter, I'm instantly more irritated realizing what just got interrupted.

"And I *am* being nice. Be glad it was me and not Dad." She turns her head to Stassie. "I *am* nice, I promise. I'm not judging you—well, other than for dating my awful brother."

I throw myself on the couch across from Sasha, and Anastasia awkwardly hovers on the spot. I pat the seat next to me until she sits, but her temperament is off; she seems uncomfortable. I fucking *hate* that she seems uncomfortable after how good our time here has been.

"Why are you back? I thought you weren't back until the day after tomorrow. It's the whole reason our flights are tomorrow."

"Charming." She grunts, turning down the volume of the TV and crossing her legs over. "It wasn't a vacation, it was a retreat for body conditioning to 'make me stronger' and, I don't know, some bullshit about being a better athlete. I spent a total of one hour on the beach. Yesterday I told him if he didn't take me home I'd never ski again, so he booked us on the next flight out of there."

I wish I could pretend to be surprised for her sake, but I'm not; in fact, this is exactly the type of shit I would have guessed if I hadn't been so preoccupied lately. But I foolishly believed he might have listened to my suggestion.

My father always has an agenda. This afternoon is another plot, because why else would you meet someone for the first time in a public place when they're already in your home?

"What type of mood is he in?"

"His usual. Like someone stuck a very big stick up his ass and he can't get rid of it." She gives Stassie an almost menacing smile. "You have any experience with overbearing parents?"

She laughs for the first time since Sash arrived home. "My parents are super nice, sorry."

Sasha sits and quizzes Stas about every single thing in her life, and to her credit, Stas answers everything honestly. By the time we're pulling up to the resort, the pair of them are the best of friends. It helps they have a common interest; now, you'd think the common interest would be being sporting prodigies, but no, it's grinding my gears for fun.

I don't get to see Sasha enough without Dad and I miss her so much. I miss the person she is when he's not around; I almost feel sad for Anastasia that the person she just made friends with is about to disappear the second Dad sits at the table. I hope she understands, and she can tell it isn't personal.

"You good?" I ask Anastasia quietly, looking at our joined hands where she's cutting off the circulation to the tips of my fingers. The maître d' walks us over to Dad's favorite table and offers us the menus. Unsurprisingly, he's late for a lunch he organized.

"I'll have a glass of Dom Pérignon, please," Sasha says, browsing the menu casually.

The guy looks at me panicked, clearly knowing who we are and not sure what the right answer is. I put him out of his misery, plucking the menu from Sasha's hands and bopping her on the head with it. "She's sixteen. Give her a juice box or something."

"She'll have a water," a deep and familiar voice says from behind me. "Hello, Nathaniel," he says coolly. "And who do we have here?"

Chapter Forty-one

ANASTASIA

WHAT'S MY NAME?

Why can't I remember what my fucking name is?

Ian Hawkins is standing beside me looking like Darth freaking Vader, with his hand outstretched ready to meet me for the first time, and I cannot remember what my goddamn name is. Nate's hand squeezes my knee; it should be a comfort, but it's reminding me that I'm not speaking when I should be.

"This is Anastasia Allen, my girlfriend. Stas, this is my dad, Ian Hawkins," Nate says calmly, moving his hand to thread it through mine.

Nate's dad looks like how I imagine Nate is going to look in thirty years. He's tall, sharp jawed with dark brown hair and big brown eyes. If he wasn't my new nemesis I might even admit that he's very handsome, but fuck that.

"Mr. Hawkins, it's nice to finally meet you," I manage to force out through the world's fakest smile, shaking his hand like we're politicians or something. He takes his seat directly in front of me and I can't wait to spend this lunch making awkward eye contact with him.

Although right now, he's more bothered about Sasha's outfit.

"You didn't want to get changed out of your plane clothes?" Ian says harshly. You can't tell that he's traveled for fifteen hours; his clothes are immaculate, hair perfectly in place. But with that one sentence, that one sneer in his teenage daughter's direction, I know everything I need to know about Ian Hawkins.

Her posture changes, she withdraws, her chin lowers. *I can't watch this.* "You look comfortable, Sasha. I wish I'd put my sweatpants on, too," I say as cheerfully as I can.

It's enough to capture his attention again—his eyes meet mine and I don't look away, as much as I might want to. I feel like I just invited him in, his criticisms, his judgment. I can see him sizing me up, it's clear in the way his eyes break from mine to scan my face, lowering to look at what I'm wearing. His mouth creeps up. "Tell me about yourself, Anastasia."

"What would you like to know, Mr. Hawkins?"

"Ian is fine, there's no need for formality. Judging by the way my son is cutting off the circulation to your fingers, I would speculate that he's quite attached to you," he says with a humorless chuckle. "How about we start with where you're from?"

"Seattle, Washington, originally. I've lived in Maple Hills for school for the last few years."

The drinks appear at the table, staff working efficiently and silently in the presence of their boss. Nate doesn't look away from his dad, scared to take his eyes off him, I think, but mutters a "Thank you," reaching for his Sprite with the hand that isn't crushing mine.

"You're welcome, Nate," a sickly-sweet voice says. We both look up at the same time, finding a beautiful blond woman placing a vase of water in front of Ian.

If I had to guess I'd say she was our age, pretty green eyes and a dazzling smile. She's looking at him with a familiarity, a *something* that makes my skin itch. An uncomfortable feeling settles in my stomach, and it whips my breath away when I realize that the feeling is jealousy. "I didn't know you were in town," she continues, completely ignoring my existence. "You should have said."

His fingers loosen and my heart sinks as he lets go of my hand, but instead he reaches toward me and tucks hair behind my ear, hand settling on the back of my chair with his finger tickling my shoulder. "You asked for no ice, didn't you?" he asks, nodding toward the drink someone put down in front of me.

I focus on the ice cubes floating and the condensation running down the side of the glass, instead of the woman Nathan has clearly had sex with at some point.

I need to stop, this is unnecessary. I don't feel like this when we're back in Maple Hills. Who he's had in his bed doesn't bother me there, but here, in front of his dad and sister, I feel the poker-hot envy creeping through my body. "What? Uh, yeah, it doesn't matter, though."

He picks up the drink and offers it to the girl. "She didn't want ice." His tone is sharp, far sharper than I've ever heard him be, and it feels weird to see him be so curt.

The girl looks taken aback as she accepts the glass from his hand, still not looking at me, but managing to look at Sasha, who's trying to hide her laugh behind her hand. Too much time passes without anyone talking.

"That's all, Ashley," Ian drawls, bored of this weird little situation going on. "Get Anastasia an iceless drink as she requested, and let Mark know we're ready to order food."

His harsh tone snaps her out of her daydream. "Yes, sir."

"And Ashley?"

"Yes, Mr. Hawkins?" she responds quickly, spinning back around to face him.

"Anastasia is part of this family and a guest. I'm going to pretend that you gave her the courtesy of actually looking at her and apologizing for the mistake, as you would with any other customer. Don't let it happen again or you'll find yourself starting the new year looking for a new job."

It's taking every muscle in my head to keep my jaw from hitting the floor. Nathan shuffles in his seat, reclaiming my hand with his. Ian pours himself a glass of water and takes a sip. "Where were we? School. What do you study?"

I tell him how I'm a junior studying business management, how I'm an only child, how I'm already twenty-one because I started school a year late after my adoption when I was five, and to his credit, he nods in the right places and asks follow-up questions.

My new drink arrives, Nate and Sasha sit quietly, probably grateful the attention isn't on them. I get a small moment of reprieve when our food orders are taken. Nate leans in, pressing his lips to my temple.

"What are you getting?" He lowers his voice to a whisper. "I'm so proud of you, baby. You're doing so well."

I don't get a chance to answer him, because Sasha tries to order a chicken burger and fries and her dad says no. "She'll have the chicken and cashew salad, dressing on the side."

"But Dad, I wa—"

"No, Sasha."

I hate this and every critical thought I've ever had about my parents weighs on me, crushing me with guilt, because my parents have never made me feel as shit as I do just watching him interact with Sasha. The words come spilling out of my mouth before I can stop them. "The world isn't going to end if she eats a burger."

For the first time since we sat here, I see a flicker of emotion on Ian's permanently indifferent face. His eyebrow creeps up and his lips purse, and suddenly, he looks nothing like Nathan. He doesn't have Nathan's soft eyes or mischievous grin that accompanies his eyebrow when it rises in surprise.

"Not that it's anything to do with you, but Sasha has a competition coming up. She needs to stick to her meal plan," Ian scolds.

"So do I, but one burger isn't going to derail her career. If she wants a burger, she should get one. I'm getting the burger," I snap back.

I don't know why I'm doing this, why I'm purposely riling up a man I want to like me, even if I don't like him. I can't help it. I want to protect her from all the thoughts that will plague her when it comes to eating, long after he stops choosing her meals.

I don't even want the freaking burger. I was going to order the salad.

Nate's hand squeezes my knee, a sign of alliance. "Can we get three chicken burgers, please, Mark? No salad needed."

Mark looks to Ian, who places his menu back on the table and gives a small nod of approval. When Mark heads back toward the kitchen, loudly blowing out a sigh of relief, I immediately feel the weight of what I just did. Sasha is looking at her drink, teeth nibbling the skin at the side of her thumb.

"I don't appreciate your insolence in front of my staff," Ian says flatly.

"Dad—" Nathan interjects.

"I'm talking to both of you," he gruffs. "You might have enjoyed your time here pretending to be in charge, but while you're eating in *my* restaurant and sleeping under *my* roof, you'll show me some respect."

Nate's body stiffens and I feel the tension brewing, but before it can progress Sasha speaks. "You're a figure skater, right? That's your sport, Stassie?"

And that's enough to capture Ian's attention, so we start the dance all over again.

NATHAN'S BEDROOM FEELS LIKE THE only safe place in the house right now.

Lunch could have been worse, I suppose, but it definitely could have been better. Nathan thinks it went well, which to me is weird and makes me seriously consider how bad things can get if this is an example of things being good.

Tonight there is a huge New Year's Eve party being thrown by Nate's dad, which the resort does every year for the guests who spend the holidays there, and our *presence is expected*.

As Nate snoozes against my stomach, I can't stop my mind from wandering to Mila Hawkins, Nate and Sasha's mom. How wonderful must she have been to produce kids like them, with a husband like that?

I remember weeks and weeks ago—before I realized how I had absolutely no chance to do anything but fall head over heels in love with this man—he told me he's the way his mom raised him. All in with his whole heart and head. Nate says she would have loved me—Lola, too—because she loved a strongheaded and determined woman.

That's how she was raising Sasha before she passed away. I can see the flickers of it in her when her dad isn't around, and I wish there were a way I could take Sash back to LA with us.

"Your thoughts are very loud sometimes," Nate grumbles from his spot on my stomach. He looks up, eyes sleepy and cheeks pink. "What're you thinking about?"

"The party," I lie.

"We're not going. It's pretentious and you'll hate it," he says, peppering kisses around my belly button. "This room has the best view of the fireworks anyway."

"Your girlfriend will probably spit in my drink, too."

He sighs heavily, resting his head against my skin before looking back up at me with a sad expression. "I wish there wasn't anyone before you, but I can't change the past. I can promise you there will be no one after you. She was never my girlfriend, though. We were kids. We went to high school together, hooked up sometimes when I came home for the holidays."

"I'm kidding, I swear. I'm sorry, I don't know why I feel jealous. I swear I don't feel like this normally and I don't care what you did before me, I promise I don't. I don't even think it's about sex, I think it's because she fits into the version of you that exists here. The one who wears snow boots and plays hockey on the lake in his backyard. You're so relaxed here and I caused the most stressful situation ever and I jus—"

"Anastasia," he says softly, interrupting my rambling. "I'm relaxed because you're here. This is the first time in years I've enjoyed being here, and that's solely because you are here with me. There isn't a version of me that is better without you by my side."

"I was thinking about your parents," I admit reluctantly. "How good your mom must have been for you to be the way you are."

He wiggles up my body until we're face-to-face and nuzzles my nose with his. "She was the best. I'm nothing like him, Stas. I swear I'll be so good to you. You'll never have to worry." The seriousness in his face pulls at my heart, and the idea that Nathan could ever be put in the same league as his dad is absurd.

"I know, Nate. I promise you that I know, and I don't doubt you for even a second. I'm very lucky and I don't take that for granted."

His mouth meets mine, soft at first, then more intense, more urgent as I sink my fingers into his hair and let him nestle his body between my legs. Love is pouring out of him, every touch soft and caring, every look and motion specifically designed for me, for us. And when he sinks into me, making me writhe beneath him, he whispers how much he loves me into my ear, how perfect I am for him, how he's the lucky one.

I lose count of how many times my body squeezes tight around his, how many times I bury my face into his chest, his neck, his pillow, how many times I have to stop myself from screaming his name. His fingers are deep in the flesh of my hips, guiding me as he buries himself so deep inside of me, I can feel him in my bones. His chest heaves, stomach flexes, pulse hammers against my lips on his throat.

And when he spills himself into me, he clings to me so tight that I'm not sure how we're ever expected to be two separate people ever again.

Chapter Forty-two

NATHAN

I LEAVE STASSIE *TETRIS*-ING OUR suitcases and head to the kitchen to grab her a drink, desperate to get out of the way so she doesn't ask me to help.

Pushing the door open, weirdly, the one person I'm not expecting to bump into is my dad. It sounds silly to say you bumped into someone in their own house, but he's never home.

I suspect he hasn't noticed me, too busy engrossed in whatever he's reading, but then he speaks. "What time are you leaving?"

"A couple of hours."

"I like her. She's strong willed. That's good. She'll need it if she wants to succeed. You love her?"

"Yes."

He nods to himself and finally looks at me, linking his hands and resting his chin on them. "She reminds me of your mom when I first met her. Bold, beautiful, not afraid of anything. She called your grandfather a pigheaded misogynist once, y'know." He smiles, and for the first time in so long, it feels genuine. "To his face as well. I almost choked on my drink, I was mortified, and when we argued about it, she challenged me to prove he wasn't a pigheaded misogynist."

I lean against the countertop, giving him my full attention, desperate to hear about Mom. "I didn't know that."

"I couldn't, obviously. Your grandfather was a bastard, for lack of a better name for him. He was very hard, and your mother didn't like it about him. I think she was the only person who'd ever stood up to him in his whole life. She was the only person who ever stood up for me, at least." He picks up the papers he was reading, and I think the conversation is over, but he puts them back down, sighing. "Anastasia loves you, too, that much is clear. A woman like her, one like your mom . . . she'll be fiercely loyal and protective. You're lucky."

"If Mom was so great, why did you do it?"

I don't need to clarify what *it* is. He knows what I'm talking about, even if I haven't said the words.

"Humans make mistakes, Nate."

"Some mistakes are unforgivable."

He nods. "I know."

Stassie burst into the kitchen, slowing when she spots the two of us on either side of the island. "Sorry to interrupt, I can jus—"

"What's up, Stas?" I ask politely, not wanting her to panic that I'm actually talking to my dad.

"I need you to sit on the case. It won't close and Sasha isn't heavy enough."

"I'll help in a second."

She nods, leaving as quickly as she arrived. I look back at my dad, but he's returned to whatever papers he was looking at earlier.

Right now, with the defeated slack of his shoulders and the blank expression on his face, I realize, for all his faults, no one can loathe him more than he loathes himself.

It feels bittersweet to be heading back to LA. Sure, putting a thousand miles between us and my dad is the best thing to do for everyone's sake, but I didn't get enough of watching Stassie go full big sister on Sasha.

I know I should be grateful for the day they did get together since we weren't supposed to see her at all, but I'm greedy. I'm greedy to see them both so happy in each other's company.

Stassie's New Year's resolution is to read more, so our entire flight back to California is spent with her nose buried deep in the book she bought at the airport.

"It's a reverse *Pretty Woman* retelling," she tells me excitedly. "She's autistic and she hires an escort to help her get better in bed. It's so good and Stella is so funny and cute."

I pinch the book from between her fingers, examining the turquoise cover, then flicking to a random page in the middle of the book. "You're reading porn in public? You're disgraceful!"

Her hand flies toward my mouth, shushing me as I throw my head back laughing. "Stop shouting," she rasps, looking around to see if anyone is listening to us. Her voice lowers, and she pulls me closer. "It's not *porn*. It's a romance book that happens to have a little bit of sex in it."

She tries to hide her face, but I hook my finger under her chin, tilting her face up to mine. I gently press my lips to hers, leaning into her ear to whisper. "Anything you read, I'll do to you when we get home."

When I lean back, I can see thousands of possibilities flashing across her face. "It's honestly not that kind of book . . . but I do have some at home that might be"—the flush of her cheeks intensifies—"of interest to you."

"I love a woman who enjoys reading."

"FUCK OFF, HAWKINS. YOU'VE HAD her for weeks, can't you share her for two freaking minutes?"

I wasn't even doing anything when Lola started hurling abuse at me. Well, I leaned over to kiss Stassie on her head as I passed the pair of them, but other than that I've left them alone. Henry, however . . .

"You're not the only one who needs to talk to her, Lola," he grumbles, crossing his arms and putting his big-ass feet on the coffee table like a petulant child. "I have stuff, too, y'know."

Crossing the room, winking at Stassie instead of going near her, because Lo fucking terrifies me, I throw myself down beside Hen. "S'up with you?" I hand him a beer while he looks at me like I've got two heads. "Your stuff? Can I help?"

"I don't have stuff . . . but I could have stuff if I wanted to have stuff. I could have more stuff than Lola. I could have more stuff than all you guys."

"No one has more stuff than Lola," Robbie whispers, looking over his shoulder to check she's not listening. "Both metaphorically and literally."

Catching up with the guys took all of fifteen minutes when we got home, but Lo can't do anything within fifteen minutes. Fifteen minutes is her minimum warm-up time.

After another hour of hushed conversation in the kitchen, Anastasia saunters over and squeezes her ass between me and Henry. "Did you have a nice Christmas, Henry?"

"You drowned," he says in response.

It stuns her a little and her head whips around to look at me, quickly looking back to Henry. "I know, but I'm okay now. Nathan pulled me out."

"You could have died." He's looking at his hands instead of her, and I don't know why I'm surprised. Henry loves Stas like she's his sister, and he's messaged me every day to check she's okay. I thought that was enough for him but clearly not.

"But I didn't and I'm here," she says softly, leaning her head against his shoulder.

He stands up quickly and heads to the kitchen, staring into the refrigerator for longer than he needs to. "Can we go to bed? I'm tired," she says to me quietly. I take one last look in Henry's direction and give her a nod, knowing the kid needs a bit of space.

Following her upstairs, we work as a team to wash, undress, and brush until we can tumble into bed. She snuggles into me, tracing her fingers across my chest. "I miss your bed."

"Want me to buy the same mattress?"

"No," she says, dragging out the *o* like she wants to say yes. "There's no point, you're graduating in six months. It'll just be something else for you to move out."

"Yeah, but you'll still be here."

The temptation to fail this year and retake it so I get to graduate with her is strong. Weird? Yes. Do I care? No. I think the Vancouver Vipers would care, though, and that's the only reason I go to class.

Anastasia uncurls herself from my body, moving to sit facing me with her legs crossed. "Nathan . . . I don't want to live here next year. Especially since you'll be in Canada."

"Why not?" An uncomfortable feeling settles in my stomach, and I wish I could go back thirty seconds and not start this conversation. "Why do I feel like you're about to tell me something I don't want to hear?"

"You probably don't, but it doesn't mean we shouldn't talk about it." She chuckles, placing her hand on my thigh. "I love that you guys seem happy with me living here. Honestly, I don't know what I would have done without you. But like I've told you so many times, I want to go back to my apartment."

"You want to live with the guy who shit-talks you constantly?" I say harshly, far harsher than I intended.

"Look, I know it might not make sense to you, and it doesn't have to. Lo has been filling me in on the stuff I've missed while I've been phoneless, and I think Aaron is finally ready to sort things out."

"Anastasia, he's been vile to you. He's a liar and a bully. You don't need him."

"Yeah, I'm more than aware! It plays on a loop in my head, but I'm not suggesting I'm friends with him. And I do need him. He's my skating partner and unless I want to start from scratch, which after two years of pain I'm not prepared to do, I need to find a way for the two of us to work together again."

"I fucking hate this."

"I know you do, bub. And I love how protective you are, but me living here was always supposed to be temporary. Do you know how hard it is spending every second with you, knowing you're leaving me in six months?"

"I don't like the idea of moving, either, but you know I have no choice!"

"It isn't what I mean, Nathan. Of course I want you to play for your dream team. Even if you weren't already signed, I'd support you going anywhere." She sighs, and that noise, the one I hear so often, the one that tells me how mentally exhausted she is with this situation, makes me hate the fact our holiday break is ending like this. "What I mean is I want to be excited for you in six months, not crying because I don't want you to move out. I think it'll be a lot easier if I live in my own place again."

She taps her fingers against her lips, and her leg bobs; she's nervous. My heart hammers. "What aren't you telling me?"

The hand on my thigh rubs up and down, comforting me before she's even given me whatever shitty news she's about to. "Aaron's been cleared to skate. I was going to tell you in the morning because it's been such a long day, but I think it means you can go back to hockey."

Playing hockey again should be music to my ears, but in reality, it feels like she's slipping away. "So we're not going to be skating together and you're moving out," I snap. "Will I just be a Thursday-night hookup, then? When you can make time for me in your planner?"

I regret it as soon as the words leave my mouth.

Her eyes widen and I watch her body tense. "You're upset, Nathan, but please don't talk to me like that."

I apologize, but the shame I'm feeling doesn't allow me to talk above a whisper.

"You're my boyfriend and I love you. I will see you as much as I possibly can, but you're jumping to conclusions. I'm hearing him out. That's all."

"You have a big heart, Stas," I mumble, pulling her body back to mine, instantly feeling better now she's back in my arms. "I don't want him to break it, more than he already has. I don't trust him, but I trust you and your judgment. I'll be there for you whatever you decide."

She drifts off to sleep quickly, and I listen to the soft sound of her breaths, letting them soothe me as much as they can. It doesn't work and I fall asleep thinking about how much I absolutely do not trust Aaron Carlisle.

THE SMELL OF FRESH FLOWERS is overpowering every single one of my senses, and I'm itching to get back in my car. The florist is taking her sweet-ass time wrapping up the peonies I picked out, and I'm painfully aware of JJ milling around behind me, mumbling to himself. "What're you grunting about?"

He tucks his hands into his pockets and shrugs. "I want a hot guy to buy me flowers."

I stare at him, waiting for his signature smirk to break, to know he's joking. "You're serious?"

"I'm just saying, flowers would be nice, y'know? The people I date always expect me to buy them flowers. It's always, 'JJ, wow, your dick is so big,' or 'you're so smart,' or 'JJ, that was the best sex of my life.' It's never, 'JJ, I bought you some flowers.' Whatever, it doesn't matter." He kicks at something invisible with his foot and wanders off to look at some sunflowers.

When I turn back to the florist, she's stopped working to listen to JJ's flower tragedy, too. I'm shaking my head as I reach into my pocket for more money. "Can I make it two bouquets, please?"

I still have the sickly-sweet floral smell stuck up my nose on the drive back home. JJ has a shit-eating grin on his face as he clings to his light blue peonies, Anastasia's pink ones resting between his knees to prevent them from getting damaged.

Manipulative little shit.

I'd love to say my desire to buy my girlfriend flowers is only because I love her, but if I'm honest, they're guilt flowers.

Beautiful, expensive guilt flowers.

I don't like how I talked to her last night, and while I apologized and I regretted what I said immediately, in my head I wanted to say a whole lot worse.

I wanted to shake her and remind her of all the horrible things Aaron has said to her, all the ways he's made her feel awful. Make her see exactly why he should be in our lives as little as possible.

But that's not fair because she knows. I've held her while she sobbed over his words; she knows exactly why she should stay away from him. I can't pretend there isn't a huge chunk of me that simply doesn't want to share her with him.

Skating with her basically every day for six weeks has spoiled me. Waking up beside her, cooking with her, even working out and studying with her has spoiled me.

What if she makes up with Aaron and she doesn't need me?

I want to build a life with her—one that'll exist when Maple Hills is a memory—so this feels like we're about to go backward. Every instinct is telling me to cling to her, interfere, protect her, but I know it isn't right. I won't be that guy; I won't just cave to myself after Anastasia has worked so hard to work on herself. She deserves the best version of me, and that version trusts and supports his girlfriend.

He also buys her flowers when he's a dick.

JJ and I went to see Coach Faulkner, and luckily, he was in great spirits. He always is after two weeks without us. He's a family guy through and through, and despite how fucking terrifying he is, he's a soft girl dad, so he loves having the holidays off with them.

He doesn't talk about his girls much. Imogen and Thea are at least in their late teens now, but I'm too scared to ask—even if it's to be polite.

Faulkner confirmed what Lols said, which was both a relief and a stress. Aaron got a clean bill of health while he was back in Chicago for Christmas; Brady emailed him this morning to say everything will be back to normal tomorrow.

"Cheer the fuck up," Coach demanded when I wasn't as over-joyed as he was expecting. "If this is about that girl, Hawkins, I swear to God . . ."

"She's my girlfriend, sir."

He sighed heavily, pinching the bridge of his nose between his thumb and finger. "Just what you needed in your senior year—a girl-friend. For the love of God, make sure you use protection. I mean it, for both of your sakes, wrap it up."

JJ snorts beside me, until Faulkner spears him with one of his famous glares. "Don't even get me started on you, Johal."

Chapter Forty-three

ANASTASIA

FOR THE FIRST TIME, I'M relieved to be waking up alone.

The conversation I had with Nate last night weighed heavily on my mind as I fought to sleep. When he nudged me this morning and said he was going to see Faulkner, I didn't fight to keep him in bed.

Even without a proper conversation, I could tell he was in a weird and sulky mood, likely riddled with guilt. He's been blowing up my phone since he left, apology, justification, apology, rant, apology. It's exhausting. But I put Nate and his worries to the back of my mind while I deal with my second—maybe joint first—favorite man.

Punching in the code when he shouts "Come in," I find Henry on the floor surrounded by paints and a huge canvas. I'm careful not to interfere with his process as I sit beside him, but I'm close enough that he has to face me. "Henry, is there anything you want to talk about?"

His head shakes, a definitive no. It's a very determined but unconvincing no, but his looks in my direction get more frequent after a while until he eventually puts down his paintbrush. "I can't stop thinking about it."

"Tell me why. They checked me over so many times, I promise I'm fine."

"I started googling statistics of people who fall through frozen lakes, then those who die because of it. Then somehow, I ended up on people who get severely injured figure skating, and I couldn't stop looking at all these things that might happen to you."

"Oh, Henry."

"I can't stop obsessing over it, Anastasia. You nearly died. I don't know how to make it stop."

"I'm sorry I scared you. I was scared, too, but I promise you I'm healthy, and it won't happen again."

"Please don't skate on frozen stuff outdoors anymore."

"I promise I won't, but I need you to promise me you will stop looking at statistics. Do you need a hug?"

Thinking about my offer, he chews on his lip a little, but then he again shakes his head. "No. I promise to try to stop looking, I just can't sometimes. It's like, once it's in my head, it burrows and burrows, and then I can't get it out. I hate it about myself, and I don't know why I have to do it."

"You know I love you, right? And that there isn't one single thing that I hate about you."

"I know you do, and that's why I worry about you. I've never had what we have before." His confession shocks the words right out of me. "I don't want to lose it."

I watch him paint until I have no choice but to get ready for my meeting with Aaron, and even then, leaving him is hard.

IT FEELS LIKE I'M GOING to a job interview as I walk through the entrance toward Brady's office.

Aaron looks as uncomfortable and nervous as I do, which makes me feel a little better. Brady's office is small, but the table is big enough for me and Aaron to sit opposite each other, with Coach to our side like some divorce attorney.

"Thanks for coming, Stassie. I know I don't deserve your time."

Brady immediately groans. "Let's not get dramatic straight off the bat, Aaron."

I try to stay indifferent and not react. "You have my attention. What do you want to say?"

"I've been cruel to you and you didn't deserve it." He sits up straight in his chair, flexing his fingers. "I haven't been the partner, or the friend, you deserve."

"You know what you haven't said to my face yet?" *Stay calm.* "You haven't said sorry. You haven't said I'm sorry, Stassie. I'm sorry I've slut-shamed you. I'm sorry I created a situation so toxic you moved out. I'm sorry I bad-mouthed you to everyone."

"Anastasia, please," Brady says, clearing her throat. "We're here to fix things. I know how much you both care about each other, let's focus on that."

"He said nobody would be able—" My voice cracks. "He said nobody would be able to love me when my birth parents couldn't. Did he tell you that, Coach? When he said he wanted to fix things?"

"Aaron." Brady's face pales, her voice strains. "Please tell me you di—"

He buries his head in his hands. "It's true, Coach. I said it all and worse. I'm so sorry, Anastasia."

"I've defended you so much, Aaron," I say flatly. "When your behavior made people think you were toxic, I told them you were misunderstood. At the same time, you were calling me a bad skater and telling people I was trying to trap Nate with a baby because I'm poor. Do you even realize how fucked up that is? What have I done to make you hate me?"

That's enough to get his attention and he finally looks up at me again. His face is blank; he's calculating the appropriate reaction, because he definitely didn't know I knew that. "My dad had another affair. Got this one pregnant and Mom finally kicked him out. She's our age, Stas. Do you know how sick that is? I'm going to have a sibling and their mom is someone I could have dated."

"Your mom doesn't deserve to be treated like that. She's never deserved to be treated like that, but I don't understand what this has to do with me."

"You haven't been around! I needed you, needed your support, and you've been nowhere. You've been partying and hanging around with guys you don't even like. I felt alone and it made me so mad at you."

All this heartache, all the tears, and the hurting. All the feelings of not being good enough, wondering if I deserve what I have, all because he didn't tell me something was wrong.

"I've been so upset about you not being a good friend that I've been an even worse friend. I don't expect you to forgive me yet, but I want to earn it. I know that'll take time, and I have an idea of how we can work through it."

Stay freaking calm. "They're words, Aaron. They don't mean anything."

"There's this therapist here in LA named Dr. Robeska. She specializes in couples, but not in a romantic way," he clarifies quickly, "people like us—pairs and teammates. My mom said she will pay for it after I told her what I'd done. Mom said this could be a fresh start for us all."

Brady nods enthusiastically, which irritates me since she was the one Aaron was bitching to about me for who knows how long. "Good communication is key when it comes to partnership. You two have had a very rocky few months, and if this pairing is going to continue, we need to get you back on track."

He knows exactly what he is doing, which is what irritates me the most. Knowing he's hitting me with something I won't be able to refuse. I've been praising the effectiveness of therapy the entire time I've known him, mainly to make him go and work out his issues. Even after everything that has happened, he's trying to manipulate me into doing something.

"Lola said you've been cleared to skate again. Is that true?"

He's nodding before I even finish my sentence, holding up his bad arm, flexing it around to demonstrate he has the movement he lost back. "Clean bill of health from the doctor. I'm ready to go when you are . . . So, therapy?"

"I'm going to have to think about it, Aaron. It's a huge commitment to make, and you've hurt me. You've really hurt the people around me, people who I love."

"You loved me once, too," he says flatly. "And I love you, as a friend, obviously."

"I think our time would be better spent getting ready for nationals. I'm not sure how I'm expected to want to be your friend again, but we can have a professional partnership."

"If I could take it all back, I would in a heartbeat, Stassie. But I can't, and I still want that friendship with you, as well as the partnership, but I need to earn your forgiveness in the right way." He takes a big, dramatic intake of breath. "By proving I'm better than I was when I was that man. I'll give you time to think about therapy. I hope you make the right choice. I really am sorry, and I'll say sorry as many times as you need me to."

Brady gives us both a speech about sportsmanship, and by the time I'm leaving the office, I'm tired and irritated, cursing the day I decided to give pairs a chance. I feel swamped by other people's issues and emotions, which is hard, since I have such big issues and emotions myself.

I'm not perfect. I am so far from perfect it's laughable, but I try my best to be a good friend. So to be told this whole mess is because I've supposedly failed Aaron as a friend is hard to swallow.

Logically, I know it isn't true, but Aaron was never going to sit there and admit he didn't even try to talk to me about it. Emotionally, I'm questioning if there's more I could have done. And now I'm annoyed at myself because that's what he wants, and I'm falling for it.

This is the problem with people. Nothing is straightforward; everyone has good and bad. Look at people like Nate's dad; is he the father Nate and Sasha need? No. But is he an evil person? Also no. It's the same with Aaron. I wouldn't be this upset and conflicted over someone that is a totally bad person.

This is where Nate and I differ because he only looks at the good and the bad. He doesn't pay attention to the murky, questionable gray area between those two points. And what I've now learned is when Nate is bothered by something, it comes out as frustration.

Nathan is waiting with a gorgeous bunch of peonies when I arrive back at the house, and I can't even pretend to be happy about it. He holds the bouquet out to me. "How did it go?"

"I don't have the energy to cope when I tell you and you make me feel shitty. Can I tell you tomorrow when I've processed it? I need a drink. I think I'm going to go out with Lola."

The surprise flickers across his face quickly, and he leans to kiss my temple. "I deserve that. Yeah, uh, take the time you need. I love you."

"I love you, too."

I THINK I MIGHT BE dying.

There's a mane of red hair covering my face when I reluctantly peel open my eyes. It smells like fresh oranges, and despite the fact I love oranges, the idea of eating an orange right now makes bile rise in my throat.

I'm wrapped around a tiny frame of sequins and pale skin, and I'm incredibly and headache-inducingly confused about where I am, because it's not with Nathan, that's for sure.

Rolling onto my back, unraveling myself from who I hope is Lola, I take in the room around me. Part of me worries for a second that we are at the apartment, but this room is far too tidy to belong to either of us.

A deep snore from the bed has me sitting up, then stopping to cover my mouth when the movement makes me nauseous. The sight of Robbie's sleeping face only adds to my confusion, but my alcohol-soaked brain deduces that I'm in Robbie's bed, weirdly, with Lola and Robbie.

I don't remember getting home last night. Well, I only remember very blurry bits that aren't helping me right now.

After my shitty day, I could feel the stress and tension leaving my body a few shots in; a few more shots in is when it started to get blurry. Every move makes my body physically throb in the worst way, and as much as I want to go upstairs and crawl into bed beside my own boyfriend, I don't think I have the strength or coordination to make that happen.

Reaching for my phone, I say a tiny prayer that Nate is awake.

NATE

You awake?

Hey, drunk girl. Yeah, just woke up.

I think I'm dying.

A bottle of tequila will do that to a person.

Why am I in bed with
Lo and Robbie?

I tried to put you in our bed but
you said I was trying to come
between you and Lola.

You guys wanted to snuggle.

Even thinking about moving is
making me nearly vomit. I have
thought motion sickness.

Watching the words on my
screen is making me feel sick.
Help me.

Want me to carry you up the stairs?
You're not allowed to be sick though.

Can you carry me really softly?
Is that a thing?

I can taste sound rn I'm very delicate.

Omw to carry you really softly.

Heavy footsteps sound on the stairs after I hear his bedroom door slam, and yet, I still can't motivate my body to move. The door lock beeps as he enters the four-digit code, and he strolls in, looking effortlessly beautiful in his boxers. I want to watch him, admire him, but the more he moves, the worse I feel, so I scrunch my eyes shut.

"I'll try not to be offended at your grimace."

"You're a work of art, bub, truly you are. Absolute ten-out-of-ten sex god. But watching you move that quickly is making me wanna hurl," I mumble through tight lips.

"Ten-out-of-ten sex god? I think someone might still be a little drunk." His strong arms scoop under my body, pulling me to his chest in one effortless movement.

"Oh my God, stop moving." I moan through the palm of my hand glued to my mouth. "How can I be drunk *and* hungover?"

"You'll feel better after some Tylenol and a shower. I take it you don't wanna work out with me this morning?"

When I glare up at his outrageously pretty face, he's trying not to laugh, which is wise, because the motion of his laughter might make me throw up on his chest.

He walks us slowly to the kitchen, sitting me on the counter gently. "You smell like McDonald's and regret." He reaches into the drawer and produces a bottle of painkillers.

"Did I eat McDonald's last night? Or do I naturally smell like a Big Mac?"

He brushes my tangled hair from my face and looks at me so lovingly that, for a second, I forget that I am an actual dumpster gremlin right now. "You ate twenty chicken nuggets in about four minutes. It was like you were in an eating competition, but you were the only contestant. I've never been more in love with you." He hands me a glass of water and puts two pills in my palm. "Do you not remember getting home? Russ picked you guys up because he was sober. You forced him to take you for food."

"I like Russ."

Nate chuckles to himself and rubs his hands up the front of my bare legs while I throw back the pills. "I know you do, you said it quite a lot. You called him 'muffin' in front of everyone. Can you guess what all the guys are calling him now?"

Oh no. Poor muffin. "Uh-oh."

He scoops me back up and heads toward the stairs, being careful not to rock me around too much. "Uh-oh is right. Poor kid, he'll get over it, though, don't worry. I think he's going to live here next year, so you'll have plenty of opportunities to make it up to him. Russ and Henry are becoming friends, I think."

Nate lowers me onto his bed and wraps me up in the covers until I'm the equivalent of a human burrito. He's being so caring, and in this moment, it's hard to think about our current differences.

"Nathan?"

"Yes?"

"I need to be sick, but I can't move my arms or legs . . ."

He frantically unwraps me and watches as I sprint toward the bathroom, and I don't know what he does while I violently expel everything in my body, but I imagine it's along the lines of being grateful to have such a graceful girlfriend.

Nate showers me, puts me back in bed, makes me food, and heads to the gym, and I stay in bed, feeling sorry for myself, with a book.

I must have dozed off because I jump when he comes through the bedroom door, looking sweaty, having apparently been gone awhile.

"You good?" he asks, dropping his gym bag at the bottom of the bed.

Before my impromptu nap, I'd been reflecting on the past twenty-four hours and quickly came to the conclusion I had an apology to deliver. "I'm sorry I was snappy with you yesterday."

"You apologized last night, don't worry about it."

"I did?"

"Yeah, about thirty times. Then you tried to seduce me, which I politely rejected—sorry. You were far too drunk to be doing anything other than sleeping."

Sinking farther into the duvet, I feel the heat creep to my cheeks. "Doesn't sound like me. You sure?"

He hums a "Yep," smirking to himself. "You were very graphic with what you wanted to do to me. Told me my dick is the prettiest you've ever seen."

Peeking over my duvet shield, he looks so happy. "It is, to be fair."

Sitting beside my legs, he rubs his hand up and down my shin gently. "Listen, you always want me to be honest with you, so I am. It's bugging me that I don't know how yesterday went with Aaron. Can we please talk about it?"

"Of course." Nathan doesn't say a word while I'm talking; he sits in silence, listening carefully. When I'm finally done, he still doesn't say anything. I shuffle nervously on the bed, nudging him with my foot. "Well?"

"Couples therapy?"

"Sports partner therapy."

"He's up to something." Nate crawls up between my legs, wiggling until he's positioned with his head on my stomach. "I don't want to upset you again. It's never about you, baby. I'm sorry if I made you feel like it was."

"I know."

"But I don't like it."

"I know that, too."

"I'm trying not to make him an us issue. I just get annoyed and it's hard to see past it."

"Nate . . ."

"Yeah?"

"Get off my stomach, I'm going to be sick again!"

Chapter Forty-four

NATHAN

THE FIRST TWO WEEKS OF term have been an absolute blur of hockey sticks, assignments, and sheer panic that Aaron is going to upset Stassie.

They started their couples counseling that isn't for couples a few days after her drunken shenanigans with Lola, and each time she comes home teary, tired, and overwhelmed.

It's normal, is what she keeps telling me. *Starting any type of therapy is difficult*—her tone is determined when she says it, her desperation to seem in control shining through like a fucking beacon on a dark night. But I remain unconvinced; she's hurting herself to forgive him and I fucking hate it.

We try to talk about it, but I become irritated, which forces her to become defensive. So we let it go because I'm not spending the rare free evenings I get with her arguing about Aaron Carlisle. She's still living with me, and she still calls it home, but her schedule is overflowing with extra practices, workouts, therapy with Aaron, therapy by herself—it's never-ending.

I can't say I'm much better. Close to two months without hockey has made me sloppy, although the time I spent with Stas has made me a better skater. I'm cleaner, smoother. I can visibly notice how much better I am when it comes to the game. I wish Stas could see, but last week Arena Two was reopened following repairs, so we packed up all our shit and moved back to our own rink.

I miss those moments before or after training when I'd see her, an elbow brush or an impatient hand on her hip and a glare when we overran. But she has a competition in a week, so the fact that the pressure of sharing the rink has been relieved for her is something I can't be mad at.

She says she isn't surprised that Aaron has returned to skating as perfect as he left it; she says it's in his blood and that, for all his faults, he doesn't let her down on the ice. She mutters that she can cope with the rest of it if he just keeps skating.

I can't pretend I don't miss being her skating partner. No, I'm not thinking of giving up hockey to be a subpar figure skater, but it was fun, and I miss that time we had together. It made it clear how much time partners spend together, especially partners who live together. The idea that she has to spend that much time with Aaron or that he's going to be in our lives that much fills me with dread. I *know* it can't be me, but I low-key wish it was.

JJ and Robbie told me I need to get a fucking grip, and they're right, but I have this unshakable *off* feeling. Henry says I'm obsessed with Aaron the way Aaron is obsessed with Anastasia, but the kid is on my side for once.

That's how I know shit is bad.

I force myself to put all the Aaron bullshit to the back of my mind since today was my first game back with the Titans, and I needed to deliver. By some miracle, I didn't fuck it up, and we won.

I'm not sure if I was nervous about being back, nervous because Stassie was watching for the first time, or because fifteen seconds before stepping onto the ice, Faulkner told me he was sending me back to Brady if I messed up.

The guys have been pumped that I'm back, and their excitement is infectious. Well, when I don't think about how quickly my senior year is flying by, and how we don't have that many games left together.

Stassie worked this morning, followed by a session with Shithead and Dr. Robeska, so I didn't get to see her before the game started, but I got her and Lo the best seats. When she was packing up a change of clothes this morning, she made a point of putting in her Hawkins jersey.

"I can't believe you've managed to convince me to watch hockey," she tutted playfully, but I know she was excited.

It was a weird feeling knowing that there was someone in the crowd just for me. I've been playing for Maple Hills since freshman year, and I've heard my name screamed plenty of times, but this was different.

Every time I went past where I knew she was sitting I felt good. It was worth getting abuse hurled at me by Robbie when I skated over to her, pressed my hand to the plexiglass, and she did the same thing on the other side.

He shut the fuck up two minutes later when I scored.

Just to add to it all, Stassie's dad texted me this morning to wish me luck. He said he'd found a bar showing the game, so he was going to treat himself to a beer—or five—after Julia made him decorate the spare bedroom. He said he'd be bragging to anyone who'd listen, so to make sure I play my best. I sat staring at my phone for ten minutes before I managed to type back a response thanking him for the support. Thankfully, I gave him a reason to brag.

I'm feeling angsty as fuck waiting for Faulkner to finish his postgame debrief. He likes to do it while it's fresh in everyone's head, no consideration for the fact we want to go and celebrate. It shows how much stuff has changed, because I remember sitting here a couple of months ago, the same situation, but I was thinking about how focused I was on hockey.

"Okay, I'm done, you can all stop looking so fucking miserable," Faulkner barks. "Don't celebrate too hard—I'm not bailing anyone out of jail tonight. See you all Monday."

Stassie is leaning against the wall, scrolling on her phone, when I finally make it away from Faulkner.

Sensing my approach, she looks up from her phone, gives me a glowing smile, and starts to run toward me. I catch her with one arm as she jumps, letting my bag slide off my shoulder and onto the floor by my feet.

"I'm so proud of you," she squeaks, wrapping her legs around me and pressing kisses over every inch of my face. "I want to drop out and be a hockey wife. My heart didn't stop pounding for one second, and when that guy bashed into Bobby, it was like I was *possessed*! I was shouting so loudly, and I didn't even understand what was going on most of the time . . . but you won!"

I lower her back to her feet and look her up and down. Fuck she looks good in that jersey; it really was my best present. "You're drunk. Please don't drop out . . ."

"I never said *your* hockey wife." She giggles. "And I'm not drunk! Well, I was, but all the stress and excitement sobered me up. You're so good, Nathan. I don't even know anything about hockey, but *everyone* around us was talking about you . . . Oh! And Dad was texting me constantly."

I don't know what to say to her as we walk toward the car, so I let her recap every minute of the game that made her ass leave her seat or made her scream at the ref, even though she wasn't sure exactly what was wrong, but she knew her boys were being fucked.

"So, you enjoyed it, then?"

"I really enjoyed it, bub."

The rest of the guys left with Lola before I left the locker room, and the plan is to go out for drinks and food. Part of me wishes we were going home, but the guys deserve this; it isn't their fault I'm boring as hell these days. The walk to the car takes twice as long as people pat me on the back and congratulate me, but we get there eventually. I wait until we're in the privacy of the car before asking Stassie the question that's been on my mind all afternoon.

"How was therapy with Aaron?"

She keeps looking straight ahead as she shrugs her shoulders, voice cracking as she speaks. "Fine, we'll talk about it later. Let's celebrate."

The anxiety radiating from her body is almost palpable. Anastasia can't hide when something's bothering her, she doesn't have a poker face. I know there is something she's not telling me by her stiff posture, the way she won't look at me, the way she's chewing on her lip. Leaning over to link her hand with mine, I try to keep my voice even. "I want to know now. The guys can wait . . . I want to hear about your day."

She twists in her seat to face me, bringing our linked hands to her mouth, and kissing my knuckles gently. Her blue eyes, the ones that were bright and so fucking happy earlier, are now swimming with *something* uncertain. "Please, Nathan. I don't want to talk about it now. Let's have fun."

"Why won't you tell me?"

"Because you're not going to like it," she whispers. Her face softens and she exhales deeply, running a hand through her hair. "And I know how you're going to react. It's making me anxious to talk to you about it. I want to celebrate your win."

She's telling me she doesn't want to talk about it. I can hear her loud and clear, but my gut is already telling me what she's going to say. If I don't confirm I'm right, I'm not going to be able to do anything tonight. "You're moving out, aren't you?"

She sighs and I know I'm right. "Dr. Robeska thinks it's a good idea. We have nationals next weekend, and she thinks it'd be good for us—Aaron and I—to spend this week getting in the zone. We used to feel so in sync when we lived together, and we've lost that. She said even if it's just a trial, now would be a good time to do it."

I'm not sure which emotion to feel as the jealousy, bitterness, anger, concern, and hurt hit me all at once. "So, the doctor that he picked and he's paying for thinks you should move back to the apartment. There's a fucking surprise. I can't believe you're falling for it."

"Don't talk to me like I'm naïve, Nathan."

"I'm not. I just don't understand how you don't see what he's doing to you! How are you forgiving him for everything he's done to you? All the things he's said?"

I feel like a broken record.

"You don't understand. You're not even trying to understand, you just want me to shut him out and I can't! This isn't like hockey, Nate! There aren't other people ready to step up and fill in. It's me and Aaron—that's it. I'm not forgiving and forgetting; I'm trying to rise above it and not throw my dreams away over hurt feelings."

"Anas—"

"No, you need to listen to me for once," she interrupts, stopping me from trying to defend myself. "I *know* that Aaron has been a terrible friend, but it takes sacrifices to be the best. I can't be the best without him, but you're so fucking determined to put up this wall between me and him that you're not listening when I tell you that I know what I'm doing. I've made my choice to try to fix things *professionally.*"

"That's bullshit. You always have other choices, Stas. You don't have to move out, you don't have to go to therapy, you don't have to do any-fucking-thing you don't want to for that man. Why should you make sacrifices for him? He doesn't care about you, and I think it's funny that he hates me, and suddenly your therapist is telling you to not live with me anymore."

"This isn't about you, Nathan. You're making the choice to not understand," she says quietly. "You're not attempting to see things from my point of view. Your sacrifice was for your team, but mine is for myself, for my future, what's supposed to be *our* future. You need to separate Aaron the friend from Aaron the skater. You need to get this thing out of your head that I'm being manipulated because I'm not."

I hate every single thing about this. I hate that I seem like the unreasonable one, that somehow Aaron comes out on top. I simply don't want her spending time with him. I get that she has to for skating, even though I wish she didn't. But her commitments are tight enough as it is without me having to share her with him. "Is he going to let you eat when you move back in with him?"

Her head drops into her hands, and the longer she doesn't answer, the more I regret what I said. Eventually, when I'm squirming uncomfortably in my seat, she looks back up. "I'm trying very hard to be patient with you because I love you, and I know deep down you're worried for me. But if you can't talk to me with the same respect I talk to you, don't talk to me at all. I have the most important competition of my skating career in one week, and I can't be preoccupied with protecting your ego, because you think Aaron fucking Carlisle is capable of undermining how much I love you."

I feel like a naughty kid by the time she's done, and I can't do anything but nod silently. She leans over the center console and presses her lips to mine, and when we eventually break apart, she rests her forehead against mine and runs her hand across my jaw softly. Everything she's said is right, and in my head, I can admit it, but when it comes to voicing it, the words won't leave my mouth.

Finally, I manage to say something, but it's not the apology she deserves. "I just don't want him to hurt you."

She links our hands back together and brings them to her chest. I can see the hurt in her face, and I can't even blame Aaron for it because this one is all me. "Can you please take us to celebrate now? Please, Nate. I want to enjoy tonight with you," she pleads, voice barely above a whisper.

I put the car into drive and do as she asks, even though I don't feel like I've got anything to celebrate anymore.

Chapter Forty-five

ANASTASIA

I ALWAYS THOUGHT THAT SKATING would be the most complicated commitment in my life.

I was wrong.

"Do you think the attitude comes with the dick or it's something they develop over time?" Lola asks, shoving a spoonful of Ben & Jerry's into her waiting mouth. Casting her eyes over to the dress we're supposed to be altering, she frowns and shovels in another heaped spoonful. "Men are the worst."

Lola is playing Angelica Schuyler in the spring production of *Hamilton*, and today the guy playing Marquis de Lafayette got himself on her bad side. She didn't want to hang around the set having her dress altered, so she brought it home, knowing that I've been fixing and adjusting skating outfits since I was a kid.

We haven't done anything to the dress yet, but we have watched three episodes of *Criminal Minds*. I have a planner full of things to do but I just can't face it, and I'm too drained to care about the fact I don't care.

I can't work out if I'm evolving or devolving.

"I think it comes with age. I don't remember being this irritated ten years ago," I grumble from behind my apple.

Being at the apartment for the last three nights has been a welcome break from going around in circles with Nathan, but I also miss him. It's such a difficult situation, because I know that he would never do anything intentionally to hurt me, but by not listening to what I'm saying, he's hurting me.

Nathan is a protector and a fixer. It's a fundamental part of who he is as a person and I love that quality in him. I love even more that he prides himself on it, and on being good to those around him. When we first argued and I wanted to avoid him, he didn't let me. After Robbie's party, when I was embarrassed about what he did to me, he purposely found me to check if I was okay.

He tried to protect Russ when it came to the truth about the rink, he took the blame for the Aaron thing to protect his team, even though it was a ridiculous decision. He challenged me on something as difficult as disordered eating because my health was more important to him than my feelings. Time and time again, Nate has shown me and everyone around him what he brings to the table.

This is why I know that, as much as he loves me, this Aaron thing goes far beyond him not trusting Aaron. This is about his self-esteem and his spot in my life as the person I need.

What I can't seem to get him to listen to is Aaron isn't replacing him. Nobody could replace him, but the more time I spend with Aaron, the more chances there are that Aaron is going to be there when I need someone, and that's the crux of Nathan's issue.

He's told me himself that there is a selfish and jealous part of him that doesn't want to share me with Aaron, and while ordinarily this would be a red flag, when we talked it out and broke it down, it feels like it's because Nate holds me in such high regard, he doesn't think Aaron deserves me.

Nathan doesn't know how to process what he's feeling because he hasn't had hundreds of hours of therapy like I have, so I'm not mad at him for not knowing how to put his thoughts into words. But he does know how to listen, and he isn't doing that right now.

To him, and the rest of the guys, Aaron is a villain. He's the bad guy of the story, the unpredictable nightmare coming to ruin everything. When in reality, Aaron is a very emotionally immature and misguided man. I've said so many times that hurt people hurt people, and it's absolutely true. He lies and manipulates people because it's all he knows.

I've spent our entire college life so far justifying Aaron's behavior, for no reason other than easiness and truly hoping that deep down he's a good person. That doesn't make me naïve; it means I've looked at the good parts he's shown me and hoped that it was the real version of him. But I've ignored red flag after red flag and that was foolish of me because I've ended up hurt as a result. Right now, my eyes are wide open, and I look at our relationship as a means to an end.

We are skaters who need a partner to skate.

I don't need or want his opinion or approval. I haven't mysteriously forgotten that his actions drove the most laid-back and calm man I know to punch him in the face. I haven't forgotten how deeply his words cut me, and even though those cuts may have healed on the surface, they're going to be privately healing in therapy for who knows how long.

I shouldn't have to scream that I'm not naïve or being manipulated for Nathan to trust my judgment. I shouldn't have to beg him to understand that there is a difference between friendship and partnership.

And if Aaron has to play the villain in this scenario, Nathan is your textbook hero, and yeah, he can keep that title because he is the hero of my story. But this is one of those gritty fantasy stories, this isn't a fairy tale. I'm not the princess; I've never been the princess, but there's no denying he's built me up over the time we've been together, and he's given me the courage to deal with something like this.

I think I want Nate to be proud of me. He tackles issues head-on, and that's what I'm trying to do, which is why since I decided to tackle Aaron, I've been super surprised it's led to arguments with Nathan. And I say *tackle* because therapy with Aaron is no easy thing. It's exhausting and it's practically corrosive. Dr. Robeska is fair, though. She doesn't take any of his bullshit or his fake pouty lips as he tries to force some tears out.

She puts him in his place, which I enjoy immensely. Like when he repeated what he said in Brady's intervention about needing me and me not being there, her first question was how many times did he try to contact me to support him. Quickly followed by how many times did we make plans where I blew him off. Of course the answer to both was zero, which led her into a segment on weaponizing our emotions.

Since I've been back at the apartment, I feel like Aaron watches every morsel of food I put in my mouth. I still believe him when he says he didn't purposely mess up my plan, and Nate has practically begged me to bring it up in therapy with Robeska.

Nate wants to be proven right, but he's also the same man who reminds me that recovery isn't about winning. It's about learning and forgiving yourself, about forgetting bad habits, and trusting the process. It isn't linear, is what he's said so many times, and I can't ignore the irony that the same could be said for this situation with Aaron.

I've found myself sending multiple food pictures a day to Nate, just looking for reassurance that I didn't colossally fuck up. Aaron doesn't say anything about my new meals ever, and when I look directly at him, he's looking at his own plate. Maybe it's in my head. Maybe he's gaslighting me. Maybe, maybe, maybe. Just another day in Maple Hills filled with too many fucking questions.

"I don't want to live here next year," I blurt out, catching Lola off guard. She puts her ice cream down on the coffee table and twists to face me, giving me her full attention. "I don't want to live in the hockey house, because I don't think that's fair to Henry and Russ, but I don't want to live here. I understand if you want to stay, though. I can't afford anything nearly as nice as Maple Tower."

"We'll move."

"What?"

"I don't want to live here, either. Let's have a fresh start."

AARON GRUNTS AS I LAND back in the cradle of his arms.

"Stop the music!" I shout in the direction of Brady, putting some distance between me and Aaron so I don't kick him in the head.

"What's wrong with you now?" He groans, following me to the edge of the rink.

"You! You're what's wrong with me, Aaron! How the hell am I supposed to concentrate when you're huffing and grunting every time you have to touch me!"

The music finally cuts off and Brady looks extra unimpressed, but I don't care. I just don't care anymore about playing nice. I refuse to take shit from this obnoxious jackass for another second.

"What're you two arguing about now?" Brady huffs, raking a hand through her hair.

Aaron shrugs his shoulders and throws me the most incredulous look. "I don't know, Coach. Anastasia seems to have an issue. *Again.*"

Heat is prickling at the back of my neck as I struggle to stop my temper from flaring. I've always associated my impatience and temper with who I am as a skater. I've always assumed it's my competitiveness—the overwhelming need to be the best—but it clearly isn't. I didn't once feel this surge of rage when I was practicing with Nate. Even when we fell down or we bumped heads for the tenth time, I took it all in my stride and we laughed it off.

I've been resting my hands on my hips in a bid to not punch him in the throat, but the skin under my fingertips is becoming sore from squeezing so hard. I know what this is about and that's probably why I'm so upset.

"Are you struggling to lift me? Is that what the noises are about? Do you need to work out more?" I seethe.

"What? No," he splutters, the pink of his cheeks spreading quickly to the tips of his ears, but then his expression hardens. "Give me a fucking break, Stas. You can't put on weight and not expect me to need a little time to adjust."

There it is.

"You bench over one hundred pounds more than what I weigh in the gym with ease. I watched you do it this morning! You added more freaking weight! I've gained twelve pounds of muscle, that's it! What do you need to adjust to?"

"I need to adjust to your fucking attitude, for one."

"You're such a dick."

"I can't practice with you when you're like this. I'm going home; we've got to perfect this and you're wasting my time."

"Bye, then!"

"Children, please!" Brady snaps.

I don't hear whatever else she says because I skate off into the middle of the rink, shaking off the rage. If he wants to put being petty over being prepared, I'm not going to stand in his way.

Chapter Forty-six

NATHAN

I'm FACEDOWN ON THE COUCH in the living room when whispering disturbs my wallowing.

I look up, finding JJ, Henry, and Robbie each cradling a cup of coffee in their hands, muttering between themselves like old women at a bingo hall. "What?" I grunt.

"Has she dumped you?" JJ says, breaking away from the mothers' meeting to sit down in the chair across from me.

"No!" I snap, moving to sit up properly on the sofa, since apparently, this is about to be a house discussion. I knew I should have stayed in my fucking room out of the way, but the gym kicked my ass this morning, and I couldn't face climbing the stairs.

JJ puts his mug down on the coffee table and holds up his hands defensively. "All right, don't cry," he says sarcastically. "If she didn't dump you, why are you so fucking miserable?"

Henry throws himself down next to me, shooting me a half-suspicious, half-sympathetic look, and Robbie appears seconds later, with a mug of coffee for me.

I definitely feel like I've been ambushed, but I suppose I should feel grateful that I've got friends that give a shit when I'm clearly in a bad mood. Sinking into the couch, sighing heavily, I down my coffee to drag the time, because where do I fucking start?

"She says I'm not listening to her. She's upset with me, but she's also incredibly understanding when I'm being a prick, which makes me feel worse. And I miss her."

"But you're not listening to her, so why are you surprised she's upset?" Robbie says bluntly.

"I *am*!" I insist. "I'm hearing her loud and fucking clear that she's giving that shithouse another chance. I listened when she said she was moving out. I listened when she said she was going to fucking couples therapy with him."

"For someone so smart, you really are a fucking mooncalf sometimes, Hawkins," JJ says, shaking his head at me, his normal mischievous grin nowhere to be seen. For once, he's being totally serious. "She's the most determined person I know. There isn't a doubt in my mind that she's going to get everything she wants in life because she's willing to make sacrifices. What would have happened if you didn't get drafted?"

"I—"

"Nah, don't give me a bullshit answer." He laughs. "You'd have used your trust fund to do absolutely whatever you wanted, and for good measure, you've got the family business to fall back on. Stassie doesn't have a trust fund. She doesn't have a family business. If she doesn't make it in skating, she's probably going to be stuck teaching, or worse, in a job she fucking hates."

"Why are you giving me a lecture on my own girlfriend, Johal?"

"Because you're only looking at the now and you're being fucking selfish! She can't be a pair skater without a pair. She's being smart, Nate. She's using Aaron to achieve her goals because she doesn't have another option. You should be proud of her for being so strong, and all you've done is get fucking jealous and petty, making her feel shit over something that's very difficult for her."

Henry and Robbie are painfully quiet while JJ rips into me. Henry is squinting at his mug, swirling around the liquid so he doesn't have to look at me. Robbie is looking at me, face blank.

"You two gonna say anything?" I grumble.

Rob shrugs. "I mean, he's right. You know he's right, that's why you look so pissed right now. You know we love her, Nate. You think I like Lola being around him? Of course I don't, but they're both big girls. Big, stubborn girls. From what you've told us, and, uh, what Lo's told me, she couldn't have been clearer with you that she doesn't want to be his friend. I think you need to decide whether you're willing to drive her away over your ego."

"It isn't my fucking ego! I'm worried about the woman I'm in love with spending time with someone who is awful to her."

"It *is* your ego," Henry mutters from beside me, not looking up from where he's still spinning his coffee. "You think he's going to manipulate her into forgiving him and then she won't need you anymore. You like being needed by her. It makes you feel important. You know Aaron hates you and you think he's going to keep her away from you. Which just shows you don't know how strong she is, or truly understand how much she loves you."

This has got to be one of the worst fucking interventions ever.

"So you all think I'm a dick, then, is what I'm hearing?"

Robbie clears his throat and laughs. "I've thought you were a dick since kindergarten, for the record."

"I didn't know you in kindergarten," JJ adds. "But I imagine if I did, I would have also thought you were a dick. You know we love you, man, but you brought her here, let us live with her and get to know her, and now we love her, too. We don't want you to ruin something pretty fucking special. That's what Aaron wants."

"I don't think you're a dick, Nathan," Henry says quietly. "I think you need to put yourself in her shoes. If you and JJ had a fight, but we had a game and you needed a defenseman that would help us win, you'd let him play. You'd put aside the drama and concentrate on the win. That's all she's doing."

"You guys have a date later, right?" Robbie says, smiling when I nod. "Talk to her about it. She needs to know you're with her on this."

"Have you three got nothing better to do than fucking Oprah me?"

That breaks the tension in the room as the three of them laugh. "JJ nudges Henry playfully, smiling. "It's a nice change from watching Henry desperately try to track down that girl Jenny or whatever from Christmas."

"You *still* haven't found her? What did you say to the poor girl? Has she gone into witness protection or something?" I joke, smiling harder when Henry glares at me like he's trying to set me on fire with his eyes.

"Sorry, Nathan. We can't all harass a girl into a relationship. Some of us need time to find out who they are first, okay? I—"

I don't hear whatever else he says over the sound of me, JJ, and Robbie howling laughing.

I DON'T KNOW WHY I feel nervous about going on a date with my own girlfriend. I watch her politely say good-bye to the doorman at the front of her building and make her way toward my car in the pickup zone. She looks fucking unbelievable. So unbelievable that we might not make it to our dinner reservation at Octopus.

It's a seafood restaurant that recently opened in Malibu, and luckily, a guy who's into JJ works there and managed to sort it out for me. I'm not exactly *for* pimping out my roommate to book a table in an exclusive restaurant, but I'm not exactly against it, either.

The second she climbs in, my car is filled with the sweet smell of her perfume. She always smells good, but right now, it's something else. Is this what happens when I don't see her for a couple of days? I'd tell her, but I can already hear her jokes about being a vampire with heightened senses.

"What are you chuckling to yourself about?" she grins, leaning over to kiss me. God, she even tastes good. I move my hand toward her face, but she bats it away before I can touch her, muttering, "Makeup."

"Vampires, uh, doesn't matter. I've missed you. You look so beautiful tonight."

"You look pretty good yourself, Hawkins. How was practice?"

We chat comfortably all the way to Malibu, catching up on the little things that have happened during our days that we don't think to mention now that we don't spend most of our days together. She tells me how she beat her PB doing squats, and now Brady is going to increase her calories again after her competition.

I tell me about Henry and Russ's budding friendship and how some of the more immature team members don't seem to like it, so I had a word with them about growing the fuck up. Frat culture is weird and can be a little cultlike, in my opinion; it's why I was never interested. I prefer to hang out with people I like instead of being forced to like specific people in the name of brotherhood.

"I will beat anyone who hurts my boys," she says sternly. I know she's not even joking as well; all five feet four inches of her would happily take on anyone to protect Henry, and now Russ.

The guy must be *really* into JJ, because he reserved us a table outside on the patio that looks out to the sea. I drop JJ a text letting him know how good our table is to score the guy some brownie points, since he's *clearly* going all out to impress.

I know that I need to talk to Anastasia about how I've acted recently, but I'm not quite sure how to bring it up. I let our orders be taken, and she fills the silence with funny stories about Lo and one of her lectures where everything went wrong. But eventually, she gives me a sympathetic smile, one that says she knows what's going on in my head. "Nate, are you okay?"

The time apart has felt a bit like a breakup, even though it wasn't, and we've still talked, but it's cemented for me that breaking up is not a reality I ever want to live. I know it's rare to meet someone who makes you feel like your whole life is brighter. I know I'm lucky that I have someone by my side who would go to war for the people she loves, and it's made me realize, right now, she's going to war for herself.

And I need to be by her side, not attacking her from a different spot on the field.

"I owe you an apology," I blurt out, definitely not in the smooth, calm way I was hoping for. "I haven't been fair and I'm sorry, Anastasia. I really am."

She slides her hand across the table and links it with mine. "It's okay. Thank you for apologizing."

"You're the most important thing in my life. I'm not sure if you know that or not, but you are, and I've been selfish. I've put you in a difficult situation, making you feel like you need to choose between us or something. You don't and I want you to know I support your goals." She nods along, letting me trip over my words and ramble quickly, telling her how I feel. She doesn't interrupt or say anything; she gives me the space I need to try to get how I'm feeling out in the open. "I *am* listening now. I promise you I am; I hear you and I get that I need to let you get on with it and handle Aaron the way you see fit."

When she senses that I'm done, she brings our linked hands to her mouth, and pecks a kiss on my knuckles. The look of relief on her face right now is overwhelming, which to be honest makes me feel worse, because she must have been struggling with this more than I realized.

I feel relieved, too; it's funny because she can be the most hot-headed and stubborn person, but when it comes to talking things out, she has the patience of a saint. And I needed that patience to fix this.

"Nobody is replacing you, Nathan. Every minute I spend skating with him, I'm thinking about how much I wish you'd taken up figure skating when you were a kid, not hockey. Therapy changed me for the better—it might with him, it might not. What happens outside of that arena isn't my concern anymore."

"I'm sorry for how I've spoken to you recently."

She doesn't acknowledge it; she squeezes my hand. "Do you want to hear something funny?"

"Right now? Yes, absolutely." Anything to get the topic on something other than me being a bad boyfriend.

"I made Aaron storm off during practice today." She giggles, bringing her wineglass to her lips. "In the middle of practice he got in his car and drove home. I had to get an Uber, but it was worth it."

"What happened?"

"He kept huffing and puffing every time he had to lift or catch me, so I asked him if he needed to work harder in the gym. Told him I know he lifts heavier than me, so what was his problem. He, uh, did not like that one bit." Her nose crinkles as she shrugs, clearly not giving one fuck about Aaron.

"I don't have anything to worry about, do I?" I say, talking more to myself than her.

"Not even a little bit. I have it all under control. You helped me be strong enough to deal with it." Her eyes look past me, and she smiles so fucking brightly that I think someone famous walked in, but no, she starts excited-fidgeting in her seat. "Oh! I think our food is coming!"

I'M RELUCTANT TO LET HER out of the car when I pull up at Maple Tower, but I have to.

"I'll be back Saturday night," she mumbles. "We can spend the whole of Sunday together, I promise."

Stassie is going to San Diego in the morning for nationals, and we decided the most responsible thing to do was to sleep in our own beds. Neither of us wants to, but she needs to concentrate on relaxing tonight, and that isn't going to be possible at my house. If I were to stay here, she'd spend the entire night anxious about me and Aaron being in the same space.

This is the right choice, even if it makes us both temporarily unhappy.

She climbs across the center console to straddle my lap, wrapping her arms around my neck and pressing her forehead against me. "I love you," she whispers, pressing her mouth to mine. "I need to get out or I'm going to end up letting you fuck me in a parking garage."

She opens my door and climbs off me, giving me one last kiss before heading toward the elevator. I watch to make sure she gets in safely, then put the car in drive, hoping that this boner will be gone by the time I get home.

Chapter Forty-seven

ANASTASIA

THERE'S BEEN A WEIRD ACHE in my chest since I arrived home and it won't go away.

It might be pre-competition nerves. I don't think anyone would blame me, considering tomorrow is the biggest thing I've ever faced. The Olympics aren't for another two years, but there are so many other international competitions I can compete at. It's how I show Team USA what I'm capable of, what I can offer, what *we* offer.

All the heartache it took to be ready for this weekend needs to mean something.

It *has* to be worth it.

Lola knows to leave me alone when I'm like this; there is nothing she can say or do that's going to make me feel better, and I'd rather be alone with my thoughts anyway. I've ticked off everything on my iPad, showered, settled down in bed with my favorite Titans T-shirt on, and that should be enough, but it just . . . isn't.

The T-shirt is fresh out of the machine, so it smells strongly of detergent. It's a smell I've always loved; the smell of clean clothes means I've done my laundry, which means I've ticked something as complete in my planner. But for some reason, the smell is adding to the ache.

It doesn't smell like Nathan anymore.

And just like that, my bed feels overwhelmingly empty, and the T-shirt itches my skin.

I understand Dr. Robeska's logic in me moving back into the apartment. She felt that my and Aaron's relationship would recover quicker if we had this time together at home, like we used to. When we talked about the things we did together outside of skating, it was clear we both had a good time hanging out together.

We needed to get back in sync, and aside from Aaron's tantrum on the ice, it has worked. I wanted to move back, too, which I told Nate before Robeska brought it up. I was worried that Nathan and I could only work being in each other's company constantly and that as soon as his NHL career started, I wouldn't be able to offer him the support he needs, which would drive us apart.

But I'm not happy here and I miss my boys.

One boy in particular.

After a few rings, I worry he's not going to answer my call, that he's busy with his friends or got his phone on study mode, but right before the line disconnects his face fills my screen. "Sorry, my phone was charging next to my bed. Is everything all right?" he says warily, the little crease in between his eyebrows deepening when he looks at his screen.

"The clothes I stole from you don't smell like you anymore."

". . . Is that a good thing or a bad thing?"

"A bad thing. A horrible, terrible, catastrophically bad thing. I miss you and it's making me unsettled."

"Baby, you *just* saw me, please don't feel unsettled. What do you need me to do?"

"Can you stay here tonight? I know you don't want to be around Aaron, but he'll be in his room, and we will be in mine," I ramble off quickly. "You won't see him. I just need you, Nate. I need you to do that thing you do where you magically make everything better."

The corner of his mouth quirks into my favorite sort of smile. It's the smile I get when I've taken him by surprise but in a good way. It doesn't happen very often because he knows me so well; it's difficult to take him by surprise, but that makes it feel extra special when it does happen. "I, uh, I dunno how I do that, but I'm leaving right now. Do you want me to get you anything on the way?"

I shake my head, watching him spring up from his bed and grab an overnight bag. "No, bub. Just you. You're all I need."

I CAN'T CONCENTRATE ON THE book I'm supposed to be reading.

I read a paragraph or two, then my eyes immediately revert to the moving dot on the map on my screen. I can't work out if it's cute or pathetic how excited I am to see his car pulling into the parking garage of my building.

I'm hanging around our front door like an excited puppy, listening for the signature ding of the elevator—while being fully judged by Lola, who's on the couch watching *Hamilton* for the tenth time this week. He doesn't even get to finish his knock before I'm pulling the door open and dragging him inside.

"Hi." He chuckles when I wrap my arms around his torso, inhaling deeply.

"You smell so fucking good," I mumble into his chest. Tightening his arms around me, he buries his head into my hair and kisses the crown of my head.

"As hot as I'm sure you two look fucking, can you not do it right in front of me? You have a room right there, and I'm trying to get my Revolutionary War on over here," Lo shouts from the living room.

I drag Nate toward my bedroom before Aaron comes out of his room to investigate the shouting and the source of the booming laugh that echoes around the apartment when Lola gives Nathan the middle finger for telling her to stop being a pervert.

That ache in my chest is getting easier to deal with every second that passes, every second that I can feel him beneath my fingertips. His finger hooks under my chin, tilting my face to his. "Are you sure you're okay?"

"I had this ache in my chest that wouldn't go away. I'm sorry to drag you back here, but selfishly, having you close makes me feel better. Am I clingy?"

He shakes his head, gently threading his fingers through my hair and pressing a kiss to my forehead. "There isn't anything I wouldn't do to make you feel better, Anastasia. I'm not sure how I'm supposed to get my smell on you, though . . ." Kicking off his sneakers, he climbs onto my bed, and I watch him fight with all my pillows until he's comfortable. I climb into his lap, resting my legs on either side of his.

"Hold your arms up," I tell him, fiddling with the hem of the T-shirt he's wearing. He does as I ask, sitting forward slightly and holding his arms above his head so I can pull the T-shirt off. He leans back against the pillows, letting me trail my fingers across the smooth, warm planes of his stomach, all the way down to his sweatpants.

Gray, obviously, because Nathan Hawkins is a man who was most definitely written by a woman.

His hands move quickly to grip my wrists, pulling them up into the air. "Your turn, Allen."

I keep my arms in the air as he bunches the bottom of the T-shirt and pulls it off my body. My nipples pebble under the heat of his glare, and when he licks his lips and runs his hands up the front of my thighs, goose bumps spread across every inch of me.

The anticipation is suffocating; his hands travel over my hips, past my waist, settling just below my breasts. Nathan has seen me naked countless times, but right now, I've never felt more exposed.

"You are perfect," he whispers, sitting up to kiss the valley between my breasts. I'm practically panting when his tongue flicks against my hard nipple and he hums happily, sucking it into his mouth. My hands grip his shoulders, and my head falls back as he swaps to my other breast, paying it an equal amount of attention. He licks and kisses his way up my neck, groaning when I grind against him, and when he reaches my mouth, I'm about ready to combust.

"I want you so badly," I whisper.

His laugh is dark, and his eyes are gleaming. "Ask me nicely."

"Nathan . . ." I moan impatiently.

"That's a good start; what else? Tell me what you want, baby."

My body is rocking against his in a desperate search for friction, just *something* that will soothe the ache between my legs, so it's pretty freaking clear what I want. His arm wraps around the bottom of my back, holding me close to him as he flips us over so I'm on my back. If I could only have one memory for the rest of my life, it'd be Nate kneeling between my open legs. His body is strong and hard, but his skin is soft and smooth. He doesn't even blink as he looks down at me, drunk on lust.

"I want your mouth."

"Where do you want my mouth?"

I trail my finger down the front of my panties, feeling the warmth and how wet they are already. His eyes follow my hand, lips tugging into a smug smirk.

"You've gotta say the words."

All the blood in my body rushes to my face. I chew on the inside of my cheek, watching him watch me. His hands are massaging my calves, so he's clearly in no rush to give me what I want. My chest is heaving, needy and impatient. "I want your mouth on my pussy."

He takes each side of my underwear in his hands and shimmies them off, pushing my legs wide and settling between them. Apparently, the time for teasing is over because he doesn't hesitate to bury his head and devour me. He's got me squirming within seconds, desperate for more but overwhelmed by how fucking good it feels.

"You like that?" he coos, knowing full well the answer is yes. My hands sink into his hair, tugging him closer, pushing him away, holding him in place, using him as an anchor to keep me on this bed.

"Nate," I cry, not quite sure what I'm crying for.

"I know, baby, I know it's good." He slips a finger inside of me, then another, curling them around, and I'm almost there. "You gonna come for me?"

My legs are shaking, and I'm floating as my entire body starts to spasm. "*Nathan . . . Oh fuck . . .*"

He leaves me dazed and breathless on the bed, while he climbs off and lets his boxers and sweatpants drop to the floor. Nathan's hands wrap around my naked thighs and tug me to the edge of the bed, navigating my ankles to rest on his shoulders. He takes the base of his dick in a tight grip, running the tip between my folds.

"Such a good girl," he says proudly, pushing the tip inside. "*Jesus Christ*, stop squeezing or this is going to be over in thirty seconds."

Digging his fingers into the front of my thighs to keep me in place, he sinks himself fully inside me.

"Stop calling me a good girl and I'll stop squeezing," I shoot back. This relationship works so well because Nathan fucking loves praising me, and I love being praised. He's gentle with me at first, slow, deep strokes that have my toes curling, but then his hand moves from my thigh, and he pairs harder thrusts with his thumb on my clit. "You're too good at this." I gasp, reaching out to try to touch him, but he's too far out of my reach.

He guides my legs from his shoulders to his hips and tugs me up, carrying me over to my bedroom door, pressing me into it. "That better? You can reach me now." He smiles, kissing and nibbling along my jawline.

I cling to him, using every last shred of energy as my body takes him over and over. The building starts in my stomach, intensifying as Nate moans and whispers praise after praise next to my ear, and my nails sink into the strained muscles of his back. His thrusts get rougher and his hands tighten on the back of my thighs. And when it can't get any tighter, the coil in my stomach bursts, sending every nerve in my body into chaos. A few more powerful thrusts and he's right there with me, grunting a string of undecipherable curse words into the base of my throat. "God, I love you."

I brush the hair sticking to my damp forehead away and cup his face between my hands. "Uh-huh," I say with a shaky breath. "I love you, too."

Chapter Forty-eight

NATHAN

THE ONLY BAD THING ABOUT having the best night's sleep of your life is eventually, you have to wake up.

It's peaceful here in the mornings, unlike the stomping up and down the stairs that happens in my house. Not to mention the arguing over who used the last of the coffee. Stassie stirs in my arms when her alarm starts blaring, grunting and grumbling when it doesn't spontaneously stop, then cursing under her breath as she feels around for her phone.

I got skilled at pretending to be asleep—otherwise known as stealth mode—when we lived together. A few nights apart has made me sloppy, though, because when she calls her screeching phone a *fucknugget* I can't help but laugh.

"Keep laughing, Hawkins, see what happens," she says between a yawn and an aggressive slap at her phone screen.

"Come here, grumpy girl." I smile, pulling her body back to mine. "How are you feeling? Can I do anything to help you feel ready?"

She rolls on top of me, resting her face against her hands on my chest. "Will you skate for me? I'll go back to sleep, and you can text me how it goes."

"I mean, I can try to bribe the judges, but I'm not sure your little stretchy body thing would fit me if you want me to skate."

Today feels monumental and I'm genuinely surprised she's

not freaking the fuck out, but as the thought enters my head, she flings her body off mine and launches herself toward the bathroom, emptying the contents of her stomach into the toilet.

Luckily, she did prewarn me the anxiety on the morning of a competition makes her throw up nine times out of ten, and not to panic it was morning sickness. She also said the vomit was my cue to leave, because from that point, she would be a nervous nightmare, and she wouldn't want me there for that.

By the time I've pulled on all my clothes and grabbed her a glass of water from the kitchen, she's emerging from the bathroom, thankfully smelling more like peppermint than anything else. "That's my cue to leave, right?" I confirm, bending over to kiss her forehead.

"Thank you for staying here last night." Her arms tighten around me. "I'd be so much worse right now if you hadn't. Good luck with your game today. I won't be on my phone, but I'll video call you when I get back to my hotel, okay? Text me your results, too."

I've been so focused on Stas's competition I almost forgot we're playing UCLA today. Hopefully, the rink-trashing drama is behind us now because the UCLA team are generally good guys. With it being so close, we see each other in clubs or parties, and other than a healthy bit of rivalry, they're one of the more fun teams to play against.

The figure skating nationals are down in San Diego and will be all weekend. The first of their routines will be today, and if they score high enough, they'll do their other one tomorrow. Anastasia was super understanding when I said I had a hockey game, so I couldn't go with her; she was ridiculously sweet and said it was okay.

What I didn't tell her is the second my game ends I'll be jumping in my car to fly down the I-5 to watch her. I give her one last pep talk, tell her how much I love her and how proud I am of her, then leave her to it.

In contrast to the calm of Stassie's place, the guys are being their normal clown selves when I get home.

JJ, Henry, Mattie, and Russ are all fully suited up, standing on the couch when I walk into the living room. Mattie uses the table as a stepping stone to jump onto a chair on the other side of the room; the table creaks under his weight but luckily doesn't straight-up collapse. I look between the four of them, waiting for someone to say something.

Robbie appears from the den, big mug of coffee in one hand, pushing his wheel with the other. He's already in his suit and I can sense the impending lecture about messing around before a game. Instead, he shrugs a shoulder and explains what the fuck is going on. "Floor is lava."

"You're fucked, then."

"Not as fucked as you. Go get your suit on, we can't be late to a home game."

It doesn't take me long to get ready, and as I'm about to get into the car, my phone buzzes.

UBER SLUT

Just set off and Brady is making us listen to ABBA

> That doesn't sound too bad.

She's singing too.

> JJ said call him, they can do a duet.

Will you still love me if I fall on my face and disgrace myself in front of the American figure skating elite?

. . .

> Yeah, probably.

I hate u.

> You're not going to fall on your face. You're going to nail it, and I love you regardless of the outcome.

Feel nauseous.

> Take deep breaths. If you're going to be sick, make sure you direct it toward Aaron.

JJ drives my car so I can text back and forth with my very nervous girl. We park and Robbie goes into asshole coach mode and demands I put my phone away to get into the zone. "You'll see her in a few hours, just get a grip for a bit, yeah?" he grunts in his most Faulkner-like voice. "I'm nervous for her, too, but we gotta, y'know, we gotta just push through it."

"Yes, Coach."

I go into captain mode as soon as we step through the doors of the arena.

It pays off because, after probably the best game we've played so far this season, we beat UCLA a very comfortable 9–3. Faulkner told me yesterday that if we won, he'd let me delay our postgame review so I could head straight to San Diego in time for the pairs short program. I'm about to head out the door when Cory O'Neill, UCLA's captain, grabs me.

"Good to see you, man," he says, slapping my bicep. "It's good to see you back on the ice. I heard a rumor you were figure skating."

"Yeah, I was, for six weeks. Another big drama. Never stops at Maple Hills, right?" I scratch at the nape of my neck awkwardly. "Director of Sport benched me because a kid on the skating team got hurt and blamed me. They were going to stop the whole team from playing until they found who was responsible, so I took the fall. I wasn't allowed to play until he could skate again."

"Oh shit!"

"It wasn't bad, y'know. My girlfriend is the guy's partner, so it was six weeks of skating and training with her. I liked it, other than my body fucking aching. They've got a competition today, actually; that's where I'm heading."

Cory's brows furrow together. "Wait a minute, are you talking about Aaron and Stas?"

Not a good sign. "Yeah, you know them?"

He nods his head, confusion apparent. "I went to school with

Aaron back in Chicago. I've known him since we were kids. You got blamed for Aaron getting injured? Stassie is your girl?"

"It was on Halloween. He showed up at The Honeypot with a busted wrist, said I'd pranked him, and he got hurt. You know our repu—"

"Halloween? Dude," he interrupts, holding up a hand. "Aaron got hurt playing football with us. We were drinking and dicking about at the beach, having a bonfire. Davey tackled him and landed on his arm . . . I didn't know he'd blamed you for that. What the fuck! He hasn't told us any of thi—"

I can see his mouth moving in front of me, but I can't hear anything over the sound of the ringing in my ears.

Everything seems to slow down as all the pieces rapidly start dropping into place. I'd made my peace with being the first person Aaron would blame during an unfortunate accident. I've been battling against this team's reputation for almost four years, and I wasn't angry about it anymore.

But he knew. He fucking knew how he got hurt, and he tried to get me in trouble for it anyway.

For what? For Anastasia? She's been single for years and he's never made a move. To get me kicked out of school? Nothing makes sense because what he did doesn't fucking make sense.

"Hawkins?" Cory asks.

"I've gotta go."

I'm halfway to San Diego before I realize I've been driving in silence. I crank up the radio, anything to drown out my thoughts, which are loud as hell right now. The main one is what am I going to do when I get there? I want to burst in there, tell everyone what he did, how he deceived the closest people to him. But *she* doesn't deserve this. This is the most important competition of her life so far. *Am I really going to set off a bomb when she needs to be concentrating?*

I've answered my own question before I've even finished formulating it—this needs to wait.

I can't imagine a future without Stassie, and sadly, her future is intertwined with him, too. Even more so if they win this weekend.

Their names are going to be recorded side by side.

He knows she needs him more than she loathes him. That's what this whole therapy bullshit has been about; he's been reminding her she needs him as a partner.

Like we didn't all already fucking know.

The rest of the drive flies by, and before I know it, I'm pulling into the packed parking lot of the Spirit Center. Stas said this is the first time in years that nationals have been on the West Coast, and I feel lucky right now that she's not on the other side of the country. Above everything else happening, I'm glad I'm here to support her, and that's what I'm concentrating on.

People are lining the halls when I make my way into the building. Trainers with the protégés, parents with their very nervous kids, and huge families wearing different skating team emblems on their jackets.

It's kind of wild that the best figure skaters in the country are in this building right now and Stassie is one of them. Figure skating for six weeks definitely gave me a new appreciation for how goddamn difficult it is.

I might still have bruises on my ass and knees from falling down.

I've got about ten minutes before the pairs short program begins, which gives me enough time to buy a drink and use the bathroom. I don't know why I'm so nervous when she's the one who has to skate.

I'm lucky to get a seat at the end of an aisle, next to a huge family all wearing matching T-shirts. Stassie and Aaron are on second in their group, but I missed the warm-up, so I haven't even had a glimpse of her. I don't manage to pay attention to the first pair that perform, my mind is too preoccupied. My seat is directly above the access tunnel onto the ice, and in my eye line I can see the back of Brady's head, so I know Stas is close.

Practically every part of the exterior of the rink is covered in cameras, with the whole competition being streamed online. The guys have all piled into our house to watch and have been blowing up our group chat with support—and horror, when someone in the last group had a nasty fall.

"*Next on the ice, from Maple Hills Skating Team, is Aaron Carlisle and Anastasia Allen.*"

I can hear my heartbeat in my ears as I watch her skate onto the ice. She looks beautiful, her long, light brown hair curled and pinned back, showing the detailed diamanté-encrusted netting across her chest and arms and down the front of her navy-blue costume. They move into the center of the rink, hand in hand, waiting for the music to begin.

A slowed-down acoustic version of "Kiss Me" by Sixpence None the Richer begins to play, and they make their first move across the ice. I've listened to this song and "Clair de lune" more times than I can count in the time we've been together.

At practice, I was with her as she glided across the ice, looking so close to perfection it was hard to believe she wasn't put on this earth just to do this. At the house, when she'd slide around the kitchen tiles, dragging me around with her, laughing, claiming we were practicing.

This song will always remind me of those moments.

I can't move my eyes from the pair as they seamlessly and perfectly deliver every move. My phone is buzzing relentlessly in my pocket, but I ignore it, unwilling to miss even a split second. They're nearing the end of the program, two minutes and almost forty seconds gone in a blink. Aaron picks her up for their final move, and Anastasia glides through the air flawlessly, landing so gently you wouldn't think she was spinning through the air a second earlier.

The pair of them move toward the center of the rink, do their final dance moves, and end wrapped around each other as the music fades. Every second of it was perfect. Not even a hair out of place.

And when the applause starts, that's when Aaron takes her face in his hands and kisses her.

Chapter Forty-nine

ANASTASIA

THERE ARE FLASHING LIGHTS GOING off all around us, and my chest is so tight I can't breathe.

I'm pushing against him, but his grip on my face is too tight, and I don't want to make a scene on the ice, since there are about thirty cameras, at all different angles, capturing this.

Capturing.

This is going to be available for everyone to see. People have already seen it; they're watching it right now. Nathan is at home watching it right now. Watching us kissing.

I'm going to be sick.

Aaron finally detaches himself from me, leaning back, looking triumphant. He holds up an arm to wave to the crowd, and it's taking everything in me not to burst into tears, right here in front of all these people. My body starts to function on its own, leading me off the ice to Brady's smiling face.

She would be smiling; we were perfect. I could feel it in every movement, every twist and turn, every moment on the ice totally in sync. Right until the end, when Aaron put his mouth on mine without permission and ruined *everything*.

I take the guards from Coach's outstretched hand, swerving the hug she tries to trap me in, and head through the tunnel away from the cameras and away from Aaron.

I can hardly see the exit a few meters in front of me as the tears line my eyes, blurring my vision.

"Stas!" Aaron shouts from behind me, and I can hear it in his voice—he's confused. He doesn't understand why I'm storming away from him when we should be celebrating our stellar performance.

A head-turning performance.

The kind of performance that puts you on people's radar—the kind of people whose radar we want to be on.

His hand closes around my bicep, stopping me in my tracks, and I have no choice but to spin to face him. I want to appear strong, give the impression that I'm not impacted by him, but I can't because the tears are streaming down my face. "We're done, Aaron. You've gone too far this time."

His eyebrows practically shoot up into his hairline. "What do you mean 'we're done'? We fucking nailed it!"

Brady appears behind him, eyes cautiously flitting between us. "We need to wait for your score. Anastasia, I know you're upset, and we can deal with this, but you need to wipe the tears away and put on a brave face for the cameras." My chest heaves as they suffocate me with their wary glances. "I know, honey," she coos. "I'm so sorry, I am. But you need to think of your career; let's deal with this after, and I promise we will."

"I don't understand what I've done," Aaron says flatly. "I don't get it. Stop crying, we need to find out where we've placed."

"No! I'm done," I say, sobbing. "I couldn't get him off me. He wouldn't stop. I didn't want to. *You* wouldn't let me go. I'm not doing it anymore, Coach. I don't want to, I don't want to, *I don't want to.*"

The exit doors open behind us, and I get the shock of my life when Nathan flies through them. I watch him approach us over my shoulder, and it takes one look at my streaming eyes to know this wasn't a stunt. It wasn't part of our routine. We weren't selling being in love for the cameras and the judges.

"Oh, here we fucking go," Aaron grumbles.

"Are you okay?" Nate asks, frantically pulling my body to his in a tight hug. His thumbs gently sweep the tears away from under my eyes as I look up at him, shaking my head.

"I want to go home," I force out between cries.

"This is fucking ridiculous. Anastasia, I'm sorry if I upset you, all right? I was in the moment. It's what the people wanted and I just wanted to deliver. I won't do it again if you're going to be this upset over a silly gimmick."

"You don't fucking get it, do you?" Nathan seethes, releasing me and stalking toward Aaron. Before I even have time to tell him not to do anything, his fist smashes into Aaron's face, dropping him to the floor. Brady is gripping Nate's arm before he has a chance to do anything more, screeching his name at him. "You forced yourself on her, you piece of shit!" he shouts down at Aaron, who's cradling his swelling cheek.

"Oh my goodness. Everyone just calm down!" Brady yells. "Hawkins, get out of here. Aaron, get up." She pulls on her hair, finally losing her cool. "Anastasia, get through the next fifteen minutes, *please*. Then we will talk, I promise you."

Aaron and I must look like absolute disasters sitting on the bench in front of the camera, waiting for our result.

My eyes are puffy, and the side of Aaron's face is swollen, although partially being covered by the ice pack a medic sourced for him. Brady is sitting between us, her hand intertwined with each of our free ones, and I can't imagine three people who want to be sitting in front of a camera less than the three of us right now.

The scores roll in, placing us in first among the skaters who have performed already, but I can't even bring myself to be excited. It's over. I sit motionless, ignoring Brady and Aaron's cheers. Her arm wraps around my shoulders in comfort, but when the light of the camera goes off, indicating the recording has stopped, I'm up and on my way to find Nathan again.

"Anastasia, wait!" Coach shouts, the sound of her shoes echoing behind me. I slow down, turning to face her, watching her jog toward me with open arms. "I'm sorry he did that to you."

"I'm done."

"You keep saying that, but what does it mean?" she asks cautiously. I can see Aaron approaching from the results room, strolling calmly like a man with absolutely nothing to worry about. "You can't quit skating over a kiss, Anastasia. I won't let you."

"I'm not quitting," I say, looking at Aaron over her shoulder as he reaches us. "I'm just not skating with Aaron ever again."

He scoffs and the urge to punch the other side of his face is overwhelming. "You'll never get another partner, and even if you do, you'll never be ready in the next two years. Are you really planning to make your Olympic debut at twenty-seven? Be realistic, *Jesus.* Just accept my apology, Stas. We'll talk about it with Dr. Robeska next week. We need to get our head in the game for tomorrow. Look how fucking good we are together! We . . ."

I let him go on and on, pitching himself to me like a goddamn salesman. And when he's finally done, smiling smugly to himself because he thinks his bullshit has worked on me once again, I look back to Brady. "I'm going solo. If our score puts us through, please tell them that I withdraw."

Aaron's hands grip his hair as reality starts to set in. "You can't go solo. Don't fucking do this to me, Anastasia. After *everything* I've done for you, for fuck's sake. Stop being such a stubborn bitch! You're not even good enough to compete alone. Oh my God. Oh my *fucking* God. You're ruining my life."

"That's enough!" Brady snaps at him.

"I'm going to find my boyfriend, and then I'm going home. Good-bye, Aaron."

"Stas, *please*," he begs.

"I've done nothing but trust you, Aaron. For nearly two and a half years, I've put everything I've got into this partnership, into our friendship. All you've done is use me and manipulate me, slut-shame me, tell me I'm not good enough to be your partner. Well, I'm finally hearing you loud and clear. You don't want me and that's fine because I don't want you, either. I'd rather skate alone and risk failing than succeed with you. Winning is absolutely worthless when it comes at the cost of having to hate myself when I'm with you."

I don't give him a chance to respond as I head back toward the main waiting area to find Nate. Part of me feels liberated, light, free, but a much bigger, more prominent part feels embarrassed and disappointed I ever thought we could have a partnership.

Standing quickly, Nate rushes toward me the second he spots me approaching. I don't give him a chance to ask if I'm okay, mainly because I'm worried I'll cry again, instead asking him to take me to the hotel to get my things.

I can't bring myself to look at my phone between the arena and the hotel, but I know it will be blowing up. Thankfully, I haven't unpacked yet, so I quickly grab my suitcase and hand my key card back to the reception desk, before hopping straight onto the freeway back to Maple Hills.

I watch my mom's name flash up for the millionth time, ignoring it until it goes to voice mail. Nathan hasn't said anything, but his hand has been moving between my leg and the back of my neck since we got into the car, stroking gently, the occasional comforting squeeze to let me know he's here for me.

The radio cuts off as my dad's name flashes up on the screen, letting us know there's an incoming call. "They're going to be mad at me. They spent so much money on this outfit a—"

"They won't be mad, baby. They're obviously worried about you. Can I answer?"

I give him a nod and he accepts the call. "Hey."

"Nate, I'm sorry to bother you. I don't suppose you've spoken to Annie, have you? Julia has been calling her but no answer. We were watching the streaming, she looked so distraught. Between me and you, Julia is very upset."

"She's with me." He looks toward me quickly, then looks back at the road. "She's asleep. She's very upset, and she's exhausted herself. We're on our way back to Maple Hills. She, uh, she wasn't very happy that Aaron kissed her. It wasn't part of the routine, and I, uhm, I'm not sure she's going to want to be his partner anymore."

I don't like the idea of making Nate lie to my parents, but I'm not ready to face them.

"I'm not surprised," he gruffs. "The ice pack . . ."

Nate clears his throat. "I punched him. But I want you to know I—"

Before he can even finish explaining he isn't a violent person, Dad interrupts. "No explanation required. Well justified, I believe. We're so proud of her; she was phenomenal until he ruined it. Get her to call us when she's awake, please. We want to make sure she's okay. We can fly to LA if she wants us to, but no pressure."

My parents despise flying, so them offering has me on the brink of tears again. The only thing stopping me is the fact I'm supposed to be asleep, and therefore can't be wailing in the background of a call.

Nate gives my thigh a squeeze. "I will. Thanks for calling."

"They don't sound mad," I say, not talking to anyone but myself.

"They're not mad," Nate confirms.

I DO ACTUALLY FALL ASLEEP in the car, only waking up when the car goes over the speed bump on the way into the parking garage at my building.

I foolishly brought all my things back from Nathan's last week, but I want some comfort items before we head back there. I can hear banging and rustling before I even open the door, and part of me is worried I'm about to walk in on Lola and Robbie doing something weird on the couch, but instead I open the door and Russ is standing in my living room, looking like a deer in headlights, holding a box labeled *SMUT* in huge letters.

"What the hell?" I mutter, looking around the room at the various hockey players in the apartment. Nathan's hands grip my waist and usher me farther into the room, closing the door behind us.

"Put your back into it," Lola shouts at no one in particular as she stomps out of my room. She closes the gap between us in two seconds, pulling me into an oxygen-stealing hug.

"What's going on?" I manage to squeak out with the breath I have left.

"We're moving out," she says nonchalantly.

"'We're'? Me and you? Where are we going?" I sound like a fool, tripping over my words as the guys all work around us, speeding ahead with what I imagine were very strict instructions from Lo.

Nathan's arms wrap around my shoulders, and he buries his head into my neck, kissing lightly beneath my ear. "Where do you think you're going?"

"All right, caveman," she tuts at him. "With the boys. Just until we find somewhere for us to live. We can't live here with *him*."

A crash comes from her bedroom, and I think I visibly see her blood pressure rise. "JJ!" she screams, storming off toward the source of the noise.

I'm supposed to feel overwhelmed right now, but honestly, all I feel is relief. I've made one huge decision today; I wasn't ready to have to make any more. I turn in Nathan's arms to cuddle into his chest, letting the chaos behind me fade away. His lips press into my hair, and he chuckles. "You ready to play house every single day?"

"As long as it's with you."

Chapter Fifty

NATHAN

Three Months Later

"STOP TRYING TO SEDUCE ME. I've got a meeting with Skinner in thirty minutes, and I need to shower."

Anastasia stops kissing her way down my torso, looking up at me from just above my belly button with those big blue eyes I fucking love. How can someone look so innocent but be so much goddamn trouble at the same time? She sits up a little, the most mischievous smile on her lips as she crawls back up my body and presses a chaste kiss against my lips before rolling off and lying beside me.

"What do you think he wants?" she asks, pulling the covers over her body so I can formulate a response, and not get distracted by the fact her tits are directly in my eye line.

"Dunno," I mumble, shuffling toward her and running my hand across her soft skin. "Probably wants to use me as a human sacrifice or something."

She nods in agreement, curling back into my body. "I can see that. Do you think your dad will let me stay here when you're gone? We can't move into our new place until the end of the school year, and I don't feel like the streets of Maple Hills are for me."

"I think he'd probably prefer to throw you out on the street, but there's a chance he won't notice I'm dead for at least six months, so you'll probably be fine."

Things with Dad are as peachy as ever. The only half-decent thing he's done recently was giving Sasha time off to let the Hamlets drive her to Denver with them to watch us play when the NCAA championships were held there at the start of the month.

We won the tournament—not like he would have noticed even if he were there. I'm glad Sasha got to see us win, alongside Anastasia and her parents. I can still hear Colin now, telling me and absolutely anyone who would listen how unbelievably proud he was. It was an emotional day all around; even Faulkner and Robbie had a little moment.

It was the perfect way to end my college hockey career, even more perfect because of who I was sharing it with.

"If you get sacrificed do I get your trust fund or does your dad take it back?" she asks, giggling when I dig my fingers into her side. "Also, do I have your blessing to marry Henry?"

"No and no," I say as sternly as I can manage. "I want you to wear black for the rest of your life and never move on."

"Urgh," she half grumbles, half laughs, squirming around. "That's going to interfere with next year's spring break plans."

She squeals, laughing as I drag her from the bed, throw her over my shoulder, and march us to the shower.

THE RIDE TO DIRECTOR SKINNER'S office seems to take twice as long as normal.

I texted Faulkner yesterday to see if he knew what it was about, but he wasn't helpful.

COACH

Hey Coach. Been asked to go see Skinner tomorrow. Do you know what it's about?

Do I look like his fucking secretary?

Well I've never seen you and
his secretary in the same place . . .

So . . .

Come see me at my office after
you're done with Skinner.

Do not bring me bad news.

My life is going to be so much easier
when you graduate in two months.

Gonna miss you too, Coach.

Skinner's office isn't in the sports building with the rest of the coaches and sports staff. For some reason, his is in the main building, right near the dean's office. I imagine it's easier for him to kiss the dean's ass if he's close by. He's on the phone when I'm shown into his office by his actual secretary, which gives me the chance to look around and confirm it's as grim as I was expecting it to be.

"Sorry about that. Nathan, hello, thank you for coming to see me. I'm sure you're wondering what this is about."

"Have I done something wrong?"

"Not exactly," he says calmly, leaning back in his chair. "Two months ago, I was approached by a student regarding the incident involving you and Aaron Carlisle."

"Okay . . ."

"She explained Mr. Carlisle had a vendetta against you and was injured off campus while drunk with his friends. He used the accident as an opportunity to tarnish your reputation."

"That's what I've been told by people who were with him, yeah."

"Of course, you admitted to being the cause, which you should not have done . . . but I've been informed it was only after Coach Faulkner had put the whole team on the bench. In essence, you were doing your best to protect your team."

Not one of my smarter choices. "That's right, sir."

"An independent investigation has been carried out and found everything the student had informed us was true. She was very thorough and was keen for your name to be cleared of any wrongdoing."

"Was this student Anastasia Allen by any chance, sir?"

He shrugs, but there is a slight smile on his lips. "The student in question asked to remain anonymous, but I wanted to see you face-to-face to reassure you the incident will be cleared from your college records. I understand you're graduating soon, but for your information, and any concerned parties, Mr. Carlisle has transferred to UCLA, effective immediately."

Oh.

"I'm sure Aaron will be very happy there. Is that everything?" I ask carefully, keen to escape on a good note.

"Yes, that's all. Oh, and congratulations on your championship win."

I give him an appreciative nod and get my ass out of there as quickly as I can. I should have known Stassie wouldn't let Aaron go unpunished.

UBER SLUT

You're in trouble.

Am I the sacrifice?

I can't be. I am very busy and important

You went to Skinner.

That doesn't sound like something I would do.

You went to Skinner and you snitched on Aaron.

All because you wanted to defend my honor.

You don't have any honor 😊

What you did to me last night is famously not honorable at all.

                                        You liked it.

Of course I did. I don't
have any honor either.

                        Aaron transferred to UCLA

Shut up!! Really?

                        Yup. Skinner just told me.

I'd have preferred
somewhere in Alaska, but
not Maple Hills will do.

Knowing I'm not going to be here next year has been a hard pill to swallow, but knowing she isn't going to have to face him at the rink or bump into him at parties makes me feel a whole lot better.

The next stop on the list is over to the sports building to see Coach. He's eating what looks like an everything bagel when I stroll in. His eyes immediately narrow, and I can see him shouting at me in his head. He eventually swallows and sort of half grunts at me. "I don't even get peace to eat my breakfast alone anymore. Between you clowns and my daughters, I am graying prematurely."

I look at his completely shaved head, nodding along in agreement. "You wanted to see me?"

He wipes his hands on a napkin and pushes his half-eaten bagel to one side. "We need to discuss your replacement as captain. It's time to start looking to hand the title over, like Lewinski did with you. Have you thought about it?"

I've been thinking about who will replace me since I got benched last year. Not being on the ice gave me time to look at the team, watch them the way Faulkner and Robbie do, and I saw a lot. "You're going to laugh . . ."

"I don't laugh but go on."

"I think Henry would make a great captain," I say honestly. "He's calm; once I'm gone, he's going to be the best player on the team; he'll always be honest; and he's not going to fuck around. He's going to be a junior, which means the team gets two years of the same captain."

He thinks on it for a minute, humming to himself quietly. "Okay. Let me speak to Robbie, see what his opinion is."

"We've already talked about it, and he agrees Turner is the best choice."

Robbie will be staying at UCMH to do his master's, so he'll be continuing to coach the team. Since the assistant coach is normally a paid faculty position, we're all hoping when he's done with school, the job will be handed to him.

A couple of weeks ago, over a shitload of beers, we sat and battled out who should succeed me. Henry has grown in confidence so much in the time he's lived with us, so I think he could handle the pressure that comes with being a leader. Aside from that, nobody can argue against him being the best player.

"Let me think on it," Faulkner says, reaching for his bagel, signifying it's my time to get out and leave him alone. "I'll see you at practice later."

Since I'm already on campus, I take a trip to the library, grab a few books I need to study for my finals, and head home.

The house is full when I get back, far too many hockey players taking up space on all my furniture. "Do you guys not have your own houses to go to? Instead of being here eating all my food and stinking out my living room?"

I get a handful of middle fingers, the odd grunt, and finally a response from Kris. "Your girl promised us pad thai."

JJ and Anastasia did the Vietnamese cooking class a few weeks ago, and since then, this place has been like a restaurant. They're determined to try as many different dishes and cuisines as they can. They cook side by side, secretly competing with each other to see who makes the best main or starter, or who makes the best side dishes. Then we sit down to eat, and they sit there smugly, enjoying all of the compliments the guys throw in their direction.

I don't mention to Stas that I'm pretty sure Bobby and Mattie live exclusively off oven pizzas, so they're going to keep showing up for food long after JJ and I have graduated.

I push through all the bodies and mess in my living room and make my way over to the kitchen. Stassie is chomping on some bean sprouts, watching the wok very intensely. "Hey, bub." She smiles. "Food is nearly ready."

I tilt her head back, capturing her lips with mine, enjoying the way her body immediately sinks into me. "You know you don't have to feed everyone, right? I don't expect you to."

She giggles and gets back to the wok. "You know I love it. It's like having loads of kids, but instead of being cute and small, they're, like, super big and drink and curse. It's nice for you guys to spend time together since some of you won't be here soon. Thai seems to be everyone's favorite—they showed up immediately."

"Anastasia Allen, do you have baby fever?"

Her jaw drops and her cheeks blush pink, eyes blinking repeatedly like she can't believe I accused her of that. "No! I'm being a good girlfriend and roommate."

I can't help but laugh. She's so fucking cute sometimes I don't know what to do with her. "You're the best girlfriend and definitely the best roommate. I love—"

"What was that about the best roommate?" JJ interrupts, pushing me out of the way of the stove. "Get out of our kitchen, Hawkins. There is culinary excellence happening here, and you're getting in the way with your unseasoned vibes."

Stas watches me with her eyebrows raised as I back out of the kitchen. She mouths *Unseasoned vibes* at me, trying not to laugh as JJ starts giving her instructions for plating up. I watch—from a safe distance—as they transfer everything into serving bowls and put it on the beer pong/dining room table. "Food!" JJ shouts at the top of his lungs, and the rest of the guys immediately start scrambling toward the den.

Lola and Robbie are already seated at the table, securing the best spots, and the guys filter in, eyes widening at the selection in front of them. The room is filled with the sound of clanging cutlery and appreciative *uhm*s, *ah*s, and *ooh*s. Stassie brings the final plate of egg rolls out, and I can't keep my eyes off her as she stands, looking around at everyone and smiling to herself.

The girl who would only eat salad, didn't want a relationship, and couldn't stand hockey players is nowhere to be seen.

She squeezes herself into the seat beside me and fills her plate full of food, groaning happily when she has a mouthful of noodles. She slaps at Bobby's hand when he tries to steal an egg roll from her plate, scowling at him to the point that he flinches. Her face softens as she turns to face me and finds me laughing at the interaction. She shrugs, not sorry in the slightest she's added to Bobby's fear of her. "Egg rolls are my favorite."

"You're my favorite," I whisper, leaning in to kiss her flushed cheek.

"Even if I had crab hands?"

"Even if you had crab hands, Anastasia."

Epilogue

ANASTASIA

Two (and a Bit) Years Later

THE SEATTLE SKYLINE IS GLOWING beneath the warm, early-evening sunlight. Dr. Andrews is running behind, but I don't mind because it gives me a little longer to admire the view.

I sometimes miss the LA weather when I'm stuck in the rain, but right now, I feel perfectly content.

"Come in, Anastasia." Dr. Andrews holds open the door for me. "I'm sorry for the delay."

"Don't worry," I reassure him, pushing myself up from my chair. "My ankles are so swollen it's nice to sit down."

"Well, you're definitely glowing if that makes you feel better. Pregnancy suits you."

"It's sweat, don't be fooled." Taking a seat across from his desk, I run my hand over my bump, hissing when I feel a tiny foot in my rib cage. "We think she's going to be a soccer player. She likes to kick."

"I'm sure with a gold medalist for a mother and a Stanley Cup winner for a father, whatever she decides to be, she'll be the best at it."

"Right now, she's the best at making me nearly pee myself."

After I graduated and moved back to Washington to be closer to Nathan, I decided to start with semi-regular therapy sessions. Therapy doesn't feel hard anymore, it makes me feel grateful. Recapping my feelings, things I've done, things I'm looking forward to, and even the things I'm nervous about. It all reminds me how much I have to feel lucky for.

By the time I'm driving home, Baby H is wriggling around, clearly as excited to see her dad as I am. Well, that's what I'll tell Nate, leaving out the fact she started break dancing on my organs when I opened my second bag of Flamin' Hot Cheetos.

When he bought me my Range Rover, otherwise known as the *sorry I accidentally knocked you up* mom-wagon, he filled all available compartments with snacks.

A wise choice since his child is hungry constantly.

Yes, I'm blaming my unborn baby for how much crap I eat when I'm sitting in traffic.

Pulling into our driveway beside my parents' car, I'm not even fully out of the car before I can hear Bunny's signature bark echoing from the backyard.

"Stop upsetting my baby," I call over the barking, waddling over to where Nathan and my dad are shooting Bunny with a water gun.

"Mom's home!" Nate shouts, causing a forty-five-pound bundle of wet, golden fluff to bounce toward me, tail wagging excitedly.

Knowing he was transferring to Seattle at the end of the season, Nathan promised me after the Olympics in February we could get a golden retriever. What neither of us planned for when we decided to become dog parents was my pre–Olympic debut anxiety causing me to vomit up my contraceptive pill.

I won gold in the women's singles.

We celebrated.

A lot.

On every surface we could get our horny little mitts on.

Six months later, I have a giant watermelon strapped to my stomach and the world's most chaotic puppy.

Nate strides toward me, closing the gap between us, aiming the water gun in my direction, a mischievous glint in his brown eyes. His shorts are low on his hips, the last of the day's rays bouncing off his tanned skin. *God, he's hot.* "Don't you dare, Hawkins."

"Welcome home." He drops his weapon to the floor, narrowly missing Bunny spinning around at our feet. Taking my face in his hands, he lowers his mouth to mine, making every single cell in my body hum happily.

Pregnancy has made everything heightened, so when I thought I was attracted to him before, I was *so* wrong. The fact my parents are here right now is the only reason I'm not trying to climb him like a tree.

"How are my favorite girls today?" Nate's hands trail down my arms gently until they reach my stomach. She's going wild like she always does when he's near us. "You want me to do the thing?"

"God, yes. We're good. We're hungry." He steps behind me, winding his arms around me until they link at the bottom of my bump, lifting to take the weight off me, and I instantly melt into him. "Oh God, yes."

I always suspected Baby Hawkins would be one big-ass baby, but I've basically been showing since conception.

RIP my vagina in a few months.

I'm all bump and boobs. Gigantic boobs that make everyone stare at my chest. I visited Lola in New York with my mom, and she spent the entire trip checking me out and debating whether she wanted a boob job.

Mom appears with a glass of lemonade, and between the two of them looking after me, I wonder why I even bothered leaving the house today. "You all packed, honey?"

I nod. "Nothing fits, so I'll just be wearing crop tops for a week."

Nate kisses my cheek from behind. "It works for Winnie-the-Pooh."

When Alex, JJ's partner, offered to help plan our babymoon, I thought they were joking. But it turns out there is a whole host of baby-related things things I don't know yet. The ones that involve me getting gifts and trips are my favorite.

"Are the baby's things packed up?" I ask, reaching down to scratch behind Bunny's ears.

Mom sighs. "You do know you'll have to stop calling him the baby when the baby gets here?"

My face instinctively scrunches. "No I won't. Firstborn." I point to the fluffy face intensely licking my ankle. I point at my swollen tummy. "Second born."

She rolls her eyes, crouching to stroke him, and narrowly avoiding the huge slobbery tongue that heads toward her face. "Come on, little guy, you're going on vacation, too!"

The intense excitement I once experienced when traveling is less intense now I'm a bowling ball, but I do enjoy bossing Nathan around from a comfortable position with my feet up.

More than two and a half years together and the man still can't use packing cubes properly.

The journey from Seattle to Cabo is seamless, and we only get stopped for pictures approximately one million times. My favorite fans are the ones who don't watch hockey, so they hand their phone or camera to Nate when they ask for a photo. He says he doesn't mind people thinking he's famous for being my boyfriend.

I can't help but laugh when he says it because he seems to mean it. I said we can work on his public image before I win my next medal; maybe it'll reduce how much he has to play photographer.

Our villa is less villa, more beach mansion, but Nate says the extravagance is necessary because he wants somewhere private where I can be comfortable.

Naked. Naked is what he wants me to be.

We spend the day on the beach, reading and napping, cooling down in the sea. Nate has made a Baby Hawkins–sized hole in the sand, the perfect size to fit my bump in, and for the first time in months, I'm able to sleep on my stomach. *Bliss.*

"STAS, YOU NEARLY READY?"

"Stop rushing me!"

I hear him chuckle in the living room. "Well, can you at least speed it up a little? We have a reservation."

Having had no choice but to wash all the salt water out of my hair, I made the critical post-shower error of sitting on the bed in my towel, with a bag of barbecue Lays and my phone. I'm now up to date with what everyone I've ever followed is doing, but I unfortunately have no clothes on and damp, frizzy hair.

Dragging my hair back into a sleek ponytail, I pull on a sundress, dab a small amount of highlighter around various points of my face, and add some mascara. The beauty of being on vacation is I can pretend this is the look I was going for, and nobody can tell me otherwise.

When I finally emerge from the bedroom, Nate is watching the Grand Prix with a beer. "Come on, we're going to be late."

His mouth opens and his head turns to look at me in disbelief. "I'm waiting for *you*! I've been waiting for you for so long!"

"That feels like an exaggeration," I mutter, putting my phone in my purse. "Should we head out?"

Standing, he guzzles the rest of his beer, still shaking his head and cursing me under his breath. "Gotta check something, I'll meet you outside."

"Hurry up, Nathan." I fight to keep the smirk from my face. "We have a reservation."

His eyes widen, then snap shut as he takes a deep breath. "I know. I've been telling you that."

The walk to the restaurant is a short one, and they lead us through the main dining area and out the back to a private beach area. Rose petals have been used to create a pathway to a lone table on the beach.

Nathan helps me tuck in my chair, before moving to sit opposite me. "I'm going to eat everything on the menu," I warn him. "It isn't going to be attractive."

"Everything you do is attractive."

"We'll see about that . . ."

I don't quite manage everything on the menu, but I make a significant dent in my meal, Nate's meal, and the bread basket. I sit staring at him while he sips his wine and people-watches. He's oddly quiet tonight, but sometimes he's like this in his downtime. Being surrounded by noise and chaos all the time at work is tiring for him, and some of the most special times between us involve us silently being in each other's company.

Sensing my eyes on him, his head turns toward me, eyes locking with mine, taking my breath away. The tip of his nose is pink from today's sun, and his normally trimmed short stubble has grown longer. Every time I look at him my pulse soars and my heart hammers in my chest, and when I think I've reached maximum capacity for how much I love him, something proves me wrong.

Falling in love with Nathan Hawkins was not something I could have planned.

No planner, iPad, or freaking sticker chart could have prepared me for my future.

My imagination isn't capable of dreaming up this level of happiness.

"You're staring at me with that goofy look you do when you're thinking too hard," Nate says playfully.

Rolling my eyes, I chuckle at his rude interruption to my inner monologue. "I'm thinking about how much I love you."

"That's funny. I was thinking about you, too."

Pushing his chair back, he stands from our table, and I watch him curiously. "What're you do—?" He sinks one knee into the sand beside me. *"Oh my God."*

As he reaches into his pocket, my heart slows down and a lump—big, but not as big as the diamond being held out in front of me—forms in my throat. Baby H is having a rave in my stomach, and tears preemptively line my eyes.

"Anastasia, you are the best thing to ever happen to me, and to call you the love of my life does not do justice to how much I love you. My existence doesn't make sense without you by my side. For the rest of our lives, in the next life, in every alternate reality, I'll be yours if you'll have me. You are my best friend, my greatest gift, and Mila—and Bunny—are so blessed to have you as their mom."

Okay, here are the tears.

"Will you marry me?"

Nodding frantically, I launch myself at him, nearly knocking him over into the sand. "Yes, yes, yes!" My hands shake as he slides the ring onto my finger, immediately taking my face between his hands and kissing the life out of me.

"Anastasia Hawkins. Wow. And here I was thinking this was just a casual, no-commitment, no-jealousy thing."

He snorts, pressing his lips against mine one more time. "Shut up, Anastasia."

Acknowledgments

MY HUSBAND, FOR BELIEVING IN me, for letting me spend our savings on funding my (very expensive) dream, and, despite having the biggest mouth ever, keeping my hobby a secret like you promised you would.

Marcy, for convincing me I could write my own book. Thank you for helping me discover my passion.

Ha-Le, the person who definitely knows *Icebreaker* better than I do. Thank you for your endless support.

Paisley and Leni, for virtually holding my hand through publishing my first book. Your hard work and creativity have made this book what it is, and I can't wait to work on so many other projects with you both.

Finally, to my crisis team, who I love endlessly:

Erin, for being my emotional support author. Thank you for your friendship, for being there to listen to all my weird, half-thought-out ideas, and for actively encouraging them all. You are the reason my "to write list" is forty-five books long. This is me putting BookBar energy into the universe.

Kiley, for being the first person to read the *Icebreaker* plot outline. Thank you for always being in my corner, for demanding chapters when I have writer's block (which weirdly works), and more importantly, for answering all my "Ki, in America . . ." messages. Your calm balances out my chaos; you are a wonderful friend.

Rebecca, for being the Canadian version of me. Thank you for making me feel like self-publishing was achievable, for listening to my random four a.m. rambles, and for talking me down when the imposter syndrome is trying to win. I feel so lucky to call you a friend.

About the Author

HANNAH GRACE IS AN ENGLISH self-labeled "fluffy comfort book" author, writing contemporary romance from her home in Manchester, England.

When she's not describing everyone's eyes ten thousand times a chapter, accidentally giving multiple characters the same name, or using English sayings that nobody understands in her American books, you can find her hanging out with her husband and two dogs, Pig and Bear.